# UNDERCOVER...
# BURNED

# UNDERCOVER... BURNED

D.K. Lange

# Chapter One

CORY SIMS LEFT CHICAGO GENERAL Hospital and sighed into the night. Not a star shown in the sky leaving it excessively dark when she stepped away from the lights. It had been extremely busy all night in the Emergency Room leaving her physically tired with aching legs, a sore back and dragging feet. For months the gangs were quiet. There was the occasional skirmish but nothing like the blood bath they saw this evening. Something stirred up the hornet's nest outside these walls and for once Cory was afraid to walk home.

She bit her lip, weighing her options. Every year since the death of her parents her younger twin sisters, Carol and Cindy, went to visit the older one in Oregon. The annual occurrence marked the first day of summer vacation and ended a week before school started. That annual event started today.

It was hard to come up with enough money for their train tickets this year. So many things happened to slowly erode away her savings. Cory sighed again rooting through her purse. Five dollars. That was all she had between now and payday which was another week away. A cab would cost her more than that. Her shoulders slumped wearily as she started the half hour walk home. Usually she enjoyed the walk but not tonight. Tonight, her senses warned, something was going to happen that would change the rest of her life. She just prayed she got home safely and there was a rest of her life.

* * * * *

Luke Patterson was a cop whose cover was about to be blown. He realized that as soon as the boss man walked in for the meeting. For two years he worked undercover to infiltrate this den of murderers, thieves and drug dealers just to find the brains behind the ring. Tonight he was supposed to meet the head of the operation. It was all arranged, and he was wired for sound. Luke prayed his taller frame, longer hair and scrubby, four-day beard would change his appearance enough to keep from being recognized but knew it was hopeless.

He was forced to surrender his gun when he entered the warehouse and cursed the fact he had no protection. Now his only hope of surviving was that those who were supposed to be listening really were listening. "I'm in trouble here. I know this guy and he knows me. This is going to get messy if you don't get your asses in here now."

Voice a low growl he backed toward a door in the shadows. With a hand on the knob he was about to make his escape when he heard the gun cock. "Well, Luke. It's been a long time since we last met. Move away from the door or I'll shoot you where you stand. You are one tough son of a bitch and I shall enjoy killing you myself."

Luke turned to face the man, curling his arm behind him, hand still on the knob. Where in the hell was his backup? "After all these years Jason, I would have thought you would've gotten over your anger."

"I spent two years in prison because of you. I swore I'd get even. I never dreamed you would make it so easy."

Luke studied his adversary. They were friends in college but that was before he knew Jason's dark side. Now the man reeked of evil, the stench of it floated around him. He was a tall, well-muscled man. His fashionably cut short blonde hair, clean-shaven and impeccable black suit made him appear as a respectable businessman. One look at his eyes would tell you different. Jason Grover was the only person Luke ever knew with truly black eyes and those eyes matched his equally black soul.

Relaxing his position against the door Luke forced a slow grin to cut across his face. "Not very sociable tonight, are you? What have you got in mind Jason? Since I don't cotton to being dead and you can't put me behind bars what are you planning to do?" Very slowly, very carefully, Luke twisted the handle of the door. His only plan at that moment was to escape. This battle of words was just a stalling tactic and he hoped Jason was just vain enough to fall for it a few seconds longer.

"I always did like your style, Luke. Cool as a cucumber under pressure. It made being friends with you so interesting." Jason leveled the pistol at Luke's heart. "Now move away from the door." He shook the pistol sideways.

Luke sensed more than saw the front door of the warehouse open and the FBI swarm in as the lights went out. Emergency lights came on flooding the building with an eerie red glow. Pushing open the door caused him to lose his balance just as Jason fired, feeling the bullet bury in the left side of his upper chest. As he scrambled in the darkness for cover he felt another hit him in the side like a white-hot poker. Damn, he was blocked in. The door he chose led to another warehouse instead of freedom.

Nothing was going as planned. Those agents were supposed to swarm the building as soon as he told them there was trouble. From what he could tell by the gunfire they were now on the losing end. Gasping for breath, he groaned from the pain in his side and shoulder. As another bullet whizzed by, missing his head by a fraction of an inch, he slid behind the barrels stacked against the wall.

"You can't escape me, Luke." Jason spoke with confidence into the darkness. "I knew there was a plant in my operation from the beginning. I also knew it was you, old friend. I planned for this night by feeding you only enough information to keep your suspicions at bay. I even stirred up the gangs which is why the Feds are so shorthanded."

Luke could hear his sinister laugh echo through the warehouse. "I planned this night knowing your habits and weaknesses. I even knew you were going to be wearing a wire. Amazing how those Feds weren't able to hear properly. Is it not?" Another evil laugh sent shivers of fear up Luke's spine. "Your buddies are dying even as we speak. You're going to die also, Luke. Money buys all the people and information I need.

"Unlike you, most care little if it's drug money. As long as there's enough to get their kids through another year of college they're willing to look the other way. Not you, though. Why is that, Luke? I knew long ago you would never look the other way. Now I'm forced to kill you to ensure you never interfere with my operations again. I could've used you on the inside however I never could buy you."

"You never will either." Luke mumbled to himself as he assessed his position. His hiding place was precarious at best. There was no going back the way he came for Jason was guarding that escape route. The front door was out of the question. When Jason's men swarmed into the building the first of those went to that door. His only means of escape was one of the many tiny windows above him. It would be risky. He would have to stand on the barrels to reach them, yet the windows didn't open. He could see that from where he was hiding. The only way out was to jump through them, and it would guarantee injury, but it was all he had. Luke judged the distance with his eyes, praying the injuries from the glass wouldn't be too severe to prevent his escape. He was hurt enough already.

As more of Jason's men poured into the second warehouse Luke knew it was now or never. He was trapped and desperately needed a gun. "Flush him out but don't kill him." Jason yelled. "I want that bastard alive, so I can have the pleasure of torturing him before I kill him."

Luke was glad for his totally black garb as one of Jason's goons almost stepped on him. Reacting quickly, he stood behind the man and snapped his neck in one quick motion. Grabbing the gun from the dying man's fingers Luke ground his teeth against the pain in his left shoulder as he lowered the body to the floor. Noise was not what he needed at this time and the sound of a falling body would give his position away in the breath of a heartbeat.

Staying in the shadows Luke tried to control the pain and nausea that threatened to overwhelm him, forcing the darkness away by shear will. If he lost consciousness now he knew he would never see the light of day and if that happened, the agents in the other warehouse died for nothing. Packing his handkerchief into the bullet wound in his shoulder he tried to staunch the flow of blood.

"Accept defeat Luke." Jason's voice echoed around the warehouse. "There's no place to go. No way to escape. No one who will come to your rescue. I made sure of that. All those who would have helped have been detained and those idiots in the other warehouse will soon be as dead as you will be."

Luke resisted the shudder running through him as he looked to the tiny windows again. It was the only way out. He just needed enough time to get from his position on the floor to the top of the barrels. As he tucked the first gun into his waistband at the back of his jeans another of Jason's goons rounded on his position.

Standing quickly, he effectively snapped the neck on the guy, grabbing the second gun. Unable to control the weight of the second man the body fell with a thud and pandemonium broke out as the man hit the floor. Luke jumped onto the barrels and dived through the glass of the small window as gunshots riddled the area he was in just seconds before.

He found himself on the roof of the first warehouse. Crouching low, he dashed across it, jumping onto the next roof. He made it across that one before he noticed the increasing pain in his hip. Gritting his teeth, he knew he had to get away and report his knowledge to his supervisor. Jason Grover had a man on the inside and his friends lost their lives tonight because of it. Luke lowered himself into the darkened alley thankful for the overcast skies which hid his position even more. Hugging the shadows, he put several blocks between himself and the warehouse, stopping for breath when he got to a quiet residential street. The houses were old, but the yards were nicely kept which usually indicated law-abiding citizens. Luke hoped so. He could hear the not-so-law abiding ones coming.

Now what? He would be seen immediately if he moved for his escape route was flooded with streetlights. He could try to return to the warehouse district and hide however instinct warned him he wouldn't escape alive. He doubted his instincts to stay alive would prevail over the pain. It had a grip on him like none he had ever experienced.

Pain searing through his body made thinking difficult. He took several deep breaths trying to clear his mind of both his pain and fear. He needed to find someplace to hold up until he was able to get help. The hospital wasn't an option. Jason would have someone willing to report to him. Where then? Pulling a gun, he waited. He was out of options. There was no place for him to go and they were coming fast.

That's when Luke saw her. He couldn't miss her. The young nurse stood out like a neon sign in her white uniform. Replacing the gun in his waistband he waited until she was right up on him. Luke's right arm shot around her waist, left hand clamping around her mouth. Seeing her frightened eyes guilt stabbed through him as tangible as the pain his movements elicited. "If you scream we're both dead." He growled into her ear. "I'm with the FBI and I have some pretty mean people on my tail. Just play along."

The plan was only half formed in his pain-fogged brain as the men cleared the alley. Luke could see the fear in the woman's eyes as the streetlights reflected on the steel of their guns. Pulling her next to him brought her face close to his. Without a clue of what to do next he was taken off guard when the woman wrapped her body next to his and kissed him.

As his pursuer's footsteps came closer she deepened the kiss, wrapping her leg around his injured one so it couldn't be seen. They were on them, Luke's mind registered. The fear in her eyes and the rapid breathing fed his guilt. Both he and this innocent woman were going to die, and it was his fault. He groaned, realizing how stupidly he acted. "Help me, big guy." She whispered. "Make out like we're lovers."

Luke responded, quickly pulling the pins from her hair and wrapping his fingers in it. "Oh darling, if only mom and dad weren't home we could be making love in the house. I can't wait until we're married. Why did I ever let your parents talk you into a big wedding?" Luke buried his head in her hair as the men sidled close.

"Damn George, you know I'm their only daughter. What would mom do without a society wedding? This is her one and only shot at impressing those uppity-ups and you know it. She's terribly upset because your parents don't have as much money as mine. Kiss me you fool. I'll drive all thought of the wedding from your mind. Oh God, I want you so bad. Are you positive your parents aren't going out this evening? I'm not sure I can wait until this weekend to have you." She rubbed her leg against his groin for effect.

Luke moaned, as much from the feelings her body next to his was creating as from pain the action elicited in his leg. She placed her arms on either side of his head creating more shadows in which to hide him, hands flat against the building they were standing next to. He felt his knees begin to buckle, pain and loss of blood taking their toll. She leaned into him, supporting him with her slight frame, pinning him against the wall. She captured his lips again as the men slid their guns into their pockets, making snide remarks as they hurried by.

Their footsteps quickened as they hurried to get out of sight. Luke refused to end the kiss, holding her with his right hand in her hair until he could no longer hear the retreating footsteps of his pursuers. He folded against her, fear and energy spent. "I'm sorry, miss." He gasped. "You could have gotten killed. Thanks."

"This isn't over yet, big guy." She licked dry lips. "We have to get you some medical help. You're going to bleed to death if we hesitate much longer."

"No." He kept his voice low even as panic rose. "They know I've been shot. They'll be waiting for me the minute I show up at a hospital. They can't afford to let me live, not after what I learned tonight and the man who shot me will have someone on the payroll. You can bet on that." He saw her worry, knowing her medical knowledge was working against him. Indecision seared across her face before it was covered.

Sighing she slid his right arm around her neck. His left arm now hung useless and the sight of his blood-soaked clothes made her swallow hard knowing what pain he had to be in. A deep cleansing breath helped steady her nerves. "All right. I've trusted you this far I guess I can trust you a little longer. You're bleeding too much to go far. Do you know someone who lives close that can help you?"

When Luke shook his head, she sighed again. "You're going to have to help me. You're too tall for me to do this alone. Lean on me. I'll take you to my home." Half pulling Luke she cut across the backs of the neighboring yards to avoid the lighted front porches and prying eyes. Leaning him against the back wall of the house she laid a steadying hand against his chest as she fumbled with the key.

Luke watched her movements closely. She looked pale and frightened. Her hand shook as she inserted the key into the lock. Long auburn hair hung in disarray around her shoulders from their acting in the alley. Hazel eyes reflected her fear as the door slid quietly inward. He knew he shouldn't allow her to become involved yet was too weak to do much else. He wasn't sure he would be able to make the step into the house. A nagging feeling of having met her tickled his pain-racked mind.

She hooked her arm around his waist and struggled to get him inside. Once there she leaned him against the wall until the door was closed and locked behind them. Then the woman disappeared into the interior of house and pulled the curtains closed. Only when that was done did she switch on the small light in the outer room.

Luke glanced around. He was in a small but clean kitchen. The house was old, probably built in the thirties but it was clean. As the woman disappeared deeper inside the house his knees buckled, and he slid down the wall, collapsing onto the kitchen floor. When the woman returned she stood in shock looking at the blood smearing the wall Luke slid down. She prayed the outer wall of the house didn't show the same signs. If it did their secret would be revealed and both she and the man she was trying to save would be found and, she knew, they would both be dead. Tucking her fear away she slowly advanced.

Luke closed his eyes as sweat broke out over his body. He fought for control over the pain searing his brain and fogging his thinking but knew he was losing the battle. The slender arm slipping around his waist startled him. Forcing eyes to open he studied the woman. She was beautiful. Standing about five feet seven she was still a foot shorter than he. Nose short and straight, high cheekbones and hazel eyes speckled with gold dust. Seeing the gold in her eyes Luke remembered where and when he met this woman. Unless she changed drastically in the past few years, which he doubted, he knew he could trust her with his life. He hoped so. He was too injured to defend against another attack.

Squatting in front of him she braced herself to lift him. "Come on, big guy. I need to get you to bed before you pass out. That won't be comfortable for either of us."

His right hand came up, unbidden, to touch her face and was surprised to feel the shudder that ran though her at his touch. "I refuse to put you in danger any longer." He whispered weakly, letting his hand drop. "The longer I'm here the more likely they are to find me. I refuse to allow you to become any more involved than what you already are."

She snorted. "You need medical care. You have to trust someone and right now, I'm it. Push while I try to lift you to your feet. After I get you to bed and the bleeding under control we can discuss the danger."

Seeing the determined look, Luke tried to comply.

Cory's heart went out to the young man she just dragged through her house and was now lowering onto her bed. Except for hearing him groan once she could detect no sign of the pain he was in. The man was tall, six feet eight if he was an inch. Black hair, brown eyes and high cheekbones revealed a strong Native American heritage. His clothes were blood soaked as were hers from being next to him. Her pulse quickened at the thought of what she had done and what she was about to do.

The ringing phone startled her. As she reached out to answer it his hand shot out, covering her wrist to stop her. Confused she watched as he put his index finger to his lips to waylay her questions, pulling up his shirt. With difficulty she covered the gasp that threatened to escape at the sight of the wires taped to his chest. Slowly she picked up the phone, lowering the receiver back into the cradle. Was their earlier conversation in the kitchen overheard?

"I need to get out of here, lady. Just put a bandage on my side and I'll go." Luke hoped she would follow his lead.

"Sit down, young man." Cory's voice was sharp and stern. "I don't know who you are or how you got that knife wound in your side, but I guess it's to be expected with all the gangs riled the way they are." She put her fingers to her lips shaking her head at him. Gathering some papers off the bedside table she shuffled through them noisily. "All right. I need to get some information. What's your name?" Again, she cautioned him to silence. Cory forced a laugh. "How about an address then?" Luke admired her cool as well as the game she played.

"Very well. I can tell by your silence you're going to be registered as another John Doe. You're the fifteenth we've had at this clinic today. The cops are already complaining." She gave a gentle laugh which caused Luke to smile. "All right tall, dark, handsome and silent. Let's take a look at that knife wound."

Taking her scissors, she cut away his shirt. Cory schooled her face when she saw the damage to his well-tanned, well-muscled body. Swallowing hard she kept her voice level. "The wound isn't too bad. The injury doesn't even need stitches. I can get Dr. Paul to look at this or I can just slap on a bandage. The choice is yours."

"A bandage will do fine. I need to get out of here."

"I hear that from all you gang members." She sighed heavily. "When are you going to learn that living is a whole lot more fun than dying?" She sighed heavily again. "Take your shirt off young man. I will get some supplies and be right back. Do me a favor next time?"

"What?"

"Go across town to the hospital. The cops have been running in and out of this clinic since these gang wars started. Dr. Paul thinks we should put in a revolving door. Besides I was supposed to be off duty an hour ago. I'm hungry and want to go home." Again, she laughed letting the sentence trail off closing the door to the bedroom as the last words were spoken.

Quickly she removed the tape securing the microphone to his chest as he helped remove the transmitter. Once it was in her hands she shrugged, giving him a 'what next' look. Luke motioned as if he was drinking a glass of water. Gently pressing the wire into his hand Cory fled to the kitchen. When she returned Luke submerged everything into the glass. "If the damn thing does work they shouldn't be able to hear now. Thank you." He whispered, sinking into the pillow, eyes closed.

Cory frowned. The man had a bullet lodged in the left side of his chest, another ripped along his left ribcage and God only knew what was wrong with his hip. "The bullet has to come out and I need to see what condition your hip is in. Judging from the amount of blood on those jeans it will probably need to be sutured. I'm going to call a friend for help."

Luke's eyes shot open and chocolate brown pools stared at her causing her to blush. "Look, Mister. I'm a nurse and the medical supplies in this house are limited. I managed to save your hide from those gunmen chasing you. I accepted your word that you're with the FBI although you have no proof. I willingly brought you to my house and now you are now taking up space in my bed. I'm just as involved with whatever mess you're in as you are. The least you can do is trust me as much as I've trusted you. I have no wish to deal with a dead body in the morning. The choice is simple. I either take you to the hospital or I call my friend. The decision is yours. Which will it be?"

Luke knew she was right. Without some quick medical attention, he would die before morning. "Friend."

Cory picked up the phone and dialed from memory. "Jasper? Thank God you are home. This is Cory and I have a problem. I need your help..."

Bending over Luke she applied more bandages to staunch the flow of blood. "No Jasper. It's not the twins. I need you to get some equipment from your old clinic and get to my house right away. Don't argue and please don't ask questions. Just get the list of things I need and bring them as soon as you can." As she named off the long list she started unbuckling his belt and open the fly to his jeans. She froze when her fingers touched something metallic knowing it was a gun. Cautiously she returned the phone to the cradle.

The man before her seemed to be drifting in and out of consciousness. After a deep cleansing breath Cory carefully removed the pistol. Running her fingers around his waistline she gently removed the one from the small of his back. "My God, mister. If you're not with the FBI I'm in deep shit." She mumbled aloud as she put both pistols in the drawer of her bedside table. Drawing a deep breath to steady her nerves she cut the rest of his clothes from his body, gaping at the ragged gash in his hip. No bullet did that damage she knew. That was caused from a jagged piece of glass. Once again, she set about bandaging the wound. Cory barely got the sheet over him when the doorbell sounded. The man's body jerked in spasms as the shrill sound echoed through the room.

She hurried to answer the door. Pulling the box of supplies from Jasper's hands she set it on the floor before pulling him inside. "Cory, this city has gone mad." Jasper's voice boomed through the house. "Not only are there gang fights but also a drug bust gone bad. Eleven FBI agents slaughtered and one missing. Not more than six blocks from here either, girl. Best you keep your daddy's pistol real handy tonight."

Cory closed and locked the door before turning to give her friend a grateful hug. "Thanks for coming, Jasper. I knew you would help me."

Jasper turned worried eyes to the woman before him seeing the blood on her clothes. "What's going on, Cory?"

Cory giggled. "Thankfully the blood is not mine. Follow me, dear heart. You'll never believe this." Jasper shuffled into the bedroom but stood rooted in the doorway. "For God's sake, Mister. Put that damn gun away." Cory ordered setting the box down. "This is my friend, Jasper. He's the doctor I called. I told you it was either going to the hospital or for me to call my friend for help. You agreed to the friend. Remember?"

Luke eased the hammer into the safety position, forcing himself to relax as he raked his eyes over the older gentleman. The doctor was a heavy-set black man with white hair whose eyes looked as if they were going to pop out of his head. "Sorry. I'm a bit jumpy."

Cory took the pistol and replaced it in the draw. Her eyes snapped with anger when she turned back to Luke. "Jasper is here to help. It was your choice. Remember? Would you rather I call an ambulance?"

"No." He mumbled sinking against the pillow.

Jasper shuffled to the bed. Lifting the bandages, he shook his head at what met his eyes. "Cory, start the IV and get fluids into him. He lost a lot of blood and will die without them. When you finish give him something for pain. Then I'll tell you how to get that bullet out."

Cory stared mouth agape. "I can't remove that bullet. That's why I called you."

"I'm a doctor, honey. If I take that bullet out I'm required to report it. Obviously, this man doesn't want these wounds reported or he would have gone to the hospital. You, on the other hand, are not required to say anything by law. Now it becomes your choice."

"I can't. What if I screw up?" Her voice trembled with fear as she stared at Jasper.

"If you screw up I die." Luke captured her eyes when he spoke. "If you fail to do anything I'll die anyway. I have nothing to lose."

Cory clamped her lips together to keep from responding and concentrated to keep her hands from shaking as she slid the IV needle into his vein. Regulating the drip, she turned to Jasper desperation showing in her eyes. Jasper laughed at her fear. "You'll do fine, my dear. Give him some Demerol for the pain and scrub up. I'll tell you exactly what to do."

Cory obeyed silently. Donning the sterile gloves the old doctor opened for her, she sat hesitantly on the bed. She knew when the Demerol took effect for the pain lines in the man's forehead and around his eyes eased. Swallowing hard she tried one last time. "You sure you don't want to go to the hospital, Mister?"

"My name is Luke and I'm positive." His voice was slightly slurred. "Go ahead." He tried to smile for emphasis knowing he failed miserably. "I'll die if you hesitate much longer and we all know that."

Jasper held Luke to the bed while Cory concentrated on his instructions, faltering only when Luke moaned. Tears of relief flooded her eyes when the bullet finally came free of his body and she dropped it into the bowl Jasper held with shaking hands. "Now what?"

"Now you sew him up." Jasper laughed loudly at Cory's frightened look. "Don't lose your nerve now, girl. You're doing fine."

Cory closed her eyes, sucked in a deep breath, letting it out slowly. Nodding, she returned to her work. When the shoulder was finished she arched her back trying to ease the pain that settled there. Only then did she realize Luke was watching her. Blushing under his scrutiny she concentrated on sewing his side together. The bullet ricocheted off a rib, following the ribcage upward. Fear showed in Cory's face when she felt the bullet still lodged just under his left arm. Seeing Jasper nod she slowly picked up the scalpel again. Her voice was gentle when she spoke. "Luke the second bullet is still in you. I have to remove it."

"Go ahead. It can't possibly hurt any worse than having the one in my chest removed." He whispered.

Cory couldn't meet his eyes. She struggled to get into a better position, yet the wound was too close to the bed. "This isn't working, Jasper." She whispered. "I can't get to the bullet while he's lying on his back and it will cause him intense pain to be moved." Tears were sliding down her face.

"Just do it, Cory. I know you can." Luke's whispered reply reached her. "This was my choice. Remember?"

At Cory's sharp intake of breath Jasper circled the bed, pulling Luke onto his side to give Cory better access to the wound. "Give him some more Demerol, honey. That will help control the pain." Once Luke was on his side Jasper saw the bandage covering the left hip. "Lordy, son. How many times did you get shot?"

"Only twice, Sir, once in the shoulder and once in the ribs." Luke mumbled as the Demerol took effect. "That's the result of jumping through the window. It was the only way out, so I took it."

"Um. Um. Um." Jasper shook his head as he pulled the dressing loose to see better. The glass had cut deep, starting at the hipbone and following down the leg nine inches in a very ragged line. "Since it's not a bullet wound I'll sew it up. It's going to be tricky and will hurt like hell." He grinned at Luke. "Missy and I will exchange places. That should give you something better to look at than this old gizzard."

Luke's smile was shallow at best. The little lady was definitely much easier on the eyes, yet he doubted he would enjoy her company any more than he did the old doctor's especially when the doctor began sewing up the leg. It was hard enough to control the pain now and Cory was being very gentle. He doubted the old doctor would be as gentle. His eyes fluttered close and he forced them to open. He was tired. Desperately tired and he could not stop his eyes from closing again.

"Finished." Cory sighed looking at Jasper. "Now what?" She knew her worry reflected in her eyes, yet she didn't care, her old friend would understand. She saw the same concern reflecting in his.

"Now we fix the hip. Find me a couple of pillows, Missy. We need to prop his leg up so I can work. After that we need hot water to clean the blood off him and see what other injuries this young man has. When we're finished we need to plan what to do with him."

Jasper was examining the hip wound when she returned from the twin's room with pillows. Positioning the leg was painful. Although no moans or complaints escaped she heard Luke's sharp intake of breath. At Jasper's bidding she hurried to give him more Demerol. Luke was practically lying across her lap before Jasper was satisfied with the position of the leg. Pain ripped across Luke's face, and Cory's heart, as Jasper probed for glass that may have been left behind. A fine sheen of sweat erupted on Luke's body. Jasper shuffled out of the room returning with a cool, wet cloth. "Wash him with that until we're finished." Jasper stated as he handed the cloth to Cory. "See if you can get him to relax a little. It will help with his pain."

As she ran the cloth over Luke's face and back, the firm, taunt, bronze muscles slowly relaxed and she was sure the Demerol had taken effect. The minute her gentle ministries ceased his muscles instantly became a hard knot again and the process would start all over. Cory felt a sense of guilt. Touching his body thrilled her. She had to keep him relaxed. It would help keep the pain at bay. The tighter his muscles were the more his shoulder wound would hurt. If he relaxed he might let his guard down enough to sleep. He needed all the sleep he could get so his body would heal.

That's what she mentally told herself therefore she failed to understand the breathlessness she was experiencing. Nor did she understand the crazy way her heart tripped in her chest. It had to be the fear this night created, she reasoned. Who wouldn't be afraid after what she had gone through especially seeing the damage to Luke's body? Anyone who was not afraid was a fool and she was far from being a fool. She heard Jasper swear under his breath as Luke shuddered against her. Her heart twisted at both the sound and the movement. "What's wrong?"

"There are multiple pieces of glass in this hip. It would help if that young man would just pass out." Jasper grumbled. "Hang on tight to him and try not to let him move while I get them out. Damn but he is going to have some terrible scars."

"Finish this, doctor." Luke gasped.

Cory pulled his face where she could see him better. "Hold on Luke. Jasper is doing the best he can." Running the cloth over his face she pushed his hair from his forehead, sighing as she fingered his thick black hair. It was shoulder length and had the slightest hint of a curl. He was badly in need of a shave and knew he would be even more handsome once the ugly beard was gone.

As soon as he fell asleep and all the wounds were tended she would have to look at the back wall of the house and more than likely would have to clean the blood from it, so Luke's hiding place wasn't discovered. She also had to clean the blood from the kitchen wall. Cory was determined to shave him after that. All this had to be done before daylight gave away her activities. Sighing she rubbed at the tense muscles of Luke's shoulder and back. So much to do before the sun rose. She was surprised when the clock in the living room struck four.

Fate certainly dealt her a strange hand this night. Even when she allowed herself to acknowledge the wild and passionate dreams she sometimes had she was sensible enough to understand they were only dreams. She was a professional and it would do her well to remember that. This man, who exuded of male virility, was only in her bed because he was injured. If not for a horrible twist of fate...Cory shook her head to stop the advancement of her thoughts and the painful memories.

Pulling herself into reality she became just that, a professional. She checked his forehead for fever. Checked on Jasper's progress and noted he was almost finished. She checked the other injuries making sure the bleeding hadn't started again. Checking the IV she saw it was almost empty. Reaching for another bag of fluid she prepared to hang it in place. Cory was careful to stretch only the upper half of her body and not move her legs under Luke as she exchanged the empty bag for the full one. What she failed to notice was chocolate brown eyes watching her from under half closed lids.

# Chapter Two

"WHERE IN THE HELL COULD that damn Indian be?" Captain Greg Waltz was paged when the bodies of his men were found. This was the bust they had waited for, planned for, the one that would allow him to retire with a good bust and a closed case. He plopped his lanky frame into his oversized chair and reached for the antacid in his drawer. He swore. How could anything so well planned have gone so wrong? Could Luke's suspicions of a mole be correct?

As he watched the bustle of activity through the glass walls of his office Luke's words came back to him. "Why not? The money is damn good. This has been too easy. No one ever questioned who I was or where I came from. Information has been handed to me on a silver platter. I'm telling you Greg we're being set up royally and I for one don't want to take the fall." Greg heard those words once before and the memory of the last time sent chills of apprehension crawling along his skin. There was no proof last time. No proof this time. All he had was gut instinct and that instinct told him Luke judged the situation correctly.

If it were true, then who was it? Who would sell out the lives of eleven fellow officers for money? How could anyone live with that on his conscience? As much as it galled him he had to consider the possibility of a mole. Who? Who would do such a thing?

Luke wanted to scrap the entire operation, yet Greg couldn't convince his superior. No matter how much he argued Major Thoms refused to listen. How could he tell someone his suspicions when there was nothing solid to back them up? The accusation was serious enough to ruin a person's career and Greg hesitated about doing that without hard evidence. There was never anything to suggest a mole was involved.

The information Luke filtered in, with relative ease as he put it, was for the smaller dealers. Never any of the bigger shipments Luke was always able to find out about. Lack of information was the reason his superior gave him for continuing the stakeout. He wanted the boss of the arms dealers and no excuses would be accepted.

Greg thought about the previous night. Since the meeting place was changed almost hourly he assigned twenty-four men to back Luke up. They were supposed to tail him until they could get a fix on his location and then surround the meeting place. At the first sign of trouble they were to rush the warehouse and get him out. The fact the meeting place was constantly being changed alerted the suspicious side of Greg. It was too much like the last time.

Then the damn gangs decided to start a blood bath and kill each other off. His superior, Major M. M. Thoms, decided twelve men could handle the operation especially since Luke couldn't get anything except small time pushers and pulled the others to help with the gang violence. Greg objected. Violently. To no avail.

Major Thoms gave the order himself. At eleven Greg got a call on his private line. Something was wrong with Luke's wires he was told. What they could hear besides static was garbled. Some tall man with blonde hair and a black suit entered the building ten minutes earlier. They were able to get pictures of everyone who entered the building yet were worried about the uselessness of the wires. Luke had no communication with them.

Luke's warning reared its head. This was too much like the last time, the time when he lost a friend and a partner. Greg ordered his men to enter the warehouse. Calls jammed the phone lines of the gunfire being heard in the area. Greg tried to pull more agents to the scene knowing they would never arrive in time. Now eleven of his men were in the morgue and Luke, number twelve, was missing.

He swallowed another dose of antacid. The sharp rap on the door brought him to his feet. Motioning the junior agent inside, he braced himself for the report. "Captain, Luke must have escaped. We found a large amount of blood on the roof of the warehouse and the one adjoining it. The window was smashed from the inside. We followed a blood trail for almost seven blocks but lost it in the residential area. He's bleeding badly, Sir."

Greg went pale. "How bad?"

"From the amount of blood we found under the eaves of one of the buildings my guess would be he's critical. If he didn't get medical help last night he's probably…" The young agent shuffled, unable to look into the stricken face of his Captain. "Sorry, Sir."

Greg sank heavily into his chair. No. He wouldn't believe that crazy Indian was dead. Luke was not dead until he was dead and without a body he was not dead. The sound of his fist hitting forcefully against his desk sounded like a death knoll even to Greg's deadened ears. Anger surged at the dead ends they were meeting. Striding to the door he bellowed orders. "I want every available agent in my office in one hour. I care little if they are on duty, off duty or on vacation. Get on the phones and get them in here. One hour, gentlemen." The glass windows of the office rattled as Greg slammed the door.

★ ★ ★ ★ ★

Jasper was finally finished and stretched the muscles of his back. "Cory, girl, go fix us all something to eat. Broth for this young man, something fortifying for us. It's going to be a long day before this is over."

Cory opened her mouth to speak then slammed it shut. Once the bedroom door closed behind her Jasper turned his attention to Luke. "Do you have some place to hide until you're better? A place Cory can go with you? She must go with you, you know. If all I heard is true she will die a horrible death just because she helped you."

Luke could see the concern in the old gentleman's eyes. It matched his own. He forced his mind to work around the Demerol Cory had given him. There was only one place he knew where they would both be safe. Drawing a deep breath, he finally nodded. "Yes. I know of one place where safety will be assured both of us. It's a seven-hour drive and I'm in no condition to help. Can she drive?"

"She can drive only she doesn't have a car." Luke saw the pain that filtered across the old man's face. He worried his white hair as he thought. "I can get a station wagon for her to use." Jasper said slowly. "These people that shot you," worried eyes met Luke's, "They will be looking for you?"

Luke sighed rubbing at the headache bothering him. "Afraid so. Not only them but also a lot of other people. I can't afford for anyone to find me until I'm better. Someone set me up and until I'm well enough to do something about it both Cory and I will remain in danger. She'll have to go with me to insure her safety."

He closed his eyes shielding his fear from the doctor's knowing eyes. There would be roadblocks and check stations he knew. Eleven murdered FBI agents would insure that. Unless his position was well hidden in the car he would never escape. A plan formed in his mind. "Does she do any camping? Have any equipment?"

The question surprised Jasper. "All the time. She helps with the local Scout Troop. Since she has a basement most of the camping gear is stored there. Why?"

"It will be needed where we're going. It can also be used to pack around me, so no one will notice when we get to the roadblocks. She'll need to wear her Scout uniform to get through the checkpoints and pack as many clothes as possible. It will still be cold at night where we are going yet hot in the day…" Luke sensed Cory in the room. Looking up he saw her, face white, staring at them from the doorway.

"I can't possibly go anywhere. I have a job to worry about." Initial shock gone anger replaced it. "I have responsibilities. I don't even get paid until next week. I have exactly five dollars to live off of between now and then. People are depending on me, not just the hospital but my sisters as well. Do you think people can just pick up and leave because you…" The ringing phone stopped her tirade. Pushing the tray she carried, none to gently into Jasper's lap, she picked up the receiver. "Hello." Anger laced her voice.

"Cory? Is something wrong?"

Cory sighed, forcing herself to loosen the death grip she had on the receiver. "No, Carrie Ann. Nothing is wrong. I just stubbed my toe while trying to get to the phone. Did the twins arrive?" She turned her back on Luke's laughing eyes.

"Yes. I'm so glad they're out of Chicago. Stories of the gang fights and the FBI killings have been on the news all night. Those killings were close to your house. We've been afraid for your safety. The twins insisted I call earlier but I was cut off. The lines have been so busy this was the first chance I had to get through. I really do wish you would tell that hospital to get screwed and leave. I know it's too impulsive for you to do but I'm worried about you."

"So am I, Sis. This time the violence has been too close for comfort. If it wasn't for supporting the twins I would dearly love to do as you suggest."

"Let the twins live with me for a while. Even if they have to start school here it would be preferable to you living so close to the violence. Damn, Cory. I know you feel responsible but there was nothing you could have done for mom and dad. Good God, Sis, get the hell out of there while you still can."

Cory sighed. She knew her sisters were worried but there was more to think about. There was the house. Her job. Her life. It wasn't much however it was all she had, and she hated the thought of leaving all she owned behind just because…She didn't realize she failed to respond until her sister called her name. "I have almost a month of vacation time coming, and I thought I would do some camping. Now that the twins are with you…"

"That would be wonderful." Carrie Ann exclaimed. "Can you do it soon? Those killings happened practically in your back yard and the twins are concerned because they haven't found the gunmen or that missing FBI agent. Oh, Cory, just pack your bags, tell the hospital to take a flying leap and come stay with me. If you leave now you could be here by late evening. You're a good nurse and I'm sure you'll be able to find another job without any trouble. Hell, your record speaks for itself. We can deal with the house and your belongings later."

Cory sighed, glancing at Luke. He seemed to be dozing. At least he didn't show any signs of the pain she knew he must be in. She started when her sister called her name again. "I'm sorry Carrie Ann, I was thinking. If I'm going to disrupt my life by quitting the hospital I'm going to do things I want to do. I refuse to move in with you just because this city has gone to hell in a basket. Since I don't have to worry about the twins I would like to…" She sighed, tears smarting her eyes. "I don't know what I want to do. I need some time alone to think about my future. Maybe I'll go camping."

"Well, whatever you do, do it quickly. It will do you good to explore new places. You never know you just might find that special man who can turn you on. You've become such a stuffy homebody since mom and dad died. You even quit dating. You need a man in your bed to drive your senses to distraction."

Luke watched Cory from under half closed lids. It amused him to see the slow blush creeping up Cory's neck and bloom in her cheeks. Never before had he known a beautiful woman who blushed. Whoever this Carrie Ann was and whatever she said had a deciding impact on Cory. Guilt stabbed him when he heard her words. He was asking the world of a woman who didn't even remember him.

"Look, Carrie Ann, I don't have time in my life for a man right now. I have my career and the twins to think about." Cory pulled the phone from her ear as her sister's laughter echoed over the line. She frowned at Jasper when he coughed loudly to cover his own laughter and her blush deepened. Turning her back to the bed she whispered, "I certainly don't need a man hanging about my bed either. I have enough to contend with. Now is not the time to discuss this, Carrie Ann."

"Sweet sister, at thirty-two you should have had several lovers by now. I can tell by your voice I've angered you but I'm serious about you leaving the city. The twins can stay with me for as long as it takes. I'll let you go but please, do get out. You know we worry about you."

Cory sighed again, her eyes meeting Luke's. "All right, Sis. I'll leave in a couple of hours. Since I intend to go camping don't be surprised if I fail to contact you for several weeks. I might just stay out until it's time for the twins to come home. If I quit without notice, I'll never be able to return to the hospital. It may be hard to get another job."

Carrie Ann's voice became serious. "I'll hold you to that, Cory. We really are worried about your safety especially now that the gangs are acting up in your neighborhood. Be careful and enjoy yourself. Talk to you when I hear from you."

Cory stared absently at the phone in her hand. Find herself a man indeed. She wondered what her sister would say if she knew she had one hell of a hunk of a man in her bed this very instant. A giggle escaped as she imagined her older sister and the disbelief she knew that revelation would have plastered across her face. If the circumstances were different she might have been tempted to tell.

"What did your sister have to say?" Jasper pried.

"Just that the twins got there safely." She replied, needlessly checking Luke's IV and multiple bandages.

"Uh huh. What else?"

Once again Cory could feel the deep red blush flood her cheeks. Her embarrassment was worse when Luke's eyes met hers. Avoiding both men's eyes she shrugged. "Same old, same old. She's worried about the news reports they listened to concerning the gang violence and the missing FBI agent. She's insisting I leave the city and all I own behind to come live with her. She's afraid something will happen to me." Her back stiffened when she heard Jasper's knowing chuckle. Anger snapped in her hazel eyes. "I'll bring you some coffee then I'll feed Luke."

Pouring coffee helped steady her nerves. Returning, she sat on the bed and fed Luke, ignoring her own meal. "I appreciate the soup however something a little more substantial would have relieved my hunger better." His voice was quiet as he watched Cory.

"Maybe by noon if your fever stays down." Jasper laughed at the anger and frustration that crossed Luke's face. "Don't expect it then for I fear the fever will hit with force long before that time. Since I have no antibiotics in my clinic there's nothing I can give you to offset the fever. Right now, we need to plan. Cory needs to call the hospital and arrange for an indefinite leave of absence so she can get her job back. I'll go to the bank and drain my savings. You can pay me back when you can."

"No." Luke growled. "I'll take care of the money. That'll have to wait until very last. First, we need the station wagon and to get things packed. We've got to get through the check stations without being detected. The Scout uniform may just be our ticket safely out of Chicago. It will also explain the amount of camping gear we'll need to hide me under."

Luke rubbed his head. His pain was returning in force and he knew he had to explain the plan before it claimed possession of his mind. "Put me in the back of the station wagon and put coolers at my head and feet. You'll need a piece of ply board to put over the coolers. The camping gear can be packed over the board and will conceal my position in the car. Everything else can be packed around that."

Panic seized Cory as she imagined Luke's suggestion in her mind. "What about the IV? How do you plan to hide that?"

"It will have to come out." At her terrified look he tried to smile. "Until we get to our destination anyway. After that you can stick me again."

Cory didn't like it. She did not like causing pain to this virile man in her bed any more than she liked the idea of running out on her responsibility at the hospital. She didn't like the idea of turning her life upside down in the blink of an eye even if it was to help the man she knew. The entire sum of her life was in this house and in her job. How would she survive without a job? Why was she even considering this ridiculous scheme? She thought herself stupid for even thinking about doing any of this. What would she have when this was over? More heartache? More anger? More bills?

Luke could see her indecision. Grabbing her wrists, he stayed the nervous flutter of her hands. "Trust me, Cory. I may be shot to hell but I'm still the good guy here." He gave her a prize-winning smile and felt the pulse in her wrists jump. "We need to get out of here in a hurry. Those drug dealers will never stop looking for me until I'm dead. That death warrant now extends to you since you helped me escape their grasp."

Cory saw the truth in his eyes. The tip of her tongue slid between her lips to give moisture to their extreme dryness. "I'll start packing but you owe me one hell of a good reference for another job when we get back because the hospital will terminate me instead of giving me a leave of absence." Guilt stabbed through Luke again. He imposed on this woman in a time of desperate need and pain. Now, she was giving up all she knew to help him further. He would make it up to her somehow providing they both made it out of this mess alive.

*  *  *  *  *

Captain Greg Waltz had the full attention of everyone in the crowded office. "From all indications Agent Patterson has been seriously injured. Since none of the hospitals or clinics report treating him it can mean one of three things. One, he is still trying to outwit the drug dealers following him. Two, they've captured him. Three, he's dead and his body just hasn't surfaced. We need to figure out which it is. Agent Luke Patterson has now become our only concern and you are all assigned to find him. One way or the other."

A young agent by the name of Fred Adkins spoke up. "Excuse me, Sir. There's another possibility. Luke could have found someone to help."

Greg was irritated with Adkins and it reflected in his voice. "Not likely. That meeting place was changed numerous times before this massacre went down. I know for a fact he didn't have time to scout the area around those warehouses. Hell, none of us did. If he's injured as severely as we fear, who do you think would come to his aid? If you met a severely wounded man lurking in the shadows would you offer aid and comfort to him? Do you think anyone would attempt to give aid with all the shots that were fired?" He knew his irritation at Agent Adkins and his concern for Luke was showing in his face.

Agent Adkins shuffled under the glare he received from the Captain. "It's just that Luke was taught well by his grandfather. He's pretty savvy when it comes to survival." Adkins mumbled under his Captain's stare. Luke had been training Fred for at least a year in his spare time and Fred respected the man even more than he respected Captain Waltz, which he held in high esteem.

A knock on the door squelched Greg's angry reply. Susan Tameron his secretary entered, confusion marring her face. "Excuse me, Sir. I know you said not to disturb you however I just received the strangest call." She hesitated until Greg motioned her in.

Irritation at having the meeting disturbed filtered across his face before he was able to control it. Greg knew his secretary wouldn't have interrupted unless absolutely necessary. "What was the call about?"

"A woman called asking for you. I told her you were in a meeting. The message was so strange I wrote it down to make sure I got it right. The woman said not to trace the call. That she had information concerning the missing FBI agent and would call back in one hour. She said for Greg Waltz to be waiting for she would talk to none other."

"She asked for me by name?" At the secretary's nod he drummed his fingers on the desk. Odd. Why would a woman ask specifically for him? It made no sense considering the situation. If he was requested by name the person had to know him. "Did she say who she was? Did you recognize her voice?"

The secretary shifted nervously. "No to both questions, Sir."

"Did you trace it?"

"Tried to. She hung up too fast. We do know it originated from the area of the warehouses. Sorry, Sir."

Greg buried his face in his hands. He knew the others were watching but he had to think. She didn't mention Luke by name but that meant little especially if Luke was alive. If he was alive why have the woman call the main office line? Why not his private line? Maybe Luke was in too bad a shape to tell her which number to call. If that was so how did she know the call would be traced? How did she know exactly when to get off the phone before the number could be traced?

Why did she know him well enough to request him by name? Did she really know about Luke or was this some kind of sick joke the woman was playing with them? News of the missing agent was plastered all over the media and Greg knew how many sick people there were in the world. Deep in his gut he knew the call was real, yet unanswered questions chased each other around in his mind.

Glancing at his watch, he took a deep breath and tied his emotions together by a thread. "All right." He nodded to his secretary, waiting until she left the room. "What happened to the pictures Agent Burns said they took of everyone entering that warehouse?"

"No help." Rafe DeAngelo stated. "The film must have been defective. Lab boys are trying to bring the images up but have yet to succeed. Every one of them are black. We found nothing on the cell phones either. The memory cards had been wiped clean on the phones. All the phones, Sir."

Shock rippled through Greg as Luke's warning screamed through his mind. "Dear God, how could that happen? All the pictures are useless? We still have no idea who these people are? How can that be?"

"Unfortunately, that's about the size of it." Rafe stated. "The only person alive who can identify those in the warehouse is Luke."

"And he's missing." The other agents winced at the anguish in Greg's voice. He took a deep cleansing breath trying to control his emotions. "I want a search of every building in the warehouse district. If nothing turns up, we extend the search to the surrounding communities. Knock on every door. Surely to God someone saw something out of the usual last night. Any information right now is more than we have to work with which is exactly nothing. Have we gotten any information from our snitches? Anything from the neighborhood behind the warehouse? Anything?"

"Not much. Most were scared inside because of the gang fights. We even interviewed the homeless and hookers in that sector. If anyone saw or heard anything they're keeping their information very quiet."

Greg sighed. He knew this was as hard for the agents as it was for him. Still Luke's warning nagged at him and he had to wonder just who among them would be selling information that cost so many lives.

"When the warehouse was entered, besides our men, how many were injured or dead?"

"Three." Rafe stated. "Two dead, one injured. We didn't get much information. He was questioned while waiting for the ambulance but was too scared to talk. Later, after surgery, he was placed in a private room. His guard was found unconscious and the man escaped. None of the nurses working the floor saw or heard anything. We're investigating the hospital personnel. The man was in no condition to escape. There had to be someone helping him."

Greg groaned. What else could go wrong? How many more blunders or problems were they to face before they were able to close this case? "I need a current report to take to Major Thoms. Hand everything you have to Rafe and then return to the warehouse district. We need to find information on Luke, and we need it in a hurry. Rafe, I want you to compile the information you receive then get it to me, but I want the information as complete as possible. If we catch these bastards I want to make damn sure nothing is overlooked to get them off when they finally go to trial."

Rafe nodded. "Do you want us to divide our forces? We could cover a greater area, but it would put us at a greater risk should another attack comes especially since we don't know who did this."

Greg looked at Rafe considering the suggestion. "No. Everyone is to pair off. We already lost eleven good men last night. I don't want any more names added to the list. It will be safer if you stay together. If Luke is alive I doubt he'll come out of hiding until he believes it's safe. Our responsibility is to make it safe for him while keeping ourselves alive." Greg stood looking over his men. "I'm going to be making funeral arrangements all afternoon. Watch for the list to show up for pallbearers. You be damned careful and cover each other. Let me know if you find anything that might help us help Luke."

Quietly the agents filed out of the office.

★ ★ ★ ★ ★

Luke knew Greg would be going crazy, yet he had to protect the woman who saved his life. Cory Sims was a contradiction in terms. Professional as a nurse when it came to taking care of his wounds or feeding him, yet she blushed like a teenage schoolgirl whenever she touched his skin. She was brave in the face of danger, evidenced by the charade she put on for the benefit of his pursuers, however this morning she was timid about escaping the very evil she saved him from. He could see the fear she tried to hide.

He knew she spent several hours outside the house washing away the evidence of his being there, his blood, and then spent several more cleaning the kitchen wall. He realized she had to be exhausted or close to it. That worried him. He needed her quick mind to help get them out of the city. If she failed at the checkpoints the agents would insist on inspecting her vehicle.

Luke hated himself for his uselessness. The only redeeming grace he currently had was that he'd be needed to guarantee her safety once they got to their destination. She would argue, of that Luke had no doubt. There wasn't any choice except for her to stay with him once they escaped. It was the only place the two of them could be totally protected from the long reaches of Jason Grover and his spies. Still he couldn't calm the guilt that riddled him knowing by not telling her everything he would be forcing her to do something that would injure her sense of morality and possibly make her hate him.

She was packing for a trip into the unknown. From her actions he doubted she remembered him, but he remembered her. Quite vividly in fact. She had been a constant source of worry for him even after he returned from his assignment, to find her parents were murdered. That worry increased when he failed to discover where she lived, needing to know she was all right after all the hurt in her life. She lived modestly he could see that for himself. Not only was the house she lived in old, but the furniture was old also. Not antiques, just old. It was hard for him to understand. What happened? Why did she leave the big house to live here under these conditions? He could understand why she wouldn't want to live in the other house. It would've held too many memories. But why like this? From what she said she was living on limited finances. He gleaned that much when she said she only had five dollars until the next payday. Had life been that hard on her since the death of both her parents? Why was her life this hard? Could Ralph had left them that financially strapped?

Shaking his head in confusion he allowed his body to sink into blessed sleep. Luke argued violently against another shot of Demerol. Cory stubbornly reminded him there was much to do before they left, and he needed to rest before they started on their long journey. Left arm useless because of the bullet wound, right arm damned near there because of the IV, Cory over-ruled his objections and had given him the medicine anyway.

If it wasn't so important his brain stay clear he wouldn't have minded so much. He reached his level of pain tolerance many hours ago and gone beyond it. Even though the pain eased it wasn't gone. At least now it was controllable.

Forcing his mind to work, he thought about their precarious position. Jasper told him before he left that the warehouse district was swarming with cops and FBI agents. If someone found the house now or remembered seeing the two of them together in the alley they would both be dead before the sun reached midday. That wasn't an option he was willing to accept. It did little to ease the guilt he harbored knowing what the situation was going to be like when they finally made it to the place he planned to take her.

Tears welled in Cory's hazel eyes when she called the hospital to ask for vacation time. When they refused she told them she wasn't returning. From the conversation he knew they gave her a hassle over the lack of notice. Guilt riddled him before but when he saw her tears it felt like a knife ripped his heart to shreds. After that she called her sisters and informed them she was going on an extended vacation, cautioning them not to expect to hear from her anytime soon.

Why did she help him? He wondered again as sleep claimed him.

★ ★ ★ ★ ★

Why are you doing this? Cory asked herself again. She was positive she knew this man. His hair was longer, and the beard distorted his facial features, yet Cory was sure he was the same man she remembered. She finally finished packing the numerous coolers she brought from the basement. They all belonged to her family although the Scouts used them more than she did since the accident.

Cory was shocked at being manhandled last night but recognized his wounds and the danger immediately. She blushed as she remembered her response to his plea for help. What must this handsome man think of her? She knew he didn't recognize her. Had she changed that much in five years? Shrugging she realized there was no reason why he should remember her. They only met once yet for her once was enough. He invaded her dreams for months afterward. Hell, he still invaded them.

They lived in a different house, in a different neighborhood five years ago. Closing her eyes, she let the memories invade her consciousness. She had just finished washing her hair and wrapped it in a towel when she went to answer the door. She was wearing cut-off shorts and a baggy sweatshirt at the time. When she saw her father's handsome partner she could only stutter. She remembered him all right.

Her father entered the hall behind her, and Luke Patterson slipped past her to talk with him. Since the floor refused to open up and swallow her she escaped upstairs in embarrassment. Even now her face flushed at the memory. She felt like a small child meeting the neighborhood playboy and acted like one. Maybe it was a good thing he didn't remember. If she had the slightest inkling he remembered that day she felt she would simply wilt away into dust. How could anyone act so stupidly over a man they just met?

She stacked the last of the camping gear next to the door, rubbing sore eyes. She didn't know what their destination was. That angered her, but Luke insisted it was safer if she didn't know. Trust him, he commanded. She knew she could. He was one of a handful of people she knew she could trust with her life, yet it tried her patience to be leaving her past behind to go into an unknown future.

Luke was too much like her father. He wouldn't give an ounce of information until they were safely out of the city. She would have done the same thing if the circumstances were reversed. Long ago she learned to keep her hiding places secret. Even her father hadn't known most of them. She sighed heavily, shaking the tiredness from her bones. She still had to pack her belongings and was badly in need of a shower. The smell of blood would be detected quicker than anything, arousing suspicions. She must do all in her power to prevent that.

Quietly she entered her room. Luke's chest was rising and falling with regularity a sure sign he was sleeping. She planned on shaving him before they left yet knew sleep would heal his wounds faster than anything. Her hand trembled when she placed it on his forehead, pushing the sweaty black hair from his face. He was hot. The fever Jasper warned about was already attacking Luke.

With a shake of her head Cory resisted the impulse to lie beside him. She pulled the bloody clothes off slipping into her robe. A quick shower sounded like heaven to her weary mind. Once the water revived her she would be ready to dress and pack. Another quick look at Luke and she hurried to the adjoining bathroom for the shower. Luke hadn't moved from his position on the bed when she returned. Another feel of his forehead warned her she would need her herbs to get him to their destination alive.

Turning to the closet she pulled her Scout shirt from the hanger. Assuring herself she hadn't disturbed the man sleeping in her bed she pulled the robe off tossing it into her suitcase and slid into a bra and the shirt. As she buttoned the shirt she realized how tired she was. Pulling panties, blue jeans and socks from the drawer she hurried with her dressing. She feared Luke would awaken and see her standing there with little or no clothes on. Once dressed, she sat on the floor, hooked her arms around her knees, pulling them close. Laying her head on her knees she promised herself only a few minutes to ease the pain in her eyes before she set to work again. God, she was tired.

Luke let her sleep. She would have to awaken soon he knew but she needed the rest. Instantly awake when she entered the room he watched her change. She was definitely beautiful. He grinned remembering the curves he could see with her back to him. Seeing her shed her uniform pants and nylons made him stop breathing. Her legs were excessively long and graceful, the panties modest and fitted against her round, shapely bottom like a second skin.

It must be the Demerol he tried to rationalize the thrill that cut through him at the sight of her just before she pulled the robe around her. He had better center his mind on keeping them alive instead of daydreaming about her lying next to him in bed, yet the thought gave him a good feeling especially knowing where he was taking her. A slow grin spread across his face as he watched Cory sleep. It was definitely going to be the most interesting recuperation period he ever had. It almost made up for being shot. Almost.

Luke drifted in and out of sleep for the next half hour. The call would have to be made soon he reminded himself and that made sleep difficult. He was taking a chance but was sure Greg was one of the good guys and they needed money to hide out on. Luke prayed his faith in Greg was not misplaced. "Cory? Wake up, sweetheart. It's time to make that call and then get the hell out of here." Luke kept his voice low trying not to startle her. He saw her stiffen but held her position on the floor. "Cory?"

"I'm awake." She mumbled. "I was just trying to get used to the sound of a man in my bed. It frightened me."

Luke grinned at her statement and stored it in the back of his mind for further consideration. He watched as she straightened her legs and back stretching the kinks from her tired body.

Yes, he smiled to himself. The next several weeks were going to be interesting. Very interesting indeed.

# Chapter Three

GREG PACED THE OUTER OFFICE waiting for the incoming call. "This woman is pushing the hour to the very minute." He grumbled, and his secretary smiled.

The ringing phone in his office was almost missed. Greg continued to pace until the secretary placed her hand on his arm. "Sir? The private line in your office is ringing. Should I answer it?"

Scowling at her grin he headed for his office. "If that woman calls again, trace it." Now what? He hated to be on one phone while the woman was due to call on another. "Waltz."

"Is this Greg?" The female voice asked. "If it is don't try to trace this, or you shall never find out about your agent. You have five seconds to decide."

"You know damned well this line can't be traced." Greg growled. "How is Luke?"

"Slow down. How do I know you are really Greg?"

"My God, woman. How am I supposed to answer that? I could be anyone and say I'm Luke's Captain."

"Exactly, so you are going to have to pass a test before I say more. Fail and I hang up and you'll never hear from me again. How long have you been assigned there?"

"Ten years."

"Good then you will know a mutual friend. He was killed after finishing an assignment. Five years ago. Car explosion in front of the office. Who was with him at the time?"

Greg sank into his chair, memory vivid. He remembered that explosion. It was one that was never solved. His voice was barely above a whisper. "His wife was with him."

"What was his name?"

"Ralph Sims."

"One more test. Pass it and I'll tell you all you want to know about your agent. Two years prior to that who was my friend's partner?"

Greg swallowed hard. Ralph Sims had a number of partners. "I don't remember who his partner was. There were several." The silence that followed while he racked his brain was strained. "Rafe DeAngelo was one of his partners. So was Luke Patterson. Hell, even I was his partner for a while. I truly don't remember who his partner was seven years ago."

"Fair enough. You've given me the name I needed. Ask your questions and I'll try to answer them."

Greg frowned at the tears in the woman's voice. "Who are you?"

"Depends on who you talk to."

"How can I be assured you really know Luke?"

"Cautious, aren't you. I guess can't fault you for that. After what happened I'd be cautious also. What if I say he's an Indian?"

"How is Luke?"

"Injured. He said to tell you it was a trap and you have a mole in the agency. He says to watch your ass."

Greg's brows furrowed in fear. "How bad is he?"

"He has been shot to hell, barely missed being captured and is currently taking up space in my...home. He says he needs money to disappear on. He's too weak to come to you. You'll have to come to us."

"Dammit, lady, let me talk to him." Greg yelled and then looked around to be sure no one heard him. He could hear the woman's muffled voice. Hand over the speaker? Why would she try to muffle her words? Was Luke really there telling her what to say? If so why was he talking to the woman instead of Luke? What the hell was going on? "Hey, lady. Are you still there?" The silence hung heavy on the line for several seconds.

"I'm sorry. He's not able to talk to you right now. Just gather some money. You're to take it to Jack's Bar and Grill outside the city. You need to be there within three hours. Do you need directions, or do you know where it's located?"

"For God's sake woman, everyone knows where Jack's Bar is located. How much money does he need?"

"Whatever you can scrape together." Came her quick response followed by a deep sigh. "I assure you that this is not a hostage situation, Captain. He's also going to need some clothes. His are no longer wearable since I cut them off to tend his wounds. It's too dangerous for me to go to his house. You're to be at Jack's Bar in three hours. Make sure you come alone, or you shall not be told where to go next."

"Will you meet me there? Will Luke be there?"

"No, to both questions. You'll be told where to go next. If you fail to come by yourself, you'll not hear from me again. Don't let anyone tail you either."

Her warning was clear. "I'm afraid that's not possible. Because of last night's massacre we've been ordered to go in pairs. I'll have to bring another agent with me. Ask Luke if he'll approve of Rafe."

"No." Her response was quick. To quick Greg decided. "If Agent DeAngelo comes with you there will be no further contact." Greg could hear the woman take a deep breath. "I'll see who Luke wants you to bring." Greg could hear her muffled curse and her voice as she talked with someone else though he couldn't hear the words. Finally, her voice came through the line. "Luke says to bring Fred Adkins. He also said for you to be very careful and not let anyone else know where you're going. He said the mole knew his every move and was responsible for the killings. He said he doesn't want to hear of your death."

"Assure him I'll be careful. I'll be at Jack's Bar with Fred Adkins in about a couple of hours. I'll be driving..." Greg frowned, hearing the phone click on the woman's end. Why didn't she let him tell her what kind of car he was driving? What kind of game was she playing? Why did she refuse to have Rafe along? How severely injured was Luke? She said he was shot to hell but how bad was he?

Sighing deeply, he returned to the outer office. Major Thoms was waiting for him, attacking when Greg arrived. "That woman has yet to call about Agent Patterson. Was that her on the private line?"

"No, Sir, just an agent from another state needing information. Maybe the woman's call was just a prank." Greg hated lying but the woman impressed him that she actually was with Luke and Luke warned him of a mole. Not once but twice. That was once too many for Greg to take his warning lightly.

"Prank my ass especially coming from the warehouse district. You let me know the minute you hear anything." The Major bellowed.

"Yes, Sir. I have to meet with the families of my dead men all afternoon. I have to leave soon to make funeral arrangements. I may not be here when she calls."

The phone rang, and Greg's secretary answered it. Covering the mouthpiece, she whispered, "It's her."

"On the intercom and trace." Major Thoms growled.

"Greg Waltz? I'm calling about your missing agent. Mr. Patterson died in the night of his gunshot wounds. He was shot in the chest and his face was terribly cut up from the glass in the warehouse. I know you are tracing. Goodbye."

"Where did that call come from?" Major Thoms growled.

"Sorry, Sir. Not enough time. The warehouse district is all we could narrow it to." Susan Tameron stated.

"Damn." Major Thoms growled as he paced in front of the desk. "We still have no clue where his body is."

Greg's voice was quiet as he watched his supervisor. "At least we know why he was bleeding so severely. God. Shot in the chest."

"I thought you needed to talk to family members." Major Thoms ground out angrily. "I suggest you get busy."

"Yes, Sir. It looks as though I have one more family to talk to. The Patterson's. Excuse me." Greg turned and left the office. What kind of game was this woman playing? First, she states Luke is alive and even called him by name. Then she calls back on another line and says Mr. Patterson died in the night. So which was it? Alive? Or dead? Pulling into traffic he pondered both calls. The woman knew too much of that he was certain. Mutual friend who was in a car explosion five years ago. He knew she was talking about Ralph Sims.

Ralph came to pick up his vacation check that day. His wife Caroline was with him. Ralph introduced her to Greg, and they talked for almost an hour about their vacation plans. They just finished backing out of the parking space when the car exploded. Greg had re-entered the building after seeing them to the car turning to watch them leave. The explosion shook the building, shattering doors and windows. That was the end of field duty for Greg. He spent two months in the hospital after being torn to shreds by flying glass. The nightmares still haunted him. Even now, five years later, he could see the car explode into flames.

The request for Fred Adkins surprised him even more. Why not Rafe? Memory hit him full force. The woman called Rafe by his last name. Did she know him? Why was she so disturbed by Rafe's presence? Luke worked often with Rafe and Greg was sure they were friends. Fred was relatively new to the agency. He hadn't been on any major assignments yet. Rafe insisted that Fred wasn't ready for field duty even though Luke said he was.

Another thought struck Greg. Major Thoms knew about the woman's call. How? He wasn't at the meeting this morning when the first call came in. So how did he find out about it? Who told him that another call was expected an hour later? He also knew it came from the warehouse district. His agitation was evident. He didn't know Luke. At least Greg didn't believe so. Not personally anyway. So why the agitation over the call that came in? He wasn't that agitated when Greg informed him of the massacre. So why now? Over a call that could very well have been a prank?

Was the second call to the outer office just a ploy on Luke's part to give him extra time to make his escape? It would be something he would do if he needed the extra time. Greg grinned. If he needed extra time it was because he was someplace close to the warehouse district. If that was the case, he would make sure Luke had all the extra time he needed.

He was holed up in the woman's house that much he understood, and he was sure Ralph Sims was another clue to his whereabouts, yet Ralph lived on the other side of the city. So how did that help him? He would have to search the communities around the warehouses himself to find the answer.

Greg slowed to a stop in front of the warehouse. Rafe spotted him and summoned the rest. "We heard from the woman again." He stretched from the car and observed the worried faces gathered around him. "She didn't stay on long enough for a trace. She did say Luke died in the night of a gunshot wound to the chest."

"Is that all?" Rafe was incredulous. "Where's his body? Where do we look? Did she say anything to help?"

Greg shook his head. "Sorry. She did say his face was badly cut up from the window glass and that he was shot in the chest. That's all I know." Greg raked his eyes over the men. All were fighting grief but Rafe. Rafe just seemed angry.

"Damn." One man muttered. "Luke was the best we had. How could this have turned out so badly? Do you think he was fingered? Do we have a traitor in our mist?"

Greg sighed deeply. "I don't know. Hell, we may never know. I want you to go over these warehouses with a fine-tooth comb. You're looking for a dead body now. He has to be somewhere close."

"What are you going to do now?" Rafe asked quietly.

"Agent Adkins is going with me to Luke's house to break the news to his housekeeper. Then I'm going to see his parents in person. This is going to rip that family apart."

"Tell them I'm sorry." Rafe pinched the bridge of his nose to stop the tears from welling. "Tell them I'll find the son of a bitch who did this to Luke. Tell them…" Rafe covered his face with his hands.

"I'll tell them. I'm sure we all feel the same way. It would be easier if they had a body to bury. Find him, dammit. Find him." Hatred for the entire situation filled his words. "Get in Adkins. You're assigned to me until all the families have been comforted."

Fred looked as if he was going to argue however at Greg's angry face he clamped his mouth shut and got into the front seat. The men moved away from the car as Greg started the engine. Silence reigned until the men were out of sight. "Excuse me, Sir, but I need..."

"Shut up, Adkins." Greg growled as he downed more of his antacid. "Your ass would still be back there with the rest of the men if you weren't specifically named to accompany me on this trip. Show me where they lost Luke's trail."

"Go down four blocks and take a left." Fred instructed. Something was wrong. Luke taught him to trust his gut instinct and it told him something was terribly wrong. His eyes narrowed on Greg. "Luke isn't dead. Is he? That's what this is all about."

"Shut up, Adkins, and keep your eyes open. Luke had faith in your abilities. Use them instead of talking because I really don't feel like discussing anything. You'll know everything soon enough." The area was crowded with police. Sliding his badge in the windshield Greg drove slowly down the block looking at every house. At the end of the street he turned around and repeated the process.

"Sir? Why would anyone back a station wagon against the door?"

Greg grinned. "I was just wondering that myself." The two exited the car and approached the house with caution. He could see the slender woman with auburn hair, dressed in a Scout Uniform, loading a variety of camping gear into the back of the station wagon. Greg gasped when the woman stood to wipe the hair from her forehead. "Corena? Corena Sims?"

"Lieutenant Waltz. Well this is a shock. It's been a long time since I last saw you. What are you doing in my neck of the woods?" Cory knew her shock reflected in her face, she just prayed she covered it well.

Greg grinned broadly as he came around the back of the station wagon. Scooping her up in his arms he gave her a big hug as his eyes quickly searched the part of the house he could see. "Goodness, I haven't seen you since..." He let the sentence trail off, embarrassed by what almost slipped from his mouth.

"It's been five years since I buried mom and dad." She said sadly. "Don't stumble over it. I've accepted their death, so you might as well do the same. I just never accepted the FBI's decision." Shrugging she continued loading the station wagon. After introducing Fred Adkins, the silence hung heavy as they loaded the remaining gear.

Cory slammed the back door of the car and then locked the house. "I see you got a promotion since I saw you last. Captain now. I'm impressed. I guess you're here for the same reason all the rest of these cops are. I heard about those agents being killed. I'm sorry for their families but at least they'll get the death benefits denied us. There's no doubt they were killed in the line of duty. Is there Captain? Not like there was with daddy." Her bitterness was evident.

Greg shuffled his feet. "I'm truly sorry for how you were treated Corena. I tried to get his case reopened when I finally got back to work. I tried to prove…"

"Tell it to someone who cares Greg. Try it on the twins or maybe Carrie Ann. They weren't responsible for the bills. I was. Explain to them how daddy devoted twenty years of his life to the FBI only to have them screw his daughters over at a time they needed help the most." Anger made her eyes bright. "He warned his superiors for months concerning an informant in the agency. After he and mom were blown into a thousand pieces they pegged him with the title of the mole. To add insult to injury they denied us his death benefits and pension. Hell, they denied us everything." Her anger brought tears to her eyes and her body was shaking with the force of her emotions. Her hands shook as she wiped viciously at her tears.

Greg gathered her in his arms again. "I did everything in my power to clear his name, Corena. Shortly after I returned to work there was a huge shake-up. Any proof I may have found got lost in the shuffle."

Cory pulled from his arms. "If what I hear is true you better start digging again. Your mole is back and its costing lives. You have eleven dead men, Greg. How many have to die before someone takes action? That's the reason I left the agency." She saw the shock in his eyes and a bitter laugh escaped. "You didn't know I was working undercover? They really did treat you like a mushroom. Didn't they?"

Greg shuffled, and Cory felt like slapping him. "I have to go." She slid behind the steering wheel gripping it until her knuckles were white. "Greg? Watch your ass. The night before Daddy died he told me who he thought the mole was. After his death I tried to find the proof. You were in a coma and the doctors thought you were going to die." She shrugged reaching for the door handle.

Greg gripped the edge of the door refusing to allow her to close it. "Who, Corena? Who was it? Give me something to go on."

She shook her head. "I never found the proof Greg. After Daddy was murdered key information turned up missing. I can tell you this. There were two of them and both of them in their own way made puppets of everyone else. Just be careful Greg and keep looking over your shoulder. I don't want to hear about your death either."

Slowly she pulled away from her life. Tears of pain and anger were streaming down her face as she tried to bury the hurt once again.

Greg was glad Adkins kept his silence. He knew the kid deserved answers, but Greg wasn't ready to give any mainly because he didn't have any. He went to Luke's house, invented some excuse he couldn't even remember, packed things he believed Luke would need and continued to Jack's Bar. They were twenty minutes early and he was toying with his food.

"Sir? Will you answer questions now?"

"As long as we're not around the other men call me Greg." He sat back, sipping his coffee while watching Fred consume his hamburger. The younger man was in his early thirties, five feet six, blonde hair, blue eyes, a little on the stout side and well-muscled. "All right. First let me explain why you're here." He related the three phone calls and some of his suspicions. "Now, ask your questions."

Fred swallowed the last of his hamburger. "Why did Miss Sims say the agency treated you like a mushroom?"

Greg laughed heartily. "Do you know how they grow mushrooms?" Seeing Fred shake his head Greg laughed again. "You keep them in the dark and feed them shit. That's exactly what they did to me. They barely gave me enough information for me to function properly once I was promoted to lieutenant. Every assignment was a struggle for the information needed. I didn't even know Corena was an agent." He worried his hair with his hands. "I was partnered with her father for several years. It was Ralph who first thought we had a mole in the agency. He warned me for months about the mole. Told that things were coming too easily. After he died I was severely injured. Once I recovered I was promoted to Captain."

Fred thought about Greg's answer. "What did she mean when she said she didn't want to hear about your death either? The 'either' is the part that confuses me."

"I've been thinking about that myself. I think she was testing me or at least my memory. I think she's the one who called. I also think she saved Luke's life last night. Make no mistake, Adkins, she is one savvy lady."

"Yes, Sir. I just can't figure out what she did with him. She would have to get him out of the city without anyone finding him. Knowing Luke, he wouldn't trust too many people with the information he was alive. I failed to see any sign of him in either the car or in the house. So, where is he?"

Conversation ceased as the waitress approached. "One of you guys named Greg?" When Greg raised his hand, she handed him a note. "There was a call for you. The man said it was an emergency and to ensure you got the message immediately."

"Man?"

"Some guy named Luke. He said it was a matter of life or death. I would've laughed if he hadn't sounded so sick."

★ ★ ★ ★ ★

Luke knew the fever would attack. Jasper warned him, yet he hoped to meet with Greg before it did. That hope failed him as his body was racked with chills. He was truly afraid he was going to die.

Cory heard his teeth chattering for the last half mile of the trip. Easing the car to a stop at the meeting place she crawled in through the back, pulling the camping gear from the plywood shielding Luke. Unrolling a sleeping bag, she tucked it around his body. "Luke, I'm going to be away from the car for a few minutes then I'll fix you something warm to drink. There will be herbs in it to help combat the fever. I'll be right back."

Luke nodded pulling the sleeping bag closer around his shoulders. The shaking increased the pain in his body a hundredfold. He had to keep his wits about him for he had yet to tell Cory of their destination. Forcing his mind to concentrate on Jason Grover he allowed anger to take control. He would find a way to hang that bastard. First, though, he had to find the mole. As long as the agency thought him dead he could stop running long enough to get well. He drifted. He knew he had. His brain and the position of the sunlight told him that much. Somewhere in that drift the shakes had mercifully stopped. The pain still existed but the shakes stopped.

"Luke? Open your eyes and drink this tea."

"What is it?"

Cory laughed. "If I told you, you would refuse to drink it. I cooled it but it will still taste nasty for I have no honey so drink it fast."

Luke did, fighting the urge to gag. Cory kept tipping the cup, forcing him to drink. Finally swallowing the last of the tea, he gasped for air. "If you're trying to poison me, woman, it would have been more humane to let me die last night. I'm so sick right now I wish I could die but I'm afraid I won't. That was horrible."

Cory's soft laugh at his growl surprised him. "Not poison, my man. It's a special tea to help fight the infection. My grandmother taught me. I'm going to start your IV now. I think I've figured out a way to conceal it when we start again. Can you tell me where we are going?"

"Reservation."

"All...right." Cory said slowly. "I've visited the one closest to here. It will take us another five or six hours to get there. Do you know any of the elders?"

"Rocky Skywalker Patterson, my Grandfather." He sucked a deep breath when Cory inserted the IV needle. "Damn. That hurt."

"Sorry grouch. It's almost time for Greg to arrive. Do you feel like talking to him?"

"No but I have to tell him what Jason said. He needs to know what happened last night."

Cory sighed deeply. "Okay. Try to rest until he gets here. Next time we stop I'm going to shave that ugly beard off you. You are definitely much better looking without it."

Luke's eyes were closed but snapped open at her words. "How would you know what I look like without a beard?"

Smiling she pushed the hair from his sweaty forehead. "Trust me, big guy. I know. Try to rest until Greg gets here."

"What about you? You've got to be exhausted."

"Tired maybe but not exhausted. I'm going to stretch out next to you." Curling into a tight ball beside him on the tailgate the warmth of the sunshine soon lured her to sleep. The dream that followed always frightened her. It always came when she was this tired. Usually she could shake herself awake. Usually. But not this time. She opened the door expecting her parents. Instead Rafe DeAngelo and Major O'Grady were standing before her. Pain twisted her heart as she listened to their words. Parents dead. Explosion and fire. No hope of saving them. Come to the office. They needed her to identify the car.

Her whimper alerted Luke and the tears tore at his heart. He struggled to turn to her. "Cory, wake up." He shook her shoulder. "You're having a nightmare."

"No." She screamed. The image fast forwarded, and she was outside the office staring at the charred remains of her parent's car. DeAngelo gathered her in his arms and she pushed him away. He groaned at her actions. "Never touch me again, you bastard. Daddy warned you he was in danger. He told you there was an informant within the agency. Why didn't you listen? Do you know why they call it a mole, Rafe? Because the bastard does everything under other people's noses. Daddy confided in you. He trusted you. You were supposed to investigate. You were supposed to be his friend. What happened, Rafe? Did someone pay you to look the other way?" Tears were streaming down her face.

As the dream fast forwarded again anger replaced the tears. "My father was not the informant, you idiot." She was now in Major O'Grady's office. "He tried to warn you. Remember? Why are you doing this? He devoted his entire life to this agency. Daddy earned that pension just as he earned the death benefits. How can you refuse to pay us? How are we supposed to pay for a double funeral? You bastards haven't lifted a finger to help this family. I have younger sisters that need to be raised. How am I supposed to do that without the money?"

Fast forward again. She was standing in front of the tombstones of her parents. "I'm sorry Daddy. I failed to find the proof you told me about. I tried Daddy. I really did. I don't know who to trust anymore. You told me I could always go to Greg. You believed in him but Daddy, they think he's going to die. I tried to get in touch with Luke Patterson like you told me however he's been shipped out on assignment. No one will tell me where he is or how to get in touch with him. Why is it that hundreds of people work at that office, but you could only trust two? Luke wasn't at the funeral, so I doubt he's been told. What am I going to do? They're trying to force me to resign. If I quit, I'll never be able to prove your innocence. What am I going to do?" Cory covered her face and cried.

Luke could hear a car approaching. Struggling to turn he shook Cory's shoulder. The action sent waves of pain coursing through him. "Cory, wake up. Someone's coming, and I can't reach the gun. Cory?" He called her name loudly this time. It seemed to rouse her from the terrible dream she was having. "Cory, honey, wake up. Someone's coming. Wake up or we may be in more trouble."

She did, sitting straight up, knocking her head against the roof of the car. Hearing the vehicle, she grabbed for the gun hidden between the coolers. "Easy, woman. That should be Greg. You all right?"

"Yeah. Just a bad dream." She rubbed at her wet cheeks. "I never should have laid down." A deep sigh escaped as she exited the station wagon. Quickly she moved items around until she was satisfied Luke couldn't be seen. "I'll be back. I'm not taking any chances with our safety." She raced across the small clearing gaining the cover of trees and watched as Greg's car moved slowly along the path. From her vantage point she could see for almost a mile detecting no signs of another car. She knew Greg would remember this spot. Her father stumbled on it one day when their cover was blown. They used it often when things got dangerous. She used it herself a few times when she needed to escape after her cover was blown. Her father and Greg Waltz had a signal they used, and Cory waited. Old habits die hard, they say. She'd hate to be the cause of Greg's death yet if he failed to give the signal… She pushed the thought aside when the car stopped, and the lights winked.

★ ★ ★ ★ ★

Fred Adkins knew they were in a precarious situation. His skin crawled between his shoulder blades. It was a sign warning him of trouble and he learned as a small child not to ignore it. Knowing what little he did he couldn't ignore it now. He saw sunshine flash on the gun barrel once and then it was gone. "Sir?" Squinting his eyes where the flash had been he searched the area quickly for the source and the person behind it.

"I saw it. Corena is no longer there. Don't make any fast or sudden moves, Adkins. Ralph always bragged that Corena Sims was a dead shot." Greg inched the car forward. "Do whatever you're told and keep your mouth shut until this thing is defused otherwise you'll wish you were never named to come."

Fred swallowed hard at the lump of fear in his throat. Who was this woman? How did she know Luke? Did she work with him? Was a partner at one time with Luke? Why did she help him if she was so bitter with the agency? Was Luke still alive?

He bit back his curiosity as they rounded a small knoll and the station wagon came into sight. Again, he saw the flash of sunlight. He ignored his urge to scan the area around the reflection. The woman already moved from her position he knew. Instead he concentrated on the station wagon. The back end was still loaded with camping gear, several pieces pulled onto the tailgate to one side. She was here long enough to cook something, yet he still could see no signs of Luke.

"Slowly open your door and get out." Greg's voice was quiet, yet Fred heard the catch in it. "Leave the front door wide open and open the back door. When you're finished, step easy to the front of the car." Fred obeyed. His movements were slow and deliberate as he put his hands on the hood of the car. He sensed she was close but damned if he could see her. He watched as Greg opened the trunk before joining him.

"All right, gentlemen, shed those shirts as well as your guns."

"Now who's being cautious? Do you think we're wired? Even I wouldn't be that stupid especially knowing you would be well armed." Greg chuckled, doing as told.

"Sorry. Daddy only trusted two people in the entire agency. That was you and Luke. Considering Luke's condition, I don't have the privilege of trusting anyone." Fred felt the cold steel of the gun press against his spine. After she patted down his jeans the gun was removed. From the sound of it he knew she was doing the same to Greg. He finally drew a breath when he heard the hammer of the gun slide into the safety position. "You can put your shirts back on." Cory came around where the men could see her. "I'm sure you understand the need for caution, Mr. Adkins. If I ever find out Luke's trust in you has been betrayed, I'll personally kill you myself." Her eyes were as hard as the steel in the gun she carried. "Luke's in the car. He's in a lot of pain and the fever has claimed him. He'll need clothes. Did you bring him some?" Greg nodded. "Good. I'm going to make sure you weren't followed."

Fred watched as she raced to the tree line and disappeared. Pulling the duffel bag from the back seat he followed his supervisor. Greg stopped halfway to the station wagon. "Luke? This is Greg. Agent

Adkins is with me so go easy with that gun. I would hate to get killed when I'm trying like hell to help."

Fred could hear another gun slide into the safety position. Even then his footsteps were cautious as they approached the station wagon. The woman said Luke was injured yet Fred strangled the gasp of horror threatening to escape when he saw Luke. From shoulder to knee the entire left side of Luke was one large mass of bandages and some of those bandages were showing signs of fresh blood.

"Thank God." Luke sighed, sinking back against the makeshift bed. "Did you bring the clothes and money?"

Luke's body felt as if it was on fire. "Yes. What am I supposed to tell your family? They'll be devastated if I tell them you're dead."

"You followed through with the second call to the main line. Didn't you?"

Greg sat on the tailgate. "I told the men the woman called and reported you dead. That still doesn't help me with your family."

"Tell them the truth. I don't know if I'm going to make it this time, Greg. Tell them that also." Luke struggled to keep his wits about him. "Jason Grover is the boss on this end. He knew about the raid. Said he knew I was a plant from the beginning. Said he knew…"

Cory was beside him. "Slow down, Luke. Your mind is working faster than your mouth. You aren't making much sense. Drink this."

Luke wrinkled his nose at the tea. Pain laced through him as Cory lifted his head and forced him to drink. As she started to lower him back to the bed a coughing spasm claimed him, and he couldn't seem to catch his breath. Every cough spread flames of pain through him.

"Help me sit him up." Cory growled at Greg. When he did she slid behind Luke easing his body against her. "Wet that dish towel with water and bring it to me." She ordered Adkins. Luke was getting worse and they had a long way to go. "Easy, Luke." She whispered, pulling the damp hair from his face. "Greg isn't going anywhere until you finish giving him your information. Take your time."

After wiping his face Cory pulled the clip from her hair. Gathering Luke's thick black hair into a ponytail at the base of his neck she secured it with her clip. The coughing finally ceased and now he lay against her in total exhaustion, gasping for breath. Greg was scared. Luke seemed to be holding on to life by a very thin thread. "Can you tell me what happened last night?" He asked Cory.

"I can only tell you what happened after he escaped." Horror quickly turned to amazement as her tale unfolded. Greg watched the two carefully. Fever claimed Luke and exhaustion was firmly set on Cory's features. She wiped the sweat from Luke's body and then forced him to drink more of the tea she made. Slowly his coughing ceased, and his breathing eased. His fear for the two increased as Luke slowly took over, telling of the events in the warehouse. Silence reigned when they were finished.

Fred broke the silence. "Miss Sims, you're in no condition to be driving. From what I can gather you haven't slept in two days and you look exhausted." At her startled look he hurried to press his point. "You can't possibly drive and take care of Luke at the same time. He's a trusted friend, Miss Sims. You're going to need help if you plan to get Luke to his destination alive."

Tears of frustration, anger and exhaustion slid down her face as she met Luke's fever glazed eyes. "Fred's right, Cory." Luke finally whispered. "Only you have the knowledge to keep me alive. They have the knowledge to protect us until we're safe. There's no way possible for you to do both. I need your help to keep from dying. The decision is yours however I vote to let them help."

Cory heard his weakness and fear and realized that he really was afraid he would die. She folded her arms gently about him trying to control the tears that threatened. "If I only knew who to trust. Daddy taught me to listen to my gut instincts, but those instincts tell me to trust no one right now. I know what happens when you trust."

"Trust them both, honey. I will kill them with my own hands if they betray that trust. That's a promise."

# Chapter Four

CORY SENSED LUKE'S HERITAGE WAS strong and that sense grew stronger as they pulled onto the Reservation. The trip had been hard for Luke and Cory got no sleep. She was kept busy sponging his body when the fever assaulted him or snuggling against him under the sleeping bag when the chills attacked.

She constantly monitored his wounds and IV. Fresh blood showed on his shoulder, yet she could do nothing about that any more than she could do anything about his raging fever or her worry that he would die before she could get help for him. In the rosy light of late evening she was glad to see the visitor's building coming into view. "Stop here. I'll see if I can get in touch with the Elder." She instructed Greg.

Cory shivered in the cool evening air. Her grandmother brought her here every year to gather herbs. They enjoyed many summer days on this Reservation, but she was never allowed to visit with the residents. She was the outsider, allowed to come only because her Grandmother was a respected elder and healer. Her grandmother died two years after her parents were murdered and Cory missed her terribly. Until now she hadn't realized how much her soul longed for the solitude the Reservation offered. Sighing she pulled her tired mind back to Luke. She smiled wearily at the startled woman behind the desk. "I need to see Rocky Skywalker Patterson, please. This is an emergency."

Cory held her impatience in check as the woman dialed the phone. After a brief conversation she turned her attention back to Cory. "Skywalker states he isn't expecting company. What's the message, please?" The dark eyed beauty asked, holding the phone close to her shoulder.

Frustrated, Cory debated. "Tell him his grandson Luke has been seriously injured and may die of those injuries. Tell him I need a Shaman to help me save his life. I don't have many herbs left that I brought with me."

Cory watched the color drain from the woman's face as she quickly relayed the message. "Skywalker is coming. You're to remain inside the building until he arrives." She told Cory in a clipped tone.

Cory sighed wearily. "That's impossible. Luke is with me and we'll be in the car. He's very ill and I refuse to leave him in his condition." As she turned she saw two very large men in Reservation police uniforms standing in the doorway. She straightened her back, anger snapping in her eyes as she approached them. "You're not going to intimidate me." She growled. "I'm walking out that door, so I can help Luke. You'll have to shoot me in the back to stop me." They didn't shoot but followed close on her heels as she left the building.

More men crowded around the car. Cory elbowed her way to the back of the station wagon lowering the tailgate. The minute she touched Luke's forehead he opened his eyes. "We made it Luke. Your grandfather should be here soon. You know they aren't going to let me stay. I'm not registered with this tribe. They will send me away when your grandfather arrives."

"There is a way."

The certainty in Luke's voice surprised her. "What have you got up your sleeve? Whatever it is, it won't work." Her eyes narrowed on him. "I'll find some other place to stay once you're with your grandfather. He'll be able to help you after I'm gone. You know as well as I do there is only one way I would ever be allowed to stay with you."

"Marriage."

His soft-spoken word startled her. "You knew that when you thought up this crazy scheme. Didn't you? Are you that desperate for a wife? Good God, man. That's not an option." She shook her head. "No. I can find someplace else to stay. There's no need to ruin your life."

"No. I have to protect you, and this is the only way I know how. Am I that undesirable as a husband?"

Cory frowned. "You would make one hell of a husband of that I am positive. I was taught marriage is forever. My parents never believed in divorce and neither do I. I sincerely doubt I could tolerate a marriage in name only. Thank you but no thank you." She shook her head emphatically. "There's no reason to even consider this. I'll find somewhere else to go. I can go to my sister's. I can go to another state and stay hidden until this thing blows over. I have my camping gear and Jasper won't mind if I use his vehicle. You need not destroy the rest of your life because of me."

The shakes attacked Luke. Cory stilled her trembling hands by pulling the sleeping bag closer around his shoulders. He grabbed her wrist, halting her movement. "I'm serious, Cory. I don't intend for the marriage to be in name only. Hell, any red-blooded man would know better than to fool himself with that farce. You're too beautiful not to make love to, especially the way you kiss. I was taught marriage is forever also. You do this and there will be no backing out once it's safe to leave here. The choice is still yours. I need you and I'm willing to marry you. If you leave me I fear I'll die. I'm not going to stay here without you. If you decide not to marry me, we will go somewhere else. Together."

The shakes attacked in force. Cory knew the only way to stop them was by body heat but too many people were around to do anything that drastic. She pulled the sleeping blanket tighter around his shoulders. The touch of her hand against his neck told her that his fever was dangerously high. His body shook so severely Cory thought he was in convulsions. His teeth chattered so hard against each other she was afraid he would break them.

"Cory. Help me." Luke's quiet plea spurred her to action, and she slid her body under the sleeping bag. She knew her face was crimson, but her concern was with Luke. She kept her face turned from those gaping into the station wagon. She no longer cared what they thought.

Gently, she curled her body over his, putting light pressure on his injured left shoulder. Blood was already seeping through the bandage and she feared he pulled the stitches loose. "Easy Luke." She cooed. "The more the shakes attack your body the more damage you do to these wounds. I'll soon have you warming up. Concentrate on controlling them. Use your mind to rule your body. Concentrate, sweetheart."

Luke focused on her words, focused on her. He could feel her heart beating wildly next to his. Could feel the warmth of her body as she lay on top of him. Could even sense her fear at his condition. She was the one keeping him alive. She was the one keeping him from giving in to the pain. She was his lifeline in this sea of pain and fever. If she left now he knew he would die. "Don't leave me, Cory. Promise me." The shakes were receding. As Cory moved from his body he captured her chin with his hand refusing to release her. "Promise me." He demanded. "I won't survive without you."

Tears welled in her eyes and spilled over splashing onto Luke's fingers. Another hand cut across her blurred vision, an older hand, touching Luke's forehead. She pulled her eyes from Luke's following the strange arm upward. His face was a much older version of Luke's with steel gray hair. Chocolate brown eyes seemed to search her very soul. "Grandfather? Cory has to stay with me. They know who I am. She saved my life and because of her kindness her life is in danger. I'm dying, Grandfather. The mole knew about me. Backup didn't come. Jason will never stop. Black eyes. See the devil there."

"Luke, look at me." Cory waited until his fevered eyes met her. "You're not making any sense, Luke. You're safe here and this Grover person can't hurt you again. You're on the Reservation and with your Grandfather. Calm down. You don't need to worry any longer."

"Yes. I do. They will kill you, Cory, just because you helped me. I can't protect you in my condition. You will only be safe if you remain here. Promise me you'll stay. Promise me you'll marry me as soon as it can be arranged. Grandfather make her promise to stay with me." His agitation was rising with his fear and fever.

"Luke. Your woman will stay with us for a while although I don't know for how long the council will allow this without a marriage. Rest now, Grandson. I will arrange for your things to be moved. Your woman will stay but the other two must leave."

Luke's confused eyes turned to his grandfather. "Grandfather? We have to protect her from Jason."

"We will." The Elder smiled. "Close your eyes and rest." When Luke did as instructed Skywalker turned toward Cory. "You will stay?"

"Yes." She sighed, covering Luke again. "He has this crazy idea that if I leave he'll die. I need to gather herbs for him. Infection is setting in and if it isn't controlled my staying here will make no difference when death visits."

Cory backed out of the station wagon stepping aside to stretch her aching muscles as the possessions were quickly transferred to a jeep. Greg was beside her, worry evident in his eyes. His hair was in disarray from running worried fingers through it. "Will he make it? Is he going to live? Can you help get him well?"

"I don't know." She replied honestly.

"Will they really force you to leave if you don't marry Luke, even though you're registered with a different tribe? Doesn't that count?"

"Yes, they will force me to leave and no, it doesn't make any difference that I'm registered with a different tribe. Some Reservations have very few rules however this Reservation has very strict rules. Grandmother liked coming here because they follow the old ways. There is much to be respected about those ways and Grandmother taught me all she knew. I won't be allowed to stay for long."

Greg watched the emotions chase themselves across Cory's face. He suddenly realized how tired she must be. Even when she was young he could never read her emotions. She was so much like her father it startled Greg. Gathering her in his arms he kissed her cheek. "Luke is a good man, Corena. He would make a wonderful husband. If you decide to go through with this I know love will grow."

She laughed softly as tears filled her eyes. "I thought you would give me the same argument Daddy would have." She watched as Luke was transferred into the jeep, cringing when she heard his moan of pain. "He would not have approved."

Greg hugged her tightly. "I just did, Corena. He would have approved of your marriage to Luke. Especially since you love him." When she opened her mouth to deny it he gave her a knowing look. "Don't deny it, woman. I can see it in your eyes every time you look at him."

He frowned as the phone conversation came back to his memory. "Luke was your father's partner seven years ago. Wasn't he?" He laughed again. "Don't answer that, young lady. That question confused me for the longest time. The blush on your face is answer enough. Follow your heart Corena. Your love will win his heart."

"Young lady? It's time to go. Say your goodbyes for they won't be allowed to follow." A police officer commanded.

Nodding, she turned to Greg. "You be damned careful, big guy. Luke thinks the mole is one of the higher ups. I think there are two. It would help if you could think up some way for a body to be found. Then there could be a closed casket funeral for him. The mole might not get suspicious that way."

As she turned to leave Greg jerked her around to face him. He sensed the others around him tense but ignored them. "Who, Corena? Who did your father suspect of being the mole five years ago? Give me a place to start. He would have done that much for me."

Cory sighed knowing he was right. She saw Luke's Grandfather from the corner of her eye and knew she had to leave. Her remaining under the protection of the Reservation depended upon him yet he didn't appear impatient as the others around her were. She sent him a questioning look and saw him nod. "All right, I'll tell you. Daddy felt Major O'Grady was the person feeding information. That was the night before he died. He told me you and Luke were the only ones he trusted. If anything should happen I was to go to one or the other of you. After they were murdered you were in a coma and Luke was undercover. I never found out where he was, so I started following the paper trail.

"I found what I needed on Major O'Grady. I even made copies and was able to sneak them out of the agency. The copies are still in my house, hidden. After the shake-up much of the evidence was hidden within the system. While I was investigating O'Grady, two other names kept popping up. I never found the proof I needed to hang their asses out to dry. I refuse to accuse them without proof, so I can't tell you who I suspected. No one would have believed it anyway." Tears were sliding down her face and she swiped at them with trembling hands. "Look closely at those you work with Greg. The same people are probably the ones that set Luke up. Find them and I will personally kill them for Luke."

The hatred in her eyes startled Greg. Never had he seen such raw, naked hurt and hatred in anyone's eyes. Who? Who was it that inspired such hatred? Who did she suspect? Why wouldn't she tell him? "I need something more to go on, Corena. Who else?"

Cory studied Greg's face finding it unreadable. "I don't have proof." She shook her head sadly. "I will tell you this much. Watch Rafe DeAngelo. Watch his actions. His every move. Read his reports carefully. Rafe writes very interesting reports. That's how I got the proof I needed on O'Grady. It took me six months, but I finally found what I needed."

It was Greg's turn to study Cory. Hard anger made the muscle in her jaw twitch as she clamped her teeth together. The gold in her hazel eyes came alive in the light of the late evening sun. He looked at Luke's Grandfather. "Do I have time for another question?" When the elder man nodded he squared his shoulders looking hard at Cory, hands tightened on her arms. "If you found the proof on O'Grady why didn't you clear your father's name?"

Cory's entire stature seemed to change in front of him. She appeared defeated. Anger turned to pain. Her whole demeanor reminded Greg of the many times he arrested someone. When the cold hard steel of the handcuffs snapped shut on their wrists the fight seemed to drain from them. That was how Corena Sims appeared to him at that moment.

"O'Grady was retired by the time I had my proof but not before he cast suspicions about my being trusted. The pressure to resign was terrible. Not a day went by that he didn't harass me concerning my ethics or morals. I couldn't resign, Greg. If I did I knew I would never be able to prove my suspicions of the other two.

"My assignments became increasingly dangerous. The day my last bust was supposed to go down I had a bad feeling. Grandmother called it self-preservation. When I tried to get out of it they told me they would only take me off the case if I resigned. As soon as I entered that building I knew it was a set-up. Tony was killed instantly." Her voice turned bitter as memory flooded her, tears flowed unnoticed down her face. "The wire I wore apparently didn't work. They didn't kill me Greg, but they enjoyed torturing me. Hours of torture. Because of that I will carry the scars the rest of my life. That's why I got out. That's why I resigned. They hurt me." She screamed at him.

As she turned away Greg grabbed her by the shoulders. His face was dark with anger. "What did they do to you?" When she didn't answer he shook her. Hard. From the corner of his eye Greg could see the men of the tribe close in on him. He also saw Luke's Grandfather stay their defense of Cory.

Anger now replaced defeat. "You really want to know?" Her hands were shaking as she opened the buttons on her shirt, her eyes never leaving Greg's face. "They cut me up. Piece by piece. Inch by painful inch. For twelve hours they kept me captive. Every time I passed out they waited until I regained consciousness. That blonde-headed, black-eyed bastard told me he was instructed on what to do. He said if it were up to him he would have just taken my virginity. He said he was told not to kill me, just record my screams and listen to me beg." Her voice had risen in her anger and shame. "He was skillful with that knife. It angered him that I wouldn't scream with the pain he was inflicting. I wouldn't give him that one satisfaction he wanted so badly, and it angered him."

She pulled the front of her shirt open and Greg could see the scars. They ran across her chest, down her left breast to be hidden beneath the bra. One long jagged scar ran across her ribs losing itself below the waistband of her jeans. He also saw where plastic surgery was done. Horrified Greg pulled her into his arms only to have her jerk away.

"It would have been better if he had raped me. At least that scar wouldn't show. These scars...no man will forgive. Not even Luke." Her hands were shaking as she pulled her attire together. "Don't tell me to follow my heart, Greg. Luke is all man and he deserves a wife he can be proud of. He doesn't deserve something that looks like me. No man does."

She turned away and then turned back to Greg. "Be careful, Captain. These men are dangerous. I ought to know. They made sure I would never forget. If they had killed me I wouldn't have to live with this terrible ache in my heart or worry about love." With all the dignity she could muster she headed for the jeep and Luke.

Luke appeared to be unconscious. After checking his wounds Cory requested permission from his Grandfather to gather herbs needed to help heal his injuries. Skywalker ordered another jeep be brought and the two, plus the driver, went to various spots Cory knew the herbs she needed grew. She knew Skywalker watched her closely, but she was past the point of caring. She had to have the herbs to fight Luke's infections.

Her belongings were unloaded when they arrived at the cabin. People were everywhere another indication of Luke's status in the tribe. Cory bundled the herbs in her arms and waited for Skywalker. Respect was shown to Elders by walking behind them. Even though she wanted to rush to Luke's side she pulled her impatience into the pit of her stomach. The mass of bodies parted allowing them entry to the cabin. It was small, just one room. A single bed sat against the wall by the window and Luke was lying in the middle, his huge body almost filling the small bed. She instinctively knew this wasn't Luke's house. The bed was too small for him to sleep peacefully in. Somehow, she could not envision him in a single bed. The handmade blankets would give comfort when the chills attacked.

A gas stove, cabinets and a sink sat against another wall. The table in the middle of the room had four chairs around it. Along the last wall a fireplace was located, the fire chasing the late evening chill from the room. Two rockers sat in front of the fireplace, a handwoven rug between them.

The rockers and rug showed gentle age from much use and Cory knew this was where the life-center of the cabin was. Whoever lived here lived a solitary life but had many friends. Tears welled in her eyes as she remembered her grandmother. Her house was much the same as this and the two spent many days and nights of teachings in front of the fireplace.

Pushing the painful memories aside Cory laid the herbs on the table as Skywalker sat next to his grandson on the single bed. Without a word Cory flew into action. While the water was heating she hung another bag of IV fluids. Knowing there were only four bags left she slowed the rate. There was no hospital on this Reservation. No way to get more IV fluids Luke would need while his fever raged. No way to get the medicines Luke needed to fight the infection except for her knowledge and the herbs she gathered. She gave a silent prayer of thanks for the knowledge her grandmother imparted.

Ignoring the crowd inside as well as outside the cabin Cory worked chopping and mixing herbs. Having no Demerol left she made tea for the pain she knew Luke would feel. Knowing how bitter the willow bark tea would taste she was pleasantly surprised when a jar of honey appeared on the table when the tea finished brewing. Grandmother used the tea often when Cory was recovering from the knife wounds and she learned the value of the tea during her recuperation yet dreaded the taste. After cooling the tea, she poured a healthy dose of honey into it to help cut the bitter taste. "Luke, open your eyes, dear. I need you to drink this." Cory knelt beside the bed, smiling when he wrinkled his nose. "This should taste better. Honey was added. The tea will help with the pain. I need to work with your wounds. It's going to hurt like hell when I apply the poultice."

Luke struggled to open his eyes and when he did they reflected the pain he felt. Cory slid her arm under his shoulders, supporting his injured shoulder as she lifted his head. Tears welled in her eyes as she held the cup. She could feel the muscles tighten with pain. He watched her, keeping his eyes glued to hers until the cup was empty. After laying him back onto the pillow she washed the sweat from his body. Only when Luke closed his eyes when the tea took effect did she rise from her knees.

Next, she turned her attention to the herbs that were boiling. Removing them from the heat she quickly added more herbs, mixing them together to form a mush. Layering strips of tape on the table, sticky side up, she put bandages on the top of the tape, spooning the herbal mush on top. With a deep breath to steady her nerves she returned to Luke's bed, removing the soiled bandages. Infection was evident in his shoulder and two of the stitches had broken open. Cory gently cleaned the wounds with hydrogen peroxide before reaching for the poultice. Luke's breathing was ragged as he fought the pain moving him evoked. His eyes opened when she touched him and now they followed her every move. Cory gently pushed the hair from his forehead. "Once I put this on your shoulder you're going to have intense pain. I'll have to hold you down once the poultice is applied." She tucked his right arm around her back. "Hold on to me, dear. I'll do what I can to help."

Luke closed his eyes, swallowing hard. When he opened them again his chocolate eyes captured hers as his right hand tightened on her shirt. Cory fought the tears that welled knowing the pain he would feel. When he nodded she lay across his chest applying the poultice. Luke's body reacted to the intense pain she warned of. His body convulsed, slamming upward against her. His hand tightened on her shirt, jerking downward and Cory felt the buttons snap off with the force of his pull. She could hear his strangled moans as she struggled to hold him onto the bed. Tears of frustration fell on his face and she shook her head violently to keep more from falling. She would be useless if she allowed her emotions to control her.

His taller frame and extra fifty pounds threatened to overpower her before other hands came to help. She grasped the edge of the bed with one hand, the rungs of the headboard with the other, the upper half of her body keeping Luke pinned to the mattress. Turning her head, she saw Skywalker working on the rib wound and she tightened her grip when she saw he was ready to apply the poultice.

Luke's body reacted again. He knew he was losing control. He tried to fight his body's reaction to the pain but failed miserably. Every time a new surge of pain attacked him his upper body convulsed against Cory. He could hear her voice and heard her prayer that he would pass out, but the pain refused to allow that blessed relief. He was vaguely aware of her gasp of pain as the poultice was applied to his leg and he convulsed against her again. Was vaguely aware that his arm was wrapped around her slender waist as he fought the white lightening coursing through his body. Vaguely aware he was holding her tightly against him. Vaguely aware of anything except his need to keep from screaming with the pain. The only thing he did know was that Cory was there, talking to him, helping him stay alive while death waltzed closer.

As the pain slowly subsided he raggedly pulled air into his painfully burning lungs. He felt hot and cold at the same time. Luke concentrated on Cory. Concentrated on her body next to his. Concentrated on her heartbeat, her voice, her being. Her heartbeat was the only thing making his beat. Her breathing kept the air moving in his lungs. Her being was the only thing keeping death at bay. When she struggled to leave him, Luke tightened his hold on her waist. When she escaped his grasp, his fear became greater than the pain. "Cory?"

"I'm here Luke." He could feel her hand on his cheek relishing the tenderness of her touch. "You need to rest and let your body heal. Clear your mind, dear, and allow sleep to come. I'll stay for as long as the council allows. Try to sleep. That will do you more good than anything right now."

Luke's eyes flew open searching her face. "Marry me, Cory. That way you'll be protected here. I'm too weak to keep you safe. If you leave the Reservation they will find you. They will kill you simply because you helped me."

Her fingers massaged the worry lines from his forehead. "I love watching your eyes, big guy, however you can't sleep with them open." She smiled as her thumbs slid to his eyelids, forcing them closed. "It's time for both of us to rest. Remember when I told you I was extremely tired?" Luke nodded. "Well, I'm past that point. I'm exhausted. I must rest before my body goes into total shutdown. I'll sleep for several days and won't be of any help to either of us. I need sleep as much as you do."

Her voice was becoming fainter as she massaged his facial muscles. Luke tried to fight the sleep she was inducing with the massage but knew she was winning and surrendered to her gentle ministries. As soon as Cory was sure Luke was finally asleep she sank heavily to the floor, laying her head on the bed next to him. Tears attacked, and Cory couldn't stop them Her hand slid over Luke's heart and she was lured to sleep feeling the strong steady beat beneath her fingers, knowing death would not visit him any time soon.

★ ★ ★ ★ ★

Luke struggled to force his eyes open. The pain he felt was minimal considering what he already endured. Shaking his head to clear the fog he felt a hand on his forehead and froze. The hand was large, not small like Cory's. Fear raced through him. Had Jason Grover found him? Was Cory captured?

"You have slept a long time, Grandson. I'm pleased the Spirits have returned you to us."

"Grandfather?" Luke finally succeeded in getting his eyes open. He looked around in panic. "Where's Cory?"

"She slept for two days after you arrived. She has been by your side the entire time." Skywalker straightened the blankets around Luke's waist. "The Elder women have taken her for a walk. The council has met and a decision concerning her has been made."

Fear gripped Luke as he watched his grandfather move to the window and look out. He waited knowing Skywalker would tell the decision of the council. Finally, he turned away from the window to sit beside Luke. "Much has happened in the four days you have been unconscious. Your woman has impressed some, angered others. Except for gathering the herbs needed to get you well she has not been allowed away from the cabin."

The fact he was unconscious for four days surprised Luke. The rest didn't. He was aware of the rules of the tribe and tromped on them deliberately to gain protection for Cory. This was the only place he knew that would provide the absolute protection they both needed. "I shall apologize to the council when I'm able to attend the next meeting. I'm responsible for the unrest and will accept any decision the council deems necessary for my actions."

"The decision has already been made, Bright Arrow." Skywalker spoke quietly. Luke swallowed hard, waiting. "The council is impressed with the knowledge your woman has of the old ways. She has been taught well by her grandmother. I'm pleased to know the woman has remembered what she was taught. Her grandmother would be proud to know the teachings were not wasted. I have missed her since she crossed over."

"You knew Cory's Grandmother?"

Skywalker knew this information surprised Luke and worried about the information he had to impart. "Yes. We were very close friends, the Grandmother and I. I know your woman also, yet she doesn't remember me. When she was tortured the doctors told the grandmother she would die. The Grandmother took her home and I helped heal the wounds. When she survived the doctors took over to do the surgery."

"Cory was tortured? What happened? When?" Luke's mind riveted on that one word, horror filling his soul at the thought. "Who? Who would torture Cory?"

Skywalker sighed moving off the bed. He paced the floor as he debated on repeating what he knew as well as what she told Greg the night she arrived. If he told Luke maybe his grandson would understand why his woman hesitated to accept marriage when she so obviously loved Luke. If he did that however he would be relaying a secret that should be the woman's to speak. Skywalker sent up a silent plea for help as the silence became heavy in the room.

With difficulty he decided to tell the secret hidden for many years. "The Grandmother came to the Reservation several years ago in desperation. She pleaded with the council for help for the granddaughter after her torture. It took several days for the council to agree to my helping since no one had seen the condition of the granddaughter."

Memory flooded him, and he shuddered when the images of Cory's body assailed him. "I have never seen such deliberate mutilation in my life. They didn't mutilate her face but the rest of her body…" Skywalker shuddered again. "That poor child endured thousands of cuts from the knives her captors used. Infection had already set in when they told the Grandmother she would die. She almost did." Skywalker stopped gulping at air as he remembered.

"Her delirium during the infection was hard to battle. She didn't plead her own case yet that of her parents. The herbs slowly conquered the infection, but her pain was five times greater than yours. Like you, she maintained her silence during that pain. Her hatred got her through much of that time. When she would feel herself sinking into the vast darkness she would scream your name. Doing that must have brought your image forward for she would calm for a while. After that whenever she would become hysterical her Grandmother and I would use your name to help calm her. I don't know how she met you or when but the day you met you touched something deep inside her heart and that helped to save her."

Then he repeated the conversation she had with Greg. "That's the reason she will not allow herself to get involved with a man. She sees herself as ugly and unlovable. The scars on her body have scarred her heart. That's why she won't be allowed to stay much longer."

Luke was thankful for the time Skywalker gave him to think about all he was told. His heart felt as if a knife was twisting inside him. Horror surged followed quickly by anger at what Cory endured. He licked dry lips, rubbing at his injured shoulder. "Grandfather? If she agrees to marriage will the council protect her? Will they allow her to remain?"

"I asked that very question. They have agreed on two conditions." Luke looked up in surprise. "Her presence here has angered many in the tribe. Not only many Elders but also many of the warriors. The decision was not an easy one. The arguments both for and against her staying were vast. That's why the conditions that have been set are harsh." Skywalker drew a deep breath releasing it slowly. Luke recognized it as a very bad sign and braced himself for the worst. "If she agrees by tomorrow to marry you, the tribe will allow her to stay on the Reservation and under the protection of the warriors."

"Understood." Luke waited. Something was distressing Skywalker. He knew it had to be the conditions set by the council and his Grandfather was hesitating in revealing those conditions. His voice was quiet, yet his senses were on full alert. "What are the conditions they demand as punishment for the anger caused by our presence?"

Skywalker rubbed his forehead as if he had a headache and sighed. "She must complete the Honored Warriors Challenge."

Shocked, Luke tried to sit up but was forced back to the bed when the sudden action brought pain flowing through him. As his body slammed back to the bed, he gasped for air as the pain attacked him in force. "Grandfather, I'm the one who caused this anger and unrest." He stated while trying to control the pain. "She shouldn't be forced to pay for my decision. I'm responsible. I should be reprimanded not her."

"I argued that point also with the council. The condition she has been given is to pay for the protection she will receive before the marriage while she is here. The other condition is for your responsibility in this."

Luke nodded. He was a high-ranking warrior and knew the condition would be stiff due to his rank. "What is my punishment for bringing her here?"

Skywalker laughed softly. "You must accompany her on the challenge. Since you're injured the time restriction has been lifted. The council knows how your woman thinks about herself. Many were around the vehicle you were brought here in. They also know about the scars and why she feels undesirable. By the time you return you must have convinced her of your love and that she is as beautiful as you see her to be."

Luke drew a sharp breath. He knew why the Elder's came up with these conditions especially now that he knew of the torture Cory suffered. He also knew what she would endure on the challenge. The Honored Warrior's Challenge was the most difficult of all challenges.

Normally it had to be completed in seven days. The time restriction was lifted and for that Luke was thankful. "This will embarrass her. If I can convince her of the marriage she'll accept the condition the council has set upon her without complaint. I don't know if she can emotionally accept my part in the conditions set."

"She is not to know the terms of your condition. The Elder's will take her away for a week of verbal teachings. That will give you extra time for healing. The women will inform her of your demanded presence the day the challenge begins. She's to be informed of the hardship so she can make her own decision concerning this marriage. She's not to know anything about your condition other than you will accompany her. Your woman must prove her love for you by helping you return. This will be your time to prove your love for her and bury her injured feelings while she is with you. If you fail she will be removed from the Reservation upon return. The teachings will be hard. Think carefully before you ask her to join with you in marriage."

Luke closed his eyes against the tears that threatened. He brought her here to protect her from harm. The pain she would endure because of his actions may hurt her far worse than any pain he ever endured himself, even with his present injuries.

# Chapter Five

CORY STARED FROM GRANDFATHER TO Grandson, unable to believe what she heard. Luke was sitting against the headboard of the bed, the blanket pulled just above his hips. White bandages stood in stark contrast to his dark tanned skin. Brown eyes watched the emotions race across her face. He just informed her that the council had given her until this evening to accept marriage or she would be forced to leave. Anger surged at the injustice of the situation she found herself in.

"You are serious? I thought this marriage idea of yours was due to the fever." She placed her hand on his forehead. "You don't have fever now." She backed away from him. "Why in hell would you even consider this? You're protected here. I can disappear. There are lots of places for me to go. Places where even you wouldn't find me. Why would you even consider giving up your life for some…some sense of honor you feel obligated to defend?" She shook her head in confusion and denial. "Destroying your life because you feel responsible is a stupid reason for getting married. That's exactly what you'll be doing, you know, destroying your life. My honor won't allow this to happen. No. Never will I marry someone just because he feels responsible for my safety." Her hands became fists and she planted them firmly on her hips. "I'm a big girl, Luke. I know how to survive on my own. I've been doing it for years. What makes you believe they even suspect I was involved? Hell, I haven't been with the agency for years."

Luke drew a deep breath, shielding his heart against her anger. "This is the only place we are both safe and you know it. You're not a full blood. You have to marry me to gain the protection of the warriors. If you leave Jason Grover will find you. Make no mistake about it. His black heart is filled with evil. His heart is as black as his eyes, Cory. He would do terrible things to you just because you helped me."

Cory turned white as a sheet, slowly backing up until she slammed into the wall, fingering the scars hidden by her shirt. Her eyes turned glassy, becoming so dark the gold specks were hidden. Once again, she was in the building where she was captured. She watched in horror as her partner was pulled from his position on the floor, blood pouring down his chest where the bullet had buried deep. Horrified she watched as the man put a spring-coiled wire around Tony's neck. "Watch this bitch." The man snarled. When he released the tension on the coil the jagged edges of the wire wrapped around Tony's neck almost cutting his head off. The gurgle of death assaulted her. Something hit her against the head and darkness claimed her. When she awoke she was in another building. The ropes binding her hands and feet stretched her until she thought she would split in half. She saw the knives coming at her as she desperately tried to escape. The man standing over her had black eyes and taunted her as he cut away her clothes. Even now she could feel his hands on her, touching her where no man had ever touched before. He laughed when he felt the membrane proclaiming her virginity.

He gloated when he told her he was ordered not to rape her. His laughter shook her to her soul when he told her it was better if she remained a virgin for when he was finished with her no man would ever want to bed her. Then he took out a tape recorder and turned it on. "Scream bitch." He yelled slapping her across the face. "I want everyone to know I completed my end of this assignment."

Then he cut her, deep cuts but not deep enough to cause death. He knew where to cut and how deep to avoid vital organs and arteries. When his torture didn't produce the effects he desired anger took control. He just kept cutting on her and cutting on her. Fear threatened to engulf her as she tried desperately to fight the images in her mind. She would never forget those black eyes. No matter how hard she tried she could never forget. Nor could she forget the shear enjoyment the bastard displayed as he used the knife against her body, watching her fight the pain he was creating.

Shaking her head to clear the image in her mind she tried several times before her voice finally worked. Even then it was shaky, and fear reflected in her words. "This Jason Grover…" She licked dry lips as she sucked in air, trying to control the fear Luke's words welled inside her. "Does he have blonde hair? Always wears a hand tailored suit? Tall guy? Maybe six feet two or three? Runs guns as well as drugs?"

Fear gripped Luke. She knew Jason Grover and from her reaction he had been the one using the knife on her. Luke shot pleading eyes to his Grandfather. Understanding dawned on Skywalker. He went to Cory, pulling her back to the bed. She was shaking with fear as he gently forced her to sit. "There's more you should know before you make your decision, woman." His soft voice drew her eyes to his. "There was a condition put upon you by the council for the protection you shall receive before the marriage."

Luke held her hand drawing her attention back to him. "If you agree to marriage you'll go through a week of teaching with the Elder Women. Then you must complete the Honored Warrior's Challenge. The time limit has been lifted yet even at that it won't be easy, Cory. Few men are able to complete the challenge because of the strain and pain the challenge presents." He waited, allowing her time to consider his words. Her emotions were schooled, and he couldn't read her thoughts. When she finally captured his eyes again he continued. "After you've successfully completed the challenge we'll be married. You will be my wife in mind, body and soul. I won't accept you as a wife in name only." Her blush told him she understood.

"It would be unfair to you." She quietly responded as she pulled the front of her shirt closer to her neck. "I'm not the woman you dream of, Luke. Marriage to me would only disappoint you." Tears welled in her eyes as her voice became a whisper. "You have no idea what you are getting yourself into. You would be terribly dissatisfied with what you get."

Roughly, Luke pulled her hands from her shirt and started unbuttoning the front. She gasped, pushing his hands away. Luke's anger surged. Not at her but at Jason Grover for what he had done to this beautiful woman. As she turned from him in shame he pulled her back. "Whatever you're ashamed of is hidden by your clothes. Take that damned shirt off so I can decide if I'll be satisfied or not." His voice was low and soft making it even more menacing.

"No." Fear gripped her heart as she tightened her grip on the shirt. "You won't like…"

"Now." He commanded softly, capturing her wrist in a hard grasp. Her breathing was ragged as she denied him again, tears pooling in her eyes. In one quick movement he released her, jerking on the shirt with enough force to send the buttons flying across the room. Cory slammed her eyes shut unwilling to see the disgust in his face. She saw it too often in the eyes of the doctors and nurses who treated her not to know it would be reflected in his eyes also. She was startled with the gentle touch of his fingers as they trailed along the worst of the scars on her chest. She refused to look at him, afraid of what she would see.

Luke quickly schooled his emotions. He didn't want Cory to see the horror in his eyes. He knew she would misunderstand thinking she was seeing aversion instead of concern. "Is this what you're worried about?" His voice was soft, confusion lacing every word. "You think it makes you less of a woman because of the scars?" He pulled the lacy bra she wore down until he could see where the scar ended tracing it with his fingers. It ended at the base of her nipple. He teased her nipple with his thumb and smiled when her body responded. Her breasts quickly became hard and taunt in response. The pulse at her neck fluttered as the blush crept up her chest and neck fanning her cheeks with color. Luke raised his right leg under the sheet, adjusting it so his body's response didn't show. Releasing her bra, he touched the scar on her side. "How far does this one go?" Fearing she would refuse to answer he slid his fingers under the waistband of her jeans, stopping at the snap as her hands stayed his actions. "Well?"

Her eyes shot open, pleading with his. "Almost to my hip." She finally whispered.

Luke released his hold on the front of her jeans. Mischief shown in his eyes. "I see nothing to turn me off as a husband." He pulled her forward whispering in her ear. "Everything I've seen convinces me even more that it would be enjoyable being married to you. Your body is very desirable, my dear. Your breasts are perfect and if you hadn't answered I would have known what the rest of your shapely body looked like. Maybe it's my scars you object to?" When her head shot up in surprise he kissed her. Slowly. Gently. Teasing her lips with his tongue, he twined his fingers in her hair, deepening the kiss as he became incredibly hard. As she responded he ended the kiss yet held her face close. "Any woman who can kiss like you do can certainly learn to love me. If my grandfather weren't here I would prove to you just how much of a woman you really are. I would prove to you, beyond a shadow of a doubt, how desirable you are. I'm so hard it hurts." Luke chuckled at the surprise he saw in her eyes.

Cory pulled away and Luke released her. She quickly drew her shirt together but not before he saw how full with want her breasts were. His knowing grin served to deepen the crimson in her face and she ran from the cabin without a backward glance. When Skywalker started after her Luke's words stopped him. "Leave her be, Grandfather. She has much to think about before she makes her decision. She needs time to weigh the pros and cons. Her answer to the council this night will change her life forever."

★ ★ ★ ★ ★

Cory stood outside the meeting hall with Skywalker beside her. Several warriors came to the cabin to help Luke dress. The pressure of his blue jeans increased the pain in his hip. When he turned pale, Skywalker left, returning a short time later with a set of buckskin clothes for him. She waited until the warriors carried Luke out before she entered the cabin to change again. She replaced the shirt he snapped the buttons from when she returned to the cabin to tell him of her decision. Since that time, she washed her hair and bathed, dressing in a pair of jeans and a baggy shirt. Skywalker frowned when he saw her attire. She informed him she packed no dresses, not knowing of her destination until they were almost two hours into their escape from the city. She knew from his reaction the council wouldn't approve of her appearance any more than he did.

There was nothing she could do about it. Dresses were a luxury she could ill afford since her parents were murdered. The twins outgrew their clothes faster than she had money to replace them. Her own attire suffered because of it. Until tonight she never worried about her appearance for she never went anywhere except to work and back. She prayed the council would not be prejudice just because of her clothes.

Luke was already before the council when she arrived. With a sigh she turned her memory to her Grandmother. Cory was the only daughter who took after her father's side of the family, inheriting his hair and eye color. The other three sisters had her mother's black hair and brown eyes, yet Cory was the only daughter who took pride in her heritage. She requested to be taught the old ways and her mother and grandmother helped teach her. When she was old enough she requested to be presented to the Elders for teaching and ceremonies.

Her father never protested when her mother talked of her heritage. Never objected to her Grandmother's teachings yet objected violently when it was time for Cory to be presented for the ceremonies. Her father's anger squelched the request. She still remembered how heartbroken her mother was with his decision. She wasn't presented until she came of legal age. Even then her father argued yet Cory remained adamant and her father finally relented.

The next several years were busy ones for Cory and her Grandmother. Cory underwent months of training, both verbal and physical as well as several of the ceremonies including the cleansing and vision sweat. Those were the times she felt closest to her Spirit Helper and learned to trust her Spirit Helper in all situations.

That made her a good agent. Her father pushed her to become a nurse but her dissatisfaction for that career showed every time she left for or returned from work. Her father finally relented and helped her prepare for agency work. Because her father worked with Greg in the drug enforcement division she was placed elsewhere. She advanced in the agency through hard work and honesty.

She was given an undercover position one night when a female was needed in a game of cat and mouse with a gunrunner. The assignment turned sour and her quick thinking and ability to shoot straight saved the life of her partner, the bust was saved, and they escaped with their lives. She was given a permanent position in the undercover unit after that. The next three years she worked undercover often. Always she protected her partner as they protected her. Her record for a clean bust brought her the satisfaction of knowing one more gunrunner was off the streets and away from the children who played in those streets. She enjoyed her job and was able to settle quickly into whatever role was needed to get her on the inside.

For months before his murder her father had been unreasonably angry at everything Cory did or said until she seldom talked about her assignments with him. They fought so often Cory finally moved from the house in tears. Then one night her father called asking her to visit. He sounded so upset she couldn't refuse. That night he confided in her about his suspicions of a traitor in the ranks of the FBI.

After the shock of her parent's death ebbed to a dull ache she tried desperately to find the evidence to clear her father's name. The harder she searched for the proof she needed the more she was urged to resign. The more she was pushed to resign the more determined she was to find the proof she needed. She refused to allow her father to be labeled as a traitor.

During that time a shift took place in her assignments. If she hadn't known of her father's suspicions she would never have noticed the shift. She would have attributed it to the success she achieved over the years even though her assignments became increasingly dangerous. She was continually partnered with inexperienced agents who were not taught the way of self-defense. Then she was assigned to make a large arms buy.

Fear welling within her, Cory concentrated on Luke instead of allowing her memories to overpower her. She listened to her father speak of Luke's virtues ever since the two were partnered. The respect her father had for Luke was obvious. Then she met him on that fateful day when she was washing her hair and he haunted her dreams ever since. His image helped her survive when her world was nothing but pain. She compared him to every man she knew or met, and everyone dimmed in comparison.

She let her mind wander to the day before when the Elder Women came to take her for a walk. She was informed that the tribe was angry at Luke's action in bringing her here. She learned Luke was a high-ranking warrior and she was allowed to stay because of his position and the respect he carried in the tribe. She thought a long time about what Luke told her. Greg told her to follow her heart and her love would be returned. Luke had seen her scars, touched them and knew the damage her clothes hid but didn't seem repulsed. His fingers trailed fire along her skin. His touch sent a lava flow to her lower belly and groin making her want to touch him, feel him, kiss him. Her heart felt like a trip hammer threatening to steal her breath away. When he kissed her, she had to fight the urge to melt into him. Being his wife would be heaven, she knew.

Yet the people who were pursuing them were still forcing him into this. He made the decision of bringing them here because he knew this was the only place she would be absolutely safe from the killers who wanted him dead. Like a true warrior he was willing to give up his freedom to protect her. Her heart thudded painfully at the realization. It was unfair to trap Luke into marriage because of her fear. She also knew how much she needed his protection. Her scars and Luke's wounds were proof of that need. From what she was able to finally piece together the same man did damage to both of them. Hatred filled her when she realized who Luke was talking about. Terrible hatred that rivaled her terrible fear. If Jason Grover ever found out who she was her death would be slow and painful.

In the end it came down to two simple questions. Did she trust her ability to survive outside the Reservation, outsmarting Jason Grover? She knew that answer. She had no doubt Jason Grover knew exactly where they were at that very minute. She wouldn't survive a night outside Reservation lands. Neither would Luke in his condition and she was sure he would insist on coming with her if she decided to leave.

The other question haunted her. Could she marry Luke simply to obtain the protection of the warriors? She knew that answer was no. Even though her marriage to Luke would assure protection she wouldn't chide herself into believing it was reason enough to marry him. She also knew now was the time for honesty. She honestly loved Luke Patterson. That was the only reason she even considered this marriage. She only hoped that Luke would eventually learn to love her back.

Hearing the trembling sigh escape Cory, Skywalker turned to her in surprise. "Have you changed your mind about the marriage to my grandson?"

Skywalker's words pulled Cory to the present and she shook her head. "No."

He pulled her face upward until he could capture her eyes, eyes narrowing at what he saw. He saw what he saw in Luke's eyes whenever his Grandson looked at the woman before him. "You are not doing this only because of the protection being married to a warrior will provide. Are you?"

Skywalker could feel her tremble. "No." She mumbled as she dropped her eyes to avoid his searching gaze.

"Look at me woman." Skywalker commanded, tapping her chin with his fingers. Swallowing nervously, she obeyed. "You agreed to this wedding because you love my Grandson. Don't you? Do not think to lie to me."

She closed her eyes again. Drawing several deep breaths, she finally opened them. "Yes, Skywalker. I have loved your grandson for a very long time. Only he never knew I existed. My only prayer is that he can learn to love me before he learns to hate me for trapping him into a marriage he will learn to regret."

Skywalker released her chin, watching as she wiped her eyes to eliminate the tears gathered there. She missed the grin that spread across his face as the door opened and she was motioned inside.

Cory sat in the middle of the half circle of Elders. She never diverted her eyes from the warrior's back that came to collect her. She dared not. She knew her courage would desert her if she were to see how many people were gathered in the meeting room. She sent a silent prayer heavenward to help her say the correct things and that she would be allowed to remain. If they evicted her now Luke was sure to leave with her and Jason Grover would find them. He would kill them both she knew. Cory wasn't willing to allow someone as evil as Jason Grover to ever hurt Luke again. As the silence grew within the meeting hall she kept her eyes straight ahead of her, face and eyes unreadable as she confronted the Elders.

The first Elder in the semi-circle spoke. "You realize the only reason you have been allowed to remain among us is because of Luke's status as an honored warrior?" It was more of a statement than a question.

Cory swallowed nervously. "Yes, Sir. I now know his status and I realize that a great honor has been bestowed upon me."

The second Elder spoke. "Luke has told us how you became involved in saving his life. Your bravery matches that of any warrior." Cory ducked her head as she felt the blush creep up her neck, "Look at me woman." He demanded. Her head shot up. He nodded. "That is better. Why did you help him? Even when you knew the risk you were taking."

Cory never moved her eyes from his. "I recognized him as a partner my father had seven years ago. I saw his injuries, the blood-soaked clothes and the men who were after him. I knew he was an agent with the FBI, and I realized the danger he was in. It was either help him or watch him die. My father had great respect for your honored warrior. The last was not an option for me."

"You are a warrior in the white man's world?"

"I don't consider myself a warrior. Others may however I don't."

"You worked undercover for the FBI?"

"Yes, Sir."

"You have killed to protect your partner?"

"Yes, Sir."

"You would have killed to protect Luke?"

"Yes, Sir."

"You have answered yes to all the questions. Why then do you not consider yourself a warrior in the white man's world?"

Without dropping her eyes, she sighed, trying to think of a way to explain. "My Grandmother was upset over my career choice. I didn't know how to explain why it was important for me to work with the agency. Seeing the fear in Grandmother's eyes I went to my tribe and requested a vision sweat. During that time, I had a vision that remained with me the rest of my life. The next day I repeated the vision to Grandmother. Grandmother smiled and advised me to remember my vision and not wander too far from the truth of that vision."

"What truth did you find in your vision?"

"I dreamed of two eagles flying over their nest guarding their children. The nest was attacked by a ghostlike image. Both parents attacked the image to defend their young. I believe that's why I did what I did for the agency. I wanted to protect the young of this country from those who sought to destroy them. The drug dealers and gun runners all seek to harm our children. Like the female eagle helping her mate defend her young from the ghostlike image I only sought to protect the children from ever finding contact with those evil people. I knew if I worked for the agency I could make a difference in this world. I also knew if I saved one child from being touched by their evil my life would have meaning."

Silence reigned after her speech. Finally, a third Elder spoke. "In your heart I see you have followed your vision to protect the young.

There is something that still confuses me. If you feel that strongly about the work you have done why did you leave?"

Unconsciously her hand came up to cover the scars that could not be seen. Her voice was very low and soft when she responded. "I was badly injured. My partner was murdered. I have twin sisters to raise. The man who…hurt me said he knew where I lived and that my sisters were still at home. He told me he would do the same to them that he did to me if I didn't resign. I couldn't allow that to happen. I could not let them injure my sisters. There was no choice left to me. I had to resign." She fought to control the tears that threatened. Cory never told anyone why she resigned letting everyone think she lost her nerve. They believed her after they found out the extent of her injuries. Many visited during the year of plastic surgeries she endured. Except for her Grandmother no one even questioned her decision after seeing the damage.

"The man who injured you and threatened your sisters is the same man who injured Luke?" The second Elder asked his eyes as hard as steel.

Cory licked her dry lips. "I believe he is the same man. Yes."

"Your sisters? They are safe from this man?"

"Currently, yes. The twins are staying with my older sister in Oregon. They go there every summer."

"Why did you not go there?"

Cory sighed. "I told Luke I could go there. I even considered the possibility. Once I realized who injured Luke I knew I could never escape from him. Luke told me he would find me and knowing what I do, I tend to believe him. I can't put them in danger."

His eyes were hard when he asked the next question. "Is that why you brought Luke here? To secure the protection of the warriors on this Reservation?"

Shock showed in Cory's eyes. "I didn't know where we were going until after we left the city. Luke didn't tell me of this destination or what he had in mind until we got here. I have repeatedly told him I would leave. He states that if I leave he will also go. He is too weak to protect us. I refuse to endanger Luke's life."

The third Elder spoke. "Once you were here and knew the rules of this tribe why did you stay? The others could have returned you."

Tears welled. "Luke was dying. Grandmother taught me the use of herbs and I had the knowledge to stop death. I couldn't let him die. I could not..." Shaking hands wiped the tears from her cheeks. "I thought his idea of marriage was due to the fever. When I realized he was serious I tried to talk him out of this. He is adamant. I also know neither of us will survive without the protection of the warriors. Even now Luke is too injured to face the evil of Jason Grover. He swears that if I leave, he shall go with me. That is unacceptable."

Into the growing silence the first Elder spoke. His question was soft, and Cory had to lean forward to hear. "Although you don't consider yourself a warrior if you had the chance would you kill this man who inflicted injury to you?"

The question surprised Cory. She never considered the possibility before. "I honestly don't know how to answer. It would depend on the circumstances I guess. If he were threatening someone I loved I would kill that bastard in a heartbeat. If I happened to see him on the street I would probably avoid contact with him. My pain and hatred for the man runs deep, Elder. Until I see him again I can't honestly tell you that I wouldn't slit his throat just to watch him bleed to death." The hatred she felt reflected in her voice.

Silence again converged over the meetinghouse. She held the eyes of the Elder who asked the last question as she nervously chewed on her lower lip. The second Elder took up the questioning. "You've had visions. That means you have been given a tribal name. What name did your tribe bestow upon you?"

"Running Eagle."

"It will remain your name while you're here. It's the name you will be known by from now on. It will help protect you." Cory nodded. "You have been told of the condition set forth from this council concerning your protection?"

"Yes, Sir."

"You accept this condition as it has been set?"

"Yes, Sir."

"You understand it will be physically as well as emotionally challenging for you to complete the condition?"

She nodded. "Yes, Sir. I understand."

"Are you willing to accept any and all decisions pertaining to this condition? The Honored Warrior's Challenge is most difficult."

Cory drew a deep breath letting it out slowly. "Yes, Sir. I accept the decision of the council. I will complete the challenge to the best of my abilities."

"Once you start this, woman, there will be no stopping. Once this meeting is over you are committed by your honor. You can't conquer your heart until you defeat your fear. You have converted fear into stubbornness. You have a stubborn streak in you that will cause much pain in the coming weeks. Only when you surrender yourself into the hands of others will you conquer that stubbornness. That's the reason for the challenge. It will tax your strength and test your fear. A woman has never attempted it, so the time restriction has been lifted. It will still be physically hard on you. You will be required to use all the knowledge your teachings have given you."

Cory nodded, resigned to her fate. "The Elder Women have informed me that this is the hardest of all the Challenges. I pray I give no dishonor to the honored warriors who have completed this challenge or those who have yet to face it."

"The Honored Warrior's Challenge is the hardest challenge you will ever face. Many of the honored warriors only complete it once because of its extreme difficulty. You will be given only a knife, a bow and a quiver full of arrows. Protection from the elements as well as food you will have to find on your own. You'll be taken to the far end of the Reservation. From there you must return to this meetinghouse. Even though the time limit has been lifted it will take many days. Now, I ask you again. Knowing all that you do are you still willing to accept the condition set upon you?"

Fear of his statement and question showed in her eyes yet her face remained unreadable. "Yes, Sir. I accept the condition set upon me for marriage by this council."

"Good. Luke's tribal name is Bright Arrow. It's important for you to use his tribal name from now on. His protection as well as yours depends on the fact that no one knows you are here. Tribal names will assure no one except the tribe knows who you are. Your teaching begins. The Elder Women will take you now."

With his words several women moved behind her. Cory started when a blindfold was slipped over her eyes. The hands that brought her to her feet were large and powerful. No woman had hands that large and Cory realized she had been assigned two warriors. The sound of people leaving met her ears as she was held in place. Silence weighed heavy until Cory could no longer hear the sound of shuffling feet. "Normally a mother presents her daughter for teaching." A woman's voice spoke softly. "I'm Luke's sister. Since you don't have a parent to help you it falls to me to present you."

The blindfold was removed, and Cory saw the woman from the visitor's center. She stood in front of Cory while seven elder women stood behind Luke's sister. The two warriors who lifted her to her feet, held her wrists, pulling her arms upward and outward until they were stretched out at shoulder height. Grinding her teeth Cory stood her ground, keeping her eyes on Luke's sister. "I am White Dove, sister to Bright Arrow. You have accepted our ways. You have willingly given up your old ways for this new one. Preparing yourself for marriage to an honored warrior is more difficult than if you were to marry a brave or a warrior. The higher the rank the more difficult the preparation for joining becomes."

Cory knew it was a warning, just as the Elder's words had been. A shudder ran through her when a knife was handed to White Dove and she started to cut the shirt from Cory's body. Tears of embarrassment welled in Cory's eyes and she shut them to gain control. Memory of another time when someone cut away her clothing while she was restrained assailed Cory. A man with blonde hair and black eyes held the knife. The cold of the metal slid along her skin, ripping the cloth, as it would soon do her body. Again, she could see in her mind the flash of light on the knife as it came closer and closer to her. Once more she felt the tip of it bury in her flesh and could hear his laughter as she fought to control the screams he so desperately wanted to hear. The warm blood running down her body, the pain the knife inflicted, the laughter, all threatened to overpower her. Her breathing became ragged as she fought to push the image away, knowing she had to stop them from visiting her.

White Dove stopped, seeing Cory's face turn pale, sensing her fear and hearing the whimper that rose in the woman's throat. Something in the woman's attitude and the sight of fear warned White Dove that Cory was remembering something which happened in the past and that something held her in the grip of terror. Her heart went out to this woman of Luke's. She went to Grandfather's cabin the day Luke was brought to the Reservation. She heard the woman screaming with terror as the nightmares attacked in force. From the look on her Grandfather's face, White Dove was certain he knew what caused the nightmares. He simply refused to say. Whatever it was, it scarred this woman's heart. Only after she sensed Cory had gained control of whatever emotion assaulted her and Cory opened her eyes did White Dove continued with the knife. First the shirt and then the bra. The knife also attacked blue jeans and underwear, falling at her feet as the material gave way. Her shoes were removed with her socks cut off. Cory was mortified being stripped naked while seven other women and two warriors watched. The blush raged in her cheeks as she stood her ground.

Once her clothes were removed a barrel was brought into the room. The clothes were put into the barrel and burned. Cory watched while her clothes burned to ashes. Once the fire burned itself out White Dove returned her attention to Cory. "The burning of your clothes is symbolic of your old life. As your clothes no longer exist neither does the life you have known. You stand before the Elders as a new babe. Explain to me the symbolism of nakedness."

Cory took a deep breath, groping for the correct words. "A baby is born into this world innocent and dependent upon others for everything he needs. He knows nothing of the world he has entered and must learn the ways of that world. I have been stripped of my past and now I stand before the Elders as I enter into a new world. I am naked as a reminder that I am dependent upon them for everything I need."

"Not bad but not quite right. You're naked as a reminder to yourself that you are born into a new way of life. Every time you hesitate or stumble in your teaching you'll be reminded of your new birth. Every time you learn well and remember your teachings you'll be rewarded, just as a child. Tonight, you have done well." White Dove nodded, and a buckskin dress was slipped over Cory's head. As White Dove tied the lacing at the side of the dress, moccasins appeared. "Explain the reason for the new dress and shoes."

"The new dress is an acceptance of me into this new way of life. The moccasins are a reminder that my life will travel a new path."

"You have been taught well, Running Eagle. Your teachings will hold you in good stead if you continue to remember them and hold them dear to your heart."

Presentation to the Elder Women in her own tribe was much different, Cory remembered. Her mother and Grandmother presented her then. She knew the Elders and it was before the time of her injuries. Before Jason Grover. Before the scars. Then there was no reason for embarrassment for there were none. She also realized the teachings would be as different as her presentation. Her affiliation with her old tribe would end with her marriage with Luke...Bright Arrow, she corrected with a hidden smile.

White Dove nodded to the warriors and they pulled Cory out the back door. There her hands were tied in front of her and she was lifted onto the back of a horse. The others mounted, one holding onto the reins of Cory's horse. Without a saddle Cory had a difficult time staying astride the horse especially with her hands tied. Eventually she figured out that if she clenched the mighty beast tightly with her knees slightly bent she could grasp tight enough not to fear falling off. The women sensed when she accomplished the task increasing the speed of the horses. One lesson learned another started Cory thought as a ghost of a smile touched her lips.

Her body ached when they reached their destination. They arrived in a clearing, close to a stream, a fire already glowing its welcome. Cory noticed that several lodges as well as four tipi's had been erected sensing this would be her home for several days. As she slid her left leg across her horses back in preparation of dismounting she noticed the slightest movement of White Dove's head. Warning bells sounded in Cory's brain. She hadn't been given permission to dismount. Sliding more firmly onto the horse she let her leg remain in position. She would have to learn patience all over again. Patience escaped her the last time. The Elders excused it as being young. These Elders wouldn't be so generous. Cory stifled a sigh. Patience was a virtue she had little of.

# Chapter Six

GREG WAS THANKFUL TO BE behind the group of mourners who were now gathered around the casket of the last man to be buried. The funeral arrangements were emotionally draining on him. Three days after the massacre his men stumbled on the decaying, mangled body. It took Greg that long to find a dead body remotely resembling Luke. Once it was hidden Greg waited. To his horror a pack of stray dogs found the body before his own men. The mutilation served to make the body harder to identify.

Greg hated this. Hated everything about this mess. Shortly after they left the cemetery an unknown man would be lowered into a grave and a tombstone with Luke's name on it would be erected. His intention was for the man's body to be returned to the morgue. He hadn't counted on the men's respect and anger. Because of the mutilation already done to the body the men took turns guarding it. From the time the body was found until now someone had stayed with it. In frustration Greg sought out Luke's family. The sad eyes of the mother haunted him, and her response did nothing to relieve his anxiety. "Let the poor man rest in peace, Captain." She said. "His body is being used to protect the life of our son. He deserves to be buried with respect. Regardless of what he was in life, because of what is happening now, he deserves a warrior's honor and burial."

Greg buried his face in his hands when she finished speaking. "Have you heard from Luke or Corena?"

She shook her head. "Nor are we likely to hear. White Dove keeps us informed. The woman's knowledge of the healing herbs has been put to use. Luke regained consciousness today and the council has made its decision." Little Fawn smiled to ease the tension lines in Greg's face. "She either leaves or accepts the conditions of the wedding."

Greg knew better than ask what those conditions were. He had known Luke long enough not to ask questions concerning the tribal ceremonies Luke underwent with regularity. His last request had been six months ago. Luke returned twenty pounds lighter and haggard looking. Greg demanded to know why a young man of thirty-five would continue to put himself through the rigors of the ceremonies. Luke gave him a lazy grin. "It keeps me in touch with my Spirit." He turned the conversation back to his assignment and his certainty of a mole in the agency.

Greg pulled his attention back to the present, studying the crowd that gathered. Several faces confused him. He recognized Rocky Skywalker Patterson the minute the tall, gray-headed gentleman entered the funeral home as well as several of the warriors who accompanied the elder. Of all the mourners an elderly black man with white hair and a painful shuffle stood out in stark contrast to the others. Another caught Greg's attention. The man was tall and thin. His blonde hair was fashionably cut, and his tailored suit fit him to perfection.

Greg would never have paid attention to him if the man hadn't stayed in the shadows. He seemed too smug, too happy, too pleased that Luke was dead. That man was now approaching Greg and he pulled his emotions together.

"It is a shame Luke died that way." His voice was soft and low.

Greg resisted the impulse to study the man, keeping his eyes straight ahead of him. His gut instinct was sounding a warning that couldn't be ignored. "Luke was a good man. He'll be missed, not only by his friends but by the agency as well. Were you friends?"

"We knew each other in college. Luke was always pulling pranks."

Greg's heart tripped in his chest. "Well, he will never pull another prank now. Whoever did this made sure of that." His hatred for the situation seeped into his voice and Greg didn't try to hide it. "It's a shame you didn't know him recently. He was a good friend as well as a good FBI agent."

"Any clues to what happened or who did this?"

Greg shook his head. At sixty-two he was getting too old for this kind of deception. The man was pumping him for information while revealing only one thing about himself. He reserved doubts about Luke's death. He stated Luke was good at playing pranks. Did he not believe the body found was Luke's? The funeral was a closed casket due to the damage to the body. Greg attended the wake and didn't remember the man standing beside him. He turned looking the man in the eyes. They were as black as death itself. "What do you do for a living?"

The man smiled at the off-handed question. "I'm in the shipping business. I tried other things for a while but finally found my niche in shipping. After a few years I branched out and I'm now self-employed. Luke should have done the same thing. If he had gotten out of the police business, he might be alive today. Tell me, Captain. How does it feel to know the FBI failed to protect someone as dedicated to law enforcement as Luke was?"

Anger surged through Greg. He knew he was being goaded, being pumped for information. This man knew exactly what buttons to push to trigger an unguarded response. "Luke was good at his job because he believed good would win over evil." Greg ground out.

The man's grin sent ice racing through Greg's veins. "It rather looks like evil took a bite out of good this time. Ironic, isn't it? The only truly unstoppable agent the FBI ever had is now stopped. Forever. Where in the world will you find someone with Luke's finesse to replace him?" The man's eyebrows arched questioningly as he stared at the anger in Greg's face.

The anger suddenly turned to defeat, and Greg looked away. "No one will ever be as good as Luke was. I've already petitioned to have his badge number permanently retired." Tears smarted his eyes.

"That's good. Since the services have ended I am going to pay my respects to the family. I hope you discover what happened."

Greg watched him go thankful for the breath of fresh air that chased the stench of evil from around him. Instinctively he knew this man was the one who butchered Corena Sims. When he returned he pulled her file. Horror rose within him at the sight of the scars she still carried yet dimmed in comparison to the feelings that assaulted him as he looked at the photos of her body after she was found. He was just as sure this man was responsible for the massacre of his men and the injuries Luke sustained. He suddenly understood Luke's fear for Corena's safety. At first, he doubted Luke's method of protection however he now knew Luke made the only decision open to him. Even now, Greg knew, it was the only option.

Greg stayed as people wandered from the gravesite hoping to get the license number of the blonde man's car. One minute the man was talking to the family and the next he just disappeared. Even though he watched, he saw no sign of a car that he drove or of one picking him up. Frustration settled over Greg as he waited for the family. Two cars were provided for their use. He was driving one and Fred Adkins was driving the other. He wanted desperately to talk to Luke's Grandfather. He needed assurance that both Corena and Luke were safe, and that Luke was recovering. He was positive the man he met was Jason Grover and just as positive Grover had doubts about Luke's death.

Luke's siblings entered the car Fred Adkins was driving while the parents and Grandfather entered Greg's car. He held his curiosity under tight rein until he had them at the house. He was being cautious but caution and Rafe DeAngelo's reports were all he had to guide him. When they were sitting in the yard under the shade of a tall oak Greg studied Luke's family. Two brothers, two sisters, parents and grandfather were sprawled in chairs, trying to get a grip on the situation they just experienced. Six warriors kept a respectful distance. Close enough to hear yet far enough away to keep their eyes on their surroundings. Luke had great pride in his family as well as his tribe. Greg appreciated that pride now.

"Luke is better."

The Grandfather's soft-spoken words were a soothing balm to Greg's nerves. "I'm relieved to hear that. He had me scared. I was afraid he wouldn't make it to the Reservation."

"He said you would be concerned. He cautions you again to be careful. His healing will take a long time. Those bullets did a lot of damage to his body. The Shaman feels it may take several months before he can return. He worries he won't be here to help you."

Greg nodded and sighed. "Tell him to be careful. Jason Grover was at the funeral today and I sensed the man had doubts. Luke was right. The man reeks of evil."

Skywalker nodded as he watched the anguish cross Greg's face. "I recognized him from the woman's description of her attacker. She has every right to be frightened of him."

"How is Corena doing?"

Skywalker shrugged. "She is with the Elder Women. Her fierce love for Luke will help her during this time as she fulfills her condition of the marriage."

Greg sighed as he covered his face with his hands choking back the questions that threatened to spill out. "Is there anything I can get for them? Anything they need?"

Skywalker's voice was quiet when he spoke. "Luke wants to see the entire file on the woman. He said to tell you he wanted the entire file, not some stripped-down version."

Startled Greg stared at the man who so closely resembled Luke. "Why would he ask that? What does he think he'll gain by seeing her file?" Greg violetly shook his head. "No. I can't do that to him. To her. His request is unreasonable. It would only serve to hurt them both and I refuse to be party to that."

Grandfather looked steadily at Greg. "He is hoping to find a way to end her nightmares. Her screams in the night tortures his soul."

"He's lucky to only hear her screams. Corena suffered at the hands of that bastard who cut her to pieces. I've seen her pictures and the damage he did was horrendous." Greg's voice failed as memory of the photo's flooded over him.

"I know what she endured at the time. I helped her Grandmother fight the infection that claimed her. Her healing was slow, and I feared she would die. It was many months before she knew where she was or who was with her. The doctors have done well concealing the scars on her body. It's the scars to her heart Luke must heal if love is to grow in their marriage. He can't do that until he knows what actually happened to his woman and he can only find that out by seeing her file."

Greg stared across the softly rolling hills that were part of the Patterson ranch, his mind in a turmoil over Luke's request. Luke bought the ranch several years ago and invested in purebred horses. He could see several mares, foals at their sides, grazing contentedly in the pasture beyond. If only his life could be as contented as those horses he could be satisfied retiring immediately. He grimaced at the thought. He was getting too old for this.

"I will have to think about his request." Greg returned to his chair. "I have to consider the impact his seeing Corena's file will have on Corena. It would upset her to know Luke saw the photos in that file. It might do more harm than good. I won't allow Corena to be hurt more than she already is."

"Do you think Luke capable of hurting the woman?"

"Not intentionally. I know what I saw in Corena's eyes the night we arrived at the Reservation. She loves Luke. I also felt the pain in her heart."

"The pain is from the torture she suffered. Luke's love for her is the only thing that will cure the pain. He can't fight the evil that caused the pain if he doesn't know what he's fighting. He must see from her file what no longer shows on her body."

Greg buried his face in his hands, trying to think. He understood Luke's request and was torn between his loyalties for both young people. It would hurt the young lovers if he surrendered the file as Luke requested yet Luke needed to know what happened to Corena especially since he was going to marry her. Greg sighed, the weight of his conscious weighing heavily on his shoulders. "All right. I'll get the file for him. He better be damned good at keeping secrets because

Corena will never trust me again if she found out I gave them to him." He lifted tear filled eyes to the pasture once more.

Rocky Skywalker Patterson nodded. "I'll stay with my son until I have the file. You are a good man, Greg Waltz. I see why my grandson has put his trust in you. This may seem like an act of betrayal to the woman, but I think you understand that this is the only way to help her. It's not an act of betrayal. Only one of love."

★ ★ ★ ★ ★

Cory curled up in pain, rocking on her shoulder. She lost tract of the days since her last monthly cycle, but she began experiencing cramps several days after her arrival and they had yet to ease. She seldom had cramps. Usually her periods came without warning except for the calendar that marked the days. The only time she had cramps was when she was extremely tired, and she passed that mark several days earlier. The teachings of the Elders had been tough, unforgiving and almost continuous. If she got two hours of sleep a day she was lucky.

Cory knew the endless hours of lessons were showing on her. She had difficulty remembering what was taught and had to bite back a tart reply when criticized for it, yet she no longer minded the lack of sleep. If she slept now she wouldn't be able to keep the nightmare at bay. What had her Grandmother done when she had cramps? She wrinkled her forehead, trying to think around the sleep that was claiming her. Tea, she decided as her eyes slid closed.

Once again, she was standing on the office steps looking at the charred remains of her parent's car. Sweat broke out on her forehead as Rafe DeAngelo put his arms around her to comfort her in shared grief. This time the hands tightened around her upper arms and Rafe's image faded. The man who held her captive now was tall with blonde hair and black eyes.

Cory fought the arms that held her. "You killed them. You killed them both." She screamed. Her fighting increased as more hands held her.

The knife gleamed in his hand and she knew fear as she had never known fear before. She heard his evil laugh as he cut the clothes from her body. "I'm not going to kill you. I'm just going to cut you up." She knew he meant every word he said when she heard his maniacal laugh. Cory fought harder as the knife came closer, the razor-edged tip opening a large wound from her shoulder to her collarbone. The next one cut across her lower stomach. She tried to escape him as the urge to double over in pain from what he was doing to her attacked her in force. "Scream, bitch." He demanded. "I enjoy hearing people scream. It's better than sex."

Cory felt something covering her mouth as the pain from her lower stomach threatened to consume her. She jerked her head away, trying to avoid the poison they were trying to get her to inhale. The knife was coming at her again, the pain the knife induced was so severe it brought only darkness and she slumped into unconsciousness.

★ ★ ★ ★ ★

Luke arrived beside his grandfather ten minutes before he heard Cory scream out. It was just after midnight and the beginning of her last day of teaching. He worried about her while they were separated. He knew from his own training that physical exhaustion was an important part of the teachings just as he knew the exhaustion would bring on the nightmares.

Her screams both startled and frightened him, and he forced himself to remain in his place as the Elder Women entered the tipi. When he heard them call for the warrior guards his fear increased threatening to sap his control. He was gasping for breath as the sound of a struggle and her frightened screams reached his ears. White Dove ran from the tipi tears on her cheeks. "Grandfather, something is terribly wrong with Running Eagle. None can settle her. We need you now."

Skywalker didn't hesitate. Soon he returned to the fire demanding Luke bring his bag of herbs, his concern obvious on his face. Luke obeyed his commands without question even though they threatened to tumble out, stirring the herbs as his Grandfather directed into the hot water by the fire. When the herbs simmered together he was handed a towel, instructed to cool the solution, soak the towel and then take it to the tipi. Luke's gait was slow and painful. His shoulder and side were healed but not his leg. It was painful to put weight on and the more he walked the greater the pain became. Forcing himself to ignore his pain he concentrated on his work that Grandfather assigned him.

Cory was caught in the grips of her nightmare. Turtle, one of the warrior guards, had a bloodied lip and his eye was beginning to swell. He was holding Cory on one side while the second warrior, Running Bear, was holding her against the floor on the other. The Elders were trying to hold the rest of her body and Cory was fighting their hold.

"Put the towel over her mouth and nose. Hold it tight against her face so she can breathe only the herbs." Skywalker demanded. "She will hurt herself if we don't stop this cycle of dreams." Quickly Luke obeyed his Grandfather's commands. It was difficult. Cory fought the towel over her face with the same fierceness she fought the hands that held her. Luke ended up gripping her head between his knees to effectively use the herb filled towel. It wasn't long before the herbs took effect.

As her body was released she curled into a tight ball and rocked on her shoulder. The other warriors helped Luke to stand and they left Cory in the care of the Elders.

"That woman of yours has a mean right hook."

Luke grinned. He experienced her strength in the car when he tried to hold her during the first nightmare he witnessed. She shoved him so hard he hit the cooler behind him and felt the stitches break in his shoulder. "They put us through very rigorous training with the agency." He stated, wetting another towel with cold water and applying it over Turtle's swollen eye and lip.

"Yeah? I'll remember that next time she has a nightmare." Turtle rubbed his throbbing jaw. "You better be careful when you bed that one. You might wake up in worse condition than when you went to sleep. Thank God I married a mild-mannered secretary."

Luke laughed. He attended the joining of Turtle to the little spitfire that was now his wife. Lightening Dancer was just as protective of Turtle as Cory was of those she loved. "Make no mistake Turtle. That spitfire of yours could hold her own against anyone that threatened those she loved."

"Probably but she never hit me hard enough to see stars. I hope this black eye disappears before Lightening Dancer sees me." He laughed heartily. "Your woman may just have a run for her money."

Turtle's good humor was returning, and Luke was pleased to see the sparkle of amusement in his friend's eyes. They straightened when the Elder Women, Skywalker and White Dove exited the tipi. Skywalker examined the damage to Turtle's face while another Elder made a poultice.

When he was finished Skywalker turned to Luke. "You're to return home, Bright Arrow. You will be sent for again. She's resting, and I need to stay with her. The Elders have decided to extend her time of teaching to allow her to rest. They will notify the Council of their decision. Go now. Take this time to exercise your leg. You'll need all your strength when you start the Challenge. I'll come for you when you are to return."

Luke held his emotions under tight reign as he limped to his horse. Something happened to Cory tonight that made the Elders decide to extend her teaching. The fact alone was unsettling in that it was unusual. He saw no signs of injuries to Cory, yet White Dove came out of the tipi while he was helping Turtle requesting the medical kit. She grabbed several large bandages before returning.

He was being dismissed yet Skywalker was needed. What happened tonight? Grandfather wouldn't be staying at the campsite if something major hadn't happened. Did Cory get injured when she fought the hold on her? What were the bandages for? Questions tumbled around in his mind begging for release. He knew better than to ask questions. If he were to know he would be informed soon enough. He still had his half of the condition to fulfill and he dared not anger the Elders with his questions before the marriage could be performed.

Cory was slow to pull herself awake. Pushing at the fog that encased her brain she struggled to sit up. The headache that attacked competed with the cramps for dominance. Doubling over she laid her throbbing head in her lap as she tried to gain control over the pain.

"Do you often have pain with your monthly time?"

Cory recognized the voice. White Dove was in the tipi. "I seldom have pain."

"Your Challenge has been delayed until this womanly time passes."

A relieved sigh escaped. "I appreciate that."

"When was the last time you had pain like this?"

Cory shrugged which sent stars twinkling in her brain. "I was… injured a few years ago. I don't remember much until several months later. My first memory was of having cramps. Grandmother made tea for me. That's the last time I remember having cramps and I doubt I have ever had them as bad as this."

"Where is your Grandmother now? I know she taught you many things and you have learned them well however she isn't with you." White Dove startled when Skywalker entered with tea. Motioning her to silence he squatted just inside the doorway.

"Grandmother died in her sleep two years ago." Cory sobbed feeling again the loneliness death left in her life. "I miss her so much. She was the only person who knew how I felt. She accepted me for who I was on the inside. It didn't matter to her that I was tortured. It didn't matter to her that I had scars and was ugly. She loved me, White Dove. No one can love me now. It's too late for me. Why couldn't he have just killed me? Oh God, the pain." She was crying hysterically as she rocked in place.

Skywalker shook his head in dismay. Moving behind Cory he pulled her face backward forcing her to drink the tea he made and then allowed her to curl back into position until her rocking ceased. He sighed sadly as he helped White Dove lower her sleeping body onto the blankets. Standing before the Elder who watched everything with curiosity he made a decision only a Shaman could make. "We shall have to bring Bright Arrow back. He's the only one who can reach through her pain to help her."

The Elder bristled. "It's not allowed. Bright Arrow is an honored warrior. He is not allowed to be around her while she is bleeding. You know this."

Skywalker snorted in disgust. "I'm sure he knows all about a woman's monthly time. I'll bring her the supplies she needs when I return with Bright Arrow. White Dove will go with me. Keep Running Eagle sleeping today. Do not allow her to awaken, Elder. Do not deviate from my orders or you shall not be allowed to see this to the end." His threat wasn't lost on the Elder. Turning he nodded to White Dove indicating he was ready to leave.

They rode in silence. White Dove was confused by the events of the last twenty-four hours. Running Eagle fought with a strength she saw only in warriors. Her screams this time was worse than those of the other nightmares. The fact she felt herself ugly was something else that bothered her as White Dove considered her to be very beautiful. Her beauty as well as her exhaustion was the first things she noticed about this woman Luke has proclaimed for marriage. Halfway to the cabin White Dove could contain her curiosity no longer. "Grandfather? I don't understand why she thinks herself ugly."

"It is because of what her captor did to her. Looking at her now you can only see a few scars. You can never understand because you didn't see her when she was returned from the brink of death." Skywalker sighed, seeing White Dove's confusion. "You will understand when we get to the cabin. I'll allow you to see what few others have."

Luke paced the width of the cabin. He left the ceremonial site hours ago. Now dawn was streaking the sky and still there was no word from Skywalker. He had done nothing but worry about Cory. Being sent away confused him. Whatever happened, Luke was sure it had nothing to do with the nightmare or his grandfather wouldn't have been needed.

The nightmare. He frowned. Something changed with this nightmare. Before when he witnessed them Cory always looked sad, tears flowing down her face. She never screamed before either. This time Luke saw terror on her face. He was sure her nightmare was of the torture she endured. The doctors described one that was so severe they restrained her to keep her from hurting the nurses. Was that what perpetuated her terror? The fact that she was being held down? He knew it was done for her physical protection, but he sensed it only increased the reality of the nightmare. He read her file carefully, forcing himself to look at the photos last. Anger threatened to consume him when he saw the mutilation. When infection overpowered her system, she was sent to her Grandmother's house to die. Six months later she returned to the hospital, undergoing a year of plastic surgery. Luke knew when she looked in the mirror she didn't see the beautiful woman he saw. She saw only the mutilated body that was evident in the photos.

How could he reach beyond that image? How could he convince her of his love? How could he wipe the memory of that torture and those scars away? How could he wipe the nightmares from her mind forever? The only thing he wanted her dreaming about was him and he wanted those dreams to be pleasant. He wanted her to know his love. A groan escaped as he folded himself into a chair. His leg throbbed with pain. He knew his pain paled in comparison to what Cory suffered. So much had changed for them since he first met her seven years ago. Arms crossed on the table he placed his head on his arms as he let that time flood his memory.

He had gone to see Ralph Sims. Ralph was his partner and they needed to plan their next move on the case. She answered the door smelling of flowers from the shampoo she used to wash her hair. He didn't know who she expected but from her blush he knew it wasn't him. She was so embarrassed that he slid past her upon seeing Ralph. They went into the living room and Luke sat where he could watch as she escaped up the stairs. He was thankful for the folders he carried. They helped hide the hard response of his body to her blush and the untouched beauty he saw in her.

Ralph informed him that Cory was with the agency and asked Luke to keep an eye on her, make sure she was doing well. Luke did.

He was fascinated with Ralph's beautiful daughter. He watched from a distance and studied her movements. Eventually he could tell her mood simply by how she performed her duties or held her posture.

Ralph was proud of Cory yet never told her. The two men argued often about it. Later, something personal sparked friction between father and daughter. Luke never discovered what it was. As the months passed that friction grew until his daughter moved into her grandmother's house. Ralph and Luke had a terrible argument that night. After both parties calmed down Ralph confided his suspicions of a mole and his concern for Cory. He was afraid she would be used as a pawn for the mole. He felt if he harassed her enough she would quit.

The next morning Luke made Ralph promise to confide in Cory about his suspicions, so she could protect herself. He assured Luke he would tell her that very night. They talked almost an hour about the vacation Ralph and Caroline had planned to take the next day. It would be their first vacation without the children. That afternoon Luke was shipped out on special assignment and he dreaded the case.

Luke found out about the explosion after he returned. He hurried to check on Cory only to discover she was deep undercover, and no one would give him any information concerning her whereabouts. Ralph's suspicions of a mole in the agency and his fear that Cory would be hurt sparked his suspicions of Cory's assignment. He searched hard for proof especially since his friend was labeled with the title of traitor.

He called Rafe and asked him about his investigation. Rafe confided that he could find nothing to prove Ralph's innocence however that wouldn't keep him from looking. Greg Waltz was having no better luck at finding the proof needed. Thwarted by the shake-up and agitated with his inability to find the proof he so desperately hoped to find Luke argued when Major O'Grady ordered him to another special assignment. The argument damned near got him fired. Knowing he would never find the truth if that happened, he backed down from the argument. To Luke the assignment was a waste of time, yet he was forced to leave. The six-month assignment turned into eight. When he returned he was told Corena Sims resigned and was working as a nurse. Luke ground his teeth together. Why had he ever accepted that explanation? At the time it seemed plausible considering what happened to her parents. Now he knew better. Luke was ordered to stay in the meeting hall, forced to listen to Cory's responses to the council's questions. He knew she spoke the truth when she told of Jason Grover's threat to the twins. He knew as well as she that the man was evil enough to carry out that threat.

"Luke?"

White Dove's soft voice startled him. He hadn't heard her approach the cabin. "Is Cory all right?"

"I don't know, Luke. Grandfather is so concerned he is approaching the council tonight. I fail to understand what happen to hurt her so badly."

"She was tortured by an evil man named Grover."

"I've seen her scars." White Dove stated simply knowing there had to be more to the story and was determined to discover the truth.

"You only see the scars where plastic surgery failed. She does not see herself as beautiful. She sees only what Grover did to her. If you're really interested, her file is on the bed along with the photos of the torture she survived."

White Dove frowned. Luke never raised his head from the table. It was as if his spirit deserted him. Going to the bed she opened the file. Pain combined with horror raged within her for Running Eagle as she forced herself to study each picture. "Now I understand why Grandfather feels you are the only one who can help her with her nightmares."

"I'm not allowed. You were there when the council set my conditions concerning her training time. I'm to watch what she goes through and help only when needed. I'm not allowed to talk to her nor touch her unless directed until the challenge begins. I dare not risk her safety by angering the tribe further." Desperation filled his voice. "I fail to understand what happened last night. I know holding her down increased the reality of her nightmare. That's why she fought so much.

But why was I sent away? I was supposed to explain to her about the Challenge and what to expect. Something more happened."

White Dove's heart wrenched at the pain in Luke's voice. "She has started her monthly flow. You know the Elder Women believe its bad luck for an honored warrior to be around a woman during her monthly time. It was the Elder Women's decision to send you away."

Luke snorted with disgust. "I dare them to try keeping us apart once we are joined."

White Dove's eyes narrowed on Luke. He still had not raised his head. "You really do love this woman. Don't you, little brother?"

"Oh God, what have I done to her?" Luke's voice reflected the despair that threatened to overpower him.

"Now is not the time to question your actions, Grandson. You did what you had to do to protect the one you love. Prepare yourself, warrior. We meet with the council in ten minutes."

The sharpness in Skywalker's voice alerted Luke to danger. He quickly rose to his feet realizing too late his mistake. The leg was weak and shot lightning bolts of pain through him. He was falling and could find nothing to stop it. White Dove, lap full of photos and papers from the file, scrambled to her feet sending the papers flying. At five feet four she was short in comparison to her brother however she wrapped her arms around Luke's waist, pulling him against her, keeping him upright until Skywalker could come to her aid. Between the two they helped steady Luke until he was able to control the pain enough to walk. Skywalker frowned as he watched Luke limp across the floor in preparation of shaving. "This is not good, Grandson."

"I'll be all right." Luke growled as he leaned against the sink. "Cory's unhealed wounds hurt worse than mine ever will."

Skywalker's eyes narrowed. "Your leg has not healed?"

Luke shrugged. "Not totally."

Seeing Luke's stubborn stance Skywalker knew it was useless to say more. After helping White Dove gather the file he tucked the envelope containing the photos into his jacket. Luke was ready by the time the jeep arrived and to his relief the warrior who was driving brought a pair of crutches with him. A sad smile crossed his face realizing he now had faster mobility. The council was waiting for them when they arrived.

The meetinghouse was once again packed with people. Brother and sister kept their silence as Skywalker presented his plan. "I stand before this council as a Shaman. I've been with the woman during the night and have seen her nightmares. She's haunted by her injuries of the past and she will be unable to complete the Challenge until those ghosts are banished from her heart." Luke looked at his sister and groaned. Too many questions would come from his grandfather's statement he knew. Would this action help Cory or only serve to hurt her worse?

"What do you propose, Shaman?"

"I propose the conditions set upon Bright Arrow be lifted and this is my reasoning as a Shaman. You recall the injuries she was asked about before she was released to the Elder Women?" The council nodded, and Skywalker continued. "This council needs to know the kinds of injuries she suffered and why. I'm commanding Bright Arrow to tell you of her life over the last five years." Luke swallowed hard. Skywalker was right in his action he just hated the feeling of betrayal that descended upon him as he began his story. He started with the day he saw her in the doorway, progressed to her father's suspicions, the parent's death and her capture and torture, ending with his own wounds and her gentle care of him. When Luke was finished he moved away from the council table.

"This woman has the fierceness of a warrior's heart, but her heart is that of a woman. Since her torture she does not see herself as a woman. She only sees the damage her captor did to her. That damage is no longer visible but has scarred her heart. She doesn't see herself as Bright Arrow sees her. She can only see these." Skywalker withdrew the envelope that contained the photos from his pocket, waving it at the council.

"Grandfather!" Both White Dove and Luke said in unison, horrified at what he was about to do.

# Chapter Seven

ALL EYES LOOKED AT THEIR stricken faces. "It's time for the truth to be known." Skywalker's voice was harsh, hard eyes glared at Luke. "Do you love this woman?"

Luke felt as if he was on a runaway train with no breaks. The truth would only serve him now. "Yes, Grandfather. I love her deeply."

"Did you not bring her here because of the evil of the man who shot you?"

"Yes."

"Is not that man the same person who did this to her?" He tapped the envelope containing the photos.

"Yes it is, however you know how we got those pictures. She doesn't know I have them and would be wounded by the action you are about to take."

"She is already wounded, warrior."

His meaning was clear. As Luke turned away from the prying eyes guilt riddled him. This situation was out of control and it was his fault. He sensed his sister's worried gaze and smiled weakly at her. From the strained silence in the room he knew the council had the photos.

"I propose the conditions on these two young people be lifted. I have heard her agony when she told White Dove of her desire to complete the Challenge. I have no doubt her honor will force her to complete it. I think we should use this time and let Bright Arrow heal the wounds hidden on the inside. To do that he must touch her as well as hold her." He tapped the envelope that held the photos once again. "Only the touch of the man she loves will heal the scars another has left upon her heart. Only then will the scars of her torture be healed. Only then will she see the woman Bright Arrow sees."

"How can you be sure this will work?"

Skywalker stared at the Elder who spoke as if he had two heads. "A few years back we had a young brave who wanted desperately to gain the rank of warrior. He wanted it so badly he worked hard to achieve the rank. The problem was the harder he tried the more mistakes he made. This council thought the young man would never achieve rank. An honored warrior worked with him, encouraged him and built up his self-worth. Still he failed. After a year the honored warrior sat him down in front of a mirror and instructed the brave to tell him what he saw. The brave told the honored warrior all he saw was a failure. The brave no longer saw a young man with knowledge. He no longer saw the hard work he put into his training. He no longer saw the warrior he dreamed of becoming. All he saw was his failures. That's how the woman is. She no longer sees herself as a woman. She can only see the scars her captor inflicted upon her body. She no longer sees herself as desirable, can't believe in her heart that she can be loved by any man. She doesn't even see her body as it is now with only a few scars showing. All she can see is this." He held up the envelope. "If the council continues with its present demands it will be responsible for the spiritual and emotional death of this woman. If so you might as well have sent her from this Reservation without protection. At least her body would be as dead as her heart. Only with Bright Arrow's help can she see her true self."

★ ★ ★ ★ ★

Greg Waltz frowned at the pile of reports on his desk. He requested them three days ago. Since most of them involved Ralph Sims they had already been transferred to microfilm and he waited to have them copied. The damned fools couldn't have sent them up as they were copied. Oh no. They waited and brought them all at once. What kind of imbeciles worked in that office? Even as he wondered his suspicion grew. Whoever was the mole, knew he asked for them and this was his handiwork.

Greg was tempted to ask Fred Adkins for help, but the man looked tired after his report. He and another junior agent spent the last two days interviewing people. They obtained a copy of the sign-in book from the funeral parlor and reviewed the names with the families. After checking off all the names the families knew they made a list of the remaining names. Adkins was advised to interview the people on the list, keeping close watch for an elderly black man with white hair and a slow shuffle. No clues had yet to turn up. Neither had the black man nor the blonde man Greg was sure to be Jason Grover. There were still twenty names and Greg refused to give up hope. That was all he had to go on.

Corena's statement concerning Rafe DeAngelo and his reports haunted him. She got the proof she needed on O'Grady from Rafe's reports. Now he was searching for the connection she found. Rafe's reports were so complete it was almost as if the man had a trap for a mind. Nothing escaped in the report. No questions remained to be answered after reading them. Greg had yet to find the connection Corena spoke of. A soft rap on the door snared Greg's attention. Rafe DeAngelo waited to be admitted and his nervous attitude warned Greg. "Enter."

Greg indicated the chair. Rafe DeAngelo was thirty-eight and one of a dozen men to survive the shake-up after Ralph Sims death. Six feet, blonde hair, blue eyes and muscular frame was a hit with the women inside and outside the agency doors.

Rafe refused the chair, absently pulling a folder from the desk, flipping through it. "We've been interviewing the people in the residential area around the warehouse district. No one seems to have heard or seen any kind of disturbance. It appears the gang violence that night kept people indoors with windows and doors bolted." Rafe suddenly stopped pacing. With a frown he turned to the front of the chart to look at the heading and then stared at Greg. His eyes were dark with anger as he approached the desk. For long minutes he stood staring at Greg. Slamming the file down, he grabbed a pen and paper. Writing quickly, he slid the paper across the desk.

"I just thought you ought to know." He tapped gently on the paper and then retreated across the office. "The men haven't given up on finding Luke's murderer but we're running out of places to look for leads. I'm going to get drunk after work. Care to join me?"

Greg frowned when he glanced at the note. It read: Luke was set up. My phone has been bugged. I need the very files you're looking at to find the proof. Be careful. People are listening to everything we say.

"Sorry Rafe. My ulcers don't allow me to drink anymore. Let me clear my desk then I'll meet you at my house. You can get drunk while I fix supper. That way you can sleep it off and not worry about driving." Greg took the notepad and wrote: Meet me at your house, placing it on the edge of the desk, turning it so Rafe could see it.

Rafe moved to the desk. "Are you sure your wife won't mind having a drunk spend the night? I'd hate to have her mad at me or you for that matter."

Greg laughed. "It won't be the first time and I doubt it'll be the last. Paula has a special room for the men who come and get drunk. Why do you think I had to build that new house we live in?"

"Good. I'll meet you after my shift is over."

After Rafe left Greg looked at his watch. There was three hours left to his shift but Rafe's mention of his wife worried him. Piling the files in his briefcase and locking it he exited the office. "I'm out of antacid. Be back soon." His secretary just grinned. He had been downing a lot of antacids lately. At the drugstore he slipped a quarter into the pay phone and dialed home. He could tell by the way his wife answered that she was angry. "Paula? Are you all right? What's wrong, honey?"

"I've been having problems with the electric. I finally called an electrician and they're now in the basement testing the wiring. We built this house six months ago. Why are we having these problems?"

Greg swallowed his fear. "Honey listen very carefully to what I say. As soon as they leave I want you to go to our room and pack everything you might need for a visit to your sister's. Pack my bags also. Take my things to the neighbors and you get the hell out of that house. I may be jumping at straws, but life has suddenly gotten dangerous. For both of us. Stay at your sister's and under no circumstances are you to return unless I tell you to return myself. I'll call as soon as it's safe. Do you understand?"

Paula's voice dripped with sweetness bringing Greg's already strained nerves to the brink of collapse. "I'm so happy you won't be coming home late. Since the electricians are finished I think I'll fix your favorite dinner to celebrate this unusual occasion. It's so rare you ever get an evening off. By the way did I tell you my brother called? He told me he was going on vacation and wanted to know if you could take time off from your busy schedule to do some traveling. I told him you were busy. He asked me if I wanted to go without you, but I knew you would object. Would you have minded if I went on vacation with him?"

Fear rose in Greg. Paula didn't have a brother. As he groped for words she continued. "Yes, dear. I'll call my brother back immediately and tell him I can go. I know you hate to decline but I also know how busy you are. They're leaving this afternoon and I'm going to miss you. It would be fun to have you go with us especially since we're going to be gone for several weeks. I have to go to the store and buy that special dinner I promised. I'll probably be gone by the time you return, and I hate leaving on an evening when you'll be home on time. Are you sure it you don't mind my leaving?"

"Paula? I love you. Be careful."

"I love you too, darling."

Greg bought two bottles of antacid and returned to his office. His wife was smart. He just hoped they were both smart enough to stay alive. The next three hours dragged by without mercy. He occupied his mind with the reports that were slowly filtering into his office concerning the warehouse massacre. There was little to go on. There wasn't so much as a footprint left at the scene to indicate who was involved. The only thing those gunmen left behind were dead agents. The photos of the scene were of no help either. They were all blank. The reports from the subdivision behind the warehouses were useless.

As Rafe stated no one saw or heard anything. He threw the reports across his desk in disgust.

Who? Who was responsible for the massacre? Who in the agency was so cold hearted as to send twelve men to their deaths? Greg tried to remember who remained at the office after Ralph was murdered. Himself, Luke and Rafe. He knew the first two were not under suspicion which left Rafe. Could Cory's warning about Rafe be true? He shook his head to clear the confusion. Rafe was as honest as Ralph or Luke. He would stake his life on it. He must have misunderstood Cory that night. She was tired and worried about Luke same as he was.

Since he couldn't concentrate he tucked the reports into his bulging briefcase. He would deal with them after making sure his wife was safely away from the house. Was he jumping to conclusions? No matter how much he chided himself for being foolish he couldn't shake the feeling that there was a bomb in his house. He had given Rafe a ten-minute head start. Now he was ready to leave.

Major Thoms entered without knocking. "Are the men getting anywhere with Agent Patterson's murder?"

Greg stared at his superior. Major Thoms was young, younger than either Rafe or Luke and a mystery to all who worked in the office. He was seldom friendly with the men and as far as Greg knew no one even knew what his initials stood for. Why did he consider this Luke's murder? Eleven agents died that day and he never asked about any them. So why did he concentrate on Luke's murder? Why the curiosity? What reason did he have to call it Luke's murder? "No, Sir. There are no leads."

"That's a shame. I understand it's getting to the men. I came by mainly to let you know that I received a report from the funeral parlor. It appears someone forced Agent Patterson's casket open before the burial crew arrived at the funeral parlor to take his casket to the cemetary. I pulled some strings and got the police report. I thought it was easier than getting a court order to dig him up. Do you know anything about that? Has the funeral director called you concerning this incident?"

Greg slowly sank into the chair, shock showing plainly on his face. "My God, why would anyone do that? Luke never wore jewelry. It was a closed casket. I'm sure he wasn't dressed in anything expensive."

"I talked with the parents. Since the laws changed forcing Native Americans to bury their dead I wanted to be sure what was in the casket. They told me he was in burial buckskins. The Grandfather provided the ceremonial array all Indians are buried with. Those included his first bow and arrow, his obsidian knife and a handmade bowl with special herbs. From the report the only thing missing was the knife."

"Grave robbers? In this day and age?" Greg rubbed his eyes. "Why would they rob Luke's grave?"

The Major shrugged. "Anyone with knowledge of Native American history knows the tradition of burying their dead with items needed for the afterlife. What is put into the casket is determined by the tribe. I assume whoever opened the casket was looking for something of value. The parents assured me there was nothing of value there." He looked at his watch. "Expect a call tonight. I should have more information. I'm sure you're anxious to get home to that pretty wife and a good meal. Just thought you would like to know about Patterson's casket."

Greg nodded absently, leaving the office. What if the Major was wrong? What if the person who opened the casket wanted to ensure there was actually a body in the casket? Why was he just now three days after the funeral being notified of this? Why was Major Thoms notified? Why was Major Thoms so interested in this particular case?

Greg checked the car from front to back before crawling inside, the memory of Ralph Sims being blown to pieces fresh in his mind after reading the files this morning. His sixth sense kicked in and he could smell death. His own. That scared the hell out of him. Senses on alert Greg constantly watched for a tail. He made several stops. One to the florist to send flowers to his wife at her sister's for he was positive she would follow his directions and leave. Another was to a fast food place where he spent thirty minutes toying over food he didn't eat. He even stopped for gas although the tank was almost full. While there he called Rafe from a pay phone. He didn't explain much, just asked Rafe to meet him in twenty minutes at the corner of his street. He was afraid to say more in case someone was listening.

After calling Rafe he called his wife Paula. She was in tears, worried about Greg. "Honey listen to me. Right at the moment I'm fine and I intend to stay that way. If anything happens you stay at your sisters and wait for me to call. I'm not stupid enough to get myself killed. Regardless of what you hear or what you're told don't believe anything unless I tell you. I might not be able to contact you for a few days so don't panic. I love you, Paula. Be careful."

"You be careful also Greg. I want you around so we can enjoy your retirement together."

"I will. I promise. I have to go. I'm going to meet with Rafe DeAngelo. I love you." After hanging up he drove around for another ten minutes, still he saw no signs of a tail.

Rafe pulled up a few minutes after Greg arrived. Still worried about being bugged he motioned Greg away from the car. "I thought you were coming to my house." Rafe questioned, sensing the caution in Greg.

"I was but something came up." Greg explained about calling his wife and the strange conversation he had.

"You don't believe there was anything wrong with the electric, do you?"

Greg worried his hair with his hands. "It's a brand-new house, Rafe. Everything was built to specs. Paula was even suspicious. What would you think?"

"Are you sure she left?"

"That's the only thing I'm sure of. After I called you I called her sister. Paula is scared."

"After what I found out today we all have a reason to be scared. Luke was right. We do have a mole." Rafe ran his hands through his hair. "You think those men planted a bomb?"

"Paula told me the electricians carried in a box that appeared heavy. Said the man carrying it was unbalanced with the weight. When he left he seemed to be carrying it with ease. That's what frightened her."

Rafe rubbed his hand along his cheek. "If a bomb was planted they would have to know you were supposed to be home. They would have to either tap into the general switches which I doubt, or they would have to tap into the phone lines. The phones, except cell phones, work off an electrical charge. A ringing phone would set a bomb off providing these people knew what they were doing. Are you expecting someone to call?"

Greg turned white. "Major Thoms came into the office as I was leaving. He told me Luke's casket was broken into and he would call tonight with more information. Whoever bugged the phones must have bugs in the office." Absently he rubbed his forehead. "But that was after the electricians came so that can't be. I don't know of anyone else who would call." Looking at his watch Greg frowned. "It has been over an hour since I left the office."

The explosion shook the ground under the two men. Instinctively both fell to the grass and scrambled for cover. Debris flew around them as a fireball shot into the evening sky. A second explosion sounded as the back half of the house blew apart. Now Rafe was on his knees in front of Greg, hand clenched to the front of Greg's shirt, eyes snapping with anger. "Damn it. What the hell was Luke's assignment that got him killed and why are you a target? What the hell is going on?"

Greg was stunned. Rafe DeAngelo's words pulled him back from an unreal world. He could hear the police and fire engine sirens getting closer and dreaded the thought of getting trapped here. "Let's get out of here. As long as they think I'm dead it may buy us some time to figure this out. Follow me in your car. I think I know where to go." Twenty minutes later they pulled into the residential area behind the warehouses. Rafe recognized the area and shuddered as he remembered finding Luke's body not more than three blocks from here. He slowed to a stop behind Greg's car. They talked to everyone on this street except for the occupants of the house they were now parked in front of. Now there was a black gentleman with white hair searching through an old red station wagon.

"Excuse me." Greg's voice showed none of the anger he was feeling but his eyes showed the anger as the old gentleman slowly stood before the two. "Are you looking for these by any chance?" He dangled a set of keys in front of the man.

"I'm truly thankful I won't have to hot wire my own car." Jasper grinned at the two men, reaching for the keys only to have them jerked beyond his grasp.

"I'll surrender the keys to your car when you surrender the keys to this house." Greg growled, his anger eating away at him.

"Now why would I want to do that?" Jasper grinned again leaning against the car.

"Because Luke and Corena are my friends and the bastard that shot Luke and butchered Corena just blew up my house. I'm in no mood for games, mister. Hand over the keys."

The old gentleman ran his hand down his cheek amusement shining in his eyes. "Um. Um. Um. Missy told me you could get hot under the collar when someone pushed the right buttons. Seeing your anger, someone must have done just that. You must be her daddy's partner. Ralph. Isn't it?"

When Greg stepped forward in anger Rafe positioned himself between the two men. "Easy Captain. It's time to back off and get some air." Turning to Jasper he glared at the man in front of him. "I don't know what the hell is going on, but I can tell you this. Ralph Sims was Corena Sims father and one of the best men I ever worked with. This is Greg Waltz, my Captain and another trusted friend. Greg's house just blew sky high and I'm in no mood for bullshit."

Jasper debated, his mind searching for something only one person would know. "Test time. How many calls were made the day after the killings in the warehouse?"

Greg answered without hesitation. "Three. One to the main line. One an hour later to my private line followed almost immediately to the main line again."

"All right. Missy was traveling with a friend. Describe him."

"Her friend was a male. He had a bullet removed from his left shoulder plus two more wounds. One on his ribs and one to his left hip."

"Very good, Captain. I'm Jasper, a doctor friend of Missy's." Inserting the key into the lock he entered ahead of the other two. He shuffled through the house turning on lights as Greg quickly locked the door behind them. "Are they both still alive?"

"Corena is being protected. Luke's fever is down but he's still having trouble with his leg." Greg saw Rafe sink onto the sofa, stunned. "Doctor, I need some help and the answers are in this house. Corena told me before I left that she found the proof to clear her father's name. She said she hid it within these walls. Do you know where it is? It might give me the answers I need to bring them safely home."

"Lordy, that's a tough one." He scratched his balding head. "There are only two places where Missy ever kept important information. There's a box hidden in her room and that computer. She brought it just after her parents were killed and spent hours in front of it for months. I don't believe she used it much since she was hurt so terribly."

"Can you get me the box?"

"I can. She keeps it in her bedroom, but you might not like what you see there. I have yet to clean up since Missy left. Too many cops around to chance it." Entering the bedroom Jasper left Greg rooted in the doorway as he moved the picture on the wall to reveal a small safe. Clicking the numbers, he soon carried a small metal box into the living room leaving the two men behind. Rafe was behind Greg. The room reeked of blood and Greg had to fight the urge to gag. It was everywhere. Rafe's face reflected his horror as he looked around. The bed and sheets were soaked. He lifted bloodied gloves and bandages from the trash can as well as the wire still submerged in water. Lifting the white uniform in the corner by the closet showed the front practically covered with blood.

From his position in the room he could see clothes under the bed. Retrieving them he laid them out. They had been cut up the left side but Rafe knew them to be Luke's. Anger surged as he looked at Greg.

"All this time you knew Luke was alive? You staged his death and that horrible funeral? You let us believe we lost a friend? How could you, Greg?"

Greg recoiled from the anger in Rafe's eyes, guilt racing along his nerves. "Not now Rafe. I'll explain everything later. Right now, we need to find the proof Corena spoke of. Luke's life isn't worth a plug nickel without it." Entering the living room, he opened the box. Inside were letters, the obituary for her parents and life insurance papers. Under that were several envelopes holding pictures. A small, single brown envelope was sealed, something hard within it. "What's this?"

Jasper grinned. "That's my gift to Missy. Those are the bullets she removed from her young man."

Rafe gasped. "Bullets?"

"Uh huh. Missy removed two from that fellow named Luke. Thought they might be needed if her man survived." Jasper grinned. "Just leave it in the box until she returns. They're safe there."

Greg nodded replacing the small brown envelope for the one with pictures. The first he looked at were pictures of her sisters. "When were these taken?"

Jasper shrugged. "Missy labeled the backs of her photos. She was a stickler for that after her parents died."

Greg skimmed through them flipping the pictures to look at the names and dates. When finished he handed the photos and envelope to Rafe. The next one he opened made his stomach churn, face turn pale and hands to shake. "My God, how did she get these?"

Rafe saw the horror in Greg's face and pulled the photos from his shaking hands. In shock, he looked at each one. They were of a woman's torso, one that was badly mutilated. The sight made his stomach churn with dread and fear for the person in the picture.

Jasper shrugged again, tears sparkling in his eyes. "We never knew who sent them. Her grandmother got a call one day from the people who bought the big house. Said there was a package on the doorstep with Missy's name on it. Since Missy was so ill I went to pick it up. No one opened it for months. When Missy was better and could tolerate the plastic surgery she finally opened it. After that all the fight drained out of her. I didn't think she kept them." He stood, facing Greg. "I can't take any more of this. Missy has been like a daughter to me and I've been worried sick since they left. Hell, Luke refused to tell either of us where he was taking her. You sure she's all right?"

Greg sighed and nodded. "I'm sure. I drove them there myself since Luke was in such bad condition. She was tired when I left her but very much alive." Greg handed the old man the keys to the station wagon and walked him to the door. "I'll be staying here for a while, so I'll need the keys."

Returning to the living room Greg found Rafe studying the pictures of Corena's mutilation. "I wish I had a magnifying glass." He mumbled flipping through them.

"Why?"

"There's something wrong with these pictures." Rafe looked around the room before going to the desk. The only thing he could find was a magnifying glass that fit over a book. Clearing a space on the desk he studied each one. "By God I think I know where these photos were taken."

Greg was lost in thought looking at the other pictures in the box. Almost all of them were of him and Ralph in their younger years. "Those are the same photo's that are in her file. They were taken at the hospital when she arrived."

"No way. There's nothing in these pictures to indicate they were taken at the hospital. I've been to this place before. I remember the markings on this floor tile. I just can't remember where it is."

Greg forced himself to stand over Rafe's shoulder and felt his stomach churn. Rafe sensed the difficulty Greg was having and covered the mutilated body with his hand. He knew from Jasper's words and Greg's aversion to looking at the photos that it was Corena Sims in the pictures. After the initial shock he forced himself to ignore the body and look beyond it. "Captain? How did the agency know where to find Corena?"

Greg sighed. "I only know what I read in her file. The bust was supposed to happen at a house. She wore a wire but apparently the wire was defective. Her backup waited fifteen minutes. When there was no contact they went in after her. All they found was her dead partner lying in a pool of blood, his head almost separated from his body. The autopsy stated he was shot in the chest but the injuries to his neck were the cause of death. No one saw or heard anything to suggest she was in trouble much less who abducted her. Thirteen hours later a call came into the office. It was short and sweet. Corena Sims could be found at the abandoned railway station."

"These pictures weren't taken at any railway station, abandoned or otherwise. Has she ever spoken of that night?"

"She talked a little after we got Luke to his destination. Corena told me they tortured her for twelve hours. She also described the man who did it. She said that..." Greg thought hard to remember the correct words. "The man told her he was instructed not to kill her or rape her. He was to record her screams and listen to her beg."

"Twelve hours. That means there's one hour not accounted for. Greg, I need a map." Rafe tapped his fingers absently on the desk. "Do you have those files you had today or are they still on your desk?"

"I have them in the car. Why?"

"I will need those too."

Greg grabbed his briefcase and a map from the car. Rafe was still studying the pictures when he returned, a frown on his face. "Since you read her file you are going to have to stretch your memory. Show me where the bust was supposed to be. Then show me where they found her." Greg spread the maps on the floor while Rafe began marking off distances with a ruler. "Give me those files." Rafe stated absently.

Greg unlocked the briefcase shoving it towards Rafe. Picking up one Rafe filtered through the first couple of pages and then set it aside before picking up the next. This continued for another twelve files before a slow grin spread across the younger man's face. "Bingo. I knew I recognized that place. Corena Sims was tortured in a building owned by one mean bastard named Jason Grover. His building is located right here." Rafe put his finger on the map midway between where Corena started her assignment and where she was found.

"This is one of those unsolved cases." Rafe tapped the file. "I was partnered with Luke at the time but when he found out who we were to interview he backed out. Said they knew each other and didn't want to blow his cover. That really pissed Major O'Grady off. Luke knew so much about Grover he helped set up the sting. Ralph helped with the interview at this very building that Corena was found in. Shortly after that Luke was shipped out on special assignment. When Ralph and I got to the assigned spot to execute the arrest warrants, everyone had disappeared."

Greg swallowed hard. "How much time elapsed between that day and the day Ralph and his wife were murdered?"

Rafe leaned against the couch. "Let me see…Luke backed down from the assignment and Ralph went with me to interview Jason Grover. That was on a Monday as I recall. Luke was shipped out Friday morning and Ralph was killed later that day. I remember Luke was angry about leaving just before a weekend. Something about a woman he wanted a date with or had a date with. I can't remember which."

Greg held his breath. Maybe he would get lucky after all. Tonight, he just might find the answers Corena searched so hard to find. Rafe sat forward looking Greg square in the face. "Before you pump me for any more information, Captain, I think we ought to lay our cards on the table. Since something is amiss here I'll go first. Luke trusted you enough to help him escape and plan his funeral. I guess I can too." Leaning back against the couch he carefully considered his words. "I know Ralph confided in you about his suspicions of a mole in the agency five years ago. The day we went to interview Jason Grove he told me he thought he was being set up. Things happened during his last several assignments that made him suspicious."

"Like what?"

"He said the information he was receiving came too easy. People, who normally would be cautious, weren't. People were confiding in him who normally wouldn't have the kind of information he was getting. Something else happened but he refused to tell me. Whatever it was made him believe he knew who the mole was. At first, I couldn't believe it, but Ralph was scared, and it showed.

"After that he made me promise to keep an eye on things. On Tuesday he sent the twins to stay with Carrie Ann and by Wednesday he had a terrible fight with his daughter Corena. The fight was severe enough that she moved in with her Grandmother the same day. I was at his house when she packed her bags and left. I was so upset over Ralph's attitude I searched out Luke and confided in him. He went ballistic. I've never seen that man angry before and I hope never to see it again.

"This was Thursday. Friday morning, I encouraged Luke to call Ralph and make peace between them. Friendships like they had were not found every day. Later when I drove Luke to the airport he told me the two had talked and everything was back to normal. Luke assured me that Ralph would make amends with Cory. After Ralph died I tried to find Luke, but Major O'Grady refused to disclose his whereabouts. All I could come up with was dead ends. Major O'Grady decided he and I should notify Corena. We went to Ralph's house and I was shocked to find her there until I saw the boxes. She was packing the rest of her things. Can you believe that little imp accused me of taking bribe money from the mole, so he wouldn't be found? That woman has one hot temper.

"The gist of it is that I never found the proof. I wanted to clear Ralph's name so badly it became an obsession for me. I failed to find anything before the shakeup. How O'Grady got the information that Ralph was the traitor I'll never know. Nothing I found would indicate Ralph, yet..." He shook his head trying to relieve the guilt he felt. "After the funeral I was shipped so far undercover I thought I would never see daylight. It was almost two years before I returned. I wrote Corena, but my letters were always returned as undeliverable. For two years I worried about that little girl, only to..." Rafe sighed, gathering his thoughts. "After that things settled into a routine again. Then Luke got this assignment and I could tell he didn't feel right about it.

We had a long talk several months ago and he was saying almost the same things Ralph said. He told me he had the gut feeling they knew his every move and he was beginning to feel like a puppet. He said he thought the mole was operating again and he was being set up.

"I started investigating on my own. Listening to conversations, reading the reports from the last two years, being friendly with the men, that sort of thing. Then the night of the gang violence I got in an argument with Major Thoms. No wonder there was a massacre. He pulled every experienced field agent off that stakeout. After what happened with Ralph I was worried about Luke. I even threatened to quit. Thoms was so angry with me he assigned me to a desk job that night. He even sat in the office all night to make sure I obeyed his orders. You can't believe the guilt I felt when I learned our men were dead and Luke was missing. Even then that bastard wouldn't release me."

Rafe's eyes filled with tears and he went into the kitchen for a glass of water. Composed when he returned Rafe continued. "When I wasn't out looking for Luke I was making calls. After we found his body..." He glared at Greg. "I should say after we found *the* body I was convinced there had to be a mole in the agency, betting it was Major Thoms." Angry he pounded his fist on the floor. "Once again I couldn't find the proof needed to accuse him. Today my phone was in a different position. Since I'm left handed I always curl the cord around the body of the phone and hang it up backward. It's easier for me to use that way. When I returned from lunch the cord was all on one side. When I picked it up to return it to the proper position for me I noticed the mouthpiece was cross-threaded.

"If I wasn't already suspicious I wouldn't have thought anything about it. But I was and did. That's when I found the bug. Curiosity got the better of me and I started poking around. Three other phones in the office were also bugged. When I came to your office I was going to ask for a leave of absence. I was determined to find the proof needed and knew it had to be in the files. It also had to tie in with Ralph. When I saw the files I needed on your desk, I decided to wait with my request for a bit longer and just watch."

# Chapter Eight

R AFE THOUGHT GREG'S EYES WOULD pop out of his head as the implication of his words sank in. "You suspected me?" Greg chuckled. "That's rich. Corena told me to watch your every move and to read every one of your reports. Stated you wrote interesting reports."

Rafe was stunned. "She suspected me?"

Greg worried his hair with his hands. "I wish I knew, Rafe. She told me your reports gave her the proof she needed on O'Grady. She also said there was a second mole, but she never got the proof she needed and wouldn't name the person. That's when she told me about you."

Hurt flashed in Rafe's eyes before it was shuttered. He nodded. "I see. That explains why most of those files are mine. I'm rather disappointed in the imp for suspecting me." He sighed. "If she had the proof, where is it?"

"All she said was that it was hidden within the walls of her house. When Jasper brought the box out I hoped it was there. We have got to find it. Corena has been hurt enough."

Rafe switched on the computer. After a while he swore. "According to this the files I can access are just household files and old ones at that. She must have a password hooked to the other one providing the proof is locked in here."

"Any way of finding the key?"

"Yes but it would take a hacker. It has to be in that box. Something this important she wouldn't leave locked for eternity without letting someone know how to retrieve the information. The Corena Sims I remember was very savvy."

Greg shook his head. "Nothing here but pictures. Most of them are of Ralph and I when we were younger. There are a few of you and some of Luke. The envelope with the bullets in it is here. Other than that and the papers we already looked over there's nothing."

"Let me see those pictures while you tell me about Luke." Rafe's attention was soon drawn away from the pictures and he laid them in his lap as he listened to Greg's tale. Greg told him everything. From Luke's suspicions to the three phone calls. To finding Luke in Corena's care to the forced marriage and her words before he left the Reservation. From the funeral and the two people he felt did not belong, to the grave robbery Major Thoms told him about before he left. Greg cut no corners with the younger man. He told it exactly how it was.

"Let me get this straight. Corena Sims helped Luke escape from the gunmen the night he got shot, bringing him here to care for him. Obviously, the bullets were removed here. There's too much blood on the bed to indicate any other conclusion. He talks her into getting him out of the city by hiding him under camping gear and now they're going to be forced to marry each other?" Rafe chuckled when Greg nodded. "What a hell of a way to become engaged. Then you said that before you left she told you she had proof on O'Grady, but it's hidden within the walls of her house. She also hints at the fact that I'm the one she suspects of being the mole. After that she suggests you need to find a dead body, pretend its Luke and fake a funeral." He shook his head in wonderment. "His parents didn't object?"

"Actually, they thought it a wonderful idea."

"Several things bother me, Greg. If she had the proof, why didn't she present it to the authorities and have O'Grady arrested? That would have cleared her father."

"I asked her the same thing." Tears welled in Greg's eyes and he shuddered when he remembered seeing the scars on Corena's body. "Those pictures you saw, the ones of Corena after she was butchered?

She still has scars, Rafe. She told me that after she obtained her proof O'Grady was already gone but he cast suspicions about her honesty. At the time I felt as if she wasn't telling me the whole truth."

"Do you blame her? What I fail to understand is why anyone would send an injured and dying woman pictures of what he did to her. Why would they even bother? There has to be some reason for the pictures as well as her not pressing charges against O'Grady. Corena obviously worked for many years to clear her father's name and wouldn't have let something this important alone without good reason. Why did she just back off from her investigation only to keep it locked in a computer?"

Greg groaned. "Carol and Cindy."

"Who are they?"

"Corena's younger sisters. Twins. I heard they came to live with her after Ralph and Caroline were killed. If that bastard threatened to injure them she would have backed away from clearing her father's name. The pictures were just a reminder of what they did to Corena, a reminder of what they could and would do to the twins if Corena didn't resign."

Rafe considered what Greg said. He nodded slowly. "I think you're correct, Captain. Corena would have protected her sisters as fiercely as she protected her partners. That would explain why she resigned." Silence reigned as both men tried to control their emotions. Rafe fought his anger while Greg fought his feelings of guilt for not being there for Ralph's daughter. Finally, Rafe spoke again. "Something else bothers me. Why would anyone steal an obsidian knife? Why break into the casket at all?"

Greg sighed. "I doubt they wanted the knife. I believe it was taken to cover up the original reason for opening the casket." At Rafe's narrowed eyes, he sighed again. "I think they wanted to make sure there really was a body in the casket. Thanks to you and the men there was. Originally we planned to return the body to the morgue in case someone came looking for that poor soul."

Rafe gave a rueful chuckle. "The men keeping guard on that body day and night didn't allow that."

"Exactly. His parents said that since they were using the body to save Luke's life it should be buried with respect. They stated they would change the writing on the headstone later. When Major Thoms told me about the objects I was surprised." Greg frowned. "Few people would have known the meaning behind those objects. Even fewer would have known Luke was an Indian who practiced his heritage. Only a small handful of people knew those items were placed in that casket. Even I didn't know Luke's grandfather put them in the casket."

"Major Thoms knew. He not only knew about them, but he also knew the symbolism behind them. Didn't he? Can you remember, word for word, exactly what he said before you left the office today?"

Greg rubbed his head in thought. "He wanted to know if there were any leads in Luke's murder. That surprised me, him calling it Luke's murder, especially since eleven members of our agency ended up in the morgue that night. I can never remember Luke claiming to have known him except on a professional level. When I informed him that we were out of leads, he commented that he heard the men were upset. After that he told me about the casket being broken into."

Rafe saw Greg turned white. "Captain?"

"I remember something else he said. After he told me about the casket he told me it was time to go. He stated he knew I wanted to get home to a good meal and my wife and that I should expect a call later. Dear God, he knew. That bastard knew a bomb had already been planted in my house hours before he came into my office. I used a payphone to call Paula, not the office phone. He probably made the call himself."

"I've had my suspicions of Major Thoms for quite some time. He showed up on the heels of Major O'Grady as I recall. The smaller busts we never had any trouble with. It was the large busts where something always went wrong. Those were the ones Luke and I had problems maintaining our cover. Many times, it was blown before we could get a clean case." Hatred filled Rafe's eyes. "That was when I began to suspect we had a mole. It was too much like that which Ralph complained of."

"Careful Rafe. We have no proof of either O'Grady or Thoms being a mole which puts us back to square one. It would make this night so much easier on both of us if we knew what Corena found."

"There's only one way to do that. We have to find out what Corena has locked in that damned computer." Gathering the pictures that had fallen from his lap while listening to Greg Rafe started putting them to rights. Some of them were where he could see the writing. As he straightened them, slight changes in the writing caught his eye. "That little imp." He grinned. "I think I just found her code."

Greg moved closer for a better look as Rafe spread the pictures out, face down. Several had markings at the lower edge of the picture. Picking these out Rafe noticed they were all pictures of Luke. "No wonder she recognized him so quickly. She used his pictures to write the codes on. I guess she figured he would inherit these if anything ever happened to her and would have spotted those marks right away. Now we need to unscramble the codes."

"That's easy." Greg laughed. "Ralph and I learned that code when we studied for the agency." Studying the marks, he handed them back to Rafe one by one. "Evil. Always. Good. Over. Conquers. Unscramble that and it should give you Luke's favorite saying--Good always conquers over evil. The codes are his words."

Rafe looked doubtful. "Awfully long for a computer file name but let's give it a try." He went to the computer and typed it in. "Access denied." He frowned. "Let's break it up." He typed in G-O-O-D and the computer came to life. "We're in." Rafe read the screen aloud. It told of Ralph's suspicions of Major O'Grady being the mole and what caused his suspicions--the ease of the information he obtained, the ability of people who were feeding him information who normally wouldn't have known. Of how Corena was to go to Greg or Luke if anything happened and how, when she needed them most, one lay at death's door and the other had been shipped out on assignment.

It told of the funeral and the paper trail she followed. It also told of her suspicions that there was at least one, maybe two moles still in the agency which she suspected but had no proof and wouldn't name them. He drew a ragged breath when he finished. His confusion was obvious. "She did suspect me. I wonder why. What did I do or say or write that would make her think I would betray my best friend?"

Greg winced upon hearing the pain in Rafe's voice. "Try the next word, always."

Quickly the screen changed. This time they were looking at a graph that listed Ralph's assignments, the partners, who was involved and who had access to the knowledge. Rafe printed out a copy of the graph. "Now we will try conquers." This was another graph. It was a timeline. File numbers were written above the dates. This Rafe also printed.

The password, over, brought up the details of who wrote the files that were listed on the previous screen. With the exception of a few, Rafe or Luke wrote them all. Again, the printer roared to life. Evil brought up a list of suspects her father investigated or arrested. One name jolted Greg to the bottom of his soul. Jason Grover. Rafe's face turned angry when Greg pointed to the name. When the printer stopped he turned to Greg. "See if you have the file of Jason Grover's bust. I'm going to see if I can compile this into something useful." Grabbing pencil and paper from the desk he headed for the kitchen table.

Greg found the report, carried it to the table and started reading. "Luke helped with the bust as a Junior Agent. Ralph states that when Luke found out they were to stake out Jason Grover he stayed in the background because the two had been college roommates for a time and he knew that Grover would recognize him. Even though Ralph made the bust he credits Luke with it. Apparently, it was Luke's knowledge of the man and his habits that allowed Ralph to trap him. It seems Jason Grover was just a small-time operator then, dealing drugs and weapons. Grover was sent to prison for fifteen years, served two and got out on appeal which overturned his conviction on a technicality."

Rafe was looking at the time line. "On what date did he get out?"

"December twelve. The bust happened three years earlier with a year between, waiting on the conclusion of the trial and the conviction."

"Date of conviction?"

Greg groaned. "June seven."

Rafe's head shot up. "My God, that's the same date Ralph and Caroline died. How did he know Ralph was picking up his vacation check that day?" Anger seeped through him. "The mole told him." He whispered.

Greg started coffee. It was going to be a long night. Rafe began setting his own time line. This time he used dates, names and events instead of file numbers. He also made a chart of information which included setting up the bust, who worked on each one, how long it took to complete, specific difficulties encountered and whether the bust resulted in a conviction.

When they were done, they sat comparing them to Corena's charts. Greg checked the files he had with the numbers Corena referred to. He had all but seven. Three of those missing files were Luke's. The other four were from different agents. The seven missing files left a huge gap in their work. Rafe rubbed at his eyes while Greg continued to study the charts. "Rafe? Who is Tom Marvin?"

"Hell, how do you expect me to remember?" He stretched in his chair. "I'm so tired I'm lucky to remember my own name much less who that was."

"Stay with me on this." Greg waited until he had Rafe's attention. "His name shows up three times. Here it is Tom Marvin. In this one, it's Marvin Toms. Here it's Martin Tom. All three are out of your reports."

Rafe sighed, rubbing hard at his eyes as he tried to concentrate. "All I remember is that he was a pain in the ass, know it all, upstart punk, junior agent who had family high up in the agency. The kid never listened to anything I told him and damned near got me killed. Only my quick responses saved my hide. Major O'Grady finally shipped his ass over to Luke. I never saw him again."

"I still don't see the connection. Everything we have is circumstantial. What is it Cory had on O'Grady?" Greg mumbled aloud.

Rafe shuffled through the papers. "We must have missed something on that damned computer because I haven't found anything in what we printed off." He wandered into the living room again, staring at the computer screen. "Where did you hide it Corena? There are no other pictures with marks on them. Only those of Luke. Is that your secret? Is Luke the key to unlocking this damned mystery?" Quickly, he typed in Luke's name. Slowly, the screen came to life. "Captain? I think you better come in here. I found something else." When Greg entered Rafe read what was on the screen. "She is writing a letter to Luke. Listen.

*'I know you were a friend to daddy, and I can trust you. To clear his name, you need to go to the Reservation. Grandmother has taken the proof there and has hidden it in a Shaman's house. Next to the fireplace, on the right, just above the mantle, Grandmother says there is a loose brick. Look behind that brick, Luke.*

*'Everything you need to hang that bastard is there. I would do it myself however I must protect my family. They already told me they would hurt my sisters and I can't let that black-eyed bastard do that. I would rather kill him myself than allow him to hurt someone I love. Be careful, Luke. If anyone should discover that you know where the proof is hidden your life will be in danger also.*

*'There is another mole. I think I know who it is however I can't prove what I suspect. Seven files have disappeared after I read them. According to records, the numbers as well as the files themselves were destroyed or never existed. Don't believe that, Luke. I read them. I know they exist only I wasn't able to track them down before I was captured and tortured.*

*'Since the only way you would have gotten the information from the lawyers concerning this file is because I've been killed. I will tell you this, look at the applications, Luke. One sticks out like a sore thumb. When I started investigating the family background I was captured. That black-eyed bastard and the one I suspect are brothers only they carry different names. That's how he knew I found the proof. I'm sorry I can't be more specific. You will have to find those files now. Take care of yourself. Love, Cory.'*

Greg paced, mumbling to himself. "Those seven missing files are the key to solving this mystery. Corena said that key information she needed had disappeared and that information was in those files she read."

Rafe stretched tired muscles. "Well, I for one am going to crash in that other bedroom. After we wake up we're going to pick up your things from the neighbors, go to my house to get cleaned up. Then we're going visiting."

"No can do, Rafe. I have got to get back to the office and talk with Adkins. He can help a lot right now."

"Afraid not, Captain. If my suspicions are correct your office was bugged. Whoever was listening heard us arrange to meet at your house after work, me with a bottle and you with food. As far as anyone knows we were blown up with that house. Right now, we are just as dead as Luke. That, my friend, is going to work in our favor."

Anger flared in Greg's face. "If we play dead there's no way of getting the reports we need. We have to get the proof out of those files, so these damned killings will stop."

"We still have access to that information, Greg." Rafe stood, stretching. "That's why we have to go visiting. Seven files are missing. Three of them are Luke's. He can supply us with a reasonable amount of information. The other four files are stuffed in Corena Sims head. Now, let's get some sleep. We have a lot of work ahead of us before this game of cat and mouse is over. I just pray that all of us survive this nightmare."

★ ★ ★ ★ ★

Something was wrong. Luke could feel it in his guts. He was waiting with Turtle and Laughing Bear for Cory's return to the tipi. It was early afternoon before she woke feeling better. White Dove and the Elders talked with Cory before Luke was allowed to see her. He knew they were conferring with her about a special ceremony before the Challenge began. Except for the Shaman no man had ever witnessed a woman's ceremonies and wasn't surprised when the three were banished to the tipi after Cory was removed. Before he left to be with Cory, Skywalker made a poultice for Luke's leg.

Unable to wear his jeans he still wore the traditional dress of buckskin shirt, breechcloth and leggings. He did not want his Grandfather to see the leg. There were two places that had yet to heal. Those places were angry red, and Luke knew his Grandfather would insist a doctor see him. He also knew Cory would insist on going with him. That would put her at risk and Luke wouldn't allow that. Turtle slid the poultice under the legging. Luke struggled with the pain but refused tea.

As the door opened Luke looked up to see Cory, face red, being returned. Turtle and Laughing Bear left as she was forced to lie down. Luke pulled her head into his lap, pulling her loose hair from around her face. "You frightened me last night when the nightmare came with such force. Are you feeling better?"

"Yes." A ghost of a smile mingled with her blush. "I didn't expect to see you. I thought you would be home resting."

He loosened her hair from the braids and was now running his fingers through its silky strands. "My half of the condition was to help with the Challenge. That way we can be joined immediately after it is finished."

Her blush deepened as she turned away from his eyes. "It's not right for you to be trapped into this marriage, Luke."

"You'll have to get use to using my tribal name, woman. It's Bright Arrow and you need to use it. As far as being trapped, I trapped you. I was hoping you could learn to love me as much as I love you."

Tears filled her eyes as she struggled to sit up. Luke's arm across her chest prevented movement. Silent sobs shook her shoulders as she ceased her struggles. "You would not love me, could not love me, if you really knew me."

"I know you, Running Eagle. I have watched you since I first met you seven years ago." He smiled at her startled look. "I watched you enough to recognize what mood you were in by your posture. I worried over your assignments. I even went looking for you when I returned and found your parents were murdered. I was worried about you."

"You never came."

Luke groaned. "I know, sweetheart. I couldn't find you. Your father told me you moved in with your Grandmother, but he never told me her name or where she lived. When I returned from my assignment I snuck into the file room and pulled your file. Your mailing address was a post office box. I hung around that post office for several days, but you never came to collect your mail." His grin broadened at her incredulous look. "I was shipped out on another assignment soon after that. It lasted longer than I planned. When I got back I was told you resigned. Still I tried to find you only they had put your file away and I couldn't find it. Oh God, Running Eagle. You don't know how hard I tried."

Cory covered her face in horror. "You broke into the file room to get my address and saw...and saw..." Sobs racked her shoulders as she curled into a tight ball.

Guilt stabbed Luke knowing it was better to let her believe he saw the photos in the file room than to have her know Greg gave them to him. He pulled her into his lap, and she buried her face in his shoulder. "I've seen the photos, Running Eagle. I know what that bastard did to you, my dear." Luke fought to keep his anger under tight control. "I know how he tortured you and why you hate yourself."

Her eyes were deep pools when she looked at him before burying her face in his shoulder again. "Then you know why this is a trap for you. You know what I look like. You know..." She stiffened, feeling the tug on the ties of her dress.

"I know what you look like." His voice was husky as his hands slipped under the leather. The feel of her skin against his hand brought an immediate response to his groin and he had to adjust her position to accommodate it. "I know what you feel like. I know that I love you."

Her breathing was ragged. "How can you? You saw the photos. You know of the scars. It's not possible to love someone as ugly as I am."

"I know you're beautiful to me." His fingers found the scar on her rib and she tried to jerk away. Luke held her tight against his chest with his left arm as his right hand continued to explore. Unhindered by jeans or underwear he traced the scar to its end. Cory's face was pressed hard into the notch of his shoulder as her shoulders convulsed with fear and shame. Tracing the scar upward he soon came into contact with the one over her left breast. She gasped trying desperately to pull away.

Ignoring her struggle Luke continued to explore. Cupping the underside of her breast, running his thumb over her nipple, he nuzzled her neck as he enjoyed the feel of her breast getting full and the nipple becoming a tight nub. "See how perfectly you fit in my hand? This nipple will be feeding our children. Until then I get the pleasure of nursing you."

The pain in his leg had eased from the poultice and he slid from beneath her to lie beside her, keeping her head pinned to his shoulder. Slowly, gently, he pulled the buckskin dress across her chest until both breasts were revealed. As the cool air touched her skin her nipples became taunt and Luke smiled. When she tried to cover herself, he captured her wrists at her side. "I told you this won't be a marriage in name only, my dear. Your body is so beautiful to me. From the day I met you until now I have dreamed of the day I would be joined with you. I plan on kissing and tasting every last inch of your body."

Her small whimper sent a jolt of guilt through Luke and he steeled himself against it. He knew of no other way to make her believe she was beautiful except to awaken the woman within. She laid perfectly still as he gathered her nipple into his mouth. The sensation rocked him and made his desire for her grow. Releasing her wrists, he gently teased her other breast as he nursed. Cory heard his guttural moan as his leg crossed her hips, could feel his hard erection and feel his tongue dancing around her nipple. Her body's response shocked her. Breast hard, nipples taunt, hot lava flowed to her groin. Fire trailed her skin wherever his fingers touched, stealing her breath away. "Please, Luke, don't."

"Don't worry, woman of my heart. I'm not going to rape you." He kissed upward, along her ribs to her collarbone, raising his head enough to avoid the neck of her dress. "The first time I enter you will be on our joining night or when you tell me you're ready for me. Right now, I'm going to explore your body. I want to know why you feel undesirable. What I have tasted so far pleases me beyond measure." Moving to her neck he nibbled at the wildly beating pulse.

Gasping at the surge of pleasure he was creating she tilted her head backward. Luke smiled at her unconscious act of surrender. The woman was buried deep and it would challenge his manhood to get her to release it. Luke always conquered his challenges and knew he would enjoy this one. His hand captured her breast, thumb teasing her nipple as he planted tiny kisses along the length of her neck. Voice husky, he nipped at her earlobe. "I love you and pray someday you can love me."

Luke kissed her closed eyes, the tip of her nose before he captured her mouth. Her lips quivered below his and her arms circled his neck, fingers intertwining in his long black hair. With her response he deepened the kiss until her lips parted. Always his hands touched her beneath the buckskin dress. He inhaled her moan of pleasure.

Exploring her mouth, he tasted the tea she drank and something else. A bitter taste he recognized from several of his own ceremonies as a crushed root and knew the taste would stay with her for several days. He realized she had completed the rite of passage ceremony. In the eyes of the tribe she was considered a woman ready to be courted.

That knowledge alerted senses other than sexual. As he continued to explore her mouth he could taste the honey applied to the inside of her lips. His Grandfather's words during his own ceremony came to mind. "Bitter is to remind us to be careful what we say to others. Words spoken in anger will bring hurt and bitterness to those who hear them. Honey is nature's sweetness. It's a reminder that gentleness and kindness will foster love and happiness."

Hearing her moan, he released her lips, trailing kisses down her neck to the pulse beating wildly at the hollow of her throat. Her hands found their way under his buckskin shirt and she was exploring every inch of his back. Eyes closed, face reflecting the pleasure his caress was sending through her, Luke doubted she even realized what she was doing. He was in control at this moment and that knowledge pleased him immeasurably. Except for following the scar from her ribs to her hip he restricted himself to everything from her breasts up. He wanted to touch every inch of her. Taste every inch of her. But not today. Today he would use her body against her defenses. He would awaken the woman in her slowly, although he was sure for her, it was all new and would seem to be a siege. As he captured her breast again, her back arched in want. Luke knew her body would respond. In his desire to awaken the woman within he forgot one thing--his leg. When her back arched her hip slammed against his injured leg. Red-hot pokers seared his brain and he collapsed against her with a strangled moan.

Immediately she stilled, the heat of passion cooled quickly by the icy grip of fear. "Luke? What is wrong?"

"Help me Cory. My leg…" Another moan escaped as she rolled as one with him until he was flat of his back.

Quickly tying her dress back together she wiped the hair from Luke's face. Cory could feel no sign of fever yet knew the pain he was in by the way his hands were fisted and the hard muscle of his jaw as his teeth clenched together. "Luke, I need to look at that leg. It should be healed by now."

Untying the legging from the breechcloth she soon had the poultice removed. The hip was hot to touch, oozing yellow infection in two places, one at the top of the scar line and one in the middle. Jasper checked for stray pieces of glass yet that was exactly what it looked like. Something was definitely imbedded in the hip and it could only be glass. Infection was firmly set in place. "Don't try to move Luke… Bright Arrow. I'll return in a minute."

Luke nodded, never opening his eyes. Cory ran from the tipi searching for Skywalker. She found him with everyone else sitting in the small clearing where she had undergone her ceremony only an hour before. Breathless, she knelt before him. "Shaman, Bright Arrow is in pain. His leg…there must still be glass in it. It's hot to touch and infected. The glass will have to be removed."

Skywalker stood, looking down at her. "You must help your warrior, woman. I will assist you and help you all I can, but he is your warrior and you must do the work."

Cory shuddered before nodding. "I removed the bullet from his chest, so I guess I can remove the glass from his leg if you tell me how. He has suffered enough pain. Will you make him some sleeping tea?" Skywalker headed for the fire ring while Cory rushed to get water boiling. In her hurry she missed the surprise her words brought to those around the clearing.

Skywalker mixed the herbs carefully as Cory watched. "Woman have Turtle give you his knife. We need to heat the blade to free it of germs."

By the time the blade was glowing the tea and poultice were ready. Pulling the knife from the coals she propped the handle against a rock so it could cool. "I'll give him the tea and then explain what must be done." When she returned her hands were shaking as she prepared the poultice. "I shall need the help of the warriors. Bright Arrow will have to be held down. Once I cut his leg open the tea won't control his pain."

"Is he angry?"

"Yes, Shaman. I gave him the tea first." She wiped the tears from her cheeks. "Was I wrong to do that?"

"No, woman. A warrior is trained to control pain. A Shaman's grandson knows the tea will prevent much of that control." He laughed softly. "You are a good healer. His deep love for you will allow the warrior in him to conquer.

Tear filled eyes looked sharply at Skywalker. "Does he really love me, Shaman?"

Skywalker pulled her face until he captured her eyes. "He loves you as deeply as you love him. You must drop your defenses to allow him to enter your heart. He has told you of his love. Yes?" Cory nodded. "Now you must open your heart and accept his love. You must also show him the depth of your love. Just as your love for him will help him heal, his love for you will heal your wounds. That's part of the circle of life. He feels badly that he has put you in danger. Both of you have a shared ghost you must conquer."

"Jason Grover."

Skywalker nodded. "Bright Arrow is haunted by his own nightmares of the man and what he has done."

"How can he…we overcome this? Grandmother taught me that if I asked for guidance in my dreams, a vision would be given me and if I listened I would be given direction."

"Did it work?"

"It did for years. Then Grover came along. I have prayed but my visions have failed me."

"Perhaps it's because you refuse to open your heart, Running Eagle. Now we must help Bright Arrow."

Gathering the knife and poultice she entered the tipi last. The sleeping tea had taken effect and the warriors moved Luke to a blanket in the center of the tipi. Cory saw White Dove's tears as the young woman stayed on the outskirts of the tipi. "Skywalker? Can you have Laughing Bear take White Dove outside? She doesn't need to see this."

While Skywalker talked with Laughing Bear, Cory rolled her blankets together to use as padding under the leg and then instructed Turtle how to hold Luke once he was on his side. Once Luke was turned Skywalker handed her the knife. Tears were in her eyes as she pushed the hair from his face. "Forgive me, Bright Arrow. I know the pain you're going to feel. I'm sorry but this has to be done." Moving to the hip she clamped his legs between hers. She knew what needed to be done but it broke her heart knowing she would be the one to cause pain to this wonderful man. Skywalker was beside her with bandages, towels and the poultice. Cory saw him nod, handing her a towel. The knife was sharp, the cut quick.

Luke convulsed, slamming against Turtle. When Skywalker saw Cory hesitate he straddled Luke's upper body as she had done his legs, blocking her view of his face. He wondered what she felt as he saw her struggling to keep the tears from falling. What horrors visited her when she used the knife? She used the towel to wipe away the blood and infection, probing with her fingers. "I found it but its deep."

Skywalker widened the cut. A first aid kit appeared, and Cory searched frantically until she found a pair of tweezers. She took a steadying breath before searching for the glass again. The tweezers were poor at best. Every time the glass moved the tweezers would slip off the smooth surface. Biting her lip Cory finally had the glass where she could grasp it with her fingers. Her hands shook as she pulled it from the muscle. The second piece of glass was easier. The minute Cory made the cut over the site it surfaced with the flow of blood and infection. "Thank God." She sighed dousing both areas with hydrogen peroxide.

Skywalker moved to retrieve the poultice. That was when Cory saw Luke. The upper half of his body was planted firmly against Turtle's legs. His hands gripping the blanket threatened to rip it to pieces. His eyes were closed however Cory sensed he was barely hanging on to his control as a warrior. Without another thought she moved around Turtle prying Luke's fingers from the blanket. She wrapped his arms around her waist as she pulled his head into her lap. There she slowly worked the knotted muscles of his arms, back and neck. "I'm here Bright Arrow. Draw your strength from me. I'm sorry I hurt you, but the glass had to come out. The leg should heal now." Cradling his head in her arms she bent over him protectively. "Oh God, Luke, I am so sorry. I love you so much that I would take this pain from you if I could. Please, honey, hang on. Draw your strength from my love. Don't let that bastard win. Please." She collapsed into tears as she held him next to her heart.

Skywalker straightened from his task. As he hurried the others out, he saw White Dove standing just inside the doorway, crying as she watched Luke and Cory. "The woman wanted to spare you this." He told her softly.

"It's not what she did to his leg that makes me cry, Grandfather. It's what she is doing for him now, for both of them, which makes me cry. These are tears of joy. Someday a man will love me as fiercely as Bright Arrow loves her. I just hope my love is as fierce as Running Eagle's is for my brother."

# Chapter Nine

LUKE TRIED TO WAKE UP, tried to fight the effects of the tea. He could feel the warm cloth inching over his body. The cloth completed its journey before he realized he was being washed. Drawing a deep breath, he rubbed his aching left shoulder. Whoever was beside him moved. "Bright Arrow, I'm going to lift your head and I want you to drink this."

No, I need to wake up. His mind screamed as his shoulders were lifted and he was forced to drink. What now? Something cool was being applied to his face. Was he being shaved? As his mind began to clear he opened his eyes to bare slits. He saw Cory, biting her lip in concentration as she completed his shave.

"Much better." She smiled washing the traces of soap from his face. "Now to fix your hair and you will be as heart stopping as ever when you wake up." He could feel his shoulders being moved into her lap and a brush being run through his tangled hair. "I love the feel of your hair, big guy. If the agency ever demands you cut this beautiful mop tell them you quit." She laughed softly as she pulled it into a clip. "You should be waking up soon. I hope so. I miss looking at those gorgeous eyes of yours. I think that's what I fell in love with first, those big, beautiful eyes. Of course, being as good looking as you are it didn't take long for the rest of your body to win my heart."

Luke knew she was talking to herself and schooled himself not to smile. Cory sighed. "Oh, Warrior. Will you still love me when this craziness is over? I'm so afraid to let you see my heart. I had a dream last night that I had to kill Jason Grover. I'm so afraid of hurting you or dishonoring you as a warrior. I can't allow you to be hurt because of my actions. The only way to protect you is to hide my love from you. I doubt I can do that much longer. It becomes harder and harder every day to hide what I feel. What am I going to do?"

Curling his arms up, he captured her around the shoulders and pulled her down to him. "You're going to give me all the love you have because I will accept nothing less. We'll get through this together and be stronger because of it. That's what love is all about." He kissed her, all the desire he felt was in that frantic connection.

Luke heard someone clear his throat and Cory withdrew from his hold, dark crimson quickly flooding her cheeks. As quickly as it came, it drained from her face, leaving her pasty white. She stood, hands fisted at her side, eyes dark with anger. "What are you doing here?"

Greg's eyes shadowed with confusion at her anger as his eyes went from her to Rafe. "I don't understand why are you so angry! We came to talk to both of you. We found the file on your computer…"

"You let this bastard in my house? You let him into my files? After I warned you about him? How could you? If I even dreamed you would do this I would never have warned you. What is the matter with you, Greg? Don't you know how to take an obvious hint?"

Greg's confusion showed in his face, as he stared at her anger. "Corena, Rafe and I worked all night trying to help…"

"I don't need his kind of help." She screamed hazel eyes so dark no gold showed. "I warned you. Why didn't you listen? His help? God help me, but I'll never need his kind of help. I saw what his help can do to people's lives. His help only ruins good people like my father. My God, Greg, why didn't you listen? I trusted you. Just like my father trusted you. How could you betray me like this?"

Skywalker, Turtle and Laughing Bear charged into the tipi. Skywalker stood in front of Cory, barring her view. "What the hell is going on in here?"

Cory was shaking with anger. "I'm leaving. I refuse to breathe the same air with that…that man."

As she turned to leave Skywalker grabbed her by the upper arms. "You have yet to answer my question, woman. What the hell is going on?"

Luke was struggling to stand. His crutches were nowhere in sight and he lost his balance when he put weight on his leg. Greg and Rafe hurried to keep him from falling. That movement drew Cory's attention. The sight of the three men side by side brought rage to her face. When she spoke she was looking into Luke's eyes. "I see now how wrong I was to trust you. I've only felt this betrayed once before and I swore I would never be hurt like that again. God, what a fool I am to trust any of you." She turned and jerked so hard against Skywalker's hold Luke could hear the lacings rip in her dress. Before anyone could react, Cory ran with Laughing Bear sprinting after her. Luke turned bewildered eyes to his friend. "My God, Rafe. What the hell did you do to make her so angry?"

"Beats the hell out of me but we have to find that woman. She holds the key to everything that's been going on and it's all stuffed in her head." Luke's hand grabbing his elbow stopped Rafe.

"No. Give her a chance to calm down then we'll track her. Grandfather send for the other warriors. It's getting dark. With nightfall comes the cold and with no way of starting a fire she'll have no protection from the wild animals or the elements. It shall be a cold night."

Laughing Bear entered out of breath. "I lost her in the woods." He bent over to help ease the burning pain in his lungs. "She's headed up the creek. Pray she changes course. A cougar was spotted in that area several weeks ago. We haven't seen it since but once was enough. There are traps set all over up there. If she gets caught in one..." Laughing Bear shuddered. "What the hell got into her?"

Cory ran into the woods like the hounds of hell were after her. She couldn't believe Greg ignored her warning about Rafe. Hadn't he read the reports? How could she have been so stupid? Stupid. Stupid. Stupid. Never should she have said anything about her suspicions. She thought

Greg would take her warnings to heart. Never in her wildest dreams did she guess Greg to be that stupid to allow Rafe into her home.

Her mind concentrated on Rafe DeAngelo. Rafe's reports gave her the proof on O'Grady. It was also a combination of his and Luke's reports that led her to believe there was a second mole in the agency. Her mind told her O'Grady could not have been working alone. She was never suspicious of Rafe until the day she was in O'Grady's office. She chided herself later for her mistake. It was Rafe's report that fingered her father as a traitor.

O'Grady leered at her when she faced him down in the office the day after the funeral. He threw Rafe's report across the desk. She was stunned when she read it. Hurt and grief threatened to overwhelm her. For a while Cory believed Rafe really had written it and she was horrified. Although her father never said he was suspicious of Rafe he did seem as if he liked the man. It just didn't make sense he would write such obvious lies about her father.

Later, when she was calmer and was able to think more clearly, she sought the proof she needed, and doubt began to form. The report she read in O'Grady's office didn't compare to those she searched through. The reports she searched were extremely complete, the text well written and the sequence of events set in order. Not so with the report she read in O'Grady's office. That report had been choppy and rather difficult to understand. Her doubt became so firmly embedded she tried to contact him. Since Luke was still undercover and not around to consult she left a message with his partner requesting Rafe meet with her. He never showed for the meeting.

Deciding he hadn't received her message she left a note on his car. The next day the note was on her windshield, his written message scrawled across the bottom. 'I refuse to talk to the daughter of a traitor.' It tore her insides apart.

Her hatred consumed her especially when she remembered how he tried to comfort her immediately after her parents were murdered. She considered Rafe to be a friend of her father's, but the note proved otherwise. Stiffening her spine, she became even more determined to prove them wrong, every last one of them. Then there was Marvin Toms. Hell, Rafe couldn't even get his name correct. Three times he was partnered with the man and each time Rafe spelled his name differently. That was when the inconsistencies began to surface. Rafe's charts were totally different than those of his partner's. Not in big ways, rather in small, barely noticeable ways yet those ways changed the entire report.

If Rafe wrote it was sunny, Toms wrote it was overcast. If Rafe wrote they talked to someone, Toms wrote they had not. Little things that changed everything. Her suspicions rocketed between Rafe and Toms. Her suspicions of Rafe chilled a bit with Luke's reports but not her anger at what he had done to her father. Luke's reports helped fan the flames of her suspicions of a second traitor in the agency. Luke was partnered with Marvin Toms on three separate occasions. Once again, the reports varied subtly but it proved someone was falsifying the records and she was positive it wasn't Luke.

Cory slowed her wild flight to a fast walk. She instinctively avoided running into trees yet had no idea where she was. Nor did she care. Her hurt was too great, the feeling of being betrayed too raw. The clap of thunder and lightning shocked her from her musings, failing to notice the gathering storm as the storm raged within her. Nature seemed as unsettled as her emotions. She sensed her future with Luke depended upon the past and her getting a grip on the hurt and anger she had for it. But how was she supposed to do that?

Slowing her steps even more she let her mind drift to the past once again. By the time she finished reading Luke's reports her suspicions of Agent Toms came into full bloom. She searched out other cases Toms worked on and found four. These were the same as with Rafe and Luke, still there was no proof against the man. The only evidence she had was the fact he was a poor record keeper. She knew he was falsifying records but without Luke to confirm her suspicions she had nothing, and she refused to talk with Rafe after finding the note. Inquiring about Toms only served to confuse. Those who hated him said he was young, inexperienced and depended on high-ranking family members to keep his butt from getting kicked out. Those who liked him, mostly women, thought he walked on water.

She thought she had proof when she investigated his background just before she was tortured. His application stated...what? She sighed, rubbing her forehead. She simply could not remember what she discovered. She remembered being found in the records room by O'Grady the day of that fateful assignment. His anger was evident. He told her how disappointed he was that she was sneaking around, trying to satisfy her curiosity about the men in the division. Then he told her of her new assignment. She was to buy a large quantity of arms that very night and her partner would be Tony Matthews. She worked with Matthews before, but the assignment surprised her. She hadn't been assigned anything in months.

Shaking the feeling of doom that descended over her she stopped to get her bearings. The storm gathered in strength and she knew she needed to find shelter before it hit. It would soon be pouring down rain. Another flash and Cory saw movement from beyond a fallen tree trunk. She froze, waiting for the next flash. When the lightening flashed again, what met Cory's eyes filled her with terror.

White Dove...and something else. Horrified, Cory picked up a rock and threw it at the cougar with deadly accuracy. Being hit in the side it backed off into the darkness in surprise. Cory ran again this time in fear not hurt. She could hear White Dove's whimper just before the lightening flashed. Her foot was in a trap, the jaws clamped tightly around her ankle. Cory knelt beside her friend frantically trying to free the leg. The cougar hadn't gone far, evidence by the chill that came over her which had nothing to do with the heavy rain that was now falling and everything to do with the blood curling scream the mighty beast released.

"Leave me." White Dove whispered in pain. "No sense in both of us dying. I'll never outrun him."

"You are my friend, White Dove. I don't have many I call by that name and I sure as hell won't leave you like this." The two women worked at getting the trap jaws to open to no avail. White Dove was weak from pain and fear. Cory was not strong enough. Combined, they only managed to ease it open slightly before it clamped shut again. White Dove's scream of pain was covered by thunder which shook the ground. Cory followed the chain that held the trap only to find it padlocked to the fallen tree. The cougar was closing in. She sensed it more than saw him. She moved back to White Dove desperation showing in her eyes.

"I don't want to die like this." White Dove whimpered, tears mixing with the rain.

Cory gathered the other woman in her arms. Pulling the rain-soaked hair from White Dove's face she tried to hide her worry and forced gentleness into her voice. "We're not going to die. Don't even think such thoughts." She scolded gently. "Right now, we have to worry about that cat and how we're going to defend our position. I need something I can use as a weapon. This damned rain isn't helping."

White Dove chuckled ruefully. "The storm is building in fury." She shivered from fear, shock and the cold rain. "The cat is very angry. How are you going to defend against something you can't see?"

The lightening increased in frequency and the wind howled around them. Cory saw the animal approaching and picked up a short tree branch. Not much, she grimaced, but it would serve as a club. She was positive Luke wouldn't allow her to run away. She just prayed she could keep the beast occupied until someone found them and both she and White Dove were still alive when they were found. The animal wouldn't retreat she knew. White Dove was a trapped meal and the cougar knew it.

With the next flash of lightening White Dove screamed with terror. The cougar was only five feet from them now. Cory advanced, closing the distance between her and the cougar. Her intention was clear. Draw the mighty beast's attention away from White Dove and center it upon herself. Fear rose within her and she clamped down hard on it. She knew she could let nothing distract her now.

Another flash of lightening brought the cougar's yellow eyes in sharp contrast to the darkness sending a shiver of fear racing through

Cory. The cougar stopped, tensing at the sight of the advancing woman. Once she had its attention Cory circled to her left, hoping the cougar would follow, putting even more distance between it and White Dove. The cougar countered every move Cory made. It was now a deadly game of cat and mouse. The cougar's scream, as his paw shot out to claw her, sent a jolt of terror along her spine. If the beast managed to make contact she would never be able to get away from it. The claws would rip deep into skin and muscle rendering her body useless to prevent another attack.

"Stay with me, big guy. I want your full attention on me." She stepped forward and the cat struck out again, missing her leg by an inch. She heard White Dove scream out but refused to divert her attention, knowing that inattention, even for a second, would mean death for her. She also had to be careful not to get too far away from the other woman in case the cougar decided to quit this game.

The cougar turned in the direction of the scream and advanced slightly on White Dove. Cory slid between White Dove and the attacker, once again trying to draw his attention back to her. "You have to deal with me first, big guy." Tapping the ground with the stick drew the cougar's glowing yellow eyes to Cory and once again she felt fear race through her. Cory sensed the change in the cougar's attitude immediately. The cat was hungry, quickly tiring of the game. It became defensive. Lightening flashed with eerie regularity as the full force of the storm hit. Cory's mind told her that even nature wanted to watch this life and death struggle between them.

The cougar screamed as it charged at Cory. Holding her ground she swung at the beast, narrowly missing him as he backed off from the danger. He screamed again, swiping at her with his mighty paws. Even that sounded different. He was angry now causing her to become even more wary of him. An angry cougar on a dark, rainy night wasn't something a sane person would or should be playing around with. It usually spelled a horrible death. She prayed someone would come to their rescue before the cougar could gain the advantage. Never taking her eyes from him she moved a foot. He attacked with more caution and again Cory narrowly missed striking him with the club. Her muscles objected from the strain of the attack stance she was in, the makeshift club felt as if it weighed a ton. Still she refused to allow the cat's attention to be diverted from herself. It would only focus on White Dove if she failed and she was determined not to fail. She had failed too many people already. She shook her head to clear the thoughts from her mind and the rain from her eyes.

The cold rain and even colder wind chilled her to the bone. Sensing another change in the cougar's attitude she tensed and then slowly backed up a few paces. She realized the action was a mistake when the backs of her legs touched the top of the fallen tree. Before she could correct her position, the animal sprang at her. Lifting the club with both hands she steeled herself to deflect the attack. She wasn't prepared for the sudden drop in the arch it took nor the weight of the animal. Thunder echoed around her as the beast hit her full in the chest, sending her sprawling backward. Pain seared through her lungs as the breath was knocked out of her. She had failed again, her mined shouted at her, and White Dove would die because of that failure. Luke's face came into view in the lightening. "I love you." She whispered as pain claimed her consciousness and her eyes fluttered shut.

Tracking Cory had not been easy, but Luke was the best tracker in the tribe. Luke's horse shied in fear at the cougar's scream. He ran a steadying hand down the horse's neck. He slowed the pace even more, not relishing the idea of facing a cougar in the dark. Then he heard it scream again. Caution filled him when he realized the sound of the cougar came from the same area, the same direction. Something was wrong. A cougar never stays in the same place unless it is occupied with finding a meal. Icy tendrils of fear tracked along his spine when he heard a woman scream. Grinding his teeth, he spurred the horse forward, the others following. He saw her in the flash of the lightening toying with the cougar. She tapped the ground with a stick drawing its attention to her. "What the hell is she doing?" He heard Rafe's strangled whisper.

Slowly, Luke pulled his rifle from the scabbard on the saddle. Then he saw another movement as Cory shifted away from the fallen tree. "My God, there's someone else up there." From his position he couldn't get a clear shot and lowered his rifle. "Stay here." He ordered the others in a whisper. "We don't want to spook that cat."

Without taking his eyes from the scene ahead he spurred the frightened horse forward. Cory circled slightly to the left and the horse shied just as the cougar screamed again attacking Cory at a dead run. Luke raised the rifle again praying for a decent shot. Cory swung at the great beast and it backed off. She moved her position again as the cougar prepared to spring. Horror ripped through Luke. Standing in the stirrups, he took aim, praying his calculations were correct as the animal sailed through the air at Cory's throat. Once the shot was fired it seemed the world went into slow motion. He saw Cory raise her arms in defense, the cougar's body coming straight at her.

A woman screamed but it wasn't Cory. It came from the opposite side from where she stood. Luke saw the body of the cougar arch with deadly accuracy, shudder in midair before it hit her full in the chest. She toppled backward, legs caught by the tree. When she landed her head hit against a rock. The cougar lay dead on top of her. Viciously spurring his horse forward it jumped the fallen tree, bringing him close to Cory. Sliding from the saddle he ignored the pain that ripped through his leg upon taking the two steps separating them. His legs folded under him when he was by her side. Her hazel eyes were glazed, and her words of love seemed to rip his heart from his chest as her eyes fluttered closed. As Luke bent to pick her up Greg stopped him. "Wait. We have to make sure there are no spinal injuries." Luke seemed locked in place. Terror filled eyes watched as Rafe and Turtle examined her.

"Is she all right? Dammit Luke, answer me. Is she alive? Is Cory all right?"

Luke raised his eyes to the woman in Laughing Bear's arms. Confusion competed with fear. "White Dove?"

Rafe chuckled. "I think Luke is in shock, young lady. To answer your question yes, she's alive. I think she just bumped her head and it knocked her out. Except for one hell of a headache when she wakes up I believe she will be just fine."

Standing he went to Luke, shaking him until his friend looked at him. "We need to get these two back to camp so they can be checked out. Let's get you on your horse and then I'll lift Corena up to you."

Luke nodded, struggling to stand. The warriors moved in to help. They all saw the risk Cory had taken to protect White Dove. They also knew the risk of the shot Luke fired. If he had miscalculated he would have hit her instead of the cougar. Luke was an honored warrior, but Cory had been the outsider. Tonight, she proved herself worthy of the honor bestowed upon her as Luke's woman. Tonight, she risked her life for one of the tribe, and it would never be forgotten. Tonight, they all witnessed the depth of Luke's love for his woman.

Cory's skin was cold when she was laid in Luke's arms and he was thankful for the blanket that appeared. No one spoke on the ride back. The wind and rain pelted them unmercifully. Luke ignored the chill that ran through his veins. His concern was for the woman in his arms, the woman he loved and hoped to marry. They moved quickly on the return trip the light of the fire was a welcoming beacon. No one spoke as Luke and Laughing Bear handed the women to the warriors who dismounted and was waiting for them. Luke's crutches appeared, and he hurried to the tipi. A flurry of activity followed.

The women's dresses were removed, and they were wrapped in several layers of blankets as the warriors were given dry buckskins to wear. Even Greg and Rafe were given something to change into. White Dove was babbling in hysterics and Skywalker was examining Cory. Luke gathered his sister in his arms. "Stop this, White Dove. Running Eagle will be all right. She hit her head and passed out. If she awakens now, it would only distress her. Stop crying, White Dove. You will make yourself sick if you don't."

She controlled her hysteria with difficulty. "I'm sorry, Bright Arrow. I went for a walk and lost track of time. My mind was on other things and I wandered too far out. I knew better than to go into that area. Everyone on the Reservation was warned of the traps. This is my fault. Now Running Eagle is injured because of me."

"It's all right, sister." Luke rocked his sister gently as he watched his grandfather work with Cory.

"No, it isn't." She wailed, tears spilling down her face. "I told her to leave me when we couldn't get that damned trap open. She told me I was a friend and she wouldn't leave me there." White Dove buried her face in Luke's chest, sobbing. "It scared the hell out of me when she faced down that cougar. She risked her life for me. Now I know how you felt when she saved you. If Running Eagle dies it will be my fault."

Luke gathered his sister tighter when her crying became harder. "You've got to calm down, White Dove." He told her firmly. "You don't want Running Eagle to wake up and find you in this state of hysteria. Do you?" As she stiffened in his arms all sounds of her sobbing ceased. When she relaxed against him, under control, he tilted her chin and gave her a lopsided grin, mopping the tears from her cheeks. "That's better. How's the leg? Are you in pain?"

"I think it's broken." She gave him a watery smile. "We'll have to find another pair of crutches for me to use."

Cory moaned, rubbing at her forehead. "White Dove? White Dove? Are you all right?" She struggled to sit but dizziness assaulted.

Skywalker gently pushed her down. "Easy. White Dove is safe and without injuries except for the ankle."

She struggled harder to sit. "The cougar."

"The cougar is dead, Running Eagle. Bright Arrow killed it when it attacked you."

"No, his leg..." She moaned, closing her eyes and rubbing at the pain in her head.

Several of the warriors ducked their heads as a grin cut across their faces. She was the injured one, yet she was more concerned with her warrior and his injuries. Luke slid across the floor. "Open your eyes, sweetheart. See for yourself that I'm fine. White Dove is here also. Open your eyes."

She did. Tears welled in them when she saw the concern in his. "I'm sorry, warrior. I guess I'll never learn to control my temper."

Luke grinned, pulling her into his lap. "I'm not the one you need to apologize to. Rafe has no idea why you are so angry with him and it has hurt him. What triggered your anger?"

"He ought to know. He wrote the report." Her head was buried in his shoulder, voice muffled as her tears came.

"What report?"

"The report he gave O'Grady stating daddy was a traitor. The one O'Grady used to keep from paying the death benefits. Don't let him deny it. I read the damned thing. It is burned into my memory as if I read it only today."

Luke looked at Rafe. The man was pale, shaking his head in denial. "I don't know what report you read, honey. I do know Rafe spent several years trying to clear your father's name. Greg, Rafe and I traced every lead we could think of. We worked on it every chance we got between assignments." Cory became very still in Luke's arms. Suddenly she buried her face deeper into his chest with a groan. "Cory? What's wrong?"

"All this time it was there. The proof was looking me right in the face and I missed it. Eleven men were murdered in that warehouse and you were damned near killed because I was too hurt and angry to see what was staring at me. I'm sorry, Luke. I'm so sorry." Her tears exploded as she tried to hide her face in shame. She held onto Luke as if he was a life jacket to a drowning victim.

The implication of her words brought Greg and Rafe from the edge of the tipi. Luke looked around, motioning with his head for the others to leave. Laughing Bear gathered White Dove in his arms, carrying her from the tipi. The other warriors followed suit. Even Skywalker left the four alone.

"All right, honey. Greg and Rafe are still here and I think it's time to put everything we know together. I want you to listen carefully to them and fill in the blank spots. We'll decide what to do from there."

Greg filled them in on the events since the warehouse massacre. Cory stopped him when he told of Major Thoms' agitation. "What is his real name?" She was now leaning against Luke's chest, the blankets pulled tightly around her in defense of her modesty and to increase the warmth she needed. She was still cold, and the chill threatened to bring on the shakes.

"Martin Thoms." Luke answered. "Why?"

"What is his entire name?"

Luke shook his head, eyes narrowed on her in confusion. "I don't believe I ever heard any other name. I only know his first name is Martin because the last name reminded me of a rotten partner I once had, and I asked if they were related. That agent's name was Marvin Toms, without the H. Why?"

She shook her head refusing to answer. "Let them finish. I need to think about this. Something…" She sighed, rubbing her forehead. "Never mind. Continue please."

Greg frowned but continued. Luke stiffened in anger when he was told Jason Grover was at the funeral and of the knife being stolen. Rafe picked up the story when Greg finished telling about the bomb in his house and the explosion. He told them of his suspicions, finding the bug in his phone, the meeting arrangements with Greg the previous evening and, once again, about the explosion at Greg's house.

Greg retrieved his briefcase as he told of meeting Jasper and finding the codes. Pulling the graphs and charts he spread out Cory's graphs and charts and then the one's Rafe made. Luke looked closely at them. Cory did not. She did most of them from memory.

"There are huge gaps in these time lines." Luke mumbled, committing them to memory. "Whose are they?"

"Three are yours." Rafe said quietly. "The other four we're not sure. That information is stuffed in Corena's head. Can you remember anything to help us fill in those gaps?"

Doubt filled Luke's eyes. "It would be difficult without some kind of information to pull from. File numbers mean nothing. You know that."

"Those are the files you wrote while you were partnered with Marvin Toms." Cory stated silently as she pulled the blanket tighter around her.

"That bastard?" Shock was in Luke's voice. "What the hell does that idiot have to do with anything?"

"Everything. He and Rafe were the two I was suspicious of. Toms, I suspected because of the inconsistencies I found in the files. Rafe, mainly because he wrote the report that fingered daddy as the traitor and the note he left on my windshield after I requested he meet with me."

Anger and confusion surged in Rafe. "You keep talking about a report I supposedly wrote. I never wrote any report concerning your father and I sure as hell never got any note from you. Hell, you never even answered the letters I sent after your parents were murdered. When was the note written?"

"Four months after daddy was murdered."

Rafe shook his head in denial. Violently. "That simply can't be, Corena. I never wrote any report. I was shipped out on a two-year assignment, three days after your parents were murdered. Luke was already gone on assignment and I had no one to return my car to the house. It stayed in the parking garage all that time."

Cory sighed, tears seeping from below her closed eyelids. "I'm sorry, Rafe. I was so hurt I never thought to find out if you were still around or if you had been given another assignment. I should have known. I shouldn't have let my anger…" She covered her face with her hands, trying to stop the tears that threatened.

"I'm sorry, Corena." Rafe pulled her into his arms, holding her tight. "I was hurt too. I couldn't understand your animosity toward me. When I returned I tried everything I could think of to clear Ralph's name. The agency kept me hopping from assignment to assignment, preventing me from doing much."

Cory pulled away, rubbing at her forehead as she settled against Luke again. "It doesn't matter now. I know who the other mole is."

Greg sat forward, watching her pale face for signs of emotions. "Who, Corena? I asked you once before and you refused to tell me. Tell me now. Who?"

"You know him, Greg. Both Luke and Rafe worked with him. Haven't you figured it out yet?" The three men looked at each other, confusion showed on all their faces.

"No." Greg growled. "Maybe I'm just stupid but I haven't the foggiest idea who set your father up. I know you said O'Grady was one of them and you found the proof. As hard as Rafe and I tried we couldn't make the connection you told me about and we did try."

Cory sighed. "All right. Listen carefully. Almost every case the men worked on involving Jason Grover, one of them was partnered with Marvin Toms. The first case, when Luke backed away because he knew Grover, daddy and Rafe went together to interview him. Marvin Toms appeared on the scene shortly after that. Hell, Rafe, the fact you couldn't get his name correct had a big bearing on me suspecting you. His reports were slightly different than yours. Eventually I realized he was the one doctoring the files. Look at the time line and how many times his name shows up. The differences continued when he was partnered with Luke."

The men bent over Rafe's graphs again startled at what they saw. "All right, so Marvin Toms was the second mole. Where is the proof?"

"It's not in the files written on those graphs." She sighed deeply. "It's in the way he writes as well as the missing files. One of those missing files is the one O'Grady made me read. The one he said Rafe wrote. The one fingering daddy as the traitor. I never saw it after that day. I wanted to get a copy of it yet was told the file and its number never existed. That's why I wouldn't resign."

Rafe groaned. "That doesn't help us, Corena."

"Actually, it does. I know the file exists. I read it. When I couldn't find it in the records room I began to dig deeper. The first thing I did was pull O'Grady's personnel file. I must say I found it rather interesting. Did you know his first wife was married to him for almost two months before he beat her so badly she divorced him? What he didn't know at the time was the woman was pregnant. She returned home, bitter, and assumed her maiden name. Apparently, she came from what O'Grady considered the wrong side of town, even though her father was rather wealthy. His business was rather...Immoral."

"Prostitution?"

That made Cory chuckle. "Nothing so fancy I'm afraid. It was from running drugs and guns. Can you imagine what that information would have done to O'Grady's chances at advancement? Anyway, he waited two years before he married again. Where his first wife had blonde hair and dark eyes, the second had brown hair and green eyes. Something in her background angered O'Grady and he divorced her also. He demanded she take her maiden name. Five months later the second wife delivered a son.

"The second wife's family was also well to do. It seems the family had ties to the governor's mansion. O'Grady could not ignore this son as he had the first. Although he visited he never took an interest in the kid until his interests turned to law enforcement. O'Grady was pressured into getting him a job by the grandparents. They threatened to expose the fact of his first wife, his beating of her and her connection with the mob."

"Marvin Toms." Luke stated quietly.

Cory sighed. "Yes, Bright Arrow. It was when I investigated his background that I found out much of what I just told you. For a long time, I couldn't remember what I found in that file. I guess hitting my head must have done some good because I remember now."

Luke held her tighter. "So far, everything you told us makes sense. How do O'Grady and Marvin Toms tie in with Jason Grover?"

"Grover was the first wife's maiden name."

The three men groaned. "No wonder Grover knew all our moves." Luke stated bitterly. "If I ever see Marvin Toms again I shall kill him myself just for the pleasure of watching him die. Damn him to hell."

# Chapter Ten

"HE DIDN'T GO FAR, MY dear. He's been hiding right under your noses. Remember when I asked you what the major's name was? You told me it was Martin Thoms, with an H. He only told you half the truth, Bright Arrow. I would bet my house his name is Marvin Martin Toms. The H was either added to hide his identity or it was added by mistake to his nameplate and he let it stay that way. Everyone says he came from a house of power and money. Greg and Rafe both stated he came along on the heels of O'Grady. O'Grady would have had a tremendous influence in who was chosen as his replacement. The files I've been chasing all these years are worthless other than to prove he doctored them. The files we need are in his personnel file."

"What is the proof on O'Grady?"

"Grandmother hid it when I was tortured. She said she took it to the Reservation and hid it one of the Shaman's houses. After she died I went to the Reservation where we were registered and asked to examine all the Shaman's houses. Permission was granted however I never found where she hid it." Cory quickly sat up eyes wide. Dizziness assaulted her, and Skywalker was sent for.

Cory smiled at his worried face. "I will be all right, Shaman. I just need something for this headache. No sleeping tea either. I need my head to become clear not fogged. Once we're done for the night I will gladly take whatever you think best." She was leaning against Luke's chest, face white.

Rafe laughed, collecting the papers. "Give her whatever she needs, Sir. This can wait until morning. She looks like she is ready to pass out again."

"No. I'll be all right." She objected.

Rafe stared at her before shaking his finger at Cory. "You may be, Corena Sims, but I'm not. Far from it. You scared the hell out of me today and I've had enough shocks over the last three days to last a lifetime. We know more than we did. We need to figure out where your Grandmother hid those papers. We need to plan our attack. All that can wait until tomorrow. All of us need to rest and begin with a fresh mind."

Skywalker returned with Turtle and enough tea for everyone. "Drink this. It will fortify your bodies while you hash this out. Luke's woman has that stubborn look in her eyes. I have seen it many times since she arrived."

Cory's hand shook so badly Luke helped her with the cup, refusing his own. He saw the gleam in Skywalker's eyes when Rafe stated they were finished for the night and grinned knowingly. He knew his Grandfather, and that the tea the other three were drinking would fortify their bodies through sleep. "How is White Dove? How badly is she injured?"

"Her leg is broken. Laughing Bear has gone with her to the hospital. She'll be back in the night. She's worried about your woman. Now drink your tea."

Luke laughed quietly feeling Cory relax against him. "I don't need it, Grandfather. What I need to fortify me is right here in my arms."

Skywalker nodded, helping Luke lay beside Cory. He knew his Grandson didn't see his worry when Luke pulled his woman, spoon fashion, against him and relaxed into sleep. Skywalker was listening outside the tipi and heard every word. His memory travel back, before the Grandmother died. She came often, worried about both the safety of Running Eagle as well as her own. Someone had broken into her house. Nothing was taken yet she could feel the spirit of evil throughout the house. The last time she came she had an envelope and stated that if the evil was to take her life he was to give it to Luke. Heartbroken after her heart attack he never thought about the envelope again. Until tonight.

Now he wondered. Did it contain the information and proof that was now lost to Running Eagle? He was positive it was when she described the hiding place. The building of his cabin had just been completed when she noted the loose brick. She joked often that it would be a perfect hiding place for things important. He remembered how determined she was the day she stuffed the envelope inside.

Determination hardened the sharp angles of his face as he headed for his horse only to be stopped by the sound of a jeep. Laughing Bear was returning with White Dove and her mother, Little Fawn. As Laughing Bear carried White Dove into the tipi Little Fawn sought out Skywalker. "We were followed from the time we left Reservation lands until the time we returned." Her voice was quiet, eyes filled with worry.

"Did you recognize any of them?"

"One. He was at the funeral. He had blonde hair and black eyes. The stench of evil swirls around him. My soul shudders when he's around me. Tonight, he came into the room at the hospital, flipping through White Dove's chart. He knows she was hurt on the Reservation and tried to get us to reveal who saved White Dove." Little Fawn sighed. "Laughing Bear took the credit but feels badly about it. He feels he has darkened Running Eagle's selfless deed. Nothing we have said will release his guilt. Will you talk to him, Skywalker?"

Skywalker nodded. "Laughing Bear is a good man, Little Fawn and very much in love with White Dove. Prepare yourself. You will be attending a second joining soon. White Dove loves him deeply yet Laughing Bear refuses to offer for her until his duties as a warrior protector is completed. If I know Bright Arrow he won't wait another day for his joining especially after what happened this evening. He was frightened by Running Eagle's bravery this night."

Little Fawn's smile was sad. "I had a vision. She will have to hold onto her stubborn bravery for the man with the evil spirit won't leave them alone. She will have to defend herself as well as Bright Arrow.

She is the one who will be his downfall and no matter how much Luke wishes it to be, he is not the one who kills him."

Skywalker sighed. "Running Eagle had much the same vision only she can't separate her vision from the nightmares that attack her."

Laughing Bear advanced. "White Dove is sleeping. Little Fawn has told you of the man at the hospital?" Skywalker nodded, watching Laughing Bear kick at the dirt with his feet. "Did I do right?"

"Yes, Laughing Bear. Running Eagle would have given the credit to Bright Arrow. You have given them a few more days of protection. We must be very careful from now on. I want someone to watch them as they have been watching us. We must keep them from finding this training ground. Also, we must now provide protection for the other two. It would hurt Bright Arrow if something happened to them."

Laughing Bear's hands clenched at his sides. "I feel useless and unworthy of their kindness after taking claim for Running Eagle's bravery. How can we help them?"

Skywalker knew the warrior was talking about Bright Arrow and Running Eagle. "We need to return to my cabin. Many things will be answered when we do."

★ ★ ★ ★ ★

Cory struggled to chase the sleep from her body. The nightmare returned only different. Where Rafe had tried to comfort her before it was Luke who now gathered her into his arms. She stayed there feeling protected until a cold chill touched her spine. When she drew back she was looking into the black eyes of hell. She pulled away and ran, not stopping until she reached the cemetery. There she cowered behind her parent's tombstones. Even still Jason found her. He was laughing as he approached, and that laughter enflamed her rage. She was the one who had the knife this time only Jason Grover had Luke. A knife at his throat cut into his flesh as he struggled for release.

The sight of Luke's blood made Jason laugh harder. Caution mingled with her protective instincts. She circled as she had done with the cougar and like the cat, Jason's attention focused on her. The deadly game played itself out in her dream. When Jason sprang at her she buried the knife deep in his chest. He was dead.

She yelled for Luke certain Jason killed him. His reassuring voice came through the gathering darkness. "I'm here, my love. I'm here." With the darkness came exhaustion and she gave in to the warm, peaceful sleep her warrior's arms induced and the steady heartbeat that assured Luke was alive.

As she struggled to come to full awareness she could hear voices just outside the tipi. Bright Arrow and Skywalker were discussing her. "I want to marry her. Today, Grandfather. I can't endure the thought of losing her. I dread the thought of spending another night without claiming her love as my own. When I saw the cougar attack last night I thought my heart would rip from my chest. I love her that much. Please, Grandfather, marry us today."

"She won't agree until the conditions are met. She does not wish to disgrace you as a honored warrior."

"She would if the council informed her she was released from the Honored Warrior's Challenge. My God, she risked her life trying to save White Dove from that damned cougar. She has proven herself more than any woman ever has. That was why the Challenge was imposed in the first place. It was the council's proof she would accept our ways. Running Eagle not only accepted our ways, but she has accepted the tribe as well. I know she'll continue to undergo the ceremonies our tribe believes in after we're married. We've talked about that a few days ago. You know they are as important to her as mine are to me. What more does the council demand of us? Please marry us?"

"I will talk to the council. I have never seen a love as deep as the two of you have for each other, Bright Arrow, however she must agree to the joining."

"Keep Rafe and Greg occupied and give me some time alone with her. I'm sure I can get her to agree." In her mind's eyes Cory could see the grin that would be spreading across Bright Arrow's handsome face.

"She will need wedding clothes and your parents will want to attend. The joining cannot be accomplished before early evening. Still, she must agree. I'll give you privacy to speak with her but remember that without her consent there will be no joining regardless of how desperately you wish it to happen."

"Yes Grandfather." Luke sounded breathless and frightened. Cory wrinkled her forehead. Was he that unsure of himself? Or that unsure of her? Both thoughts distressed her almost as much as they excited her. "Grandfather? If she becomes stubborn about completing the Challenge will you talk to her? She'll listen to you."

Skywalker's laugh covered Cory's. "Yes Grandson. I will tell her the reasons for the Challenge and the conditions imposed upon you. The decision is still hers."

"I'm going to fix Running Eagle something to eat. They say the way to a man's heart is through his stomach. Not for this warrior. It was the blush that started in her neck and crept all the way to her hair that convinced me she was the woman for me." The voices drifted away as they put distance between themselves and the tipi.

Cory bathed in the knowledge she was truly loved and closed her eyes, relishing the fact. The smell of frying bacon made her tummy growl. Stretching lazily, she realized suddenly that her dress was gone. Scrambling to her feet she searched frantically while trying to keep the blanket around her.

"What do you think you're doing, woman?"

Cory blushed, drawing the blanket tighter around her. "I can't find my clothes and I need to help prepare the meal."

Between the crutches and his long legs, the distance that separated them narrowed quickly. "Not today will you be preparing a meal for anyone to eat." Bright Arrow growled as he narrowed the distance between them. "My God, woman. You have a knot on the back of your head the size of a goose egg. Your dress was as muddy as you were. The women have washed it and it is now drying."

Confusion etched her face, as she pulled tighter on the blanket. "Muddy? Then who…"

Luke watched the blush surface from under the blankets and spread its wings across her face. He wanted to hold this woman/child of his but kept the distance between them close yet far enough away so not to temp him. His intention when he entered the tipi was to kiss her senseless, raise her sexual awareness until she couldn't think straight and then get her to agree to the wedding. The hazel eyes flecked with gold had a half frightened, half expectant look to them. Luke controlled his grin with difficulty. She expected him to kiss her. Quickly he changed plans. "After you fell asleep last night I gave you a bath and washed the mud and leaves from your hair." He picked up a thick cord and wound it around his fingers. "It needs to be brushed. Since you have a two-fisted death grip on that blanket I'll do it for you."

Surprise mingled with a new blush. Her eyes betrayed her feelings, relief mingled with confusion. Luke laughed. "Do you really think I would take advantage of a defenseless woman? Especially one who is afraid to let the blanket loose? Not this warrior." He fought to resist the impulse to kiss her when she blushed again. "Sit down. I want you to listen to all I have to say, for you have a decision to make. I need to talk to you and will brush your hair while I'm doing it." He whispered while running his fingers along her cheek.

Wordlessly she obeyed. Luke sat behind her, pulling the tangled hair down her back. She closed her eyes while she listened to the reasons why the council insisted she take the Honored Warrior's Challenge. He asked her to marry him. Told her how much he wanted to be married. Wanted her. Loved her desperately. Every time his fingers touched her face or neck while he worked the sensation sparked a firestorm, igniting a lava flow through her veins straight to the parts of her body newly awakened yet still untouched. Still unknown.

"Corena Sims, please marry me? Today. It's been hell sleeping so close to you, knowing we could be sleeping together. Join with me so I can join with you. I'm only a man who loves you and I want to prove that love to you every minute of our lives. Say yes, my dear."

Hearing his declaration of love thrilled her soul and other parts of her body. There was still one thing that needed to be settled she knew.

Reversing her position on the floor she searched his dark brown eyes. The chocolate seemed to have melted into deep pools, so intense were his emotions. The sight of him made her breath catch in her throat. His hair was loose and hung like a raven's wings around his shoulders. The bronze of his skin was deeper from his time in the sunlight. He wore no shirt, just breechcloth, leggings and moccasins. Doubt of herself increased as did the pulse in her neck. Unable to stop herself, her hand snaked out from beneath the blanket and traced the muscles of his chest. "I'm afraid you won't be satisfied with me. You've had many women in your life." She tried to gather her thoughts.

Luke sensed she was struggling for words and forced himself to remain quiet. He had battles of his own to fight at the moment. Pleasure fog had control of his brain at the feel of her hand sliding over his body. His body reacted instantly and then hardened even more when she ran her tongue over dry lips. With difficulty he captured her traveling hand. He sucked several deep breaths to clamp down on his growing need.

Cory sighed. Tears were in her eyes as she captured his eyes again, her hand trembling within his. "Oh warrior, I have never been with a man. I'm not experienced in the ways of giving you pleasure. You will be sorely disappointed tonight."

Keeping hold of her hand he ran his fingers across her face again. Her eyes slid shut and her defenses seemed to melt with his touch. "Do you love me, woman?"

Longing was in her eyes when she looked at him. "Yes warrior. I have loved you for a very long time."

"Will you join with me?"

"You will be..."

Luke kissed her to silence the words. It was soft and short but full of promise. "The question requires only one answer. Yes or no?" She ducked her head, tears on her cheeks. Tipping her chin upward he waited until she looked at him. "Once we are joined I will become your teacher. Me and your body. It pleases me greatly that you've never been with a man. Virginity is a woman's gift, a gift only she can give.

It's a gift between two hearts and the most special of all gifts a woman can give her husband. You captured my heart the first day I met you. I dated women after that, but I kept wishing they were you." He raised the palm of her hand to his lips and kissed it.

"This evening after we are joined, don't let fear dictate your responses. Let your body and your senses rule your head. Pleasing me is easy. Watching your uninhibited response to my touch pleases me. The way your fingers explore my body pleases me. The way your breasts fit my hands and your nipples become tight with want pleases me. The fierce heart that loves me pleases me." Luke lowered her hand, putting it against the breechcloth. Her fingers instinctively tightened around his erection. "Does this feel like a man who's disappointed knowing you're inexperienced?" His voice was husky as he kept her eyes captive. "Or does it feel like a man who is going to enjoy teaching his wife? There's much to be done to prepare for the joining, woman. I need an answer soon."

Her hand moved up the torso of his body, over the washboard muscles of his stomach and chest, sliding around his neck. The action was strictly responsive to his words, Luke knew, yet he had to strangle a moan of pain as he became even harder. With her movement the blanket opened enough for him to glimpse her breasts, taunt and firm.

"They named you correctly, Bright Arrow. The arrow you've embedded in my heart has brightened even the darkest times in my life. I love you, warrior. If you're sure, I would be honored to make this our joining day." She kissed him as she wanted to kiss him for years. As his tongue slid between her lips, hers pushed it back following his inside. Her fingernails dug into his flesh just below his neck as she explored his mouth with passion.

Luke broke the connection by pushing gently on her shoulders. "Easy, woman. You keep this up and I'm liable to lose what little control I have left. Making love to you right here, right now, would be heaven on earth but I promised not to do that until we were joined. Be warned, woman. Tonight, we will be joined in body as well as in name. You belong to me, Running Eagle. I will allow no one to hurt what is mine."

His kiss this time was soft, full of longing and promise. Cory snuggled closer to him, holding tight to his neck as her senses reeled out of control. Movement at the doorway made her go rigid. Skywalker's voice surrounded them. "Breakfast is ready. Come and eat."

★ ★ ★ ★ ★

Fred Adkins knew what he had to do and hated the thought. He sighed thinking of the call he received from Major Thoms. He was shocked to silence when told Rafe DeAngelo had been visiting the Captain and the house was now a smoldering pile of rubble. Shock quickly turned to grief when he saw the Captain's house. It was nothing more than a big hole in the ground. Major Thoms ferreted him out offering condolences. Fred thought the Major really cared about his men until he saw his superior talking to the tall man with blonde hair wearing an expensive suit. The Major was talking with Jason Grover. All day at work he wondered what his next move should be. There were seven names on his list and the elderly black man with white hair and a shuffle had yet to surface. His decision was made when Major Thoms called Fred to his office. "I'm trying to wrap up Agent Patterson's murder case. I understand you've been working on leads."

Fred drew a deep breath. "I'm sorry Sir but I haven't had much luck in the leads department. I honestly think I've been chasing my tail on this thing."

"Nothing on the list you were given?"

"No, Sir. The Captain was grasping at straws there. Almost all the people on the list were business acquaintances. Agent Patterson apparently invested in purebred horses. Many on the list were people he bought horses, feed or saddles from or sold horses to. The rest have been people he knew in college. Women mostly."

"Patterson had a lot of lady friends, did he?"

"He had a lot of friends, Sir. I have yet to find any close friends especially any close lady friends." He shook his head. "I'm chasing down leads that go no place."

Major Thoms' eyes lit with interest. "What about a young woman named Corena Sims? Was her name on the list?"

Stunned Fred pulled his emotions into check hoping he hid his surprise well. "No, Sir." He wrinkled his forehead as if thinking when actually he was praying. "I don't remember that name being on the list. No one I talked to said anything about a woman named Corena Sims. Did she know Agent Patterson?"

"Her father did and was partnered with Agent Patterson when first assigned to this agency. He was a Junior Agent at the time." The Major tipped back in his chair drawing his hand along his chin. "I thought she knew him. Maybe I was wrong."

"Should I investigate this woman?"

"No. I don't believe it would help. It just surprised me she wouldn't come to the wake of one of her father's partners. I thought maybe her name was on the list. It might be just as well to let sleeping dogs lay." The Major started pacing the large office. "Do you know anything about a man named Jason Grover?"

Fred's skin crawled between his shoulders. Bad sign he cautioned himself. "Grover?" He wrinkled his forehead again. "No, Sir. I fail to recall that name being on the list either. Should I check him out?"

"No. He was a college friend of Patterson's." Major Thoms turned and stared at Fred. "You really are out of leads."

Fred sighed heavily. "Yes Sir I am. I was going to ask the Captain for a few days off. My sister is sick and asked me to help with her kids. You see she's divorced and doesn't have a phone. She has three kids. The little tike isn't old enough to go to school and with no help she's worried about his care. Since I'm not accomplishing much here I thought maybe the Captain would approve some time off. Now, I'm at a loss as to what to do." Tears welled in his eyes as he thought of Greg.

"Take it easy, son. I can approve your leave of absence. Do you wish to go now?"

Fred shook his head. "No Sir. It's only another two hours until the end of my shift. I would like to finish my reports before I leave. There may not be much to put into them, but it needs to be done."

"No problem. How long will you be gone?"

"Probably only a few days. I want to be back for Captain Waltz and Rafe's funeral." Again, a flood of emotions surged through Fred. As he struggled to control his own emotions he could detect no trace of emotions in his superior and wondered why.

"Fine. I'll make the arrangements. Pick up your letter before you leave today. If you need more time just call and leave a message with the secretary."

"Thank you, Sir." Fred rose to leave. As he stumbled from the room guilt surged, threatening to overwhelm him. He hadn't exactly lied to his superior. Not exactly. Caution gained the upper hand and he simply failed to tell Major Thoms everything he knew.

Returning to his desk he noticed a repairman removing the mouthpiece from Rafe's phone. When he saw the man tip the phone up, catching something that fell from it his suspicions rocketed as the skin between his shoulders began to crawl again. After the man left Fred lifted his own phone. Working quickly, he removed the mouthpiece to find what he knew he would, a listening device.

Damn. No wonder whoever blew up the Captain's house knew both Rafe and the Captain would be together. His suspicions rocketed again. Major Thoms knew too much. Was he in on all the murders? He shuddered when he realized that his superior was probably a major factor in the deaths of so many.

Who else? It wasn't possible for one man to be holding all the strings in this game of death. So who? Looking around he mentally checked off each agent he saw, rejecting all. He suspected none of them. They all worked together to find any clue that would lead to an arrest in this case. That meant it had to be someone who could move in and out of the agency without notice. Mentally he checked them off. The cleaning ladies. The security guards. The secretaries. His eyes narrowed when he saw Captain Waltz's secretary stand, glance around and then go to Major Thoms office. The skin between his shoulder blades crawled as he watched her slip through the door. He knew her name was Susan Tameron and she had been there before he arrived in the agency. If she was part of the mole's system where could he find out about her? She transcribed reports he knew. Did she also change them to suit the needs of others?

Suspicion raced along his spine as he completed his paperwork. There wasn't much. Most he finished late last night after returning from the devastation that was the Captain's house. The urge to confirm or refute his suspicions overwhelmed him. Fred glanced around the office. Another Junior Agent entered; one Fred was only vaguely familiar with but liked immediately. "James? I need to go to records to check on something. Do you need anything?"

"Unless you can tell me how to conquer the anger I have over the deaths that have happened over the last month, no." He rubbed at his eyes. "I'm sorry, Fred. The death of the Captain and Agent DeAngelo has been a tremendous strain on me. What the hell is happening?"

Fred didn't answer as he gathered his papers together. What could he say? They were all feeling the strain. All were feeling the anger at the lack of leads. All mourned those who died. As he was exiting the office Susan Tameron left Major Thoms office. "Going somewhere?"

"To the records room." Fred mumbled. "I need to add something to one of my reports."

She smiled sweetly at Fred making his suspicions gnaw again. "No need for you to bother with it. If you tell me what needs to be done I can do it for you."

"I appreciate the offer however I need to have something to do to occupy my mind. It's just a minor detail yet I feel I should include it. Agent Patterson taught me how important good records were to the closure of any case. Since I want to be as good as he was..." Fred choked back his grief, taking a deep breath to steady his nerves. "Thank you for the offer but I need to do this myself."

A sympathetic smile crossed her lips. "I understand. If I can be of help just ask. I really don't mind especially since everyone is busy trying to solve the mystery of all these deaths."

Fred left, trying to clamp down on his anger. If his suspicions were correct the woman didn't understand at all. After requesting his files, he sat at a small table reading through them. At first, he couldn't find anything wrong until the small differences began to surface in his mind. The crawling of his skin forced him to return to his office and retrieve his notes. Before leaving he stopped in at Major Thoms' office for his letter of release for vacation time.

Returning to the records room he compared his notes to the files he requested earlier. The supple changes became glaringly blatant. If Luke hadn't triggered his suspicions he would have thought the errors to be typing errors. Now his suspicions were confirmed. Taking those pertaining to the last month he requested copies be made.

While he waited he sat mulling over the situation he now found himself in. He needed to find out how Susan Tameron fit into the picture. How? She was a secretary so there would be no files of hers to compare. His eyes narrowed in thought. She would've had to fill out an application to work here as well as have a security screening done. Could he get the information from personnel? He sincerely doubted they would release her file. There would be no reason for him to seek that kind of information.

"Here you are, Agent Adkins." The man at the records window, copied files in hand, drew his attention. "I'm surprised you came for these yourself. Usually Miss Tameron comes after the records you agents need."

"Does she come often?"

"Often enough. She is one hot lady. Don't you think? I wish she would pay more attention to some of us around here. I keep asking her for a date, but she always refuses. Says she doesn't date the men she works with." He sighed deeply. "I understand her birthday is coming up. If I knew where she lived I would send her a dozen roses. Maybe that would make her see how much I like her." He leaned against the counter eyes distant with his thoughts.

Fred grinned, his eyes shining as an idea began to develop. "Maybe I could sneak up to the personnel office and get the information for you. Do you know anyone there who will let me into the files for a few minutes? Someone that will find himself busy just after I get there?"

The man laughed. "Great idea. I happen to know a certain lady who has been a friend for a long time. Just a minute." He grabbed the phone punching buttons. After a quiet conversation he turned back to Fred. "All set. Ask for Wilma. She'll help you. She's an older woman with gray hair. Can't miss her. She is the only one working there with gray hair."

Fred arrived breathless. Wilma already had the file pulled and left him in a windowless office with pen and paper. After quickly writing down the address he went to the copying machine and copied the file as well as the vacation letter Major Thoms gave him. With the information safely tucked into his pocket he left. As soon as possible he called his sister warning her of the situation. She worked on a small-town police force and cautioned him to be careful. After packing he spent the night tossing and turning. As much as he grieved for his Captain and Rafe DeAngelo he hated the thought of breaking the news to Luke Patterson and Corena Sims.

His grief served to put his senses on high alert when he left the next morning. He could detect no one following him yet his skin was crawling. Going straight to his sister's he arrived in time for an early breakfast. She must have seen him pull up because she was in her robe, her hair disheveled as if she had just gotten out of bed.

Two hours later the sensation passed, and he continued to the Reservation. Now he swore silently as he pulled to the side of the road. Frustration etched his every nerve at the thump, thump, thump of the flat tire. Damn. Would nothing go right today? This was the second flat tire he had in less than three miles. Now he would have to walk to the Reservation. His shoulders slumped at the thought of the remaining five-mile trip. Once he arrived he would have to convince someone there to allow him to speak with Luke and Corena. He just hoped someone would remember him as well as remember he was a friend. Traffic was light. Walking in the mid-morning sun was hot yet Fred was glad for the solitude. It gave him time to think about how he was going to break the news of the deaths of Rafe and Greg to Luke and Corena. So deep in thought was he that he almost jumped out of his shoes when a horn sounded behind him.

"Agent Adkins? What in the world are you doing out here?" The woman on the passenger side asked.

"Mr. and Mrs. Patterson? Has something happened to Luke? Dear God, please tell me he's all right."

"You look horrible." Luke's mother stated. "Get in. It will be much cooler on you."

Fred nodded knowing they would help him talk to Luke. Parked on the side of the road, engine running, air conditioner on high, they listened as Fred explained the strange turn of events. They exchanged knowing looks when he told them about the explosion. Fred missed the exchange, wallowed in grief. "Now do you understand why I need to talk to Luke and Cory? Greg told me how devastated Luke was when he came off assignment to find Cory's parents were murdered. I think it would be easier for both of them if they heard it now instead of later."

"Luke says you're an honest man, Mr. Adkins. We were just going to visit those two. You'll have to stay overnight because both Luke and his woman will be going through a special ceremony today. You can talk business tomorrow." Two Hawks, Luke's father, told him.

"Yes Sir." Fred glanced at Luke's father. "I guess unhappiness can wait another day."

★ ★ ★ ★ ★

The headache nipped at the fringes of Cory's being since early morning. She toyed with breakfast until Skywalker and the Elders took her to the ceremonial circle. There the council assured her that she had proven herself worthy of their protection. The two now had permission to be joined.

The ceremony she was undergoing was in preparation of her joining. The smoke, herbs and fragrant oils used for the ceremony served to bring the headache forward from the edge of her mind to a dull ache. As the women combed her hair in preparation of braiding the headache bloomed into more than a nuisance and she closed her eyes against the nausea that rose. Each time the comb hit a tangle white lightening shot through her brain. She bit her lip until it bled fighting the headache.

"Running Eagle? What's wrong?"

Cory opened her eyes at the sound of White Dove's worried voice. The world was spinning, and she clamped her eyes shut against it. Her stomach lurched as the ground beneath her feet opened up and left her falling into nothingness. "Running Eagle, drink this." Skywalker's voice split the pain that enveloped her. Shoulders and head being lifted returned the lightening to the darkness behind her eyes. "We're going to take you to the hospital for x-rays."

"No." She forced her eyes opened to plead with Skywalker. "This is my joining day. Don't ruin this for us."

Luke entered her line of vision, kneeling beside her. "Running Eagle, the joining can wait until you're better. You need to be examined."

"I refuse to go. Not today." The fine lines of her face hardened with determination as tears ran down her cheeks. "This headache won't prevent us from being joined."

Luke gathered the weeping woman into his arms holding her tight against him. "Darling, I want you as my wife, but I hate seeing you in pain." His distress was evident.

"The tea will control the pain. Once we are joined I'll go if need be but not now."

"Once we are joined I'll be your husband, Running Eagle. I will take you to the hospital myself if need be."

"No." Her voice rose in panic. "Someone might recognize you. You can't be protected off the Reservation." She clung to him desperately afraid she would lose him to the evils beyond Reservation lands. "I knew that's what you would say. That's why I didn't tell anyone about the headache. I can't bear the thought of losing you now. Promise me you won't put your life in danger because of me."

When her crying became harder Luke gently pulled her head back forcing tea between her lips. They named this woman correctly he realized with a grin. A female eagle protected its own to the last breath within her. Cory couldn't fly but she could run like the wind and, even now, she was protecting her own. Just as the female eagle.

When her crying subsided, he pulled her away from him enough to kiss her passionately. He ended the kiss, thrilled to see her eyes shining with anticipation of all the kiss promised. "Sleep, woman. We will soon be joined. You need to rest."

As her eyes slid shut Skywalker picked her up to carry her to the tipi. "If the headaches continue she will need to be seen." He spoke quietly. "I will get the clinic to help."

"If you still think she needs to be seen after the joining I'll take her. I didn't promise her anything about not going."

# Chapter Eleven

FRED ADKINS LOOKED AROUND IN utter amazement. It was a good thing he was seated when Luke appeared because the force of his grief threatened to overwhelm him at the sight of his friend. Fred respected this man, considered him a true friend. Although he was happy Luke was getting married, the secret he carried hurt his heart.

Luke's eyes narrowed watching Fred. "Something is troubling you, my friend. It shows in your eyes. Out with it."

Fred shook his head unable to look Luke in the eyes. "A lot has been happening at the agency. I promised your parents I wouldn't discuss business on your wedding day. I refuse to break that promise."

Luke grinned. "I appreciate your promise, Fred, so I won't pry. I made no such promises, however. Stay here. There are a few things you need to see." Struggling to his crutches he slowly hobbled away. Luke entered the tipi where Greg and Rafe were dressing. "You guys didn't tell Fred Adkins you were still alive. Did you?" The surprised look that passed between the two men answered Luke's question louder than words causing laughter to bubble over. "The poor man looks like he has lost every friend in the world. I believe you should talk to him before he grieves for much longer."

"Fred is here?" Greg asked incredulously.

"Yes. He said he promised my parents not to talk to me about business today. I think he came to tell me of your untimely deaths. It would do the young man a world of good if you would appear again. At least for him." Luke left the tipi first eyes shielded as he watched Fred. The younger man stood as the two advanced toward him. All color drained from his face, mouth open in shock when he saw the ghosts of Greg and Rafe. Luke knew then his suspicions were well founded. Fred Adkins came to break the news of the two deaths.

Skywalker laughed. "They did not tell him?"

Luke chuckled. "No, Grandfather. I guess they were so scared they failed to tell anyone. Fred is now our only contact with the agency."

"I have something to give you. I planned on giving it to you as a joining gift however I think you ought to take it now so not to injure Running Eagle."

The sad tone of Skywalker's voice alerted Luke to additional trouble. "Running Eagle is still asleep?"

"Yes and will probably be so for several hours yet after drinking the tea I made for her. I don't wish for her to know what is in this."

Luke finally turned looking Skywalker in the eyes. What he saw shook his soul with dread. The older man was fingering an envelope and pain filled his eyes as he met Luke's. Luke nodded turning to the tipi. "Whatever it is I guess I ought to deal with it now. I don't want Running Eagle distressed today. She has had more than one person should endure." When Luke was seated Two Hawks entered behind Skywalker. The look on his father's face warned him even more. With a sigh he held out his hand for the envelope.

Skywalker refused to relinquish it. "Before I give you this know that I stood guard at the tipi last night while the four of you were talking. I heard your woman say her Grandmother hid important papers in a Shaman's house. The Grandmother was a very good friend of mine, Luke. We had a special relationship."

Tears welled in Skywalker's eyes. "She came one day after a package arrived at the house Running Eagle's parents owned before they died. She stated there were…pictures in the box along with a warning. It stated simply: remember. She returned the pictures to the box, resealing it. Returned all but one. The one she brought to my house. Later when your woman was better Running Eagle opened the box."

Skywalker began to pace, the silence becoming thick in the tipi. Finally, he had his thoughts gathered. "Running Eagle bought a computer and spent long hours working out her graphs. The same ones you saw last night. She had a hard time remembering things after her injury and was afraid she would forget important events and worked desperately to record all she knew. There was a small panel on the wall that move easily when touched and she hid her evidence there.

"The day Running Eagle had her first surgery to hide the scars the Grandmother came home, finding that someone had already been there. Nothing appeared disturbed at first but then the Grandmother began noticing small things that should not have been. Pictures were reversed in their positions on the mantel. A glass was in the sink that was empty when they left. The clothes in the drawers were ruffled. Things like that. The Grandmother was frightened. She knew Running Eagle had proof on her parent's supervisor. Rushing to the wall she pulled it from the hiding place, put it and the picture that Running Eagle never saw and brought it to me.

"That was shortly after I moved into the cabin. We had laughed about the loose brick next to the fireplace when she helped me move. She even stated that it would be a good place to hide something important. The day she came with the envelope she made me promise never to look inside. I was instructed to give it to you if anything should happen to Running Eagle or the Grandmother. She trusted both of us."

Skywalker sat next to Luke. "I'm sorry, Bright Arrow. I never did look inside the envelope. I just assumed it was her will. Last night after listening to the conversation I realized how stupid I had been. I retrieved it and gaining the courage I needed to break my promise, I looked." With a shuddering breath he surrendered the envelope to Luke. "Don't let Running Eagle see the picture." He pleaded.

Luke's hand trembled as he lifted the flap. Inside were four pieces of papers wrapped around the picture. Luke looked at the picture first. It was one of Cory after she had been butchered yet it wasn't taken at the hospital. Pain ripped through him once again upon seeing the damage. He had to cover her body with his hand before looking closer. This picture was different from the ones he saw in her chart. The blue tile on the floor was swirled, blood pooling around her body. Cory was still tied up. Anger surged. The bastard had taken these after he cut her up and before she was found. Returning the picture to the envelope Luke took a steadying breath before he turned his attention to the papers. They rattled from his anger when he unfolded them. The first was a letter, the handwriting crimped and shaky. He knew instantly the letter was from Cory's grandmother. Another deep breath steadied his nerves.

*Bright Arrow,*

*I know that my son-in-law as well as my granddaughter trusted you with their lives. If you are reading this then something has happened to Running Eagle or myself. I prayed that by stealing this information I would have saved that dear, sweet girl. I guess I was wrong. Even though she has quit the agency they are still after her. God forgive me, but I can't allow them to go free. I pray you will know what to do with this. Be careful Bright Arrow. What you have in your hands will get you killed just as it has killed my wonderful family. I can only look down from heaven and try to keep you safe once this information is in your hands.*

It was signed simply, Grandmother. Sadness surged through him as he replaced the letter next to the picture. The next was neatly folded yet Luke could see where the wrinkles had been smoothed out as if someone had wadded it into a ball. His mouth was dry when he opened it, his sadness turned to anger when he read it. It also was a letter. The pen flowed freely, the handwriting flowing across the paper. A cold chill swept over Luke. He recognized it as belonging to Jason Grover. This one was addressed to Major O'Grady.

*Father,*

*I hope you were impressed with my handiwork. It's a good thing you got Luke Patterson away on assignment. I would hate to have to kill him as I did the Sims family. He taught me so much while I was in college. It would be a shame to kill him before I tortured him, but I would have done it. The bomber wanted to get even with him, and I had to exert a lot of influence to keep him under control.*

*I know you'll keep your end of this bargain. I expect to spend as little time in this hellhole as possible. I've bought my way into a cell with another who has benefited your operation greatly. If you fail to change the records and get me off, I'll personally see you receive the same treatment Ralph Sims received. Don't do anything about Luke Patterson at this time. I will deal with him when I'm released. I have a lot of time to plan for his torture and untimely demise.*

There was no signature. Luke clamped down hard on his anger. Putting the second paper at the back of the stack he noted the third was also a letter. This one was also addressed to O'Grady and Luke clamped down hard on his rising anger.

*Father,*

*Have done as you ordered. Torturing Corena Sims was a pleasure last night. I hope you're satisfied with the results of my handiwork. I didn't rape her as per your orders however that piece of meat would have been worth your anger. You owe me another virgin, father. I hope you're satisfied. The bitch will never talk. Threatening her sisters was a wise decision on your part.*

*Enjoy the tape of her screams. If you are playing it now, you'll notice there are none. She refused to give either you or me that pleasure. No matter how hard I tried she kept her screams inside. She must have been taught by the same people as Luke Patterson was. Amazing how anyone can keep their pain from conquering. Luke would have said she had the heart of a warrior. Fate is truly strange. Luke taught me that, years ago. I have never forgotten it.*

*Partner that idiot half-brother of mine with anyone who comes close to my operation. He can keep us both informed through his sister. Your payment for your consideration of my safety will arrive within a few days. For now, enjoy the bitch's silence.*

*Ironic, is it not? All you wanted was to see the end results and listen to her screams. One you did, the other you'll never have the satisfaction because of her stubbornness. How nice it must be to have stubborn people like her and Luke working for you. Such a shame to be disappointed. Isn't it?*

As Luke put the letter behind the others, questions assailed him. How did Cory get the letters? She was in critical condition after her torture and he knew there was no way for her to have obtained the letters on her own. Who provided her with them? "Grandfather? Did the Grandmother say how Cory got these?"

Skywalker had started pacing when Luke opened the envelope and now he turned to look at the letter Luke held up. "No. I remember she said some of the warriors at the other Reservation were angered over what happened. She mentioned that they intended to obtain jobs at the agency and seek answers. Maybe one of them found it."

Luke nodded flipping open the next paper. The handwriting this time was crimped and small. Someone named Crazy Wolf signed it.

*Running Eagle,*

*I believe I'm suspected and know my time here to be limited. I've been working with the janitorial services. I found this note in Major O'Grady's trash and slid it into my pocket before I emptied the can. The tension here is easing since you're so sick. There are whispers of major changes about to take place including here in my service. I may not be able to obtain much more information for you as they are talking about layoffs and I will be the first to be laid off. I pray this is what you need. Be careful cousin. Talk around here suggests your Grandmother and you are being watched. These men are extremely dangerous. Don't take chances. Wait until you have someone you trust to help you.*

Slowly, Luke lowered the three letters into his lap. This was the proof Cory spoke about. Yet it was more than that. It was also proof of Jason Grover's involvement in the cover-up of her torture. He suddenly realized Cory didn't know the name of the man who butchered her until after she arrived on the Reservation and he used the name. Memory surfaced hard of the day she asked if Grover was blonde with a handmade suit.

With a sigh he turned to Two Hawks. "Father, please release Fred Adkins from his vow of silence. I need information from the agency as soon as possible. Once you talk to him please ask that he, Greg and Rafe join me here. I want to get some plans laid before Running Eagle awakens from the tea Grandfather gave her."

After Two Hawks left, Skywalker turned to Luke with tears in his eyes. "Bright Arrow, I'm sorry to hurt you like this on your joining day."

"No, Grandfather. You've done the correct thing. Now is the time to plan. I need to be assured Running Eagle won't awaken until those plans are made."

"Too late." Her angry voice met him. "I awoke to find Fred outside talking with Greg and Rafe. Whatever plans you need to make had better include me, Bright Arrow, or I shall refuse to be joined with you."

Luke groaned. "I didn't mean that as it sounded, my dear. I didn't want to distress you when you will become my wife in just a few short hours. Forgive me."

Anger quickly dying she stood behind him, wrapping her arms around his neck, letting her hands rub over his chest, distracting him, tempting him and he had to put tight control over his need. She noticed the papers in his lap. "I see someone found my proof." She looked at Skywalker. "Grandmother must have loved you deeply. I'm hurt that my presence and injuries prevented her from doing something about that love."

"I loved your Grandmother also, Running Eagle. It was by mutual agreement we didn't join. She wanted to be close to the family she had remaining, and I wanted to be close to mine." He watched the couple's reaction closely. Luke appeared shocked, yet happiness shown in Cory's eyes. "That didn't keep us from loving each other whenever we had the chance. I pray I made her last days here on this earth as happy as she made mine. Our love was as strong as your love. I miss her greatly."

"Grandmother was very happy those last few years. I often wondered if she found someone to make her feel whole. I'm honored to know that someone was you." A sad smile crossed her face. "In my suitcase there's something of hers that never really felt as if it belonged to me. Now I know why. There is a small locket with a garnet stone wrapped in leather. Next time you go home please take it. It was intended to go to you."

Skywalker had tears in his eyes. "Thank you." He whispered as he kissed her cheek. "I shall keep it only until you have a daughter. The stone was your grandmother's favorite. I made the locket for her, inserting the stone after the first time she shared my bed."

"She never took it off. The sisters wanted to bury her with it, but I refused. I knew it was intended for someone and removed it when I added the spices and things she would need on her journey just before they closed the casket. I never wore it but have carried it with me everywhere. It gave me the feeling she was with me somehow, that she was protecting me. I have my warrior to protect me now, so you are welcome to the locket. It belongs to you."

As Skywalker hugged her they heard a cough from the doorway. Turning around to see who entered she missed seeing Luke tuck the envelope with the picture under his leg. "You look well, Cory. Much better than the last time I saw you." Fred shuffled uneasily.

"Come in. I'm so happy you could come to share this special day with us. Skywalker found what Grandmother hid. Perhaps now we can get some answers. Since the agency is getting very short handed we also need to plan for the mole's downfall and arrest."

As the men gathered around Luke, he took her hand, squeezing her fingers. "Honey, would you find those charts Greg has? His briefcase should be in the tipi where he has been staying. They might be needed."

She bent close to his ear. "I've seen the letters, my dear. I'll give you time to bring the men up to date. I'll stay with White Dove in my tipi while you do so. Send for me for I want to help with the plans to bring those bastards down. Promise me you shall alert me?"

Luke kissed her. "I promise. Thank you." He watched until she left the doorway, dropping the flap behind her and then he told the men how Skywalker found the envelope. "There's a picture in the envelope Cory doesn't know about. Her Grandmother requested in her letter she not see it either." He swallowed hard. "It's not a pretty sight."

He saw Greg turn pale and seemed to shrink away even though he never moved. Rafe held out his hand and Luke surrendered it. The muscles in his cheek twitched as he looked at the picture. "This is worse than those in her house." He whispered feeling his stomach roil. Taking several deep breaths, he finally managed to force himself to look past the mutilation. "The floor design is the same, so it had to be taken in the same place as the others. We know this building belongs to Jason Grover. Ralph and I were there just prior to Ralph's murder. That tile is unmistakable." He sighed deeply as he handed the picture to Fred.

Fred hid his revulsion well. After several deep breaths he sat staring at the picture. "Since I haven't seen any of the other pictures I'm rather at a disadvantage here however..." He pulled the picture closer. "Rafe, look at this. What do you make of it?"

Rafe leaned over Fred's shoulder as Fred pointed to the edge of the photo. "Sorry. My eyes must not be as good as they once were. What are you looking at?"

"Something…It's so hard to see…I wish I had a magnifying glass. Whatever it is the image is blurred."

Luke slid across the floor to look over Fred's shoulder. "The image is blurred for a reason. Grandfather, do you have a mirror?"

Skywalker nodded rushing from the tipi. Luke took the picture again but had to put his hand over Cory's bloody body before he could concentrate. When Skywalker returned he took the mirror handing it to his father. "Hold that will you?" His attention was not on his father or the mirror. "The man who took this was behind those in the image. Someone beside Jason Grover was in that room. I think…" His face became pale as he arranged the mirror, so the reflective side was toward him. Turning the picture around, he positioned it in front of the mirror. Rafe groaned. Fred gasped. Greg looked as if he would pass out and Luke's features took on a murderous look. "That bastard." He growled. "No wonder there was so much blood on the floor. They left her there until he arrived."

"Who, Bright Arrow?" Two Hawks whispered. This was the first time he had seen the damage to Cory's body and the sight sickened him.

"The image Fred saw was a reverse image. It appears as if there was a mirror on the wall or that the wall was very shiny." Luke shrugged as he studied the reflection in the mirror. "Regardless, when the person took the picture he caught the image of those in the room in the photo. With the mirror their images became identifiable. Jason Grover is there, knife in hand. O'Grady is there, patting Jason on the back. Major Thoms is there, standing beside O'Grady."

"Who took the picture?" Skywalker asked.

Luke shrugged, confusion showing in his face as he was looking at the image in the mirror. "It would have to be someone they all trusted. It doesn't show up here, however. The person must be just out of reflective range."

Fred groaned. "Put the picture away, Luke. I think it's time to tell you what I found out yesterday. You better send for Corena. She needs to hear this."

Cory entered cautiously, seeing the grim faces of those around her. Sitting next to Luke she held tightly to his hand. The silence grew heavy as Fred fumbled in his pocket, retrieving the papers he had copied. "I was called before Major Thoms yesterday. He asked all kinds of questions. Two in particular disturbed me. He was asking about the investigation and asked if I found a man named Jason Grover or a woman named Corena Sims." He shot her an apologetic look when she inhaled sharply.

"That got my suspicions up. As I was sitting at my desk I noticed Greg's secretary enter his office. I knew he couldn't be working alone… that he had to have someone who could help him. I also saw someone take a bug out of Rafe's phone. I began checking and found my phone was also bugged. That in itself was enough to send warning signals to my head. I finished my reports and told Susan Tameron I was going to the file room to add information to one of my reports. When she offered to do it for me the warning bells sounded again." He sucked a deep breath. "I found what I was looking for."

He spread out the reports he copied as well as his notes. "They are slightly different. Nothing really noticeable. If I weren't looking for something already I would've thought them to be an error on the typist's part however that typist was Susan. Later I was able to get into the personnel file room. I made copies of Susan Tameron's security clearance as well as her application." He handed them to Luke.

Looking over his shoulder, Cory gasped. "Convenient." Luke growled handing the copies to Greg and Rafe. Anger tightened the muscles in his jaw.

"God." Greg groaned. "She was Major Thoms' connection all along. She was the one who fed Thoms the information about the call Corena put in. That's how he knew so much. She's Thoms' half-sister."

Fred nodded. "Apparently her mother delivered Major Thoms first then got married and had Susan. How Major Thoms got mixed up in this mess is beyond me."

Cory laughed. "Let me give you a history lesson, my friend. It goes back to Major O'Grady. He was married twice. The first wife's maiden name was Grover. He beat her senseless before he divorced her insisting she use her maiden name."

"Grover?" Fred croaked. "As in Jason Grover?"

"The same. Next, he married a woman whose maiden name was Toms, without the H. Once again, he divorced her insisting she use her maiden name. If you had looked into Major Thoms file you would've seen that he applied under T-O-M-S not T-H-O-M-S. I believe he added the H to hide his secret." She shrugged. "Anyway, his mother married again to a man named Tameron. Susan Tameron must have been hired after I left the agency and so I had no knowledge of her until now."

"So what do we do now?" Fred asked seeing the anger growing in the faces around him.

"Now we plan." Luke growled. "I want to catch all those bastards and it needs to be done all at the same time. I want none of them to escape justice. First, when is Greg and Rafe's funerals supposed to be?"

Fred cringed. "Two days from today. I'm supposed to be on the honor guard."

"Good." Luke nodded with a satisfied grin. "Let's see how they like ghosts. I feel like playing with their minds. They've done enough of that so this ought to be fun."

"Bright Arrow?"

Luke kissed Cory. "Don't worry, my dear. You'll be there to help if I get in trouble. Tonight will belong to us. Tomorrow we are going to make an appearance at the wake." He chuckled. "You're involved up to those pretty ears of yours anyway, my dear. I want you to attend the wake. Grandfather? What was I buried in?"

Skywalker's eyes narrowed on Luke. "Traditional burial clothes. What are you planning on doing?"

"I plan on making them believe in ghosts. What else? Since my leg still hurts I'll be forced to stay in the background, allowing Major Thoms only one glimpse of me however one glimpse should be enough to send him running to Jason Grover. Running Eagle will have to play this scene without a script however."

"I don't understand, Grandson." Confusion etched the old man's face. "Surely you're not thinking of sending her to face Jason Grover without protection."

"If she stays in the crowd she'll do fine." He turned to Cory. "Your father was proud of your quick wit and quick thinking. Major Thoms, as well as Jason, will try to pump you for information. You'll have to use all your courage and that quick mind of yours not to give away our secret. Can you do this?"

Cory bit her lip before nodding her head. "The Elders once asked me what I would do if I ever met Jason Grover again. At the time my hatred ruled. Now I would like to get even. Yes, Bright Arrow. I can help set the trap." Her eyes deepened with thought. "I think I know how to keep myself safe. I just claim poor memory which is not truly a lie. Much was lost to my memory after I became so sick."

"What are we supposed to do?" Rafe was scared. He could see many things happening that could go wrong with this idea that would get both Luke and Corena killed.

"You're going to stay on the Reservation for now. You'll make an appearance late the next night, with Greg making an appearance the day of the funeral." He turned to Greg. "I need you to call your wife. I'm sure she's worried sick about now. I want you to warn her. She's to see your ghost and I want her to faint or at least come close to it. I want her to go into hysterics, pointing to where you were. Be sure to get your butt out of there before someone comes after you. Cory, I want you to stay with Greg's wife tomorrow. As many people as there will be around her at the time it should provide you with enough protection to keep you safe until I can come get you."

"That will bring their defenses up, son." Two Hawks stated. "How will it catch them?"

"The proof is already in our hands, father." Luke gave Two Hawks a warning look. "We just have to get them to start watching over their shoulders. Major Thoms knew Greg and Rafe were both partners with Ralph. He also knows Cory knew Greg personally. It would be expected for her to show up at the funeral and I'm sure they shall be looking for her to appear."

"How do we catch them?" Fred asked.

"You'll have to do that, my friend." When Fred stiffened his back, Luke grinned. "While we're keeping them wondering I want you to send a telegraph to the main headquarters in Washington D.C. Use a land line to contact a Captain Richard Stevens. If they give you any trouble tell them I told you to call. Richard is my cousin, so the name Patterson will get you through to him in a hurry. He knows about our problem with a mole so not much information will need to be given. Tell Richard to meet us at the airport, that we'll be bringing the proof ourselves. Then get someone you trust to buy Cory and I plane tickets. Buy them under the names of..."

"Mr. and Mrs. Wolf and Violet Summerfield." Cory grinned. "That was Grandfather and Grandmother's names. No one will trace us that way."

Luke kissed her quickly grinning when she blushed. "Agreed. Buy them under Mr. and Mrs. Summerfield. It may take several days before we're able to return. Until then be damned careful what you do."

"How do we keep Running Eagle protected while she's in plain sight?" Skywalker asked worriedly, seeing that flaw as dangerous.

"Fred will have to introduce himself to her. No one must suspicion that they already know each other." His hand tightened on hers. "Stay with the crowd, honey. Don't allow yourself to be without someone around you every minute you are there. Paula, Greg's wife can help with that."

"Where are you going to be?"

"I'll be at your house." Luke grinned. "Last time I was there I hurt too damned bad to do anything but dream about you joining me in bed. Have Fred bring you home. If they try anything I'll be there to protect you." His eyes turned dark with anger. "It would give me great pleasure to return some of the pain we endured."

Cory nodded. "Since we no longer have Jasper's car how do we get back to the house?"

"Not a problem." Rafe chuckled. "I know a kindly old gentleman with a red station wagon who is worried sick about you. One call should bring him here in a heartbeat. Since the Reservation is being watched we'll have to find someplace for you to meet with Jasper and then transfer the camping gear there. Most can probably fit in Mr. and Mrs. Patterson's car. You only need enough to hide Luke. The problem is where Greg and I are going to hide."

Greg looked at Fred. "I know."

Eyes wide, Fred shook his head. "I only have a one-bedroom apartment. How do you expect the three of us to sleep with only one bed?"

Rafe laughed. "We've been sleeping on the ground in these tipis since we arrived. Do you really think sleeping on the floor could be any more uncomfortable than that?" At Fred's look of doubt Rafe laughed harder. "God, it will be good to be alive again. I want to be there when they arrest those bastards. Promise me, Luke, that this won't go down without us."

Luke ground his teeth together against the anger raging through him. "That's a promise you shouldn't have to ask for. All of us have reason to see these bastards fall. That will be granted before we tell Washington what's going on. Never fear. We'll be together when this thing goes down."

"Grandson, I know there is much to think about however it's time to prepare both of you for the joining." Skywalker stood pulling Cory to her feet. "Once I turn Running Eagle over to the Elders I will return to prepare you with Two Hawks help."

Seeing the blush spread across Cory's cheeks he was instantly hard at the sight of the blush. Luke kissed her hungrily. "I need to get ready also. When next I see you, it will be the time we are joined. Do you have any last-minute doubts?" Seeing the shake of her head he sighed, a sigh of relief and kissed her one last time before Skywalker escorted her from the tipi. "Soon my love." He whispered to her.

Cory followed Skywalker, excitement shining in her eyes. White Dove and her mother, Little Fawn, were waiting for her. After slipping into the white buckskin dress and knee-high moccasins she knelt between the two women. "First your hair." Little Fawn stated. Pulling a long coil from either side of Cory's face they encased the hair in white leather strips. When the coils were finished White Dove brushed the remaining hair into a soft cloud while Little Fawn placed a medicine wheel hairpiece in her hair to the left of her face.

"This wheel is a symbol of our unity with God, the universe we live in, as well as each other. It's a circle, symbolizing the circle of our lives together and is encased in white leather to show purity of heart. It has crossed bars in the center. Those are symbolic of the four elements of this earth, water, fire, sun, and land. The crossroads are symbolic of the paths that our lives can take as well as the two individuals who are joined by the circle. The center is connected as you and Bright Arrow will be connected once you are joined. The feathers are from birds and will give wings to your love, so you can touch the sky together. It's placed to the left of your face, closest to the heart."

Love showed in Cory's eyes as she hugged her soon to be mother-in-law. After returning the hug she pulled Cory's face where she could see her eyes. "I'm glad to finally meet the woman who saved two of my children. Of the five of my children I never thought Bright Arrow would be the first to be joined. Since it is I'm glad it's someone who loves him as much as he loves you. I'm thrilled to have you for my daughter."

A delicate blush stained Cory's cheeks. "Never doubt my love for your son, Mrs. Patterson. I never believed in love at first sight until I met Bright Arrow."

"That's how it was for me when I met Two Hawks." A knowing smile lit her face. "I have a gift for you. It's always passed to the first woman who marries into the family. That's you and I couldn't be more thrilled or honored to release it to you."

Tears sprang to Cory's eyes as she looked at Luke's mother. "Whatever it is it should go to White Dove. She's your daughter."

"White Dove was never eligible. It goes to the first woman who marries into the family." A tender smile crossed her face as she placed a choker around Cory's neck. "It was given to me. Now I pass it to you. It's a talisman for fertility. Without having son's the choker can never be passed along to the woman who married into the family."

The blush returned, deeper this time as Cory fingered the choker. It was five strands wide. The bone hair pipe was offset with turquoise nuggets. The disk at the front of her throat was abalone with more turquoise and feather streamers. Bending forward she gave Little Fawn another hug. "Thank you. Not just for the choker but for having the man I love. He's so wonderful. You and your husband can take pride in the way you have raised him."

"Every tribe has a different ceremony, so I must tell you of our joining ceremony. You will stand before Bright Arrow and the lacing on the left sleeve will be removed. The front of the buckskins will fall." Little Fawn watched as Cory's hand slid to where she now knew was a scar. "You must not try to prevent that from happening, Running Eagle. Bright Arrow will put his mark upon you while proclaiming his love for you. Once that is done you will do the same to his chest." Cory drew a deep breath before nodding. "Once the marks are dry which doesn't take long, the front and back of your joining clothes will be laced back together. After that Skywalker will join you in blood. Do you know how this is done?"

"Yes. He will draw the point of his knife across our palms and then bind us together to let our blood mix as one. That's done in the joining ceremony of my tribe also. It shows the world that I and Bright Arrow have found our life mates."

"Good. Skywalker was concerned this would hurt you because of your past. Most of the time this leaves a scar." Little Fawn extended her left hand. A light pink scar showed proof of her joining with Two Hawks.

Cory traced the outline on Little Fawn's hand, tears gleaming in her eyes. "This scar I'll be proud to bear, Little Fawn. It's like the ring of marriage. It's an indication that marriage is forever. It will be done in love, not anger or hatred. When I see this scar, I will know that my warrior loves me, and I'll never be ashamed of it. He will bear the same scar, an indication of my love for him. We will be as one this day, Little Fawn. I only hope my children will be as wonderful as their father. I pray they shall be proud of what they are."

"Stay true to your heritage and grow with Bright Arrow through the ceremonies. You will be the best parents you can be, my dear. Bright Arrow has told us you wish to continue with your teachings and the ceremonies. I'm pleased to know my grandchildren will have parents who believe in their heritage."

The Elders entered. "It is time."

As Cory stepped outside Skywalker pulled her to him. "Bright Arrow knows how embarrassed you'll be about the ceremony. He has asked the council if the actual ceremony can be done inside the tipi with the celebration following in the clearing. The family, the council, your friends and the witnesses will be there however it won't be like having several hundred people watch."

"Bright Arrow doesn't mind?"

"No, Granddaughter. His only thoughts are to be joined with you."

Cory sighed with relief. She felt she could do all without hesitation except the painting. That worried her for she was afraid she would disgrace her warrior because she couldn't control her embarrassment which she knew would surface. Offering his arm, he escorted her to the other tipi. "How is the headache?" He whispered when they got close.

"It's still there just tucked back to the fringes of my brain. The tea helped. As long as I can keep it at bay I'll be fine. Thank you for everything you have done for us."

Stopping at the flap he looked her in the eyes and smiled. "No need to thank me, my dear. It is you who deserves the thanks. You have saved two of my grandchildren. No matter what I do for the rest of my life that blessing can never be repaid. I loved you before and now I love you even more."

The blush that adorned her cheeks complimented the excitement dancing in her eyes. Turtle and Running Bear stepped to either side of her. "We get the pleasure of presenting you to Bright Arrow." Turtle said with a peck to her cheek. "When I was joined with Lightening Dancer she was embarrassed during the paintings." He whispered in her ear. "Keep your eyes on Bright Arrow. Think of nothing and no one but him. Blank your mind of everyone around you but him. You'll do fine."

As she nodded she could hear an elder address the tribe. "People of the tribe. You are here to help celebrate the joining of an honored warrior, Bright Arrow. He has professed his love for Running Eagle, and she has accepted him for her own."

Skywalker's voice reached her next. "Running Eagle was brought to our tribe because of the danger Bright Arrow's injuries brought to her. The council was angered because the laws of the tribe had been violated. Ceremonies as well as completion of the Honored Warrior's Challenge were demanded before the joining. Since Running Eagle has proven her loyalty to the tribe the council has agreed the ceremonies are to be completed as Running Eagle deems herself ready. Since she has shown her devotion to this tribe by saving one of our own, at great risk to her own life, the Challenge has been deemed unnecessary. If there are objections by the tribe now is the time to voice them."

Cory held her breath and closed her eyes in fear as the silence lengthened around her.

# Chapter Twelve

HEN SKYWALKER SPOKE AGAIN CORY released her breath with a rush bringing a chuckle from her two guards. "No one has spoken against this joining. Running Eagle will now be taken to the tipi." She waited beside Turtle and Laughing Bear until she felt a light squeeze on her elbow. Back stiff, eyes straight ahead, she drew a cleansing breath before nodding.

At the sight of Luke her steps faltered as her breath lodged in her throat. He was dressed in a white beaded buckskin shirt, breechcloth, leggings and moccasins. His black hair hung loose around his shoulders. A small portion of hair on the left side of his face was enclosed in white bindings as hers was.

High cheekbones and dark tanned face gave a fierceness to his features against the white of his clothing. His chocolate eyes burned with passion making her heart flutter wildly in her chest. An eerie feeling of having stepped a hundred years into the past assailed her as she walked between her warrior guards.

Turtle and Laughing Bear took her to Skywalker and then retreated into the crowd. Skywalker stood before her, tilting her head until he could capture her eyes. "Bright Arrow has proclaimed his love for you before this council. They have yet to hear your words of love for Bright Arrow. Do you love this honored warrior?"

Cory licked dry lips. "Yes, Elder. I have loved him for many years. I have never loved another for none stirred love within me as Bright Arrow has."

"Through that love will you join with him? Stand beside him when times are bad? Bring his children into this world? Grow old with him?"

Cory hated the blush she knew was fanning the heat in her face. "Because of my love for him I will gladly do all those things."

Skywalker smiled releasing her chin as he turned to Luke. "Bright Arrow you have heard the words of love spoken by this woman. If you accept her words as honor stand before her."

As Luke advanced Skywalker moved to Cory's side. Her lungs refused to function correctly. Her breath was coming in short gasps as she looked up into the face of her soon-to-be husband. His eyes captured hers and she could not pull away from their hold. Even as she listened to Skywalker's words she couldn't tear her eyes from his.

"All things of value within this tribe carry a mark of possession. The most valuable possession anyone can have is the love of another. Once two people are joined they belong to each other, never more to be two individuals but a single entity."

Luke saw Skywalker move behind Cory, saw her stiffen as he removed the laces on the left shoulder of her dress. He sensed her embarrassment when the front and back of her dress separated revealing the scar. Still he refused to release her eyes. He knew most of her breast would be exposed. It needed to be, so he could place his mark upon her.

White Dove hobbled beside them. A tray full of bowels with different colored paints was handed to her when she steadied herself on her crutches. The silence grew strained as the two remained locked in eye contact. Finally, she saw the slightest nod from Cory. White Dove battled the grin that threatened. Her brother was very smart where this woman was concerned. Luke was speaking to his woman through his eyes. In that silent communication he allowed her time to compose her emotions, conquer her embarrassment in front of those invited into the tipi and prepare herself for his touch.

Luke broke eye contact to pick up the first bowl yet Cory's eyes never left his face. "Running Eagle, my mark is known by all in this tribe. I put my mark on you today with pride and love." While he spoke he used the paints, exchanging one color for another. His movements were quick but precise. "With my mark know that you are forever my woman. By this mark everyone will know I claim you through love. Rest assured I will love you, care for you, provide for you and protect you until my dying breath." When his words were finished so was the mark on her chest.

Skywalker then moved behind Luke removing the ties at his left shoulder. As the buckskin separated a ghost of a grin could be seen on Cory's face. Turning to White Dove she picked up a bowl of paint. "Bright Arrow, this tribe does not know my mark but soon all will know what it looks like. It was given to me in a vision years ago. By putting my mark of love on you, you shall know the depth of my love. Your arrow pierced my heart many years ago. The brightness stayed as a light when my way was dark. Know that I claim you with love. Know I will be proud to bear your children. I will be there when you need me most. If I'm not at your side when you need me, look inside your heart and know I am there. Look to the sky, my love, for my eagle will be soaring high above and know I am with you in love and spirit until my dying breath."

Once again when the words were finished the mark was finished. Skywalker stepped beside them both. "You have proclaimed your love to each other. Your marks are now plainly visible. Know you now, once the paint is removed the mark will remain in your hearts forever. Know that children will bless your lives with happiness and wonder. Give them love but give love to each other more, for they will leave and only the two of you will remain. They wear no mark because they do not belong to you. They are your gift to others." He nodded to White Dove. She handed the paints to another before turning to Running Eagle, quickly lacing the front and back of her dress together. Skywalker did the same to Bright Arrow.

Once their attire was back together Skywalker stood between them facing Cory. "Running Eagle, you now wear the mark of Bright Arrow's love for you. You are joined in spirit. I shall now join you by blood. Hold out your left hand." Cory, her eyes captured again by Luke, held his eyes as she extended her left hand. A sharp inhale of breath was all the indication Luke had that Skywalker made the cut from thumb to small finger.

Skywalker spoke again. "The cut is at an angle to remind you that your life is only half. Bright Arrow is the other half. It is placed on the left hand of the woman because woman is the symbol of love and the left hand is closest to the heart where love can always be found."

White Dove held the bleeding hand as Skywalker turned to Luke. "Bright Arrow, your other half is waiting. The man's right hand is the symbol of strength. It is the right hand that is cut. Hold out yours." Luke obeyed feeling the hot, burning sensation of cut skin. "The cut is the same as your woman's."

Taking both hands, he placed them together, cuts pressed tightly against each other. "I have united you in blood. Give her your strength and she will give you her love. The mingling of these two is the only way you can be complete. Without one, the other will fall. Stand beside her always for only then will you share the love you have for each other."

Little Fawn and Two Hawks stepped forward as Skywalker retreated, taking the lacings from the couple's hair. Little Fawn smiled as she tied Cory's wrist to Luke's fingers. Two Hawks tied Luke's wrist to Cory's fingers. The third was handed to White Dove who tied their palms together. Two Hawks grinned at the couple. "You are now bound together as one. Your blood flows between you as one. Your lives are joined from this minute on as one. From this time on you shall be known as belonging to each other as long as you live. I am proud to pronounce Running Eagle as my daughter."

Amid the cheers of those within the tipi Luke pulled Cory tight against him, capturing her lips. His kiss held his promise of the future, conveying his need of her as well as his love. A path opened in the crowd when Luke ended the kiss and the flap was raised. Luke's smile was broad when he escorted his new wife from the tipi to more cheers from those of the tribe outside. A great feast was set in the clearing as the sun painted the sky with brilliant colors of red, blue and gold as it slowly gave way to the encroaching night. Cory giggled when she had to feed Luke the meal. "What's the matter? Have you never learned to use your left hand?"

Luke snorted. "Not to feed myself with. The bindings won't be removed until after I have claimed your body." He whispered. At her delicate blush he bent forward and whispered in her ear. "When I have you alone I will show you how well I can use that left hand." His grin became wider at the love he saw shining in her eyes, and he groaned with need when the blush stained her cheeks.

Presents appeared as the table was being cleaned. White Dove knelt beside Cory. "Running Eagle, I want to give you my gift before I rest my leg." She slipped a small knife with a sheath in Cory's hand. "The game you play will be dangerous. This knife will fit into your boot however it will kill with the accuracy of any bullet. I know Bright Arrow has thought of all the ways possible to protect you, but I would be honored if you took this as part of your protection. Be careful sister and take care of that stubborn brother of mine." With a quick kiss on Cory's cheek White Dove hobbled away.

"How did she know?"

Luke watched frowning as his sister went straight to the arms of Laughing Bear, tears on her cheeks. "If I were to venture a guess I would say mother and father told her. You'll find that little happens in this family that is not shared with all." Luke mumbled. "It would only be right since she loves you as much as I do. She is correct when she says this is a dangerous game."

Cory grinned seeing the direction Luke's attention was centered. "They will be good together, husband. She loves Laughing Bear as deeply as I love you." When his startled eyes met hers, she laughed until tears filled her eyes. "I believe there will be another joining once you are safe. The confrontation with the cougar scared more than you silly. Laughing Bear hasn't let her out of his sight since that night. He hovers around her as a mother hen hovers around her chicks when there's danger about. I think Laughing Bear fears she'll be hurt again."

Luke shook his head in wonder, watching Laughing Bear and White Dove enter the tipi together. A slow grin spread across his face as mischief shimmered in his eyes. "The moon is rising as is my need for you. The presents can wait but I doubt my control is strong enough to resist you much longer. I want you, Running Eagle. I want you as my wife. I want your body as I now have your heart and blood." The blush was deep as she stood. The blush quickly fled when Luke struggled to gain his feet only to topple sideways. Quickly she grabbed him around the waist, pulling him next to her to keep him from falling. Others rushed to their side but stayed back when they saw Luke wave his hand at them.

"I think it's time for you to rest your leg." She stated anger lacing her words. "Why didn't you tell me your leg was hurting? This day could have waited…"

Luke silenced her with a kiss filled with promise. "You wouldn't wait because of a headache. I couldn't wait and refused to. The leg is just stiff from sitting. It hurts but not as much as the rest of me is hurting for you." He nipped her ear playfully.

Her anger wasn't abated, and she shrugged off his teasing lips. "Talk to me Bright Arrow. Is your leg still infected? Is that why you still use the crutches? Is that why you hurt so much and are not able to walk?"

Luke sank back into his chair forcing Cory to follow. "Grandfather looked at the damage to my leg. He's already warned me that I may never have full use of the leg again." Luke drew a ragged breath forcing his fear to the pit of his stomach. "That glass did a lot of damage, Running Eagle. This may end my career as an agent. I didn't want to tell you until I could get a professional to look at it."

Luke let Cory think about his words. He was shocked when he saw the tears in her eyes. "I know this is going to sound selfish but I'm glad you won't be working undercover any longer. There are other things you could do besides being a desk jockey. You would make one hell of an instructor and can teach the new agents how to keep themselves alive in dangerous situations. The thought of being without you for months on end really scared the hell out of me. I've been praying to be brave enough when you leave on assignment and not break down in tears of worry until after you left. I knew my tears would hurt you as much as leaving would."

Luke chuckled as he kissed her tears away. "Not selfish, my little Eagle. At first, I was angry with God as well as the situation I found myself in. All I know is how to infiltrate the bad guys. It's all I've ever done. Then reality set in on me. I was thankful I would no longer be forced to leave your side. I'll be there to protect you this way and watch our children grow. Even though my life is turned upside down I know this will help to keep us together. I never thought about being a training officer, however. That would give me something productive to do with my life as well as keep the meaning of my life within my work. Too many have already died because of lack of proper training." He kissed her again. "What will you do once we are all safe? What do you want to do?"

She turned her face away shrugging. "I have no idea what I'll do. Since I left the hospital without notice I can't return there. It really doesn't bother me because I hated being a nurse. Always did. That's why I hounded daddy to help me get into the agency. It was hard to break into the 'all men's club'. There was no one who taught women how to keep their cover from being blown. Daddy taught me all I know about working undercover. All that stopped when O'Grady declared daddy a traitor. My position was taken away, my security clearance was downgraded, and I worked as a secretary for months. That didn't bother me either because I swore I would find the proof I needed to clear daddy's name and it gave me access to the files I needed. I never allowed myself to dream past that time." She shrugged. "I guess I shall just stay home and be a nobody."

Luke grinned as he struggled to his feet. "Never a nobody, my dear. Tonight, I shall prove that to you." Once again Cory supported him when he swayed. When his crutches were brought she tried to remove the lacing to allow him use of both hands. "No." He growled, slipping his crutches under his arms. "Just help me. We can make it together. The lacings are not to be removed until after the joining of our bodies."

A deep blush fanned her cheeks, yet she didn't argue farther.

Luke hobbled painfully to the tipi. Once they were inside Cory helped lower Luke to the floor while indecision of what to do made her hands tremble. "Luke..."

"No words, woman. Only touch." Slowly he began untying the lacings at her shoulders. Her eyes were closed, and he could see the hint of fear filter across her face. His voice was soft when he spoke again. "It will be slightly painful the first time I enter you, Running Eagle. It will only last for a few seconds and then you will never feel pain again with our joining." His sharp intake of breath when the front of the dress fell forward made her eyes fly open. His fingers trembled when he touched her. "My God, woman. You are so beautiful. I have dreamed of this day for so long. When I failed to find you I feared those dreams would never be fulfilled. It's hard to believe you are really mine after all these years. I love you so much."

The hunger in his eyes made lava pool in her loins. Slowly she removed the lacings from the sides of the shirt and then those at his shoulders. The shirt fell away revealing smooth, tanned skin. She couldn't resist touching him. As her hand slid across the washboard muscles of his chest her excitement grew as the look of pleasure surged over Luke's face. A small grin of mischief crossed her face as her hand reached the ties of the breechcloth. Luke's breath was coming in short gasps, his eyes closed tight in expectation of what she was doing. Cory pushed him gently against the bedding. Lying on top of him she shuddered with the force of emotions that flooded her when her breasts touched his skin. Her hand traveled down his ribs thrilling her even more when she heard his strangled moan of pleasure. Quickly she untied the breechcloth, slipping her arm between them to untie the other side.

Luke was hard. Hurting hard, she knew. She could feel his erection and the sensation sent her senses reeling. Once the breechcloth was untied she slid her hand inside, wrapping her fingers around his hardened manhood. His moan served to excite her more than she thought possible. "Know this, husband. From this day forward no other woman will ever touch you as I'm touching you. The only woman who will ever feel you like this is me." She ground her pelvis into his erection. "I will fight for you until the day I die."

Luke turned her onto her side pushing at the dress. When she kicked it off her legs his hand trailed along her skin leaving tendrils of fire where he touched. "Be prepared to touch me often, wife, for you are the only one I will seek to warm my bed." He kissed her deeply as he pushed the breechcloth from around him. With the removal of the ties to the breechcloth and nothing to hold them in place the leggings slid down as he moved his leg over hers.

His frown when he encountered her boots made her giggle. "Shall we finish undressing, my husband?"

Luke snorted as he struggled to sit. "This has got to be the most difficult time…"

Cory laughed when she saw Luke's blush, surprised that he would be embarrassed. "I'm not stupid, warrior. I know you've been with other women. That doesn't bother me as long as they stay in the past. You will just have to teach me what pleasures you and have patience." She helped remove the last vestiges of their clothing, frowning when she saw the red, swollen line that ran down his leg.

"Teaching and patience go hand in hand, my dear." He murmured in her ear as she tossed their clothes together. Pulling her back down to the bedding he traced the worry lines in her face. "Don't think about my leg this night, Running Eagle. This night I make you my wife as I have dreamed about for so long. When we get to Washington D.C. I shall have the leg looked at." Capturing her lips, he let his free hand roam the curves of her body. When he thumbed her nipples into tight peaks he inhaled her moan of pleasure. As her free hand roamed over his buttocks he captured it, bringing it and their bound hands to the sides of her face.

She submitted to his hold until he suckled at the very nipple he just thumbed into hardness. Her back arched and she struggled to gain release of her hand. Luke smiled around the nipple. 'Not tonight' he thought. 'Tonight, I will prove to you that I'm a true warrior for I will conquer your fear as I have your love. I will teach you how to be the woman you are, my dear. Then you shall never worry about how your body responds to mine. I will show you what true love is, and I'll wipe those horrible memories from your mind and your dreams forever.'

When her back arched again he quickly tucked her free hand under her body, knowing that if she touched him, his firm control would be shattered. "Now, my little Eagle, I'm going to show you how to soar." He whispered as he nuzzled her neck. "When you float down I will climb the heights with you, and we shall soar together."

Slowly he worked his hand down her body until he could part her womanly folds. She stiffened as his fingers gently rubbed her nub but not for long. Soon he was once again inhaling her moans of pleasure. Cory arched against him, her body pleading. Luke did not deny her. He suckled first one breast then the other.

As he scooted down her body, trailing kissing along the tight muscles of her stomach to her hips, she once again stiffened when his mouth replaced his fingers on her nub. "Luke?" She exclaimed with a mixture of hesitancy and excitement before she gained a greater height.

His name this time was breathless, and she struggled harder to free her imprisoned arm yet the weight of her body against her arm refused her release. "Not yet, my dear. But soon. I'm going to take you over the edge first." Rubbing his fingers around the opening he felt the moisture his lovemaking was creating. A smile creased his face as he inserted two fingers within her, stretching her in preparation of his entry.

Luke fought for control as her body enfolded his invading fingers. She was tight, hot and moist. He knew the moment she felt his fingers. Her eyes opened wide with the blush high in her cheeks. Luke ignored her reaction, bringing his mouth to follow his fingers. Her head buried in the bedding as her hips rose to meet his onslaught. Her strangled moan was almost more than he could resist. His grin grew when he felt her insides spasm around his fingers. 'Over the top, my dear.' Luke thought as he moved his fingers inside her as his tongue continued its assault. She shuddered, her bound fingers tightening on his wrist. "Luke…I'm going to explode." Her words made Luke smile again, as his tongue brought her over the edge. Only when she was soaring did he stop to watch the pleasure etched in her face.

Her breathing was ragged as she floated down from the heavens. Luke stretched out to watch as she finally touched earth again. Tears welled in her eyes. Startled Luke gently kissed them away. "What are those for?"

"You received no pleasure. You're still hard and…" She folded her body against his.

Luke laughed softly pulling her face up. "That was only to prepare you for the invasion of my body, my dear. I did receive pleasure. Feel how hard I am? Next time it will be my body and not my fingers that will invade your womanly sweetness and we will meet our height together. We will soar to the heights together."

Once again, he allowed his hands to assault her body as his mouth claimed hers. "I told you I would taste every last inch of you." He whispered before capturing her breasts again. "I will do it again and again, my lovely wife. Every day of our lives together if that's what it takes to release the inhibitions you have."

Cory rose quickly to his skilled tongue and hands. Lava was flowing through her veins threatening to ignite her body from the inside out. Her heart was beating so quickly she had difficulty catching her breath. Butterflies had taken up permanent residence in her stomach. "Luke, join with me." She whispered frantically.

Unable to control his own need he was helpless to resist her pleading. Bracing his weight over her, he captured her lips as he slipped inside her. This time as her warmth surrounded his erection it was her that inhaled his moan of pleasure. She felt full inside and moved to accommodate his hardness. The action brought him inside of her with force. She could feel him straining to hold himself still as her body adjusted to his. Cory felt the sharp pain he warned her of before she was consumed with a fire of her own. Her hips rose in rhythm to meet him and he knew he was lost. Luke strained to hold onto his release. Pleasure fogged his brain with each mind-blowing thrust. Somehow, she managed to free her non-bound arm and it was now wrapped around his waist pulling him tighter against her. As he struggled to slow her frantic pace, to hold on to his release, he realized it was she who conquered.

When he felt her body spasm around him he surrendered, his explosion beyond his control, his body shuddering as she milked every last seed from him. Collapsing against her, breathing ragged, he tried to roll to his side knowing he was too weak to accomplish even that.

Cory was the first to recover. As one she turned him onto his back. "I love you, Bright Arrow." She whispered planting tiny kisses along his neck and chest. Luke moaned with pleasure when her hand began exploring his body. "You invaded my dreams since the first time I met you and no matter how hard I tried I could never banish your memory. When I realized it was you who grabbed me the night of the shooting I knew I could never banish you. You were already buried deep within my heart, the same heart that hurt when I saw your wounds. The same heart that cried when I thought you didn't recognize me. The same heart that feared you would die and leave me without anyone again. The same heart that loved you."

Luke pulled her against him, wrapping her tightly in his arms. "I was so frightened I would be recognized by Grover's gunmen I took a chance you would help me. I really didn't recognize who you were until we were in your house together. Even then I didn't believe you recognized me. I was hurting too bad to know much of anything other than I knew you would help me and that you offered a safe haven from Grover's men." He was startled when he felt the warm tears falling on his chest. Gently he pulled her face where he could see her. "What is it, Running Eagle? Why the tears?"

Quickly, she wiped the tears away. "I'm just being silly. I guess it's the stress but..."

Luke sucked in a deep breath, rubbing the tense muscles of her back. "You miss not having your family here on this special day. Don't you? Is that why you cry?"

"I miss not having my parents and grandmother, yes. I know they're watching from heaven and I'll have to accept that." She wiped at her tears. "I told you I was being silly. I have you to hold me now. I have you to fill my days as well as my nights." Bracing herself on her arm she wiggled up his body until she could capture his lips. Hungry for him again she explored his mouth, running her tongue over his teeth and lips. As his hand tightened around her waist she deepened the kiss. When her hand started traveling his body she inhaled his moan of pleasure. That moan ignited the lava within her. She was grinning when she ended the kiss. She was determined to explore his body as he had done to her.

Luke was surprised with the quickness Cory brought him to hardness. He was even more surprised when she tugged his arm from around her. The kisses she planted along his neck set his heart to hammering and he closed his eyes, enjoying the sensation she was creating within him. God, he loved this woman.

Cory straddled him, kissing the pulse bounding in his neck. Her eyes were shining when she moved to the nubs on his chest. As she suckled him she could hear the growl of pleasure that purred in his chest. Stretching beside him she curled her leg on top his erection, rubbing gently as her hand ran lightly along his ribs.

When Luke tried to turn over she blocked his attempt. "My turn." She whispered. "You've explored my body, given me more pleasure than I ever dreamed possible and now I shall return the experience."

Pleasure fogged Luke's brain as he surrendered. He didn't think it possible to be so hard after just making love, but he was. He became even harder when Cory wrapped her hand around his erection. His lungs burned, and he tried to draw a deep breath. "Running Eagle…"

Cory grinned when Luke failed to continue. Curiosity got the better of her. She was strangely calm now Luke was no longer making love to her. "What do you taste like, husband?" She whispered. Her grin became wider when she heard his moan. His eyes were closed, face flushed with pleasure. Running her hand lightly over his ribs she followed her fingers with kisses. Mischief gleamed in her eyes when she held his erection again. Slowly, watching the pleasure on his face, she wrapped her lips around him and suckled on him.

Luke shuddered when his world spun with bright lights of pleasure. Her mouth was warm and insistent. "Running Eagle. Stop." He gasped, tugging at her. "If I'm going to come I want to do it inside you. Sit on me."

"What if I don't wish to stop?" She asked breathlessly. "What if I wish to taste you like you tasted me? What if I want to continue doing this?"

When she replaced her lips around him, he shuddered before pulling her next to him and rolling on top of her. "That will be left for another day, my dear. Right now, I want to be inside you." The want in her eyes belied the grin on her face. Luke nuzzled her neck before assaulting her breasts again. She was soon drowning in the tide of feelings he was creating, fighting to keep her moans from being heard. Luke chuckled as his hand found her nub. "Don't fight the feelings, my dear. Soar with the eagles but let me hear how much I please you." He whispered nipping on her ear. "The greatest pleasure for a man is to know beyond a shadow of a doubt his woman is enjoying what is being done to her. It heightens the pleasure."

"This was...supposed to be...my turn." She gasped as fire threatened to burn her from the inside out. "Stop, Bright Arrow. Let me do this."

Luke did stop. As one he rolled again pulling her on top once more. "Just remember." He growled. "I want to be inside you when I explode and not in your mouth either."

Cory struggled to settle her rapid heartbeat and drew a long, ragged breath. "I will." She mumbled capturing his lips again. "I love you, Luke. More than I can ever say." Again, her lips traveled down his body until she captured his erection. Once again, she was calm now Luke was no longer in control.

Luke wrapped his free hand tightly around the blankets they lay upon, wanting her to stop at the same time he prayed she would continue. When his fingers tightened on her wrist she moved from his erection back to his neck. Straddling him she slowly lowered herself, feeling the fullness as he was buried deep within her. She closed her eyes, enjoying the feeling while trying to adjust to the fullness of him inside her.

Luke didn't move. He was afraid to. After several calming breaths he opened his eyes to see Cory watching him, a smile on her face. Reaching up he captured her breast in his hand. Her head fell back as he rubbed the nipple into a tight peak. Curling up he snaked his arm around her waist, pulling her on top of him again.

She gasped with pleasure when her nipples rubbed against his chest. She gasped again when his hand slid between them and he rubbed her sensitive nub. "Stretch over me, sweetheart. I want to nurse on you." He whispered. Mindlessly Cory obeyed. As his lips surrounded her nipple she wiggled which caused him to bury deeper inside her. Luke let her set the rhythm. She was slow at first but as her need grew so did her rhythm. Luke knew he was losing control and tried to slow her frantic movements, but she wouldn't be denied. When her muscles clamped down on him in spasms Luke connected with her in a frantic kiss as he exploded within her. They inhaled each other's moans of bliss.

Without a word she loosened the ties that bound them, curled tightly into his body, head over his heart and fell into a deep and peaceful sleep.

# Chapter Thirteen

CORY NERVOUSLY TUGGED AT THE black skirt she was wearing as she stepped to the door of the funeral parlor. Her father taught her that mental preparedness was ninety five percent of keeping her cover safe. She worked all afternoon trying to gain that mental preparedness.

A gentle smile slid across her face as she remembered how difficult Luke made that. Taking a deep breath to steady her nerves she entered the funeral parlor. Fred Adkins was by her side instantly. "Hello. My name is Fred Adkins. Have you come to honor Greg and Rafe?" His voice was loud enough that several heads turned.

"Yes." She gave a ghost of a smile to Fred as she looked around. "Is Mrs. Waltz around? I would like to express my sympathy."

"Right this way, Miss…"

"Sims. I'm Corena Sims." She held out her hand pleased when Fred followed her lead. "Are you a friend?"

"I worked with both Captain Waltz and Rafe DeAngelo." He was escorting her into the main room. "I'm sorry we had to meet under these sad conditions. The men had a lot of friends. How did you meet them?"

"My father worked with them. It's a shame for them to die that way. Good men should die with honor."

Paula was approaching, holding her hands out to Cory. Tears were in her eyes as she held the younger woman. "I'm so happy you could join us, my dear. I knew you would come. How are you, my dear?"

"I'm doing well, Mrs. Waltz. I'm sorry for your loss. Greg was a good friend to my father as well as a partner." Cory stiffened when a man entered her line of vision.

Sensing the change Paula turned, motioning the man forward. "This is Major Thoms, Greg's boss. Major, this is Corena Sims. Her father worked with Greg."

"Miss Sims. It's nice to meet you."

Cory swallowed hard when the Major took her hand. Slowly she pulled it from his grasp. "I'm sorry for your loss, Major. I'm afraid I didn't keep up with things after daddy died. How long have you been with the agency?"

"Since Major O'Grady retired, my dear. I took over his position. A lot has changed since that time."

The devil danced in her eyes. "More changes are to come." At the look of surprise in his eyes she swallowed her laughter. "It will be difficult to find good men to replace Greg and Rafe. The new men coming in to replace them will make a tremendous difference with those left to work with them. The new people will create great changes in the office." Another man stepped behind Thoms causing Cory to swallow the fear and bile that rose within her.

"Major Thoms. You shouldn't keep this lovely lady all to yourself." The man admonished, shoving gently on Thoms' shoulder. Grabbing both her hands he drew her into a secluded corner. "May I introduce myself? My name is Jason Grover. I knew both men. Who do I have the pleasure of addressing?"

Corena tried to politely reclaim her hands from his only to have his grip tighten. "I'm Corena Sims. My father used to work with Greg and Rafe. I thought it only right I should come tonight and express my sympathy to Mrs. Waltz."

"I'm glad you did." Jason purred stroking her fingers as his eyes narrowed on her. "You seem familiar. Have we met before?"

Cory shrugged, once again trying to free her hands from the grip of Jason Grover. "If we have I don't remember. You see, I was severely injured several years ago, and the loss of blood affected my memory.

Much of my past is nothing more than a blur. My memory is focused during the last three years. Anything before that time, are only scrap pieces of images that pop into my mind. I'm sorry."

Jason turned her hands over in his, gasping at the cut on her left hand. "My goodness. What happened?"

Cory blushed. "Nothing much. I've been camping since the riots started. I'm afraid I was rather stupid while chopping ice for my drink. My hand slipped down the knife I was using." She shrugged. "It'll heal."

"You should have a doctor check this out. It may leave a scar."

She looked into the black eyes of the man that made her feel dirty simply by his touch. Swallowing hard she finally found her voice. "It will only be one of many."

Jason tugged on her hand. "Let's see if we can find a first aid kit. I'll help bandage this."

As he tried to pull her from the room she retreated, pulling her hands from his with force. "I have already treated the wound, Sir. I need to go to Mrs. Waltz. Thank you for your concern but it is nothing to worry about."

"It's amazing how much that wound looks like one obtained when a person is joined in the Indian ways." His eyebrows arched toward his perfectly combed hair. "Do you happen to know any Indians or been to any Reservations recently? It might help jar your memory."

Cory was deep in thought. Finally, she sighed. "If I do I'm afraid I don't remember. How do you know so much about Indians?" She started walking back to the center of the room praying Jason would follow.

Clasping his hands behind his back he did follow her. "I had a college roommate who was an Indian. He was very proud of his heritage and we talked often of his tribe's ceremonies. Did you know they swear protection to one of their own or they put special items into caskets when their warriors die?"

"Amazing. I didn't know that. What kind of items?" She was once again beside Fred. "Mr. Adkins, Mr. Grover was just telling me about the Indians and their strange practices. He was just about to explain what they put in a warrior's caskets upon their deaths." She turned back to Jason, feigning interest when every instinct told her to run. "Please. Continue. It's an interesting subject. Maybe I should check a book out on it in the library."

"I would also be interested in knowing, Mr. Grover." Fred turned to the man who radiated evil. "Especially since Luke Patterson was a Native American. He was a special friend and mentor to me."

"Who is Luke Patterson?" Cory turned bright eyes to Fred. "His name seems familiar."

Jason glared at Fred. "He was with the agency for years." Jason stated before Fred could speak. "He was killed in a bust gone bad."

Cory sighed. "So much tragedy. When was this?"

This time Fred answered, his eyes becoming teary. "The night of the riots. Twelve good men died that night. Now the Captain and Rafe's names will be added to the list of those killed in the line of duty."

Cory patted his arm. "I'm sorry for your loss, Mr. Adkins. When my parents died, I..." She scrunched her face up as if trying to remember. Finally, she waved her hand in the air, sighing deeply. "I can't remember what I did after they died." Another sigh. "Sometimes it's hard to remember any part of my life past the last two or three years." Tears shimmered on her lashes. "It is so difficult when a person can't remember. So much is lost to me. I wouldn't have remembered Greg and Rafe worked with daddy if it hadn't been..." She sighed, shrugging again. "No matter. I remembered and now I'm here. They've aged since the time my father took pictures of them. I had to go through the family album to finally convince myself I should be here. Such a waste."

"You're here. That's all that matters." Grover patted her shoulder. "What do you do for a living, Miss Sims?"

"I used to be a nurse however I resigned before going on vacation. I had difficulty remembering things. My memory loss is becoming worse, you see. The doctors are hopeful the medicine will help. Right now, I have plans only to travel."

Again, Jason's eyebrows shot up. "I've traveled quite a bit. Any place in particular?"

"I don't know yet. Wherever my feet takes me is fine with me. If I hadn't cut my hand and needed the first aid kit I left on the table I wouldn't be back yet. I hope if I make new memories I won't miss the old ones so much."

Fred's hand rubbed her back in sympathy. "They have food and drinks downstairs. Would you like something?"

"No, thank you. I need to say goodbye to Mrs. Waltz. Streets confuse me in the dark." With that she stepped away from the two men. Jason, she noticed when she reached Paula's side slid immediately to Major Thoms' side. "How are you doing?" She whispered to Paula.

"Fine. Is Greg really all right?"

"Healthy and unhurt." Cory whispered. "He's worried about you and sends his love as well as a warning to be careful. He's told you what to do tomorrow?"

"Yes, but I hate this."

Cory kissed her cheek. "You would hate it even more if he were caught now. His life is still in danger. This was the only way to get a message to you. Hold to the truth that good always conquers evil. Luke should make his appearance before long. Play your part well for I don't want my husband to be injured again."

Paula's eyes twinkled as she looked at Cory. "Congratulation, my dear. Luke is a good man. I'm so happy for the two of you."

Seeing Major Thoms and Jason approaching Cory pulled her emotions into the pit of her stomach. Her face was composed when they reached her side. Major Thoms took her hands squeezing them lightly. "Miss Sims, Jason has told me you were getting ready to leave. Can one of us offer to take you home? It would be no trouble."

Cory shook her head. "No thank you. I appreciate the thought however my doctor says it's best for me to do this. He feels that even though I get lost I will learn to remember better if I stretch my memory." She smiled. "Besides I like being lost. You see so much of the city that way." Turning back to Paula she clasped the older woman's hand. "I'm sorry for your loss, Mrs. Waltz. You must forgive me however I can't remember your first name."

"Paula." She squeezed Cory's hands in return. "Thank you for coming, dear. You be careful out there. Many idiots run the streets this time of night. Perhaps I could get Fred to take you home."

"Fred?" Cory chewed on her lip as she contemplated the name Paula mentioned.

Paula nodded in Fred's direction. "Mr. Adkins. He's very nice and I think you would be good for each other. He is terribly depressed since Greg…" Tears filled her eyes. "Come. I'll ask him." She pulled Cory with her as she headed toward Fred. Jason and Thoms followed, frowning. "Fred, would you please accompany Corena Sims home? She has a terrible time with getting lost. It would relieve my worry greatly if you would do this for me."

Fred took Cory's hand as he gave Paula a weak smile. "It would be my pleasure, Mrs. Waltz. It's the least I can do…" He sucked a deep breath.

Without another word Cory allowed Fred to pull her to the front doors while Paula turned to Jason and Thoms. "I'm so upset. How am I supposed to pay the bills? How am I going to survive?" Her voice died away as Cory left the building on Fred's arm.

"That was close." Fred murmured as he handed Cory into his car.

Cory giggled, excitement showing in her eyes. "We're being watched. Pull down the drive and around the corner. I want to watch when Luke makes his appearance. I want to make sure he doesn't get injured. We'll pick him up at the end of the block."

Fred ground his teeth together as he started the car. The skin was crawling between his shoulder blades as he maneuvered the car down the block. Cory was sitting close to him, watching out the rearview mirror when another car slid to a stop behind them. He was stiff with surprise when Cory slipped her arms around him, kissing him passionately. "Play along." She hissed. "We have a tail and they're watching us."

Guilt riddled him as he wrapped his arms around Luke's wife, pulling her tight against him. The tap on the side window told him Cory was correct. He stiffened, pushing her away from him, quickly pulling his suit jacket into place before turning to the person outside the window. He swallowed hard seeing Major Thoms' angry face. He took a deep breath as he slowly rolled down the window.

"Just what the hell do you think you're doing, Agent Adkins? You're supposed to be taking this woman home not molesting her."

Before he could answer Cory put her body in front of his, right hand on the wheel, face in the window and eyes snapping with anger. "I beg your pardon, Sir. What business is it of yours who I kiss much less who kisses me? I may not have much of a memory but by God I know when I'm attracted to a man and when I'm not. Is there some problem with my kissing Mr. Adkins? I like him. You may be his boss, but you have no control over his private life."

"Your father wouldn't have approved, and you know it."

"My father? My father has been dead for..." She scrunched up her face. "for a long time. Mr. Adkins was just being kind. I like him."

Thoms, anger showing in his eyes raced around the car jerking the door open. "Get out, Corena. I'll take you home myself. Fred return to the funeral parlor."

Cory sat back in the passenger seat arms crossed over her chest, huffing. "You're not my father and I'm a big girl. I don't want you to take me home. I want Fred to take me. At least he doesn't yell at me."

"Stop being such a child." Thoms yelled. "Stop whining and do as I say. Get out of the car this instant."

"No." Cory stamped her foot on the floorboard. "What do you plan to do, Major? Do you think you can assault me? I would press charges in a heartbeat if you did. If you touch me I will scream my head off. I want you to leave me alone." She huffed, pushing back against the seat, chin jutting out in stubbornness. "I like Fred. There is nothing you can do about it. As I said, I'm a big girl and can make up my own mind."

"Corena Sims, I must insist."

Cory saw a flash of gold buckskins move from behind the tree. "Fine." She huffed, slipping her legs over the edge of the car. "I'll go home with that biker guy I saw over by the tree. At least I wouldn't have to worry about getting poor Fred in trouble." She leaned over, kissing Fred on the cheek.

"Biker guy?" Thoms asked peering into the darkness beyond the streetlight, confusion showing on his face. "What biker guy?"

"That one." She pointed to the tree. "Hey mister. Will you give me a ride home? This idiot is bothering me."

Luke stepped from around the tree dressed in burial buckskins. "I want my knife." He howled into the stillness.

Cory looked in confusion. "What knife? Boy, this night is really getting spooky." Fear crossed her face as she slid back into the car. "On second thought, maybe I will have Fred take me home." She cried as she slammed the door shut, pushing the locks down on her side before crawling over Fred to lock the doors on his side.

"I want my knife." Luke howled again before the light bulb popped and the street went dark. Thoms turned white, running to where Luke had been only seconds before.

"Get us out of here." She hissed after quickly scanning the darkness. She could see no sign of Luke and breathed a sigh of relief. "We'll pick him up later, after Thoms leaves the area. We don't need to draw any more attention to ourselves or to Luke."

Fred nodded, put the car into gear and hit the gas. He had a hard time controlling his own fear that rose in him when he saw Luke step around the tree. An eerie feeling crawled along his spine to settle between his shoulder blades. Even though he knew Luke was not a ghost his performance made a believer out of him. As they turned the fourth corner he relaxed his grip on the steering wheel. "You're good, Corena. When this craziness is over are you going to return to the agency? You could go back into undercover."

Cory snorted. "I doubt it. My security clearance has been destroyed thanks to O'Grady. I always wanted to teach new women recruits. That will never happen now." She shrugged while trying to banish her anger. "It would take quite a bit of explaining but maybe I can get my job back at the hospital although I hated it there. I've always hated being a nurse." She sighed deeply. "A lot depends on Luke. I love him too much not to be there for him. I will probably end up being a housewife although I hate the thought but will probably love every minute of it even though spending days alone doesn't sound in the least bit interesting to me. I just wish I knew what to do about the twins when they return."

"What about them?"

She shrugged. "They have one year left before they graduate high school. I hoped they would go to college however I could never afford to send them. Carrie Ann wants them to live with her in Oregon. My poor sisters have been shuffled around a lot since my parents died."

"What do they want?"

A deep sigh escaped her. "I honestly don't know. It was different before I was married. I only dreamed of Luke loving me and never planned to marry so raising the twins never troubled me even though money was always a constant consideration. They will need lots of things that will cost once graduation approaches and with no job that may present a problem. Now there's Luke to consider as well as the twins. My house is way too small for all of us to live in comfortably. I thought to sell it but without a job I would never get a loan."

Surprise filtered across Fred's face as he pulled to the side of the road two blocks from where they last stopped. Switching off the engine he turned to her. "Why not live at Luke's house once this is over?"

Cory laughed ruefully. "His apartment is smaller than my house. Do you really think the four of us can survive being piled together in that tiny area? No thank you. The twins need room to move about. Besides Luke only has a one-bedroom apartment." She was watching the subdivision for signs of Luke and missed the look of amusement that crossed Fred's face. "I wonder where he is."

Fred got out, stretching as he scanned the area. A feeling of dread was beginning to settle in the pit of his stomach as his skin crawled between his shoulders. Luke should have met up with them long before now. "How long have we been driving around?"

"Over a half hour. Something must have happened to Luke. Give me your gun, Fred." She put her hand out even as her eyes searched the darkness around her.

Shock showed in his face. "He could still be trying to evade Thoms. We should give him more time."

"Time is something he may not have. Give me your gun, Fred. Now isn't the time to argue." Hesitantly he placed the gun in her hand. "Stay here and be ready to help me if I call." Slipping off her shoes she faded into the shadows of the night.

Cory melted into the shadows, her black skirt, blouse and nylons helping to hide her position even more. Senses on alert for any sound she raced back to the place she originally saw Luke. Slowing her frantic pace as she approached the tree she scanned the area watching for signs of the direction Luke would have taken.

Bending close to the ground she scurried forward peering around the tree. Major Thoms car was gone, the light still dark. Breathing a sigh of relief, she knelt, surveying the ground. She could see where the grass had been disturbed. Two sets of prints could be seen in the soft dirt around the tree, one hard soled, the other soft soled. One print of the soft soled showed deeper in the soil and Cory knew Luke left that when he limped away. They pointed to the center of the subdivision. Tracking Luke was hard in the dark. She could only spot scanty signs of his passing. The grass was laid over where his leg dragged, flowers with broken heads, always leading to the center of the subdivision. She could find no signs that Thoms had followed after the first several feet and she was thankful for that small gift.

When she came around a dark building a car approached. She shrank back around the house before the headlights could reveal her position. As she hugged the building her hand came into contact with something warm and sticky. Fear surged through her when she realized it was blood. Was this from Luke's leg or from another injury he suffered? Did Thoms shoot him again? She rejected that having heard no sound of gunshots. Although she saw no other signs of blood she knew that which was on her hand had to be Luke's.

Grinding her teeth against the fear that swirled around her, she sucked in a sharp breath to steady her runaway thoughts. "Luke?" She whispered. "Where are you warrior? Give me some sign, sweetheart."

Cory heard a hissing sound as the car circled the subdivision. She pushed tighter into the wall as it swung in her direction. When the car passed her without detection she moved to the next house. Ducking under the lighted windows she hurried toward the position she heard the hiss. "Luke? Where are you?" She whispered again.

"Over here Running Eagle. At the back of the next house. Stay low. They're coming around again."

Cory fell to the ground, hidden by the flowers that were in full bloom. She could hear people inside talking, commenting about the frequency of the car which passed in this quiet neighborhood. Her breath lodged in her throat when she heard the man suggest the woman call the police. Once the car turned the corner she hurried to the next house thankful the windows were dark.

"At the corner, Running Eagle. I hurt my leg. You'll have to help me."

Sliding beside him she gathered him in her arms, breathing a prayer of relief. "You scared the hell out of me. How bad are you hurt?"

"That bastard shot at me." Luke grunted. "He missed but only because I dived behind another tree. I think he was shooting at shadows because he fired off another three rounds after the one he fired at me. When I landed my leg hit the tree. It hurts like hell."

"You're also bleeding. I found blood on the house three doors down. How am I going to cover that?"

Luke moved to look around the house. "Is it noticeable? How much blood is there?"

"Not much but enough to raise suspicions if anyone happens to look really hard. I can try to wipe it off and then return for you. Whatever we do we need to do it quickly. The people in the last house are worried about that car. I heard them talking about calling the police."

"Help me over to the house with the blood. If we make it that far, we'll worry about our next action." Luke struggled to gain his feet only to plop back to the ground with a groan. "Maybe not."

When the car circled again Cory risked detection to look at the injury. Luke strangled a moan as she pulled the legging down. Her concern reflected in her eyes as the car passed their position. "You've torn the stitches loose Skywalker put in." She stripped off one of her nylons tying it tightly around his thigh. "If I help do you think you can stand? We need to move."

"If I don't we'll both be dead."

Cory grimaced at the guilt that laced his words. Wrapping her arms around his waist she pulled him to his feet, steadying him when he swayed. When he nodded she put his arm around her neck, half pulling, half carrying him to the previous house. She propped him against the wall trying to decide how to get him around the lighted windows without detection.

She could hear the man and woman inside. "Go to the back window, Millie. Watch for that car to come by again and see if you can get the license number. I'm going to the kitchen to call the police."

Cory sent a silent prayer of thanks heavenward as she moved back to Luke. "We need to hurry. Those people are all in another part of the house now and we can get by their house without being detected." She lifted him back into her arms. Pain shuddered through him with each step he took. After she got him to the car she would have to come back and check for signs of blood, she knew. Her first concern was getting Luke close enough for Fred to help.

She could hear the police sirens coming closer as she moved to the house where she found the blood. Not much, she noted, quickly wiping it away with her skirt. Once again, she pulled Luke along. Flashing lights darted along the darkness as both the car that was circling the subdivision and the police car pulled to the side at the far end of the street throwing eerie shadows around them. Cory leaned close to Luke and whispered in his ear. "Hang on, Luke. We have to cross this street and then cut through the next subdivision. Fred is waiting for us."

"I'm trying, Cory. I hurt so damned bad." He drew a deep breath as she leaned him against a tree.

"Rest. I need to check behind us."

"No." Luke hissed.

"I have to. If any of your blood is showing they will know you're alive and not a ghost. They'll never stop looking for us if that happens and you know well I am correct. Too much is planned to ruin it now. It won't take long. I will be right back." She kissed him quickly and then ducked below his arms and disappeared into the night.

Luke closed his eyes against the pain only to have them open a few seconds later when he heard a noise close to him. Slowly, his hand moved to his back withdrawing the knife he had hidden there. "Bright Arrow." Turtle's voice reached him. "We're here to help." As he lowered the knife Turtle came around the tree. "Where is Running Eagle?"

"My leg is bleeding. She went to cover our tracks."

Turtle motioned with his hand and three more warriors came from the darkness, Laughing Bear among them. Kneeling next to Luke he examined the leg, frowning when he heard Luke's strangled moan. Turtle turned to the others. "Running Eagle has gone to cover their tracks. Laughing Bear will come with me while you get Luke to Agent Adkins. Tell him to get Luke to Running Eagle's home." He whispered. "Your house is being watched. We'll bring your woman home." He assured Luke.

As Turtle started to rise Luke grabbed his arm in a viselike grip. Turtle swallowed hard as he knelt beside Luke again. "Kill them if you must but don't allow them to hurt Cory again." Luke's eyes were hard with anger.

Turtle nodded. "You'll have to carry him. Take him now." He commanded softly before rushing in the direction Luke told him Cory had gone. The two men almost missed seeing her for she blended in so well with the darkness. She was nothing more than a shadow that moved. They approached the darkened house with caution only to find she had already disappeared. "Now what are we supposed to do?"

"How in the hell should I know?" Laughing Bear hissed. "I failed to catch her last time she ran. What makes you think I can catch her this time?"

"You never could nor would." Cory whispered coming around the corner of the house. "I could have easily killed both of you if I had not recognized the two of you. What are you fools doing here?"

"Skywalker sent us." Turtle peeked around the corner at the two cars down the street. "They won't be there forever. Bright Arrow is on his way to your house. Are you ready to leave before things get worse?"

"Yes, but that may be impossible right now. Jason Grover arrived a short time ago and he has several men with him. They are searching the area as we speak. I found a way into this house. Follow me."

Silently she slid around the house leaving the other two to follow. After a quick look around, she flipped up the window screen, pushing up the glass. A small hop took her over the top. The others followed as they heard people approach. Cory moved through the house on silent tread gaining the front room in time to hear Jason Grover's voice. "So you saw Luke's ghost. Since I don't believe in ghosts you will forgive me if I doubt your story."

"How did he know the knife was missing then?"

"Someone must have told him, you fool." Jason growled. "Use your head, stupid. If that was Luke's ghost why did Corena see him?"

"I have no idea. All I know is I shot right at him and he just disappeared without a trace."

"Did you find any signs of blood?"

"No. What did you do with the knife?"

"I have it. The next time that bastard is buried it will go with him. Right in his heart. How he managed to survive I can only guess. I thought at first it was that Sims woman who came to his aid however since talking with her tonight I think her mind is so far gone she wouldn't have known him even if she saw him. You'll have to get Adkins to tell you where he dropped her off. I think I'll make a return visit to see if I can shake her memory loose. I want to see the fear in her eyes again. This time I won't be under orders not to rape her. She is one beautiful piece of meat I will enjoy taking." His laugh set shivers of fear up her spine.

A hand wrapping around her mouth startled her. "Shhh. If he hears you he'll find us." Turtle whispered in her ear.

Laughing Bear followed their movements around the house until they were out of sight. When he returned he found Running Eagle with her face buried in Turtle's chest, sobbing harshly. Kneeling beside the two he rubbed her back. "I thought they found us when she whimpered. We need to stay here for a while until they move on. Bright Arrow and Running Eagle are supposed to be at the airport by two this morning. Will we make it back to her house in time for the flight?"

Cory drew a deep breath before lifting her face. "Yes. I refuse to let those bastards win. The first step to stopping them is to get to Washington D.C. and get some power behind us. Then we'll watch them fall."

# Chapter Fourteen

THE STEWARDESS SHOWED THEM TO their seats before taking Luke's crutches. "Is there anything I can get for you? Coffee maybe?"

"No, thank you. My husband and I just need a little rest. It has been a busy night."

The stewardess pulled down two pillows and blankets. "I hope you have a chance to sleep. The weather all the way to Washington is clear so we shouldn't hit any turbulence. If you need anything just let me know."

Cory nodded, watching with fascination as the plane prepared to take off. Luke closed his eyes almost as soon as he sat down. The pain medicine she insisted he take was taking effect. She kissed his lips as she covered him with the blanket. His hand came up to capture her neck. "You told me those damned pills wouldn't make me sleepy. You lied, woman."

"I did not." She grinned, kissing him lightly on the lips. "I said they don't make me sleepy. They don't. I never took them. Grandmother didn't believe in pills and I used the herbs she kept on hand instead."

"You still lied."

"Does your leg hurt now?"

"Hell no. Nothing hurts. I barely have enough feeling in my body to move. I hate feeling like this."

She kissed him quickly as she turned off the overhead light. "Rest, husband. We will be in Washington by the time you wake up and our busy day will start again. By this time tomorrow night, you may need another pill whether you like it or not." She kissed him gently again as his eyes closed.

Luke was too tired to care as sleep claimed him. He was confused when he awoke. Something heavy was lying on his shoulder and his right arm felt numb. Years of training set caution to his movements as he slowly opened his eyes. The flight attendant came quickly to his side. "Your wife is sleeping, Mr. Summerfield. I was just going to try to move her. She looks terribly uncomfortable."

Reality rushed in on Luke when he saw the stewardess. Turning slightly, he held Cory with his left hand while he struggled to get circulation back into the fingers of his right hand. "Lay the pillow in my lap and then help me lower her onto it. She probably won't wake up."

"That won't be comfortable for her or you."

Luke chuckled, fully awake now. "We've slept in worse positions since knowing each other. This will just be another."

The stewardess helped lower Cory onto the pillow Luke placed in his lap. Cory struggled to awaken until Luke folded her against him. The stewardess was impressed the way this newly married couple helped each other. She remembered reading that they were going to D.C. on their honeymoon. She was glad to see the love shining in the handsome man's eyes for the woman as he tenderly fingered her hair. "We should be landing in about fifteen minutes. While the other passengers leave the plane, I'll bring your crutches. If you leave last there will be less chance of getting hurt. Can I get you anything?"

"Coffee?"

"Coffee it is."

Luke sipped at the coffee wondering how he was going to get Cory out of the office long enough to show Richard the picture. He hated to see the pain he knew would be in her face if she ever saw it. Anger surged threatening to choke him.

"Bright Arrow?" Cory's soft voice floated up to him. "Is something wrong? I can sense your anger."

Luke smoothed the hair from her face. "Only at Jason Grover. I'm sorry I put you in danger last night."

She straightened, grimacing when her muscles balked at being disturbed. "How close?"

Her long hair was in disarray and she never looked so cute to Luke as at that moment. "We should be landing soon. Are you all right?"

"Better than you are husband. I want you to have that leg looked at while we're here. We can talk to Richard while we wait on doctors." At the sight of his tight lips she kissed the twitching muscle in his cheek. "You know as well as I that you need medical attention. Get it done now so we can see this thing through to the end together. You'll be in terrible pain if you wait and that may interfere with the plan. If the leg becomes infected and the fever returns, you will not be well enough to finish what is started."

Luke sighed knowing she was correct. "All right. I'll go to the hospital but they're not going to admit me. Whatever they want to do will have to be done in the Emergency Room or we leave right away."

Cory chuckled as she heard the stewardess over the intercom informing them to fasten their seat belts in preparation of landing. After landing the stewardess arrived with the crutches as promised. "What does your cousin look like?" Cory asked, her hand nervously pleating the ends of her shirt as they left the plane.

Luke laughed quietly. "You can't miss him."

Cory took a deep breath as she stepped into the main building. She glanced around but her attention was mainly on Luke. His face was white, and his breathing was ragged as he stopped again to rest. "Cory." His soft whisper came to her. "I think I need to sit down."

She was beside him instantly trying to keep him from falling. She knew he was going to pass out just by the look of him. Kicking the crutches from under his arms she slowly lowered him to the floor. Kneeling beside him she lowered his head between his legs, forcing herself to ignore the people around her. Someone handed her a wet towel and she rubbed it over his face as well as his neck. "Open your eyes, big guy. We need to get you to your cousin. He'll know where to take you for the best medical care we can afford."

"An ambulance is on the way even as we speak." The man next to her stated. The deep voice which sounded so familiar brought her head up. She was looking into an exact duplicate of Luke. Her surprise must have been written in her face for the man chuckled. "I'm Richard Stevens. I presume you're Luke's wife."

"Cory?"

"I'm here, Luke." She pulled the upper half of his body up, leaning him against the wall. "Feel better?"

"I feel like a fool. Is Richard here?"

"Open your eyes." Richard chuckled. "I'm right beside you. I have an ambulance on the way. Whatever happened, you can tell me later."

Luke nodded, holding tight to Cory's hand. "Remember, woman. I will not stay in the hospital. ER only or I go home."

Richard laughed shaking his head in disbelief. "Never got over your fear of hospitals. Have you?" The sirens drew his attention. "The ambulance is here, Luke. Young lady? If you give my partner David Watts, your luggage claim tickets he will meet us at the hospital with them." With another chuckle Richard waved the paramedics over to their position.

★ ★ ★ ★ ★

Cory stared at the two men trying to decide if she could trust them. Luke was going through a series of x-rays and MRI's so there was little to occupy her mind besides worry. Richard Stevens requested she explain all that happened while they waited. Richard could pass as a twin to Luke with the exception of his hair being two inches shorter. David Watts was another story. He was older, much older, with gray hair and a quiet attitude that told Cory he knew much more than he was saying. He held authority in his stature and his silence confirmed her suspicions that he held some higher rank than that of a field agent.

He was surprised when she asked for his ID but relinquished it without comment.

When she handed it back, Richard chuckled. "Trust me, Cory. He is one of the good guys." He was actually Richard's superior. "I trust him as Luke trusted Greg or Rafe. I met both men while visiting Luke at the ranch. Can you fill us in on what's happening?"

Cory did, starting with her father. As she spoke she pulled the graphs and charts from the briefcase. Richard noticed the envelope, picked it up and had to school his face when he saw the contents. Quickly he stuffed it under the other papers while Cory looked worriedly toward the hall for the doctor. She just finished explaining how Luke injured his leg again and their rescue by the tribe's warriors when the doctor came into view. She rubbed her sweaty palms down the front of her shirt as she stood.

"Mrs. Patterson?" The doctor called looking warily at the other two men. "I need to talk to you about your husband."

"This is Luke's cousin and a friend of the family. What you have to say to me, they are allowed to hear." She said smoothly. "How is Luke?"

"He told us several pieces of glass were already removed from the wound on his leg. I'm afraid we found another. It's deep in the muscle, at the same angle as the bone and will need surgery to be removed. The surgeon is currently talking to your husband however he is adamantly refusing to sign the operating permit. We need you to sign it, so your husband can be taken directly to surgery before more damage is caused by the glass."

Cory gathered her hair into a clip. "I would like to see those x-rays before I agree to anything. Richard and David will come with us."

"I need to ask you about the other two wounds, Mrs. Patterson. They look suspiciously like bullet wounds."

Cory laughed softly. "That's exactly what they are, doctor. I would like to see my husband now."

As the men stood Richard slipped the envelope with the picture into his pocket. The staff refused to allow him in with Luke earlier and was grateful Cory included them. He had a lot of questions for his cousin.

The doctor's back was stiff with anger as he led the way down the hall. Luke's angry eyes met them. He was now in a hospital gown, another doctor examining the leg while a nurse attempted to start an IV. From the look of it she wasn't having much luck.

"What do you think you're doing?" Cory demanded looking at the nurse. "If you don't know how to do that then stand back and I will start the damned thing. His veins are big enough to float a ship in." Amusement laced both pairs of chocolate eyes when Cory pushed the nurse aside. "I'm sorry Luke. Had I known the nurses were this incompetent I would have done this myself before I went to talk with Richard." With quick, effective movements, she slid the needle into the vein, quickly taping it in place. The doctor examining Luke's leg stared at her in shock. When she was finished she looked the doctor in the eyes. "Now, I presume you are the surgeon. I want to see the x-rays."

"There's one piece of glass left, and it lays along the bone. It will need to be removed."

Richard and David moved to Luke's side when the doctor moved to the lighted screen holding numerous x-rays. "Did you find the envelope?" Luke whispered while fear was heard in those words. "Cory didn't see it. Did she?"

"Yes I found it and no, she didn't see what was in it. Whose reflections are on the wall?"

"There are three. The man with the knife is the bastard that cut Cory up. The older one next to him is Major O'Grady, now retired and the younger one is the current Major, Thoms. Hold it to the mirror. They show up well and there is no mistaking who they are."

At Major David Watts look of confusion, Richard slipped him the envelope. With a grin he pulled the hospital gown back and examined the damage on Luke's skin. "Got hurt bad this time. Didn't you? I thought I taught you better."

"Those are bullet wounds." The doctor stated the obvious, a dark frown on his face as he moved back to Luke's side. "He told me he was with the FBI. You need to talk to him about this injury. I assume you are his supervisors?"

"You can assume what you want." Cory stated firmly, anger making her eyes hard. "I want to know about my husband."

"Your husband needs surgery, not only to remove the glass but to try and repair the leg. If left unattended he'll never be able to work as an agent again. He is stubbornly refusing to sign the permit."

Cory slipped her hand into Luke's. "Can the glass be removed here in the Emergency Room without taking him to surgery?"

"It could however the repair can't be done here. It would also be very painful. He needs to go to surgery."

"Can you guarantee you can fix the leg?"

The question startled the doctor. He hesitated at the hard look in her eyes. "I need to take him to surgery to try…"

Anger sparked in her eyes. "The question requires only one of two words, doctor. Yes or no. Can you guarantee you can fix the leg?"

"There is never any guar…"

"Yes or no, Doctor." She ground out.

The doctor ran frustrated hands through his hair. "No, Mrs. Patterson. I can't guarantee I can fix the leg. I can only try. The glass did a tremendous amount of damage. I'm surprised this man is able to walk on the leg at all considering there is still glass in it. I want to try to fix the damage while I'm getting the glass out."

"That will be hard to do considering the glass will be removed here or I will remove it once we get to our motel room."

Shock shined in the doctor's face. "It's obvious you have some medical knowledge Mrs. Patterson but I doubt you have the knowledge to do something like this. My God, woman, do you know how much pain your husband will suffer? Even with pain medicine to control it?"

Cory leaned close to the doctor's face voice menacingly quiet. "Who do you think removed those bullets from his body, you idiot? He suffered lying in my bed while I probed for those bullets and then suffered more while I sewed him back together. It was even worse when the glass was removed, not once but twice. If you do it here, in this room, he'll have medicines I didn't have to keep him comfortable. The choice is yours, but he will not be admitted to any damned hospital. We have only been married for two days, doctor.

"So far in the past month my husband was shot twice. Injured further when he jumped through a window to get away from those wishing him dead. A cougar attacked me, and he was shot at again last night. I'm tired, both physically and mentally and I really don't give a tinkers damn what you think you can do. I'm only interested in results. When I leave here my husband goes with me whether that piece of glass has been removed or not. Now the decision is yours and that decision is simple. Do you remove the glass here in this room where you have the medicine to control his pain or do I remove it when we get to ours?"

The doctor retreated from the anger in her eyes. "Since both of you are determined, I'll remove it here. You, Mrs. Patterson, will have to stay in the waiting room until I'm finished. I request you leave the room now."

Luke struggled to sit up, anger radiating from him. "Cory, get me out of here."

"Mr. Patterson!"

Luke jerked the front of the doctor's shirt so hard the man almost fell across the bed. "You're not going to touch me unless my wife remains with me."

"Luke, release him." Cory commanded softly prying his fingers off the doctor's shirt. "I think he understands I won't leave your side."

The doctor nervously looked from Richard to David as he straightened his attire. Seeing he would get no help from the other men in the room he nodded to the nurse. "Bring me everything I need. Be sure to get a scrub suit and mask for Mrs. Patterson." He looked at Richard. "Are you two staying?"

Richard chuckled. "No doctor. I'll leave my beeper number with your nurse before I leave. I have some planning to do at the office. Cory? I'll be taking the briefcase with me. Let me pull my men together and brief them. When the hospital notifies me, I'll return to take you and Luke to my house. Both of you need to rest for a few days while we pull this thing together within the agency."

When she nodded, the men left. "That woman is a wildcat where Agent Patterson is concerned." David mused. "I've never seen anyone whose eyes reflected anger so vividly. So, what was in the envelope?"

"Your eyes are still as sharp as ever, Major." Richard's grin did not meet his eyes as he exited the room. "Look for yourself." He heard his supervisor gasp as he stopped at the nurse's station. When they entered the car, Richard slid behind the wheel. "I believe from what I heard in that room the woman in the picture must be Luke's wife. That would explain why he didn't want her to see it. After seeing the picture can you handle an interview with Luke tonight, or shall we get someone else?"

"It's been a long time since I worked the field. I believe it's time to get back into that line of work for a while." He looked at Richard, eyes filled with confusion. "Can I ask you something?" Seeing Richard nod David tried to form his thoughts into tangible words. "Do you really believe what she told the doctor?"

"Which part?" Richard grinned. "Grandfather called me after they left. He wanted to be sure Luke saw a doctor about his leg while he was here in Washington. What Cory told the doctor was an abbreviated version of what happened. She not only helped Luke escape after he was shot she removed the bullets from him while he was lying in her bed. Once they were at the Reservation she saved Luke's sister by facing down a cougar. When Agent Adkins called I had him fax me a copy of her file. It's under the seat if you're interested."

Something in the way Richard's voice became quiet warned David and he sucked a deep breath. Apprehension filled him as he reached below the seat. Silence reigned as he read the file. "This is Luke's wife, Cory?"

"Yes. The man who did that to her is the same person who shot Luke. Now you know how dangerous these men are. We'll have to be very careful in the next few weeks. Too many good men have already lost their lives to the evil of Jason Grover."

Major David Watts had the images made into individual photos before calling his men together. After bringing them up to date on what Cory told them he passed around the pictures. "As you can see from the damage done to the woman in the photo we are dealing with some very dangerous men who get enjoyment out of hurting people."

Silence reigned as the men adjusted to what they were seeing. "Who is the woman?"

"She was an agent. Since her recovery she resigned from the force. Her security clearance has been reactivated as well as her status with the agency. What you see here is classified, gentlemen. Her husband is also an agent injured by the same bastards who did that to his wife. He is very protective of her as she is of him. Don't think that because she's a woman you can dismiss her. Both she and her husband will let you know right away if you anger them. Since you have worked with Richard Stevens I must warn you, the men are cousins and look like twins. When you look at Luke Patterson you would swear you were looking at Richard. Now, we plan. I'll turn this over to Agent Stevens."

Richard stepped forward. "As the Major stated these men are very dangerous. I talked with my cousin when we were alone last night, and he filled me in on all that happened. His wife doesn't know of our conversation concerning her and Luke wants to keep it that way. He also filled me in on a plan the two of them have been working on. Because of Corena's fear of Jason Grover slipping from our fingers they want to bring them down all at one time. Jason Grover by the way is the one that butchered Corena."

"Can she be trusted?"

Richard looked out over the concerned faces of his men. "She can be trusted enough to give her life for you. Any of you. A copy of her file has been pulled. Anyone who doubts her ability, or her devotion is welcome to review it. Luke and Corena will be here in one hour to explain their plan. Luke has requested no one mention the photos you have before you and I think you can understand why. Corena is very sensitive to the scars she carries. That's why they aren't here now. I'll answer all questions I can concerning her at this time."

"How experienced is she?"

"Corena Sims Patterson never lost a partner the entire time she worked for the undercover unit in the Chicago Office until the day she was captured and tortured. She was one of a handful of women to work that unit and she worked most of the assignments where a woman was needed. Major Watts called several of the men she was partnered with. Although Corena has never taken credit for any bust they all credit Corena's ability to keep a clear head in an emergency and her deadly accuracy with a gun to saving their asses. Each one stated they put her in for accommodations for bravery."

Richard tried to think of the right words. "Corena is one of those people who does her job every day to the best of her ability and in such a way no one notices she's even there. Her partners say she has a gift for reading a situation…a special sense about her that warns her when there's danger. That gift and the courage to go in under fire to save her partners are what endeared her to those she worked with. It was also the reason for their request for the accommodations of bravery they each put in for her."

"She is decorated?"

"No. We investigated that also. All the letters are in her file. It appears her supervisor at the time, Major O'Grady, managed to stop all accommodation requests from ever going farther than her file."

"This Major O'Grady. He's the one Miss Sims worked so hard to prove as a traitor?"

Richard smiled. "Call her Corena, Cory or Mrs. Patterson, gentlemen. Corena married my cousin, Luke Patterson, a week ago. She is very proud to be his wife and she will correct you immediately if you call her Miss Sims. To answer your question, yes. She finally had the proof she needed when she was sent on her last assignment. I know many of you wonder why she didn't press the issue once she found the proof or why she resigned. Several things happened.

"Corena was and still is raising younger twin sisters. When she found the proof, she was sent on the assignment causing the destruction you've seen. While she was recuperating a box was delivered to her house with pictures similar to that one, warning her to silence. Her captor told her he would do the same to the twins. What would you have done?"

A murmur ran through the room before the next question was raised. "Captain, if her last assignment is the one where this mutilation occurred how disfigured is Mrs. Patterson?"

Richard grinned. "I'm going to wait until you meet her and let you decide for yourself."

"Captain? If Corena is going to be working on this case which I assume from this talk that she is and will be heavily involved, what happens if she freaks?"

Richard sighed. "Corena will be allowed to see this to the end. All feel that is her right considering what happened to her. I have deliberately withheld much of the information concerning this case because I feel Luke and Corena can explain it better. This is something Corena has worked for over the last five years. Her only reason for working with us now is to clear her father's name. As you can tell from the pictures her life was ruined. Without her we would still be working on suppositions and guesses. To answer your question, I sincerely doubt that will happen. I'll be working with her and I'm fully prepared to pull her off the case if she becomes a threat. Once again please wait until you meet her before making any decisions. I wouldn't put myself in the position of getting my head blown off if I didn't believe she could handle anything that was thrown at her. Next question."

"How involved will the other three, Captain Waltz, Agent DeAngelo, and Agent Fred Adkins, be in bringing this case to a close?"

"Very involved. Luke and Corena insisted on it before they would tell us what happened. Major Watts did a background check on all the men and all check out to be good guys. As with any situation like we're involved in they must also be watched however I have met both the Captain and Agent DeAngelo several times and believe they are on our side."

"We are going into this situation blind, Sir. Is there a contingency plan in case something goes wrong? Will we have time to scout the area after we arrive? If something should go wrong will we know who to depend upon for backup?"

Richard chuckled as the questions flowed around him. "Slow down, gentlemen. As I said before I have refrained from giving you much information because I want Luke and Corena to explain the plan they have devised. If any of your questions aren't answered after they're finished feel free to ask them. Knowing Luke, he has already thought about many of the things you have questions for and can settle any fears that may arise. For now, please stick to those questions concerning Corena."

"It's obvious you admire this young woman, Sir. I'm concerned about placing my life on the line with her. I know from experience how losing a partner affects a person's thinking. They either become so upset over losing the partner they judge a situation too quickly and react from fear or they hesitate a second too long and another partner dies. I would feel better if she didn't come along."

Once again Richard waited for the mumbling to settle down. "Let me tell you what happened in the last month." Richard told how she saved Luke from the gunmen, removed the bullets and then told of her experience on the Reservation. Eyes became wide when he told of the cougar attack and chuckles went around the room when told how she faced the doctor in the Emergency Room. "She won't let any of you down, gentlemen. She is a special lady even if her past is filled with pain. I'll be working with her and will be placing my life in her hands once this thing gets started. I trust her, and I think you will also. Any other questions?"

When no further questions surfaced Richard stood, seeing Luke hobble into the outer room with Corena at his side. "Very well, gentlemen. Since they are here I shall do the introductions and turn this meeting over to them. I think you will be satisfied with the plan."

Richard controlled his laughter with difficulty seeing the shocked looks on the men's faces when Luke entered. Once Luke was seated Corena took his crutches and placed them against the wall then stood behind him. "Gentlemen, this is Luke Patterson and his wife Corena

Patterson. First they are going to tell you about their investigations and then they'll explain the plan they've devised to catch these people." Richard brought a stack of files to the desk, pushed an overhead projector forward before lowering the screen behind the couple. With a nod to Luke he retreated into a corner of the room.

Luke drew a deep breath, rubbing at his left leg. "First we need to go back five years. How long the mole was in operation before that we don't know. Five years ago, Ralph Sims told me he thought he was being set up. He said information came too easy and he had gone to Major O'Grady with his suspicions. O'Grady told him he was losing his nerve. Ralph was due to arrest a small-time drug dealer named Jason Grover." He nodded to Cory and she placed an overhead film on the projector and the image of Grover appeared on the screen. "This man is Jason Grover. He is without a doubt the most heartless bastard I have ever known. Ralph was worried because Grover swore vengeance the day Ralph arrested him. The day Grover was convicted, Ralph and his wife were blown to pieces outside the FBI building in Chicago."

Cory took over. "After daddy's death the FBI sent me a notice stating the funeral expenses wouldn't be covered because of an investigation O'Grady was doing into my father's assignments. When I faced O'Grady concerning this he told me that my father was the mole and threw a file across the desk at me. I was determined to prove the agency wrong. Daddy had already fingered O'Grady. I just needed the proof. While I was searching for that proof I came across many things that indicated another mole was working with O'Grady. The harder I looked the more O'Grady tried to destroy my reputation within the agency. My assignments became more dangerous and I was always paired with inexperienced agents. When I was successful in completing them, I was assigned a desk job. Unfortunately for O'Grady it gave me the time and access I needed to find the proof on him."

She drew a deep breath before continuing. "Major O'Grady was married to two different women. One was named Grover. The other named Toms. The Grover woman came from the bad side of town.

Her father was one of the city's major drug and arms dealers. She gave birth to this man." Cory nodded her head toward the screen.

"The Toms woman came from the rich side of town. Her father worked closely with the governor. She gave birth to this man." She swapped Grover's picture for that of Major Thoms. "Both men were sired by O'Grady however neither carry his name for when he divorced the wives he insisted they resume their maiden names. Eventually the second wife married a man named Tameron and gave birth to a girl, naming her Susan. She is currently working as a secretary in the agency under the direction of Major Thoms. She is another we must capture." Once more Corena changed pictures.

Luke continued. "I was assigned by Major Thoms to go undercover for a gun running sting operation. Grover was the head of the operation and bragged that he knew I was a plant just before he shot me. I warned Captain Waltz of a mole for some time. Like Ralph, the information came too easily. The night of the riots Major Thoms pulled every experienced agent off the bust and as a result, eleven good men are now dead."

Seeing Luke's eyes darken with distress Cory knew how hard this was for him. She continued. "Greg Waltz was also investigating especially after he met with myself and Luke when I finally got Luke out of the city. Rafe DeAngelo found a bug in his office phone warning Greg of the same. That evening they made arrangements to meet. Suspicious of events that happened when Greg talked to his wife, she was sent to stay with her sister while Greg delayed his return home. They were on the corner of the block when the house exploded around them. Right now, Luke, Greg and Rafe are considered legally dead. That will work in our favor."

Luke had his emotions controlled again. "Six nights ago, I made a ghostly appearance at Greg and Rafe's memorial service however my wife had already left with Agent Fred Adkins who is another trusted agent and Thoms followed them. I made a special appearance for his sake." He chuckled. "That scared the hell out of him. Scared him enough for him to take several shots at me. Thank God his aim has not improved over the years, but I did hurt my leg again which prevented me from escaping as planned. My wife came to my rescue." The men in the room cleared their throats to keep from laughing when a blush fanned Cory's cheeks. "When she went back to cover our tracks she was almost caught by both Thoms and Grover. She can tell you about that for I was already on my way with Agent Adkins."

"Both Grover and Thoms were together. I could hear them talking. Thoms believes Luke is a ghost however Grover is convinced Luke is still alive. So far, my part in the rescue is not known which will also work for us. Grover wants to find me so he can…" Cory licked dry lips as she sucked a deep breath. "Part of this plan is to let him find me. I've already surrendered my proof on O'Grady but there is no concrete evidence on Thoms or Tameron. The only way to catch them is to trap them. That's what we're here to explain." She turned off the projector, standing in the corner.

Luke continued. "O'Grady is retired and living a comfortable life. We can pick him up anytime. The problem is the other three. Thoms and Tameron follow the instructions given them by Grover. Jason Grover is the brain behind the moles. Make no mistake about it. Since taking his grandfather's place he can reach places others only dream about. After his short stint in prison he has never been captured again.

"Only twice do we know for certain that Grover personally supervised a job. Once when he captured my wife and once when he shot me. Because he's so slick at getting away we need to capture them together. If he escapes…" Luke closed his eyes for a few seconds and then continued. "Corena has devised a plan to catch all three. I want you to remember what's said for all our lives depend upon your performance once the plan is put into motion. Since this plan is hers I'll let her tell you about it."

Cory blushed when all eyes turned to her. "When I went to the memorial services for Greg and Rafe I encountered both Major Thoms and Jason Grover. I had a convenient loss of memory that night. When we return, and the trap is set, my memory will return. I'll go to Major Thoms and tell him I remember Grover and name him as the one who…" She took a deep breath. "name him as the one who captured and tortured me. I'll tell him I'm willing to swear out a warrant for Grover's arrest."

"Won't that put you in greater danger?" David Watts gasped while trying to tamp down on his fear.

Cory grinned evilly. "That will put my right in the middle of this mess. Yes. I know I no longer carry status with the agency, but this is the only way to get the three of them together. I'm sure by now they know I have the proof I need on O'Grady they just don't know how much I have stuffed in my head or what I have on them. They won't allow me to live. Luke and I have argued over this but it's the only way to ensure the safety of your men and still take them down at the same time."

Watts shifted uneasily. "I don't like this one damned bit, but let's hear the rest of your plan before I decide."

"Thank you." Cory's smile was sad. "I plan on meeting him at my father's grave. He's buried in the middle of the cemetery and there will be more than enough places to hide your men. I need to have a wire, so the conversation can be recorded. I'll tell Thoms I'll hand over the proof on O'Grady at that time."

Luke saw the tears brimming on Cory's lashes and gave her time to compose herself. "Thoms will believe what he's heard and is assured to call Grover. This is something Jason Grover won't miss. I know him, and he takes great pleasure in torturing and hurting people. He'll be there, and you can bet he'll be watching everything from the time he gets the call to the time he arrives. His caution and intelligence is what kept him out of prison this long. Once his position is known regardless of whether or not Thoms is around I want that bastard taken down. If the other two get away, we'll deal with that later. Grover is the dangerous one. He needs to be taken out first or he will disappear without getting justice."

"What happens if they fail to show?" A man in the back asked.

Cory snorted. "Have no fear of that, gentlemen. They know I'm holding all the cards. O'Grady knew. That's why he ordered Grover to capture me. Thoms was puppet to O'Grady as well as Grover. That's also the reason why they will never pass up the opportunity to kill me." She stepped forward. "Make no mistake about it, gentlemen. Jason Grover has no heart. He is dangerous to the health of all who get in his way. I'm willing to put my life on the line to capture this bastard and clear my father's name. I only ask three things of you. Protect my husband, capture Jason Grover and try to keep me from getting killed. This man cut my partner up just to listen to his dying breath. He will do no less with any of you. If something does go wrong be prepared to shoot to kill for Grover won't give you a second chance." The room was quiet when she moved behind Luke once more, placing her hands on his shoulders.

Major Watts slipped another film on the overhead projector. "The cemetery is old with only four entrances." He pointed them out. "I want twenty-four-hour surveyance on all the entrances the moment we arrive. I want that cemetery wired for sound and video. Everything that happens that day must be recorded so there is no doubt in anyone's mind what happened. I want two men to each entrance. If anyone comes I want to know about it immediately. Due to the age of the cemetery most of the tombstones in this area are large enough to hide behind. Just because the action will take place in front of Ralph and Caroline Sims grave be sure to watch your asses. Jason Grover won't walk into anything smelling like a trap without first scouting the area. He is just as likely to kill you as look at you."

Turning off the projector he turned slowly to his men. "Agent Patterson has made arrangements through his grandfather to house all of us for the duration of our stay. You will have three days before the plan will be put into effect. On the fourth morning we'll go to the cemetery while Mrs. Patterson goes to the office. We must be ready when Corena sets the trap into motion. Any questions?" When no one spoke, he turned to Luke. "I need to make arrangements to get things started from this end. You look like you need to rest that leg."

Luke grimaced when he tried to stand, sitting back heavily in the chair. Richard stepped forward at the same time Cory did. In one swift motion she had Luke on his feet. "Captain take Luke and Corena home. Luke needs to rest that leg if he plans to help capture these guys. That's an order, Luke." He stated when he saw Luke was ready to argue.

Cory looked worried, Luke was scowling, and Richard was laughing when they left the office ten minutes later.

# Chapter Fifteen

L UKE WAS, ONCE AGAIN, IN the grips of fever when they were met at the visitor's center. She had the antibiotics the doctor at the hospital ordered yet she saw few signs that they were working. "I'm sorry, Grandfather." Cory sighed as she pushed the wet towel over Luke's face. "I didn't think to take my herbs with me. Washington has nothing but concrete and well-manicured lawns. I could find none to help Bright Arrow."

"Lone Wolf said much the same since moving there." He patted Richard on the back, ignoring the stares from the others. "You can tend Bright Arrow's wounds when we arrive at his house on the Reservation."

At her suspicious look he laughed softly. "His house, Running Eagle, not mine." With a movement of his hand the warriors began unloading the luggage into the waiting jeeps. Skywalker turned to Richard. "Have your men divide up with the warriors for they will be staying with them while helping here. You and one other will stay at Bright Arrow's house. Greg and Rafe are also staying there awaiting your return. It will give you time to discuss this plan and devise a plan in case something goes wrong."

Skywalker laid his hand on Luke's forehead, frowning before turning to Cory. "Lone Wolf called and told us about the glass and fever. I have already gathered the herbs needed to tend his injury." His voice held caution. "He won't be able to go with you, Running Eagle and that will worry him all the more."

Cory worried her lip. "I know, Grandfather. He must be kept sleeping when the plan goes into action or he will insist on coming."

Skywalker lifted her head, eyes narrowed as he studied her. "You have seen something. Tell me what was in your vision."

"Not here. I will tell you when we're alone." She whispered. "Not here. Please, Skywalker? I don't want Bright Arrow to hear."

He released her, tamping down on his curiosity. The ride to Luke's house was longer, the house sitting in a small clearing. Skywalker smiled at the gasp he heard from Cory. "He has four bedrooms in the house." He spoke quietly as they pulled to a stop. "The master bedroom will be more comfortable for him than mine. The warriors will hold him as you apply the poultice. It will be much like the last time."

Tears filled her eyes as the warriors gently lifted Luke from the jeep. Greg and Rafe waited with her until the last of the men entered. "He will survive, Cory. Between your knowledge of herbs and your love for him there is no doubt in my mind." Rafe whispered, squeezing her hand for encouragement. "His love for you will keep him fighting to live."

Nodding, she pulled her emotions together before entering. She only had enough time to see the spaciousness of the living room before Richard stepped to her side. "Skywalker is fixing the poultice now. Once the injury is tended we all need to talk about this plan. Nothing can be left to chance. I do not want to have any of my men injured or dead. Besides, my cousin will kill me if anything should happen to his lovely wife."

Nodding, she moved to Skywalker's side. He was waiting for her beside a doorway she assumed to be the bedroom. The warriors had removed Luke's clothes and he was covered except for his leg. Tears threatened when she saw how infected it was. "I'm ready." She whispered to Skywalker.

Richard helped hold his hips while the other warriors surrounded the bed. Luke's eyes captured hers. "I'm sorry, Bright Arrow." She cried as she placed his arms around her waist. "This will hurt as much as the last time." His hands threatened to tear her in half when the poultice was laid against the injury. Anger threatened to consume her when Luke faded into unconsciousness from the pain.

Richard pulled her from the bed, taking her to the outer room while the warriors covered Luke. Skywalker, a cup of tea in his hand, was beside her when she finally folded onto the couch. "Drink." He commanded. "This will strengthen you."

Suspicion crossed Cory's face as she remembered the last time he told her that. "No thank you. I need to keep my wits about me. My life hinges on my ability to think clearly."

Skywalker laughed at the confused faces around him. "It is not sleeping tea, Running Eagle. Few besides Bright Arrow will sleep tonight. The warriors wish to listen to your plan as do Greg, Rafe and I."

Cautiously, Cory accepted the cup of tea. Before explaining the plan, she turned to Rafe. "Luke told me you recognized the building which they tortured me in. I need to know where it is."

"Corena." His eyes reflected his concern as he shook his head. "I can't do that to you."

"Don't refuse me, Rafe." She laid a reassuring hand on Rafe's knee. "When I go to Major Thoms the morning we enact this plan, I'll need something I can feed to him, so he believes what I say. If he asks me where I met Jason Grover and I can't name the building he'll know this is a trap. I need all the information I can get. This time, it's stuffed in your head."

Seeing Richard nod, Rafe sighed. "I recognized the floor tile you were laying on. It was a blue rose pattern on terra-cotta tile. Ralph commented on it when we were there, and Grover bragged he had the tile imported for the building." He got up to pace. "Do you know the tall skyscraper on the corner of Fifth and Pine streets? The one with the mirrored glass windows?" Cory nodded. "That's where that bastard cut you to pieces. From the pictures I would say he did it in his office." Cory rubbed at her forehead as memories assaulted her. Seeing her face go white Rafe knelt in front of her. "I'm sorry, Corena. I knew this would hurt you."

She gave him a weak smile. "It's all right. I needed to know. Thank you, Rafe. Now, I need to tell you the plan we will enact in a few short days." The men listened as she explained the plan she devised. Silence hung heavy around the room when she finished. "I only pray things go as planned."

Greg sat forward. "What is your contingency plan should this go sour? If somehow this plan backfires?"

Cory shrugged. "I'll have to kill the bastard myself." She growled. "I refuse to live my life in fear and I'm tired of running. Bright Arrow may never be able to work undercover again but he can work as a trainer. I had a vision, Greg. In the vision Jason Grover had Luke. Something was coiled around his neck, drawing blood. We battled, and I traded my life for his."

"Running Eagle…" Skywalker's voice reflected his worry as he came to her side.

"Don't argue, Grandfather. This is the only feasible plan, and everyone knows it. Without me Jason Grover will never come to the cemetery. The other two are minor players in this horrible game. I have to be there to protect Bright Arrow. The vision showed me that much. I'm scared but there's nothing I can do about it. Grover and O'Grady are to blame. In four days my father's name will be cleared, and my husband will be safe from the evil that threatens his life. Greg and Rafe can resume their lives. It will be over one way or the other. Four days."

She stood, stretching. "Right now, I need to get some sleep." Tears shined in her eyes. "Just keep Bright Arrow asleep, Skywalker, until this is finished. If we are blessed after this is over, I'll return to be by his side forever. If not, don't let him spend his life grieving for me." Shaking the tears from her eyes she walked past the men to enter the bedroom.

★ ★ ★ ★ ★

Cory stopped at Susan Tameron's desk. "I need to speak to Major Thoms, please."

Tameron smiled, sending icy tendrils of fear up Cory's spine. "May I please ask what this is in reference to? Major Thoms is rather busy today and may not be able to see you."

"You may however I'm not required to answer. Tell the Major that my name Corena Sims and I remember. Everything. He will see me. I can damned well guarantee it." She moved to a chair and, with more calm than she felt, sat to wait.

It didn't take long before Tameron was standing in front of her. "The Major will see you now Miss Sims."

A vague smiled crossed Cory's lips as she followed Tameron into the office that was once O'Grady's. Major Thoms stood. "Have a seat Miss Sims. Your message intrigues me. Do you mind if my secretary stays?"

Cory shrugged. "I came seeking your help. You may have heard I was investigating the death of my father five years ago. I finally found what I needed. The proof that there were traitors within this agency. I found it the same day as my last assignment. That was the day I was tortured. After I recovered I remembered little of what happened to me or what was in my past. The doctor told me it was because of the loss of blood and that someday there would be something that would trigger my memory causing it to return. Seeing Jason Grover the day of the memorial service triggered the return of my memory."

Thoms' hands were shaking as he shuffled the papers in front of him. "I see. Just what do you remember?"

"All of it. I remember who butchered me and killed my partner that night. I remember where I hid the proof I found. I even remember thinking there was another mole in the agency and of looking for the proof of my suspicions. Because of that I'll surrender the proof at a place convenient for both of us. I don't trust many in this agency especially after what happened to me. I think you can appreciate that fact. I may be unusually cautious, but I have to be after being tortured. I'm willing to swear on the stand to what I found. The proof is irrefutable, and the traitors will go to jail for a very long time. I'm also requesting a warrant for arrest to be issued for Jason Grover."

"I would like to see this proof before I go through all the paperwork of getting an arrest warrant. Do you have it with you?"

"Do you think me a fool?" Her eyes snapped with anger. Cory drew several cleansing breaths. "My parents were blown apart when their car was bombed. I told some of my memories to Greg and Rafe but my memory at the time was shaky at best. Now they're dead." She shook her head. "No, Major. I'm no fool. Since all I ever wanted was to clear my father's name I will meet you at the cemetery. At their graves I'll surrender to you all the proof I have providing you have the arrest warrant in hand for both Major O'Grady and Jason Grover."

"Major O'Grady?"

Cory almost laughed at his wide eyes that showed his shock, his hands trembled, and his face turned white. "Yes. Major O'Grady. You see, he was the mole that got my parents murdered. I have hard evidence and that evidence will clear my father's name."

"Who else have you told about this evidence?"

"No one. After Greg and Rafe were murdered I was afraid to say anything. Once I returned from the memorial service and my memory returned in full I needed time to gather the information I hid. I don't want any more deaths to occur because of what I found. Do you meet me? The choice is yours. You can help bring down the most wanted man in America or I shall seek help from the main office."

Major Thoms stalled. "Without proof it will be difficult to get an arrest warrant."

Cory snorted the angles of her face hard with irritation. "Don't stall, Major. I'm going to give you one hour to appear at the cemetery. After that I'll be gone, and you'll never get the evidence you need to make the next rank advancement in your career." She stood, smoothing the wrinkles from her shirt. "Do you meet me?"

"Sit back down Miss Sims. I need something more than your word these two people were involved. Even if I could get an arrest warrant the attorney will want proof. How do you know Jason Grover is involved?"

"He's the one that butchered me. Look in my file, Major. The photos from the hospital are there. You will be able to see the damage that Jason Grover did to me. I even have the note he left for me. Shall I tell you what building they took me to? He took me to Fifth and Pine. The building has those fancy windows that look like mirrors. The tile on the floor is terra-cotta and has a blue rose pattern on it."

Thoms swallowed hard. "All right. What do you have on O'Grady that will help me get the warrant?"

"O'Grady is the father to Jason Grover. After he divorced his wife she resumed her old name. O'Grady also ordered me on that last assignment. That's all I'll say for now. Meet me in one hour at the grave of my parents and I'll show you everything I have on the two men."

Major Thoms nodded slowly. "All right. I'll meet you if only to find out what you think you have. The information you have given me is extremely sketchy and I doubt I can get the arrest warrant until I have everything in my possession."

"I'll have to think about that." She stated cautiously, eyes narrowing on the Major. "Once I release my proof there will be no other copies and that puts me in a dangerous situation." She sighed deeply. "Meet me in an hour. Come alone." She saw Susan Tameron stiffen. "Since I don't know if the mole is still working I'm cautious. I think you can understand that feeling. I don't want to die today."

Major Thoms shuffled papers, thinking quickly. "I need to have my secretary, Susan, with me. I need a witness to what is discussed. I trust her." Cory worried her lip, indecision written on her face. "No one would believe what was said without witnesses, Miss Sims. You trust me enough to release the information to me. I trust her enough to keep her mouth shut about the happenings around here."

"All right." She sighed deeply her eyes narrowed in thought. "I'll agree to your secretary however I don't want anyone else to come. Since Greg and Rafe were killed I'm extremely cautious about the information I hold."

"I might have to bring one other person with me." Major Thoms stated hurriedly. "If you have the evidence you say you do, I want some back-up. I don't wish to die today either."

"Don't turn this into a flea circus, Major. I will disappear if you do." Her warning was clear. "I will see you in one hour." Turning smartly, she left the room, the two within glaring at her retreating back.

"Do you believe her? After all this time she has a convenient memory recovery? I don't like this at all. How do we know that she can be trusted? How much do you think she knows?" Susan whispered.

"I think the little bitch knows exactly what she claims she does." He sat heavily in his chair fear showing on his face. "Jason isn't going to like the fact her memory has returned. Neither is father." He worried his hair with his hands, his mind a tangle of thoughts.

"Do you think she knows about us?"

"Stop fidgeting, Susan. If she knew about us do you think she would be so brazen as to waltz into this office and proclaim she had proof? That would be a foolish thing to do. Use your head, woman. From what I remember of Corena Sims she was anything but a fool. We'll just have to meet her."

Susan paced nervously. "I guess you're right. If she should ever discover… I hate this."

"Well you never hated the money Jason supplied." The Major growled while reaching for the phone.

"What are you going to do?" Susan screeched.

"I'm going to call father. He'll know how to handle this." The continual ring of the phone caused his frown to deepen. Slamming the phone onto the cradle he glared at it. "Father isn't home. Now what?"

"Call Jason, you fool." Susan hissed. "Tell him what the woman said and verify what she told you is true."

"I was there that night. Remember? Everything she said is true, right down to the design of the floor tile." His hand shook as he reached for the phone. "Jason does need to know. I just hope his anger is not directed at me."

★  ★  ★  ★  ★

Peace flooded over Cory as she waited behind the tombstone of her parents. She was surprised to realize that she wasn't even frightened over what would soon happen. "This is for you." She whispered, gently rubbing the smooth marble surface. "Today, daddy, your death will be avenged." She stiffened slightly upon hearing the car approach. With a deep cleansing breath, she scanned the occupants of the car. Major Thoms was getting out of the driver's side as Susan Tameron exited the passenger side. Another man in a trench coat, collar up with a hat that hid his face got out the far side from the back seat. The man glanced around, searching. Cory knew this had to be Grover. She doubted he would stay behind.

"Miss Sims, I'm glad to see you. This proves you weren't just blowing smoke when you entered my office this morning." Major Thoms said as he approached.

She shifted her position behind the tombstone when the Major and Tameron blocked her view of the man who remained by the car trying to keep all of them in her line of sight. Every time she moved Thoms would shift again blocking her view. "I never blow smoke, Major. You should know that by now. Do you have the arrest warrants?"

Thoms shrugged raising his empty hands. "There wasn't enough evidence to convince a judge to issue them."

Cory laughed bitterly. "Where is your father? I'm surprised he didn't show up especially since you were the gofer for the mole."

Surprise crossed his face as fear showed in his eyes. "Just give me the evidence and we can all go our separate ways."

"I told you I was no fool, Major. You should have listened. Shall I tell you where your father is at this moment? Trusted men are currently holding him in a secret location. Your fall will be just as complete as his when I have Jason Grover arrested for the murder of my partner, and attempted murder."

"You seem so sure, Miss Sims. I wonder why."

Caution ruled her movements as she leveled the gun over the top of the tombstone. "Remove your hands from your pockets, Major. Tell your sister to drop her purse and have the other man step to where I can see him, or I will shoot you right where you stand."

When Susan Tameron tried to run Cory shot over her head stopping her in midflight. The gun instantly came back into position, pointing directly at Thoms' heart. "I'm no mood to be fucked with, Major. Why did you set Luke Patterson up? He was the best agent this agency ever had and will be hard to replace. Why order him killed?"

"He got too close, Corena." The man at the car sneered. He had moved during the ruckus and was now standing to her left, hands below the tombstone he stood behind.

She shifted her position slightly to bring all three into view. "Well, if it isn't Jason Grover. Now why is it I knew you would come? Raise your hands and get over here with the rest of the trash."

Jason laughed when he pushed the hat from his face, blood showing on his hands. "I'm afraid not, bitch. Tell your backup to come forward or Luke will be the next one you watch die." His black eyes glowed as he jerked up on Richard while his laugh echoed around the cemetery. "I see you really do remember my wonderful toy. Do you also remember what this same wire did to your other partner? As I remember he lost his head over it." He laugh was maniacal, his black eyes watching her closely.

Slowly Cory lowered her gun but kept it in her hands, praying no one would become trigger-happy at this point. "So, it's a standoff. Do you think his men are going to let you get away without trying to save him? You're the fool if you think I came here with only Luke to help me. You're surrounded, Jason. There's no way for you to escape except by surrender."

"Not me." He growled pulling Richard beside him. "I'll tell you what. I'll stake Luke to the ground and order these two idiots to back off if you'll do the same with your men. I've always been fascinated with you and your damned control. Face me. One on one. If you win you get to figure out how to release Luke before the wire cuts his head off. If I win," he shrugged. "I'll kill you."

She took a deep breath. "Luke. Don't struggle against the wire. It's spring action and will do exactly as Jason says." She warned all who was listening before returning her attention to Grover. "Now what?"

"You come with me and I'll show you how a real man feels. Once I'm finished I'll release my old college friend here or at least release the wire around his neck." Jason laugh sent chills over her skin.

Cory stepped around the tombstone keeping the gun pointed at Jason. "Tell you what, I'll come with you only after you release Luke." She could see the distress her words brought to Richard's eyes and shot him a warning look.

"I think not." Jason laughed as he stepped forward dragging Richard with him. "Tell your men to step forward where I can see them." He jerked tighter on the wire. "Now, Corena."

She circled away from the tombstone. "Gentlemen, as you can see we have a standoff here. Put down your guns and stand where this bastard can see you."

"Wired as well." Jason's eyebrows shot up, his grin looking more like a sneer as he nodded his appreciation. "Father always said you were smarter than most in the agency. I give them three seconds or Luke dies."

"Do as I say." She screamed. "Drop your guns and stand where Jason can see you or Luke will die."

Slowly, seven agents stood, throwing their guns in front of them. "Good, now drop your gun, Corena."

She stood her ground. "Not until you release Luke. If he dies you die. Plain and simple. You already killed Greg and Rafe. I won't have Luke injured further. We are still at a standoff, Jason. So? Now what?"

Jason's hand tightened on Richard's shoulder dropping him to his knees. "On the ground, old friend." He whispered. "Once the tension is released you'll be dead anyway. Until that time I'm going to make you watch what I do to that bitch." Raising his head, he growled at Thoms and Tameron. "Collect their guns. I want them to watch knowing they can do nothing to stop the death of this bastard Corena thinks so much of."

Cory laughed. "He's not the bastard. You are. No matter how much money or power you accumulate you can never change that fact."

Jason forced Richard to the ground, removing the knife from behind his back. "What do you say, Corena? Shall we finish what was started years ago?"

Cory swallowed hard at the fear that raged through her. "What do you have planned, Jason? Do you think I'm stupid enough to allow you to rape me in front of all these people without a fight?"

Jason stabbed the knife into the handles of the wire, trapping Richard on the ground yet keeping the wire from springing. "No, I suggest a competition. Just you and me. Winner gets to do with Luke whatever they please to do."

Cory gasped knowing that any movement on Richard's part will result in the untimely removal of his head. "Don't move, Luke. Don't even twitch or that thing will spring." She cautioned as she lowered her gun.

Jason's evil laugh threatened to overpower Cory as he gained his feet. "I always knew you were too soft for this game. Only your stubborn will to live allowed you to be here today. Kick the gun away and face me."

Cory did, and a calm descended over her as she looked into his evil black eyes. "Your brashness surprises me considering I have nothing to defend myself with. You said one on one. I don't consider this a fair fight. Or is it that what you are afraid of? Fighting fair?"

Jason removed two knives from the coat before pulling it off. One he threw at Cory's feet. "When a possession was in dispute the Indians would stake the prize to the ground and fight to the death." His eyebrows rose as he stepped across Richard. "Since Luke seems to be important to you we shall do as your ancestors did." He kicked Richard in the leg causing blood to flow from Richard's neck. "Here is the prize you must die for, bitch." Another evil laugh echoed around the cemetery.

Quickly Cory snatched up the knife, circling as she did with the cougar. "Not today." She hissed. "Today you will die. Remember Luke's saying? Good always conquers over evil. It will conquer today, you bastard." She jumped at him, arm raised, knife ready to kill.

Jason was surprised by the attack and they both fell, Cory on top of him. He moved enough the knife took a deep bite from his left arm instead of burying in his heart. Pushing her away he rolled. "So, the bitch can fight."

Cory saw the anger growing in Jason's eyes even as his voice remained soft. She stayed cautious as she circled Richard's body again praying the anger would work in her favor. "I can see why O'Grady never claimed you. You're a spawn from hell, Jason and I'm going to send you back there."

"Not today, bitch. Today I will remind you how it felt all those hours while I used this knife on you. You didn't scream then but I'll listen to you scream today before I'm finished with you. I can guarantee that."

When he came at her, Cory sidestepped bringing the knife down on his back. "My turn, bastard. That is only two of those you placed on me."

Caution entered his eyes as he watched her go into attack stance. He circled, looking for a weakness. He knew of only one and that was Luke. As he advanced toward her he kicked Luke in the ribs bringing blood to flow freely from around his neck and pool in the hollow of his throat. Richard clamped his lips tight to control the pain.

He laughed when Cory cried in anger. She stepped over Richard. "I'll kill you for that." Her warning was low, yet everyone heard her in the stillness. She knew those who surrendered and was now being held at gunpoint, were only half of those hidden within the cemetery. The others were waiting for their chance to save those around her. They would never get the chance. Jason had Richard and she was now in a death struggle with him. One would die this day at the very least. If she died Richard would also die. Only she knew the secret to the wire that was around Richard's neck.

"Give it up, Grover and I'll make sure you spend the rest of your life in prison. You would hate being on death row. It is such a tension filled place and you always liked things to be calm and organized."

"Death is always present in life, bitch. I thought I taught you that the last time I had you in my hands."

While he talked Cory attacked, hurtling herself at him. Her weight forced him to the ground, and he struggled desperately to throw her off him. His hand to the side of her face accomplished that. She struggled to her knees, shaking the fog from her brain while Jason struggled to staunch the flow of blood from his ribs. He reacted next trying to kick her. Cory saw the attack coming and rolled away from the impact. She tightened her hand startled when her fingers didn't encompass the knife. As she struggled to her feet she searched for it.

"Looking for this?" Jason sneered flipping the knife in his hand. "Now it's time to die."

He attacked again, and again Cory avoided him, kicking him in the leg as he moved by her. "Not very good. Are you? No wonder you have to hire people to do your dirty work. What's the matter, Grover? Didn't daddy take enough time with his bastard son when he was little? He didn't teach you very well, did he?"

The anger Cory hoped for ignited in Jason. His eyes and face reflected it. He was like the cougar and was quickly tiring of the deadly game they were playing. When he attacked this time, he anticipated her move and plowed into her, knocking her backward and the breath from her lungs. "My turn." He snarled.

Cory saw the knife coming at her and kneed him in the groin. When he groaned with pain she rolled out from under him. Jason grabbed her hair jerking her back to the ground. As she fought for release Jason's words entered her consciousness. "I'm going to kill you for that, right here on the grave of your parents. You will die, Corina. The way I wanted you to die all those years ago. Isn't it ironic that the daughter should join them, dying on their graves?" His laughter echoed around the cemetery.

The pain radiating through her right shoulder told her she was stabbed. Fear raced along with the pain. She needed a weapon and she needed it now. As another attack of burning pain ripped along her ribs memory flooded her mind of her wedding day. White Dove's image came to her, the image of the knife given her for protection. She struggled harder trying to pull up the leg of her jeans. When the knife was finally at her fingertips she saw Jason kneel over her the knife glinting in the afternoon sun. "Not today, you bastard." She screamed. "Today, you die." With all the strength she had left she thrust with the knife. When she felt it sink to the hilt into the tender flesh of his stomach she pulled it upward, feeling the warm, stickiness as Jason's blood poured over her. Shock registered in his black eyes before he tried one last time to bring his knife into a killing blow. That was denied him as she pushed his dead body away from her.

Struggling to gain her feet she saw the others surge forward in the confusion, pulling the guns from the stunned hands of Susan Tameron and Major Thoms. The area surrounding Richard filled with men. "Don't touch him." Cory screamed as she crawled to his side. The men stepped back uncertainly. "Easy, big guy. You move or one of these idiots tries to release that wire and it will be the last thing you see before you die. Don't move or even take a deep breath or the wire will trigger."

Slowly, she lowered herself to his side trying to keep the pain from showing in her eyes, yet she knew Richard saw it. The others stood around Richard, fear and indecision showing in their faces. She could see none in Richard's eyes. She didn't expect to either. He was too much like Luke, too much the warrior. "The first thing I'm going to do is release the knife that's in the handles." She gasped, trying to keep the fog from claiming her as she wiped the blood from her eyes. She knew her eye was cut from the blow Jason landed to her face. She looked at Richard. "The pressure must be maintained, or this thing will cut you to pieces." She raised a bloodied face. "Major Watts? I need help."

White faced David knelt beside her. "I've never seen anything like this. What do you want me to do?"

"Exactly what I tell you or Richard is dead. Hold firmly to the handle to the wire. If you release the pressure from around his neck the wire will activate, and his head will be removed. I have little strength left to do this and only I know how to release this death trap without anyone getting killed." The tension around her became thick enough to cut. Cory struggled to keep her brain functioning as she swiped at the stickiness running down her face. "Ready?"

David nodded. Holding tight to the handles he watched Cory struggle to release the knife. Other hands helped her, tanned hands with long sensitive fingers. Gasping, she looked into Luke's worried face. "Don't say anything about me being here, woman. Grandfather has already bitched me out. Just tell me what to do. Rafe and Greg are here to help."

"Pull the knife out of the handle. David? Keep the tension tight on the handle." When it was free she crawled next to Richard's head putting her fingers under the wire. "I've only seen this done once that was successful. I refuse to let you die, Lone Wolf. David will have to slowly release the pressure while I put counter pressure on the wire. Bright Arrow will have to pull you out as the circle is enlarged. Don't try it on your own. It will only cause additional injury." She turned tear filled eyes to Luke. "I must get my foot on the back of the wire before you attempt to move him. David will have to help on the other side. Once he's free we must carefully release the pressure, or my hands will be cut off."

"Running Eagle let me do this." Luke pleaded.

She shook her head, as much to deny his plea as to shake the fog from her mind. "No. Lone Wolf will die if this isn't done correctly. Do as I tell you." As with the day of their joining Luke captured Cory's eyes and refused to release them. Silent communication passed between them as the silence in the cemetery became strained. Richard watched, seeing peace enter the two. He finally understood what his Aunt Little Fawn told him about the love these two shared. It was special.

Finally, Luke nodded. "I'll help with his head while Greg and Rafe help move his body. Be careful, woman. You're injured enough as it is. Between us there have enough injuries to last a lifetime."

Cory kissed him quickly and then nodded at David. "Easy." She cautioned, feeling the wire bite into her fingers. Slowly the wire loosened enough for her to slip her hands beneath it. Richard could feel it bite into the back of his head and clamped his teeth together against the pain. As it lifted farther Cory brought her foot next to his head. "This is the tricky part." She whispered. "I have to get my foot over the wire at the same time your head is lifted. Don't do anything but lie there. Luke will have to lift your head for you. Any movement on your part will only cause more damage."

After a deep breath she nodded to Luke. Slowly Luke lifted Richard's head as Cory slipped her foot over the wire. He could see blood dripping from her palms and knew she was cut. His heart twisted at the sight of her. Blood covered her from hair to knees yet he couldn't tell how much of it was hers and how much was Jason's. He could only pray while she concentrated on removing the wire from around Richard's neck.

Once her foot was firmly on the wire she drew another deep breath. "Very good. Now Luke, you need to turn him slightly, so I can place my foot closer to the middle. David? Get ready. Once I have my foot where I need it, Richard will need to be rolled my way and you'll have to place your foot on the wire. Hold it tightly. Richard is almost free, and I want no mistakes to happen now. Too little pressure and this contraption will trigger."

When she nodded Luke turned Richard. He had to clamp down hard on his concern for her injuries when he saw the grimace that crossed her face as she moved her foot to the center of the wire. Blood flowed freely down her fingers, dripping on the ground. When she nodded again they turned Richard close to her leg. "Now, David."

When David was in position Richard was returned to his back and she smiled at him. "As soon as this wire is wide enough to clear your head, Bright Arrow will help you out. Then comes the hard part." His startled look made her giggle. "I fear it won't be much better on David and I once you're free. This device Grover loves to use is like razor wire. The spring is manufactured into it. If we're not careful it will wind around our hands or legs, cutting deeply. We'll deal with that once you're free. Ready?" She giggled again seeing Richard struggle to answer her. "Don't move, my friend, not even to nod. You don't need any more injuries or scars than what you will have from this damned wire. Just be prepared to gain your freedom." David slowly released the pressure again when she nodded.

The pressure on his foot was tremendous and he knew the pressure on her hands had to be straining her muscles, but he could detect no sign of weakening. "Try it." She gasped. David feared the opening wasn't large enough, but Luke managed to turn Richard's head enough for the man to be pulled to safety. As soon as Richard was free Luke crossed the wire and knelt next to his wife. Their eyes met, and he could see the terror in them. "Now what needs to be done? How can I help you?"

"Now we try to free ourselves without letting this thing cut us to pieces. I'll need your help to hold tension on the upper part of the wire, Bright Arrow. My muscles are objecting to the strain and I sincerely doubt I will be able to keep up the tension much longer." Tears shimmered on her lashes and her voice reflected her exhaustion. Luke didn't hesitate, slipping his hands above David's foot. "Now the tension needs to be tightened until it is once again coiled tight as a snake. The trick is to release hands and feet before the thing strikes."

"Wait, Cory." Rafe was beside her, hand on her shoulder. He feared she was becoming too weak to escape. "Let us get some stones to place over the lower section of the wire. It will hold the lower wire in place while releasing your feet. It'll be easier to remove your hands when the time comes."

Tears were sliding down her face. "Hurry, Rafe." She whispered. "I'm afraid I can't hold much longer."

The men behind her  scrambled to carry a heavy grave marker. Rafe and Greg pushed it over the lower wire. "Try that."

"David, release your foot. If the wire doesn't move, I'll release mine." Everyone held their breaths as David followed Cory's directions. He could tell no difference in the tension he was holding on the handle. "Very good." She breathed. "Now it's my turn." Tension settled over the group as she slowly pulled her leg from danger. "We'll at least be able to walk out of here." She giggled with the release of tension that fear instilled in her. "Now if we can only shake hands when this is over…"

Luke knew Cory was going into shock from her rambling words and the giggles she was fighting. "Running Eagle, hang on, honey. I know your hurt but we need to finish this." Luke took a deep breath to settle his fear as much to help his aching muscles. "What now?"

She refused to look at Luke knowing it was her fault he was still in danger of injury. "Now we count to three and roll away from this thing. David must do the same for when the tension is released on the wire it will jump like a snake, coiling around itself and the weight until its one very tight ball." Another deep breath and she nodded. "I'm ready."

Luke said a silent prayer. "I'll count. When I say three all of us will roll." He looked at David. "Ready? One. Two. Three."

When the three rolled away the wire sang into the tense silence, rolling several times upon itself. The men stood mesmerized until it stopped moving.

# Chapter Sixteen

D AVID WAS WHITE FACED WITH worry as he sought out Richard. The paramedics had Richard's neck wrapped in bandages, IV started and was loading him on the stretcher when David appeared at his side. "Are they all right?" Richard's voice was raspy but working.

David turned to look at the two. Cory was wrapped in Luke's arms, her head buried in his shoulder as the effects of shock racked her body. "She's one hell of a woman, Richard. I thought you were a goner when I saw Grover pull you around that tombstone. Then when she faced that bastard with nothing but a knife…" David shuddered. "Do you think he'll release her so she can be treated?"

Richard's chuckle was painful. "I doubt that at this moment either of them even know that help is here. Approach them cautiously, David. Wounded animals react instinctively, and they are both wounded right now, in both body and soul."

David didn't have to. Greg and Rafe were already approaching the couple. Rafe knelt a safe distance from Cory. "Luke? It's time to get this little lady some medical attention." He had to repeat it twice before Luke raised his head. "It's all right, buddy. Let's get Corena taken care of. The ambulance is here."

"How bad?"

"We won't know that until you release her." He scooted forward, gently pulling Cory out of Luke's arms. "The paramedics are here, and we need to get her to them. Greg will help you up while I carry her."

Luke's shoulders slumped as he released her. She was unconscious he knew. Her limp body frightened him. Greg pulled him to his feet, and he limped painfully to the ambulance. The medics surrounded her, blocking his view. "Get in Bright Arrow." Richard commanded. "She needs the help neither of us can provide. How are you feeling?" Luke shrugged his eyes glued to the backs of the medics.

Richard spoke again. "Get in and let these guys wrap your hands. David won't let them take her in the ambulance without you."

Luke nodded again knowing Richard was right. There was nothing he could do for Cory at this moment. He felt useless especially when she had been there for him, nursing him back to health. When Richard repeated his name, Luke crawled into the back of the ambulance with his cousin. His eyes never left the area where Cory was. Richard's eyes narrowed on Luke's leg. "Is that your blood or Cory's?"

Surprise marched across Luke's face as he stared at his leg. The pant leg was covered with blood, the crimson widening even as he watched. "Mine, I'm afraid to say. I never even noticed. I don't know how I got hurt."

Richard grinned. Not surprising, he thought to himself, considering what happened this day. Gently so not to heighten Luke's agitation, he patted Luke's arm. "Let them look at that also, cousin. If I know you, you'll insist Cory be seen first. If she knows you're injured she will refuse until you are cared for."

Luke nodded absently, looking out the open back doors of the ambulance as the medics worked on his wife.

★  ★  ★  ★  ★

"Mr. Patterson?" The doctor called, pushing open the door where Luke and Richard were anxiously waiting. "Your wife is awake, but she is refusing treatment until she talks to you." The doctor looked from one to the other of the men. "Twins?"

"Almost." Luke laughed. "We're both going to see my wife and you'd better not argue."

From the hard look in both men's eyes the doctor knew there was no sense arguing. Leading the way to the room he watched as the worry in her eyes turned to happy tears. Her sharp eyes missed nothing. Not the bandages around one man's neck or the bandages on the hands of the other. Her eyes riveted on the cut in Luke Patterson jeans. "How bad?"

Luke shrugged. "Not bad." Luke grinned kissing her deeply. "I tore a couple of stitches loose. How bad are you?"

"They want to admit me." Tears streamed down her face. "I want to go home, Luke. Refuse to allow them to keep us separated. Please Luke? I just want to go home."

Luke gathered her in his arms, sliding beneath her head. He held her close while she sobbed out her fear. "Running Eagle, no one is going to separate us again. I want you to let them work with your injuries, however when I leave here you'll go with me." When her eyes, shining with tears met his, he grinned. "Sound familiar?"

A smile quivered on her lips as she relaxed against him. "Have the doctor tell you what's wrong with me. They gave me something for the pain and my head is swimming." Her eyelids slid shut as sleep claimed her.

The doctor moved to the side of the bed. "Considering what I was told happened today your wife is extremely lucky the injuries are not more serious." He pulled the sheet down showing her right arm. "The arm has mainly a surface cut. No stitches will be needed however I will have to tape it closed. Movement of the arm will be painful while that injury heals. There shouldn't be any scar providing infection doesn't become a problem. Her hands are severely injured. More so than yours. The cuts are deep enough to be concerned about infection but not deep enough to suture. That is one of the problems with hands. I'll send some cream home with you. I want both of you to use it. Since her hands are worse than yours she'll have problems using them. She probably won't be able to dress herself, to use a fork or even hold onto a glass for quite some time until her hands heal."

He lifted the left side of the gown. "There's another cut on her side. It runs close to the scar that already exists. That one will definitely need to be sewed and will leave another scar." Replacing the gown, he pulled the shoulder of the gown down. "Her right shoulder is cut, also needing stitches." He covered her pulling the sheet over her. "She complained of pain in her leg, but I can find no sign of injury. There are no cuts and the x-rays show no signs of fracture. I believe she bruised it somehow in the scuffle. The cut on her face and near her eye should heal without any trace of scars." The doctor turned looking at both men. "All things considered this woman is extremely lucky. Her injuries will heal, and I can detect no signs of injuries to the baby or anything that would affect her carrying it to term."

Luke turned white while staring at the doctor. Richard sank heavily into a chair. "Baby?" They said in unison.

"Yes. Baby. It is standard procedure to do a pregnancy test on any injured married female not using protection. From what she said, you have been married for about a month and a half. I had a sonogram done on her when the blood work came back positive. According to the tests your wife is about four weeks pregnant. As I said, I can see nothing wrong with the baby. I have yet to tell her she's pregnant."

Luke was grinning from ear to ear. "Mother's choker really does work." He chuckled when Richard laughed. Controlling his excitement with difficulty he turned to the doctor. "Please don't tell her. I want to be the one to break that happy news to my wife. God, a baby. Did you hear that Richard? I'm going to be a daddy. Thank God I will never have to be sent undercover again and can stay home to help raise my child."

The doctor looked doubtful but grinned when he heard Luke's happy words. "I'll not say anything providing you get your butt out of here and get something to eat." When Luke shook his head in denial the doctor placed a hand on Luke's shoulder. "Your wife will sleep through all of this. Since its obvious you're not going to allow us to admit her I want to keep her sleeping until after you get home. She will be in intense pain, young man. Think of her welfare as well as your own. Get something to eat. It will be several hours before I finish repairing all the damage her body sustained today."

Seeing the stubborn look that entered Luke's eyes Richard stood. "The doctor is correct. We need to eat and then I want you to tell me how you escaped from Skywalker." When Luke hesitated, Richard gently lifted Cory from his lap. "Move. She's bleeding again and if she loses too much blood she will have to stay."

Luke moved as if in a fog beside Richard. "A baby, Richard. Cory has blessed my life in so many ways." He whispered. "I wonder how Running Eagle will react to the news of the pregnancy once she knows."

"Better than you, I hope." Richard laughed as they entered the restaurant. The others stood, their concern showing in their faces. Questions assaulted them as the two claimed their seats. "Settle down, gentlemen. I'll tell you how Corena is after we order. Right now, she's still in the Emergency Room and the doctor is working on her injuries."

While Richard ordered a meal for both Luke and himself, David watched Luke, curiosity blazing in his eyes. He could detect no sign of worry, only…excitement. His eyes turned to Richard. "Luke will be all right, Major. Now let me tell you how Corena is doing. She will live with two additional scars. One is near the first scar on her ribs. The other will be on her right shoulder where he cut her with the knife first. It will be small and hardly noticeable. Her hands will take a long time to heal and she'll need help with everything until they improve. The slice on her arm, face and eye should heal without scars. All told we were all lucky today and I owe my life to my new cousin."

Everyone waited with baited breaths, looking from one to the other. David finally broke the tension. "There's something else. Give."

Richard laughed. "Luke's turn."

"Luke?" Rafe asked. When his friend didn't answer he put both hands on Luke's shoulders pulling him until he could see Luke's eyes. "Luke? What else?"

Slowly a grin slid across Luke's face. "You are not going to believe this, but Cory is pregnant. I'm going to be a daddy." His eyes were shining with happiness. "The doctor hasn't told her yet and I asked him to keep it a secret. I want that pleasure. She is going to make such a wonderful mother."

Rafe quickly recovered from his shock. Slapping Luke on the back he grinned. "You stud. Congratulations." In a loud voice he ordered drinks all around.

"Not for me." Luke objected. "I have to get Running Eagle and take her home. I also have to call Fred. I'm sure he has already heard about today and I don't want him to worry needlessly. He should know that all is well."

Greg coughed, bringing Luke's attention to him. "I already called. He's a nervous wreck. I invited him to dinner with us and he should be arriving...about now."

Fred approached the table hesitantly. Luke chuckled. "Come on over, Fred. I want you to meet these guys." He laughed when Fred got close enough to see Richard. "This is my cousin, Richard. My mother and his mother are sisters. We were born on the same day only five minutes apart. I'm older."

Fred took his seat cautiously watching Luke. Never had he seen the man express his emotions so openly and he wondered what caused him to drop his defenses. Greg laughed, patting Fred on the back. "Never worry, Fred. Luke is just excited about the new agent we'll be getting before long."

"Oh?" He sucked a deep breath. "Another shakeup is going to happen?" Fred hid his surprise by taking a drink of his water.

"Nothing so drastic." Rafe laughed as the waitress brought their food. "Luke is going to be a daddy."

Fred choked on his water and would have dropped his glass if Richard hadn't grabbed it. "Cory is...is..."

"Pregnant." Luke nodded. "We're going to have a baby. Isn't that wonderful?"

"Great. That's great." Fred mumbled trying to bring happiness into his face but knowing he failed miserably.

Luke sobered instantly eyes narrowed on Fred. "What's wrong? Out with it, my friend. Something is bothering you."

Fred looked directly at Luke. "Have you told her you own the ranch?" Seeing Luke's look of confusion anger surged. "That woman of yours has been worrying about where you, she and those twin sisters of hers are going to live. She thinks you still live in that damned apartment. If she hasn't talked to you about it yet, then you don't know how worried she is. Not only that but she's worried what she's going to do with the rest of her life since she lost her nursing job. Did you know she wants to train female agents? Did you know she's worried about where the money will come from that is needed to send those twin sisters to college? Have you talked to her about any of this? God, man. Corena may not be as excited about this as you expect her to be. She wants children but not when she's worried about how you will accept being married to a poor woman."

Luke sat back, contemplating Fred's words. He had not discussed any of the things Fred asked him about nor had he considered her feelings about their future. He just assumed he would provide for the family. All the family, including the sisters. Hell, he had enough money to send the sisters to college and still allow Cory to do whatever she wanted in life. "I guess I just assumed she knew."

"Well she doesn't." Fred's anger was abating. He dabbed at the water on the table unable to look Luke in the eyes. "I'm sorry, Luke. I've been crazy with worry ever since I saw Corena enter the office this morning and then saw Thoms and Tameron leave shortly after her departure. My worry overloaded my mouth. I apologize."

Luke sighed. "No, Fred. A true friend speaks the truth when truth is needed. The doctor said he was going to give Running Eagle enough medicine to keep her sleeping tonight. I'll return with her to the Reservation. If she's feeling well enough tomorrow I'm going to take her to the ranch. By tomorrow most of her concerns should be put to rest."

"Most?" Richard's eyebrows shot up.

"She knows her security clearance is ruined. Without it she'll never be allowed to work at the agency again especially as a trainer. I just pray she'll be satisfied being mother to our child, yet I know she'll want to do something until the baby comes. She quit her job at the hospital the night I was shot, and she won't be allowed to return there since she didn't give the required two-week notice. Employers frown on people who quit without notice. They have already told her she would get a poor reference from them." He groaned as he buried his head in his hands.

David opened his mouth only to close it when he saw Richard shake his head in warning. "Buck up, Luke. Neither of you are going to be working for several weeks yet. She won't even be able to look for a job until she heals. Maybe something good will happen for your woman."

"I hope so. Her life has been a living nightmare since her parents were killed." Luke drew a deep breath calming the anger churning in his stomach. "Let's eat. Running Eagle should be ready to come home by the time we're finished. I'll need to make arrangements to get both of us back home."

★　★　★　★　★

Cory came to awareness slowly. Her body throbbed with every heartbeat reminding her she was still alive. Running her hand along the other side of the bed she failed to feel her husband's body next to her and fear welled up inside her, the fear of having lost him threatening to choke her. "Luke?"

"I'm here, sweetheart. I have breakfast ready."

She groaned. "I'm not hungry."

"To bad. Grandfather has been haunting the house since we arrived. He's insisting you need nourishment to make you heal. I have your clothes ready and once I get you dressed Richard will help you into the dining room."

She raised her hands, a frown on her face when she looked at them. "I really am not hungry, husband."

Luke's laughter brought her eyes to his. "The doctor said you would need help with everything until your hands heal. Not to worry. I'm prepared to feed my beautiful woman." When she stuck out her tongue at him, he laughed harder. "Out of bed, woman. People are waiting to welcome you to the land of the living."

"I don't feel well. I don't want to visit with anyone." She snapped at Luke.

Luke bent over the bed and kissed her soundly. His chocolate eyes seemed to dance with merriment. "Sorry, my dear but Richard only gave me five minutes to get you dressed. Unless you want him to carry you into the dining room bare ass naked you better cooperate."

Her eyes popped wide open. "He wouldn't dare."

"Yes I would, little lady." Richard's voice came around the door. "You have exactly two minutes to let my cousin get you decent and then I'm coming in."

Cory strangled her indignation as Luke helped her into jeans and a sweater. "I'm perfectly capable of walking." She hissed. "I don't need to be carried."

"Sorry, those are Grandfather's orders."

"You don't look sorry to me, you idiot. I'm not a child and I hate being treated like one."

Luke kissed her again to curb her anger as he held her face in his bandaged hands. "Then stop acting like one."

Richard knew she was seething with anger by the hurt look in Luke's eyes. "Shame on you." He scolded, lifting her in his arms. "Luke has been worried sick about you. You really are acting like a child and I had plans to take the two of you someplace peaceful where you could be together without being disturbed. Instead I feel like spanking you."

The tears sliding down her face stopped his entry into the outer room. "I'm sorry, Lone Wolf. I just feel so useless. There's so much to worry about I just feel overwhelmed. So much needs to be done and now I'm hurt and…"

Richard sat on the edge of the bed settling her in his lap. "Have you talked to Bright Arrow about this?"

"No. He's been worried about staying alive and helping me clear daddy's name. I didn't want to dump more worry onto his shoulders."

Richard clamped down on the response that came unbidden to his lips. "Now that this craziness is over you can begin planning the rest of your lives. Dry your tears, little lady. It's time to eat. Afterward we are leaving the Reservation. Don't argue with him or me. For once just do as you're told without reacting with anger."

Tears threatened again when she was taken into the outer room. The house was packed. It seemed as if everyone on the Reservation was in the house. Although she tried to capture Luke's eyes he avoided looking at her. Shame raced through her knowing Lone Wolf spoke the truth about hurting Luke. It seemed to take forever before she was seated at the table, a plate of food in front of her. Cory choked on every bite of food Luke fed her. Conversation swirled around her, but she didn't hear a single word. She was ashamed of herself for her words of anger and the hurt she caused to Bright Arrow. That made the food go down hard and she struggled to keep the tears that were threatening from falling.

Luke took her hand, leaning close to whisper in her ear. "Eat, honey. Lone Wolf is going to take us away from here, so we can talk in peace."

"I'm sorry I hurt you." She whispered tears on her lashes. "I'm just so worried and…"

Luke's arms came around her, pulling her tight against him. "Mother? Pack us a lunch to take with us please. Running Eagle needs some time away from this crowd. Lone Wolf, I think it's time to leave."

As they left the Reservation, Cory sat stiffly between the two men trying to decide how to approach Luke with her worries. Luke's hand rubbing up and down her leg did nothing to help clear her mind. Instead it brought images of their times together as husband and wife. The sight of the big, rambling ranch house shocked her. "Whose place is this?"

"Mine." Luke grinned when she turned to stare at him. Gently he tapped her mouth shut. "My parents have been staying here since I was injured. They've been taking care of the livestock for me."

"Livestock?"

"Yes, my dear. I have several head of purebred horses, many with foals at their sides. After I show you the house I'm going to take you riding. You do know how to ride. Don't you?" She nodded in amazement causing Luke to laugh. "Good. I want you to pick out the rooms you think the twins would like. The warriors said they would help move most of their belongings into the house before the twins returned from their summer vacation with Carrie Ann. Anything you think they won't need we can store."

"Or burn." Cory whispered. "The furniture isn't very good, Luke. Most is worn out. Why didn't you tell me?"

Luke sucked a deep breath. "I thought you knew. When I realized you didn't know I was afraid you would hate this place and want to continue living in your house."

She punched him lightly in the chest wincing when pain radiated up her arm. "Silly. I was trying to think of a way to sell it and get a bigger house but without a job that was impossible. No bank would give a loan to an unemployed woman. I knew all of us wouldn't fit into the one I own. Now I can sell it and send the twins to college."

"You could do that." Richard stated, pulling the car to a stop at the front door. "You could also let them apply for the scholarships they are eligible for through the agency. Now that you've cleared your father's name they can apply for them and the death benefits will finally be paid even if it is five years late. His pension will also be opened for you and your sisters and that should help with the expenses."

Cory shook her head. "Luke cleared daddy's name. He knew who to go to with the information I gathered. I have him to thank for that."

Richard chuckled as he lifted her from the car. "Still giving someone else the credit that belongs to you?"

★ ★ ★ ★ ★

Excitement shined in Cory's eyes. The twins were coming home today, and Carrie Ann was coming with them. It had been three weeks since Jason Grover was killed, and the bruises had finally faded enough to be covered by makeup. Her hands were still sore but healed enough to do most things without help. Luke's leg was healed yet he still had a limp. A specialist examined him and told him what they already knew. The limp was permanent, and he would never be able to work undercover again.

Cory was never sick and for that she was grateful. Luke told her about the baby the first night they stayed together in the ranch house. Now she was putting the final touches on her attire and her hands fluttered nervously over her dress. "Luke? Do I look all right?"

Luke entered the room. He wore a black suit with a blue shirt, a black tie hanging over his shoulders. "You look good enough to eat." He grinned appraising her outfit. She was still sleek, the baby not yet showing on her flat stomach. She wore a light blue dress that matched his shirt, the silky material hugging her curves making him fight for control of his wayward body. Her high heels still put her a half head shorter than he. Slipping his arms around her he watched her in the mirror. "I'll have to beat off half the men tonight."

"Where are you taking us?"

"It's a surprise, my little Eagle. If I told you it would be a surprise no longer." He straightened. "Hold still. Mother gave me a necklace for you to wear." She gasped when he wrapped the ruby and diamond necklace around her neck. "Beautiful." He murmured wrapping his arms around her. "Just like the woman I married."

She struggled to turn in his arms. Capturing his lips, she gave promises of the night to come. He finally pushed her away, groaning as she giggled at the bulge at the front of his suit. "Keep that up, woman, and we'll be late picking up your sisters. What would they think of me then?" His husky voice whispered in her ear.

Cory laughed at his warning. "I have nothing to put around your neck, so I guess I ought to tie this tie of yours. You never could manage a simple tie."

"Hell, those things were invented to choke a man."

"No more uncomfortable than these heels you insisted I buy. We could go comfortable and wear jeans."

Shock shown in his face. "If you did that I wouldn't be able to admire those beautiful legs that support the rest of your beautiful body." He groaned as the blush stained her cheeks. "Come on, woman. We need to pick up your sisters. My reservations won't wait forever."

She grinned. "So we are going out to dinner."

Luke gave a mock groan. "You'll get no more information out of me." Kissing her quickly he held her elbow as he steered her to the door.

Cory pumped him for information the entire trip to the airport. He stayed back when the reunion with the sisters resulted in squeals of happiness. Luke escaped long enough to load their luggage before going back for the women. Questions flowed so fast he could not have answered half of them even if he was inclined to, which he wasn't. He grinned when they pulled up in front of the restaurant. Cory eyed him suspiciously when a footman opened the door for her, handing her out. Luke circled the car throwing the valet the keys.

"Mighty fancy for a homecoming." She whispered.

"Your sisters are impressed." He chuckled seeing their wide-eyed stares. When Cory started to say something, he kissed her soundly. Wrapping her hand around his elbow he led her inside. The restaurant was packed, and they were led to the only table open, one in the middle. "It's a good thing I made reservations, or we would have to wait forever."

Nervously, Cory took the seat the waiter held for her. She could feel the eyes watching them and hated the fact they were drawing attention. Her suspicions surged when the waiters brought their drinks and meal before they brought a menu. Bending to Luke's ear she whispered frantically. "Luke, what are you up to? No one ever brings a meal before people place an order. Something is wrong here."

"I already ordered for us. Before we came." He tugged nervously at his tie. "This is a celebration, my dear. Be kind to this old man and just be happy."

Cory gave an unladylike snort. "Old my ass."

"Eat." Luke commanded.

She did eat. Since becoming pregnant she was ravishingly hungry as well as easily tired. The food was done to perfection and Luke was a perfect gentleman to all at the table. Soon the feeling of being with family and being well loved helped relax her. She was giggling at something the twins told her when she noticed the stillness that enveloped the room. Suspicion rocketed when David Watts stood on a platform at the front of the room, microphone in hand. One look at her husband and she knew she was being set up. He was grinning like a Cheshire cat. "What have you done?"

Luke swallowed hard, but his grin remained. "Nothing. I'm just following orders."

David Watts cleared his throat. "I want to thank everyone for coming to our annual awards ceremony. This has been a tragic year especially for the agency here in Chicago. Eleven good men died needlessly because of a traitor within our ranks. We almost lost three more to that evil. First I would like to call Greg Waltz to the stage."

Greg stood nervously adjusting his tie. His wife Paula beamed with pride. When Greg ascended the platform, the applause was deafening. David continued when the room quieted. "Greg Waltz is the Captain for the Chicago office and I will turn the microphone over to him."

Greg cleared his throat. "This will be one of my last official duties before I retire. First, I would like to call all four daughters of Ralph Sims to the stand, please."

"Luke?"

Luke grimaced at the fear he heard in Cory's voice. "I don't know anything other than I was ordered to bring the family." He whispered while holding her chair.

Nervously the four women approached the platform. When they were standing at Greg's side he gave Cory a supportive smile. "As most know by now Ralph Sims and his wife were murdered five years ago after a sting operation. We now know the traitor in this office was involved in the bombing. Thanks to his daughter, Corena Sims Patterson, the proof of his guilt was found, and he has now been convicted to two life sentences in prison." Cory shrunk behind the other three. "It is with great honor that I present the daughters with the FBI Memorial star and the Medal of Valor for their father." Rafe brought forth a small box handing it to Greg before pulling Cory from her hiding place. He placed her next to Carrie Ann.

David brought a plaque up next. Greg read the inscription. "To the daughters of Ralph Sims, in memory of his heroic deeds and to express our deepest sympathy at their loss through the death of their father, it's with deep appreciation that this award is presented this day for the dedication he has shown the FBI." Standing before the sisters he presented the plaque to Carrie Ann, pressing the other two medals in Cory's hands, kissing her tear-wet face.

Cory stumbled back to her seat, wrapping herself in Luke's arms as the standing ovation roared around her. Luke finally pulled her away, brushing the hair from her face. "If you don't stop crying, my love, you will ruin this shirt." As she tried to sop at the wet spot showing on his chest he laughed gently guiding her to the chair.

Greg continued. "I now call Luke Patterson."

Luke's face reflected his shock when he stood making Cory giggle. He shot her a warning look as he headed to the front. "Luke Patterson is one of those men we almost lost. His quick thinking is the only thing that got him out of the massacre alive. He was terribly injured while escaping. He'll never again be able to work in the field and we are now forced to restrict his movements to the office. Although he continues to be on sick leave his new position in the Chicago office has been confirmed."

He turned to Luke. "Agent Patterson, you have been promoted to the rank of Captain. Your new assignment is to train those idiots out there to keep their asses from being blown apart." He pinned the bars on the lapel of Luke's suit amid applause. When Luke started to leave

Greg laid a restraining hand on his arm. "There is another award this young man deserves. Corena Sims Patterson will you please come forward and help me honor your husband?"

Cory's blush was high on her face when she stepped to Luke's side. The entire room was hushed as Rafe once again brought forward a box. The medal, nestled inside a dark velvet lining, winked in the overhead lights. "This is also the Medal of Valor. Luke Patterson escaped with his life only to help plan the capture of those traitors within this agency." He turned to Luke. "Luke Patterson it's with great pride that I award you the Medal of Valor." Pulling the medal from the velvet he handed it to Cory. Her face was shining with pride as she pinned the medal to the lapel of his jacket. Another standing ovation greeted the two as they returned to their seats. "I'm so proud of you." Cory whispered kissing him hard.

David returned to the platform. "I would like Captain Greg Waltz to return to the stage with his beautiful wife Paula. I also want Rafe DeAngelo to return to the stage and to stand next to Captain Waltz."

Cory grinned seeing the embarrassment in their faces. "I'm glad to see I'm not the only one who blushes." She whispered snuggling deeper into Luke's protective embrace.

"I take this time to honor two men who have worked for the agency for many years. We almost lost both of these men to evil when the house they were supposed to be in blew up. They worked to put the evidence together Mrs. Patterson collected. From there they helped in the capture of those men. Paula, would you do the honor of pinning both men with the Medal of Valor?" Giggles bubbled up when the men blushed deeper and threatened to boil over. Cory had to stuff her napkin against her lips to keep them inside. Luke didn't succeed as well. His chuckle was covered by the applause that went around the room.

David waited until Greg and Rafe were seated. "I would like to call Captain Richard Stevens to the platform."

Surprise filtered through Luke. "You didn't know any of this was going to happen?" Cory whispered.

Luke shook his head as Richard gained the platform. "Captain Stevens was injured when he was captured by Jason Grover. His family is here and once again I ask that Luke and Corena Patterson come to the platform to present his Medal of Valor." Luke heard the gasp that usually follows when people saw how much the two men looked alike. Once again Cory struggled to stifle the giggles.

David handed the medal to Cory. She smiled as she pinned it to Richard's lapel. He was wearing a dark blue suit with a light blue tie. She didn't hear what was said as she kissed his cheek. "You deserve this. My thanks for everything you've done for me."

Richard lifted her off the floor in a hug. The blush was high in her face as she struggled to keep her dress from riding up. Luke was trying desperately to strangle the laughter that threatened to overcome him when she hurried to stand next to him. "It's my pleasure to announce that as of today, Captain Stevens has been assigned to this office." Cory squealed with pleasure as she hugged Richard again. David was finally able to continue once the cheers and applause finally died down.

David had to cough to keep from laughing. "Hold onto your hugs, Corena. There's more to come and from the look on your husband's face he's not too appreciative of the attention his cousin is getting." Her face flushed a deep red as she hurried to grasp Luke's hand as laughter abounded around her. "One last announcement before we release Captain Stevens. I wish for all to know that he has now been stripped of that title." He heard Cory gasp. "As of this day Richard Stevens will carry the title of Major."

Cory's happy squeal echoed over the room as she hugged Richard again. "I'm so happy you will be around for a while. I want our..." Her face turned white when she realized she was about to announce to the world they were going to have a child.

Richard kept her between himself and Luke as they left the platform. "I know about the baby, Running Eagle." He whispered. "Did you really think Bright Arrow would keep the secret for long? He's just as happy about the baby as I am. Thanks for being here."

"Don't run off too far, Major Stevens. I would like all three of you back up here." When they turned confused faces to David, he laughed. "Give a man an advancement in rank and he hesitates to obey a direct command." The room echoed with laughter as the three, once again, ascended the stairs, confusion marring their faces.

"I want everyone to know these awards have been a well-kept surprise. Greg Waltz, Richard Stevens and Rafe DeAngelo were told of Luke Patterson's awards but not of their own. Captain Patterson, I'm afraid was simply ordered to appear with his new family." He glanced over his shoulder. "That was done mainly because these two seem to read each other's minds and I didn't want either of them to know about tonight's awards. In keeping with the events of tonight there are still a few awards I wish to present.

"Corena Sims Patterson it's my pleasure to inform you that your security clearance has been reactivated with full privileges. It is also my pleasure to inform you that your sick leave was approved from the day you were captured. A check for those years will be sent to you."

David saw Cory sway and Luke tighten his arm around her. He waited until color returned to her face. "I want Major Stevens to come forward please." When Richard was beside him David placed his hand over the microphone. Cory tried to back behind Luke when she saw the grin on Richard's face. Luke's arm prevented that.

Richard took the microphone. "I have just been informed as to why I was ordered back to the platform. Apparently while I was recovering from my injuries many people have been working very hard to get your security clearance approved, Corena. Since this was an unusual case it ended up at the White House. The President has signed the order for you to return to work for the agency."

David handed him a document with the official seal of the nation. "It states here that you are ordered to return to the services of the FBI at such time the doctor releases you from sick leave. You are to be promoted to the rank of lieutenant and will help Captain Patterson in the training of new agents." He brought the paper forward placing it in her shaking hands. "Congratulations, Running Eagle." Richard whispered as he kissed her cheek.

David spoke into the microphone. "Captain Patterson will you please return the favor your wife gave earlier and place her bars on her dress?" David grinned when Luke, after pinning on her bars, picked her up, giving her a deep kiss. While she was wrapped in Luke's arms David motioned Richard to his side and then for Greg, Rafe and Fred to come up. As Luke lowered her to the floor David cleared his throat. "Agent Fred Adkins stand behind Lieutenant Patterson and make sure she doesn't leave the stage. Captain Patterson step forward to the mike please."

Cory had a death grip on Luke's arm and refused to let go. He pulled her to him looking deep into her eyes. The silence lengthened as the two stood locked in silent communication. Finally, she drew a deep breath and released her grip. Luke kissed her quickly before going to stand beside the other men.

David stepped closer to the edge of the platform. "I'm going to let Lieutenant Patterson's partners tell you about her. It's as much their story as it is Corena's." One by one her partners came forward telling the crowd about her assignments and how, if not for her, they would be dead. When one finished another took the microphone, the first coming to give Cory a hug and a kiss. The platform behind her was full when the last one finished speaking and Cory was crying so hard the crowd was swimming in front of her. In the silence of the room Luke took the microphone. "Now it's my turn." He swallowed hard seeing the tears running down Cory's face. "I want to tell you what happened the night of the massacre."

Cory covered her face with her hands and then folded into Fred's shoulder when he pulled her next to him. Fred released her only when Luke came to hold her. Richard was talking now, describing in vivid detail how she saved his life by putting her own in danger. He also came to give Cory a hug and kiss before releasing her back to Luke.

David stepped forward again. "Usually the next award would be given on the steps of the White House. We knew Luke would never be able to invent an excuse to get his wife there without raising her suspicions, so we did the next best thing. Would everyone please rise for the President of the United States?" Cory's gasp of shock was audible over the scrape of chairs as the crowd stood. The entire room came to attention when the President entered.

# Chapter Seventeen

"WELL, LIEUTENANT. IT SEEMS YOU have a list of credits longer than most of our most honored service men." He smiled trying to ease the fear he saw in her face. "It is my privilege and great honor to award you two medals this night. The first is the Medal of Valor."

David stepped forward opening the box. The medal twinkled in the overhead light. The President removed the medal from the velvet and stepped in front of her. "It is an honor and privilege as President of the United States to award you this." He slid his hand under the edge of her dress pinning the medal in place.

"It is also my honor to present you with the Presidential Award for Distinguished Service. This award is seldom given and only when a person has been severely injured in the line of duty. You were reinstated when you were in Washington D.C. seeking help." At her look of surprise, he laughed. "I advised Major Watts not to tell you. This was a dangerous situation you were proposing, and I wanted you to have a way out if you decided not to go through with it. Since you completed the terrifying task of capturing Jason Grover and the spies that were in the Chicago office it only shows how deep and true your heart runs. This award is given for both times you were seriously injured. First at the hands of Jason Grover when you were captured and tortured and then at the hands of Jason Grover when you fought for the life of Major Stevens." After pinning the medal below the other he stood back and saluted her. Cory's hand trembled as she returned the salute.

"There is a second award that Mrs. Patterson deserves. This award is seldom given and it is with great honor that I award it to her tonight. Lieutenant Corena Patterson, it is with great pride that I award you the Presidential Medal of Freedom with Distinction. It is the highest award a President can give to a person not of military standing. You have been honorable in the service of the FBI and distinguished yourself with not only those you worked with but within the FBI itself." Cory's face was white as he stepped toward her once more. Richard brought a box that he opened for the President. The President removed the medal as Cory was held in place by Luke. The President went behind her, placing the medal around her neck and securing it at the back. "Now you join the ranks of few. I'm proud to know there are people out there that are devoted to the good citizens of our nation." He faced her once again. "Thank you for your dedicated service to a grateful nation."

"Since I'm here I'm going to give two more awards." David opened another box. "Captain Patterson with great honor and pride I award you the Presidential Award for Distinguished Service for the injuries you sustained the night of the massacre as well as your part in capturing Jason Grover." Luke returned the salute he was given.

David appeared with another box. "Major Stevens it is with great honor and pride that I award you the Presidential Award for Distinguished Service for injuries you received when you were captured by Jason Grover as well as having a major part in that man's capture. It's good he is off the street for all times." He saluted Richard. After receiving the return salute, he stepped away. "I know you don't know who put you in for those gentlemen, however I think it only appropriate you are told who sang your praises."

Cory turned white shaking her head at the President. When she started to retreat, David's hand snaked out to stop her. "No, you don't, little lady."

Richard and Luke both stared at her. "Running Eagle?" They said in unison.

The President chuckled when she hid her face in her hands. "When my secretary called the Washington office Major Watts warned she would react this way. Since she requested my silence as to her responsibility I didn't hesitate to agree." He pulled her hands away from her face. "I kept my promise. I didn't tell them, my dear. You did. Captain? With your permission I would like to kiss your wife." Luke nodded grinning when Cory blushed deep red.

After kissing Cory's cheek, he turned to Luke. "You are a very lucky man." He looked again at Cory. "In more ways than one. Congratulations, Captain." Turning to Richard he shook hands with him also. "Congratulation, Major. I'm proud to have signed your promotion." At the look of surprise, he laughed. "This group obviously made sure their secret was safe. I personally promoted all three of you." Stepping back, he saluted them as a group. "Take care of each other." He commanded before leaving.

The room erupted into applause as the platform became packed with people. Everyone was patting them on the backs and congratulating them. Cory tugged on Luke's jacket her face flushed with embarrassment. "This is embarrassing. Please get me out of here. I want to go home." She pleaded.

Luke nodded, whispered to Fred and Richard before pulling her from the room. The car arrived at the same time the twins and Carrie Ann appeared with Fred and Richard. Greg and Rafe were right behind them. "You're not staying for the party?" Greg asked astonished as Luke handed Cory into the car. "This is a celebration for you as well as a retirement party for me. You can't leave. Paula has yet to speak with you."

"I would really rather not." She smiled sweetly at him. "Since I've become pregnant I find I tire easily." She yawned for effect. "I usually don't stay up this late." She yawned again. "My doctor warned me I would be excessively tired and to get plenty of rest."

"Can your sisters stay?" Richard asked. "I'll make sure they get home safe and sound."

Cory grabbed him by the tie pulling him close so only he could hear her whispered words. "You had better, big guy. The way Rafe is looking at Carrie Ann I'm going to hold you to that statement."

Richard laughed. "I'm the one who is supposed to be giving the orders. Remember? So my first official order is for you and Bright Arrow to return home and go to bed."

"Are you ordering us to sleep?"

Richard laughed at the mischief he saw dancing in her eyes. "I would never order a husband and wife to do that. Especially not you two. I'm not fool enough to think that order would be obeyed." He laughed again when he saw the darkening tinge of her cheeks in the overhead streetlight.

"Bet your ass, cousin." Luke grinned starting the car. "Let's go home dear. We have an order to obey."

Richard laughed harder as he closed the door. "Looks like I'm taking everyone home. Cory is feeling rather...tired."